NOT EXACTLY ROCKET SCIENTISTS

and other stories

BUD SCHILL, JR.

and
JOHN MACILROY

and
ROB HAMILTON

PAGE PUBLISHING, INC.
New York, NY

First originally published by Page Publishing, Inc. 2017

ISBN 978-1-68348-851-4 (Paperback)
ISBN 978-1-68348-859-0 (Hard Cover)
ISBN 978-1-68348-852-1 (Digital)

Printed in the United States of America

CONTENTS

LESS THAN DIVINE INTERVENTIONS

MORE MISADVENTURES

EPILOGUE

To all our great friends from a gentle youth,
and to our wonderful wives.

FROM THE AUTHORS

Let's get it out in the open, right off the bat.

We were goofballs, and magnets for mischief. Pinheads, really. Boys who managed to screw up just about everything, everywhere: scouts, camp, school, dancing lessons, church, vacations, team sports, bowling, first dates, and summer jobs. You name it. We annoyed our parents, teachers, coaches, ministers, scout leaders, and counselors. Adults, wherever we could find them, and girls in general, all sputtering in disbelief as we drifted from one witless antic to another.

Everybody.

Now, we didn't set out to make a mess of things, and at heart we were good kids. But like boys everywhere, we engaged our small world in haphazard and zany confusion. We weren't uncaring, just careless. We weren't dumb, just clueless. We weren't sacrilegious, just easily distracted in church. We weren't irresponsible. Well, maybe a bit.

HERE'S THE BACKSTORY.

We have been friends forever, and it's been magic from day one. Two of us walked into our first day of kindergarten together, joined later by the third. Several of the characters you will soon meet were in that first class too—great guys like Scott "Suds" Estes, David "Spike" Hughes and Billy Fitzsimmons. Sherwood "Woody" Thompson, Jim "Bay" Basinger, John "Nils" Ohlson, and Tony "The Lesser" Intilli were other early buddies, joined later by guys like Scott "Wiener"

McQueen, who moved from Cincinnati (and the only one of us who could spell that town correctly), and Ted Hellman, who had nudged over from Springfield in sixth grade, and could spell everything *but* Cincinnati. In junior high, we found a whole new cast of characters to add to the fun. You will meet Bobby "The Duke" Ellington, Billy Jaeger, "Big Al" Schultheis, George Freund, "Moo" Morgan, Donnie Hohnstine, and Terry O'Brien, as well as lots of innocent bystanders. Although we lost a few prized buddies to private school along the way, we found new friends in scouts, Little League, church, and even camp.

You will not, however, meet many girls, as we really messed up there. It was like we all had borrowed metal colanders from our moms' kitchens, putting them on our heads in a futile effort to pick up signals from an alien female planet. No signal. No clue. No hope. But you will meet a couple of our dogs, who were mostly goofballs, too. At least they seemed to understand us.

The three of us no longer relive our tales when we are dining out, ever since the night we lost all control and were politely asked to enjoy our dessert "elsewhere," and this in a place *run by a friend.* Our book is a shared remembering of some of these stories, and time has certainly softened some of the rougher edges, and blurred some realities. We have likely mixed up some people and places, simply forgotten others, and even changed a name or two. Like a good fish story, some of our capers have grown a bit over the years. We may not have always been able to separate these creative liberties from the truth and, well, stories *are* stories, but in their retelling we intend to embarrass no one but ourselves.

Which we think we do quite nicely.

Our wives know all these stories, and after listening patiently for years, finally suggested we start writing them down. Frankly, we think it was purely a defensive ploy on their part, except we called their bluff. They may yet regret their suggestion, but we don't. We have loved reliving our adventures, and now writing about them. We like to think that many of these stories capture something of the universal magic of youth—that they could have occurred almost *any* place, and maybe even *any* time. But they *do* spring from a certain place and a certain time—our youth in a small New Jersey town in the 1950s and early 1960s.

And it was a pretty good time. We came on the scene after the struggles of a world war, in which we lost relatives, but before Vietnam, in which we lost friends, along with our innocence. And way, way before Hurricane Sandy, in which some of the places of our favorite memories were simply, and sadly, *washed away*.

We know now, of course, that the times were far more complex than we ever imagined, and that we were just one tribe among many. We were largely unaware of social changes just beginning to emerge all around us. Our victories were scarcely noted, our failures rarely the stuff of tragedy, and our disappointments pretty common. But it was not a youth without meaning and consequence. And many, many laughs.

And our little town was pretty neat, too. You may even have heard about it, as it grew up too, long after we left.

But in our day, our town—we'll get to the name shortly—was home to about 6,000 good folks, and the three of us, too. It boasted its own post office, apparently with the first zip code—07078—ever granted to an unincorporated village. We have no idea if that's true, but we have always doubled down on this zip code myth, with some cool story that a former Postmaster General had lived in town, and pushed it through. Come on. If you were the Postmaster General, wouldn't you call in a chit for your own zip code?

Our town was then, and still is, known for its top-flight public schools. It continues to deliver graduates to top colleges, although you may soon conclude that those considerable resources were wasted on the three of us. In fact, at our first business lunch—where we were hoping to interest a *real literary agent* in our work—and well before any actual food arrived, our prospective agent, having just read the manuscript, actually did ask us directly, "Just how did you clowns even get into college?" We think the better question may be how did we even get out of high school, but we hired him on the spot anyway—our newest best friend, the tireless Jerry Rudes.

Our adventures started in our elementary school, the Glenwood School. It had, and still has, a wonderfully classic look—red brick, with white door and window trim, and the obligatory white cupola crowning the roof, along with a sturdy flagpole dead center on the front lawn. It looked, in fact, remarkably like the plastic school building you may have gotten one Christmas for your Lionel train set, only Glenwood was two stories tall, already had a second wing, and didn't sport a plastic nail-polish-red brick shine. By third grade, we all walked to school. And by fifth, we could ride our bikes, which was a *very big* deal.

The town itself sported a number of welcoming churches, a classic brick railroad station, real sidewalks, a couple of cool parks, a bird sanctuary, and traffic lights only when you crossed into "the township." You see, we were linked in some strange jurisdictional way to a mother ship, the Township of Millburn. This whole township idea seems a Jersey thing, and the relationship of the Township to our village was kind of like the gravitational physics of a binary star system: no one really knows how it works, but the village and township have been orbiting around each other for a very long time.

The three of us grew up in small homes just a short walk from the "Village Center," with its block-long collection of small shops, on one side of the street only. Although the line-up would change over the years, we remember a gas station, small pharmacy, dry cleaners, grocery, hair salon, realtor, and our favorite shop of all, a marvelous newsstand-candy store called "Haggett's," which sat right next to the post office. The whole block was tied together in a kind of two-story faux English style, sporting a nice white stucco and dark wood trim livery. Most people could walk from end to end in about a minute. We, of course, did not believe that a straight line was the best choice between *any* two points, and many an adventure started somewhere along the block, often after a chance meeting—maybe at Haggett's, or at the gas station where we pumped air into our bike tires (and later bought our first gas at maybe eighteen *cents* a gallon), or even the S&S grocery store when we were on some errand. But once off mission, and off that straight line, these adventures could last for *hours*.

Today, the town has about 13,000 people, and you may remember it from the Philip Roth novel, *Goodbye Columbus,* although the movie version, with Ali McGraw, shifted the action to Westchester, New York. Or you may know it as the home of a well-known and impossibly upscale mall, which was once just a woods full of mystery and mischief for our gang. Or maybe you know it as a haven for high-end Wall Street Wizards, who can today enjoy a pretty easy commute into the city. These folks have really upped the ante in town, and few of us could buy our old homes today.

But here on our pages we welcome you to our remembered Short Hills, New Jersey, and our youth, long ago.

Back then, pretty much running the whole show was the Greatest Generation—those men and women who had suffered through terrible wars and economic hardship, only to pick up the pieces without a fuss, with the dads (mostly, back then) marching off to jobs and taking charge at the local scout troop or Little League or church. Some of our mothers worked, and others didn't, but they were there too—making our lunches and stitching our homemade sports jerseys—as we stumbled through our boyhoods. They learned to fix our bikes, and even our broken spirits.

Together, this Greatest Generation drove us to ball games, bowling, scouts, first dates, and even something awful called dancing school.

We just drove *them* nuts.

They deserved better, but our adventures all made for a lifetime of stories and, as you will learn, most of us turned out OK after all.

If we have succeeded at all in this collection, you will find some of our stories funny, some a little painful, and others bittersweet. Many of them take place as we played our sports. If, as someone has said, play is really about how we all learn to read other people as well as the world, these stories may reveal quite a bit about our time, and ourselves, and that is why they come early in our book. Our next stories take us through misadventures in our schools and the painful wrongs visited upon our teachers, who, like our parents, deserved much better. Perhaps, as the next section, the Church Trilogy, suggests, we had hoped to right those wrongs by good deeds in church, except things just didn't work out that way. Once again, our hearts were in the right place, but we routinely screwed up even in this sacred refuge. Summer was also a great time to mess around, and mess up, and our last grouping of stories shows how mayhem, mischief, and misadventure followed us there, too.

Of course, only through the patience, grace, and love of the adults were we boys able to "grow up gently." Our sometimes comedic, sometimes bittersweet journey rested squarely on the broad shoulders of the adults who did their best to move us along in some responsible way. So we close our book with an epilogue, written as a tribute to our parents, teachers, coaches, and everyone else of the Greatest Generation. We think of it as a thank you, and we like that story the best.

Finally, in our brief Afterword, you will learn how it has all turned out for many of us.

In reading our book, we hope you will recapture something of the fragile magic of your own youth, the enduring miracle of friendship, and the gift of gently remembered stories told over the years with both laughter and tears.

Our stories follow no particular narrative order and generally stand on their own. If you think we have stuffed too much fun into the collection —the idea of "too much" still foreign to us—feel free to roam around our misadventures at will. We just hope you will find a few that will hit the mark. Enjoy.

Bud Schill, John MacIlroy, and Rob Hamilton

BY WAY OF INTRODUCTION

It was an especially wonderful time to be a noisy moron.

- Bill Bryson, *The Life and Times of the Thunderbolt Kid*

NOT EXACTLY ROCKET SCIENTISTS

As a kid in the 1950s, I always figured the first person on the moon would be Alice Kramden. Her TV husband, Ralph (Jackie Gleason), began threatening to send her there in 1956. Of course, he never did. But thirteen years later, on the day my first child was born, July 20, 1969, the United States put a man up there. A lot of stuff happened in between.

For instance, I was shooting baskets with schoolmates on October 4, 1957 when I heard that Sputnik—the world's first artificial satellite, not much larger than our basketball—was launched into orbit by the Soviet Union. This event led not only to the founding of NASA and a new political, military, technological, and scientific race between the two superpowers, but to the refinement of what had already been a fascination among boys my age with space travel, which, up until then, had been the province of fiction only.

Our fascination had originally been sparked by Buster Crabbe, who, banking off his fame as an Olympic swimming champion, starred in several *Flash Gordon* movies in the late 1930s. These were the space movies we watched as kids in the early 50s. Flash, his girlfriend Dale Arden, and a stiff named Dr. Zarkov were constantly matching wits with Ming the Merciless, the evil ruler of the planet Mongo. Ming's only sympathetic, reliable, and relatable characteristic was transparent lust for Dale.

During this era, we had a lot of cowboy heroes, such as Tex Ritter, Hopalong Cassidy, The Lone Ranger, Roy Rogers, Gene

Autry, Lash LaRue (who eventually taught Harrison Ford how to use a bull whip for his role in *Indiana Jones*), Wyatt Earp (whom we called "Quiet Burp"), Bat Masterson, Kit Carson, Paladin, Wild Bill Hickok, Zorro, and my favorite, The Cisco Kid. But we had only one space hero—Flash Gordon. And he let us down, since his movies, made over a decade earlier, were so stupid.

Back to Ming. He wasn't an interesting space villain like Darth Vader or a mutant like Jabba the Hut. He was just a jerk, with the elongated face of Vladimir Lenin, eyebrows shaped like boomerangs, a goofy hood and a pointed collar always turned up. (Ming the Merciless bobble heads, by the way, are available online!)

But more than the two-dimensional characters, what made the *Flash Gordon* movies so lame were the fake rockets. They would take off from fake sets in a prone position and arc upward after skidding across the ground for about ten feet without wheels. And the pilots and passengers could climb into them and ascend within seconds, as though they were running out to the grocery store in a DeSoto. It was all too clear that the rockets were miniaturized and puppeted. My friends and I figured that even though we were unlikely to ever need a rocket of our own to do battle with a dork like Ming, we could make better ones than the producers of the *Flash Gordon* movies. We set about to do just that.

So for a time, in addition to being cowboys, we were rocket boys, but the trajectories of our rocket careers were both shallow and short, spanning the period from 1956 to 1959.

We started out making a fleet of paper rockets, which were always lined up on our bureaus and floors, ready to be launched into outer space. But the only way they could take off was if we threw them, which we did often—and more than occasionally into someone's eye or a bowl of soup. Even our dogs would cower or hide when they saw us pick one up. The only critter who wasn't afraid initially was my mother's parakeet, Peter, who taunted us from his perch, protected by his cage. Although occasionally the tip of a paper rocket would hit the back of his mirror, causing him to flutter furiously and then quickly jettison a load of parakeet poop.

Eventually, some of my friends and I tried to figure out how to make a rocket that would actually take off on its own. We experimented with several suspect substances for our fuselages. For reasons I don't have to explain here, neither paper towel rolls nor balsa wood worked particularly well.

We thought we had the answer when we came upon some unused electric conduit pipe, which we liberated from one of the new houses being constructed in the neighborhood. We figured that if we took about a foot of this stuff, glued wings onto it (made from spare parts from crashed balsa wood airplanes), attached a silly putty point to its tip, poured the right fuel into it, and lit the fuse, we could cause the hodgepodge rocket to fly. This overly simplistic approach turned out to be wanting in several key particulars, among them the fact that we had no clue what fuel to use. We certainly didn't have access to real rocket fuel, so we had to improvise. We made a poor choice—gunpowder.

Today, kids don't have cap guns. They have water pistols and Nerf Blasters that shoot sponge balls or little darts with suction cups on the tips. Back then, we had unlimited cap guns and unlimited caps. These came in rolls, approximately a half-inch wide, of perforated red paper (sometimes yellow). Every half inch or so, there was a raised bump in the paper that concealed a tiny amount of gunpowder. You'd put the roll on a spool in a cap gun and with each pull of the trigger the spool would rotate the span of one cap. This placed the cap under the hammer of the gun, which, when it hit the cap, caused a small explosion which emitted a spark, some smoke and a cracking sound. Nothing, of course, came out of the barrel, so we weren't really shooting anything. Just pretending. But with real gunpowder.

Our ill-conceived plan was to stockpile as many caps as we could and mine them for gunpowder for our rockets. We would stretch a roll of caps out on a counter top and cut into each little bump, and sometimes into the counter top, with a razor (a tool in ready supply) and scrape out the gunpowder. Conceptually, this made sense; in practice, it didn't work so well—about two out of three times, the cap would explode. If it didn't, we would get about one grain of gunpowder.

Today, parents would be very nervous at the sight and sound of caps. But in the 50s, our parents bought us as many boxes of caps as we could handle. We got them for Christmas, birthdays, Arbor Day, or just because we asked. We would say, "I sure could use some more caps." Not, "I'm running low on gunpowder." So, although our caps were never in short supply, the gunpowder yield was minimal in comparison to the labor involved. After a while, we realized the pace of collection was too slow to fuel our plan to beat Alice Kramden to the moon. Since we were reluctant to try to extract gunpowder from our firecrackers (they were too valuable), we needed another source.

During the 50s, most boys were totally unsupervised. If we weren't in school, we were free-range. Our parents had no idea where we were. They sent us out in the morning and figured we'd show up for dinner. We could be out playing ball, climbing trees, chopping down trees, throwing snow balls at moving cars, shooting bows and arrows, throwing rocks at glass bottles, tossing knives and spears, shooting BB guns, making bonfires, putting pennies on train tracks, setting off fireworks (more on that later), riding our bikes into town, riding our bikes into other towns, crossing dangerous highways, swimming in quarries, driving go-carts, climbing on the rafters of new houses, etc. Our parents didn't have the corner of a clue where we were, nor could they find us, unless we wanted to be found, as there were no cell phones.

If we were inside, the mischief could be even worse, especially after one of the toy companies (it might have been Hasbro) invented chemistry sets for kids.

We all had chemistry sets, but since we were young boys, we hadn't yet taken any chemistry courses. So, we were teaching each other and making stuff up. We would mix substances that had never been combined in world history, and then we would light them on fire. For several years, our basements smelled like rotten egg factories, and there were burn marks everywhere, including on the linoleum, the walls, and the curtains. It's fair to say that no one thought of us as pre-med students or future brain surgeons.

Grant Griggs and his family had just moved into a house two doors up. Grant had an early credibility problem, in that he claimed that once his father had parachuted to safety from a small plane, clutching Grant's sister, Pussy, in his arms with Grant holding onto his legs. We had trouble buying this. So when Grant told us he knew how to make gunpowder, we were skeptical. But it turned out he did.

Grant explained that gunpowder is a simple mixture of 75 percent saltpeter, 15 percent sulfur, and 10 percent charcoal. We had, or could get, all that stuff, although we were iffy on the calculation of percentages. We pooled our supplies and then ordered refills of ingredients. Over time, we accumulated enough gunpowder to supply a small army.

But there was no big payoff here, because we came to appreciate that gunpowder is a substandard rocket fuel, in that it doesn't propel rockets. It blows them up.

This we learned on our first attempt. Grant, Charlie Berger (who lived two doors down on the other side), and I had stuffed a lot of gunpowder (an unstable hybrid obtained from caps and chemistry sets) into a piece of conduit, fitted out with a cardboard point wrapped in tape and a cardboard barrier at the base, through which we inserted a fuse. We balanced the vehicle inside a piece of metal gutter that had come detached from the house of Dodd Potts, who lived between Charlie and me. We lit the fuse, figuring our rocket would travel at least a few hundred feet. We backed up, anticipating the glory.

Nothing happened. We had heard of delayed reactions, so we waited. Eventually, Charlie worked up the nerve to topple the gantry with a small rake so we could check the fuse. It had fizzled. I forget what we made the fuse out of, but whatever it was, it didn't hold the flame. It took us about twenty minutes to figure out how to put together a better fuse, which we made from "fusing" fuses we had in our firecracker arsenal. We lit the new fuse and stepped back. Just barely far enough.

After the explosion, the drainpipe was back at Dodd Potts' house (but on the roof), and the only thing left of the rocket was a black spot on the grass. The rocket had dematerialized.

We had to start over. We went with the conduit again, and the drainpipe (which we retrieved using a ladder). We diluted the gunpowder just a bit and put a few drops of water in it to "slow the burn."

The second explosion ruined the drainpipe for future use and sent the rest of our contraption to Neverland. We found pieces of conduit imbedded in the garage door, and we had to go to the very back of the yard (behind a tree, and technically not on our land) and dig up a piece of sod to patch the area of the front yard that had served as the launch pad but now was missing.

We wrote both of these failures off as bad luck. But we didn't much care, as we weren't planning on growing up to be rocket scientists.

Since we kind of liked explosions, we proceeded with that model, but in another medium. Howitzers.

One of the secrets to propelling an object a long way, and straight, is to make it travel the first few feet in a controlled direction. That's how rifles work, and why they are more accurate than handguns. As this realization hit us, we were staring at the perfect "rifle barrel"—one of the metal pipes from the swing set in our backyard. We figured my sister and her friends didn't need the swing set anyway. So we removed one of the legs. This required some tools, and some strength, but we were boys. We could do anything. We planned to replace that leg later.

The pipe was about twelve feet long. After we cut the top off with a hack saw, we separated the bottom from the chain holding it to an iron stake in the ground, but we left in place a pin that was soldered across the base. This we considered to be perfect to hold in place anything we might put down the tube as a potential projectile.

But first, we had to select a propellant. Having given up on gunpowder, we knew we needed something that would burn, and emit fumes, and not blow up. Who thought of this, I can't remember, but we came up with the solution of using match heads. Not the little ones in the cardboard folders, but the big wooden ones.

We bought several boxes of wooden matches at the A&P. We snapped off all the heads and scrapped the wooden sticks. We tightly packed the heads into a piece of conduit tube and lit a few of the heads at the bottom. Quickly, they all ignited. In the process, we noticed a huge rush of fire and fumes. We wondered if this might be a good rocket fuel, but we were now building a howitzer, so we stuck with that theme.

We obtained a rubber cup of some kind. We knew better than to use plastic. This one was hard rubber. I think it was the lining to a hole at one of the local golf courses. Anyway, we taped it to the base of the swing set pipe, which we had propped up on about a 45-degree angle through the remaining uprights of the now unsteady swing set. We drilled a hole in the base of the cup and inserted a fuse. Then we angled the pipe toward the sky, shoved a giant marble down the muzzle, and lit a fuse leading to the match heads.

The result was thrilling. There was no explosion, but rather a *WHOOSH* as the fuel ignited and the marble rushed into the sky.

Behind my house were woods that, to us at least, seemed to stretch for miles. Actually, they stretched for a few hundred yards before banking up past what we called "the sand pit," which then sloped up about fifty yards to Mt. Ararat Road, which had a few houses on it. Tony Intilli and Billy Fitzsimmons lived up there. They were both participants in many of our capers.

Next to the sand pit, and on the edge of the woods, but down on our level, was a haunted house. It had been abandoned years earlier. Most of the windows were broken. Our parents knew we went over there all the time, but they didn't seem too afraid of either the ghosts, the rotten boards, the exposed nails, or the broken glass.

Anyway, we decided we would use the haunted house as target practice for our howitzer. From my backyard, we zeroed in on our target. Adjusting for windage, we took aim. After the *WHOOSH*, there was a *THWAAP*, as the marble whacked the side of the house. After another trip to the A&P, we repeated the target practice.

We were now emboldened. Confident of our firepower, and our aim, we decided to take on a trickier task—hitting the house up on Mt. Ararat Road between Tony's and Billy's. This house was twice the distance to the haunted house and up about fifty yards higher. We assumed the marble would never get there. It did, and when it hit the aluminum siding, the echo lasted for what seemed to be an eternity. We listened for a phone call, or a siren, but silence set in. We sent up a scout who reported that no one was home, and that although there was a slight dent on the side of the house, there was no major damage.

We felt badly about whapping the house and wanted to turn our scientific skills to a more noble purpose, one that we figured our parents would appreciate. We thought about trying to shoot Sputnik out of the sky, but there was no Internet back then and thus we couldn't get access to the orbital charts. So, naturally, we turned our attention to tent caterpillars.

Tent caterpillars never really hurt anyone, although it is said that when eaten by a mare, they can cause an abortion. One or two tent caterpillars in isolation can be kind of cute. Thousands of them in a huge, ugly tent in an apple tree in your front yard can be annoying, particularly if they keep falling on your head and going down the back of your shirt.

Tent caterpillar nests were very prevalent in our town in the late 50s. They drove us nuts. The creatures were everywhere, and their abodes were eyesores. About 10,000 of these creatures decided to build a nest in our beautiful front yard apple tree. My father remarked a few times about what pests they were, and how, when he got the time, he was going to do something about them. We beat him to it.

We were to learn, though, that exterminating tent caterpillars can lead to adverse consequences, particularly if you use "cherry bombs." If caps would make modern parents nervous, cherry bombs would freak them out. These were red, cherry-sized tools of obliteration. They packed the wallop of at least a dozen firecrackers. Each cherry bomb had a green fuse about an inch long. Once that monster was lit, you'd better get far away, fast. A similar device of about the same explosive strength was an "ash can," which was a silver cylinder about two inches long with a fuse coming out of the middle. Throughout America, hundreds of teenage boys have been expelled from hundreds of schools for lighting either a cherry bomb or an ash can and flushing it down a toilet.

On a day when my parents were both out, Billy Fitzsimmons and I decided to take action. The nest, which was a dense, white gossamer, was about fifteen feet up in the tree and about a foot and a half across. We knew we couldn't pry it loose, as it was too sticky. Although we had not seen this done, we heard that some fathers had been successful burning the tents. We weren't sure about that, but we decided to give it a go. Then we had a great idea. Let's burn the nest and also blow it to smithereens. In laying out this plan, we decided to try another rocket.

This took about an hour. We got some rags and soaked them in gasoline from the lawnmower can. We took a long bamboo pole that Billy had, got on a wobbly stepladder, and draped the drenched rag over the tent. Desiring to make sure there was enough gasoline, we repeated the process with another rag. We poked at the rag so that it went around most of the tent and allowed some of the gas to seep in.

We didn't have time to build another rocket. So we went into our stash of fireworks, which included some small "skyrockets." These harmless devices were mounted on skinny sticks. When they took off from the ground they emitted sparks and traveled about forty feet. We took a small swab of rag and tied it around the tip of a skyrocket.

Then genius struck. We got two cherry bombs and an ash can. One by one, we stuck the fuses into the hollow end of the bamboo pole and reached up, penetrating the nest with the pole. When we retrieved the pole, the explosive device remained inside.

We placed the skyrocket on the ground, lit the rag on top, then the fuse, and hoped the skyrocket would carry its flaming payload into the tent caterpillar nest. It didn't. It carried the burning rag past one of the other branches and onto our front porch. In a panic, we managed to extinguish the fire before any noticeable damage occurred.

Then we got another skyrocket, affixed another soaked rag, lit it and took more careful aim. For the first and only time in our rocketry history, the device went straight up. It lodged into the gasoline-soaked tent, which immediately went ablaze. Anticipating what was about to happen, we cleared out.

With only milliseconds between them, the explosions were deafening. Two cherry bombs and an ash can. The nest was obliterated, as were two branches of the apple tree. In every direction—up, down, left and right—burning pieces of nest and rag flew, and either flaming or already crisp tent caterpillars went everywhere. They were on us, on the car belonging to a neighbor named Mickey Silvane (who my father was convinced was really Mickey Spillane, author of the Mike Hammer detective mysteries), on our picture window, on Dodd Potts' roof, in our garage, in the street, in other trees, in our pants cuffs, and in our hair.

Charlie Berger had not been in on this project, but he heard the explosion and, from two doors down, yelled, "Sweet!"

Pussy Griggs saw it and ran to tell her mother.

When my parents returned, there were repercussions, starting with the mandate that we clean all the windows and apologize to the neighbors. But my folks basically took it all in stride, and I think my father was relieved both that no one was killed and that he now didn't have to deal with the nest.

Except for a few other dangerous experiments with gunpowder and various propellants, in which the co-conspirators included Bob Stultz and Tim Haslam (whom we called "Hasbro" and later "Bro"), and in which there were some close calls (after one of which Bro couldn't feel his arm for two days), we all kind of drifted away from these scientific pursuits. Haslam and I decided we wanted to become lawyers and began advising some of the others on statute of limitations issues.

At about 9:45 a.m. on February 20, 1962, while on spring break from high school, I was standing with my father in an orange grove between Ft. Lauderdale and Hialeah at the moment John Glenn took off from Cape Canaveral on Friendship 7 for the first ever Earth orbit, and we could hear the rocket above us. We knew this was a big deal. Throughout the next few hours, we listened to the radio to make sure the mission was successful, which it was.

We had, of course, witnessed, on television, the "up and down" rides, in 1961, of Alan Shepherd and Gus Grissom, but this was a four-ring orbit, which was a huge accomplishment by a nation whose president made it a priority to put a man on the moon in that decade. We were lucky to have experienced up close (albeit from an orange grove) this milestone in rocketry and space travel.

But by 1962, my personal career in rocketry, and that of most of my friends, was long over. We had proven ourselves to be total misfires in that field, as well as in all things involving chemistry and weaponry. Along the way, we had dabbled in fireworks and chemistry sets, and with a howitzer and a series of doomed rockets—all to no positive gain and substantial economic, environmental, and entomological loss. It was fortunate for our country that we had no designs on careers with NASA. After all, we were not exactly rocket scientists.

GOOD SPORTS ALL

We made too many wrong mistakes.

> - Yogi Berra, after the Yankees lost to
> the Pirates in the 1960 World Series

BANNED FOR LIFE

It was Halloween 1960, just a few days before JFK was elected president. We were too old to go out trick-or-treating, although I remember going out that night anyway, wearing just a football helmet, to bolster my candy supply. In fact, I'm pretty sure that Mischief Night (the night before Halloween) was the night several of us (I think I recall that Johnny O'Reilly was in the posse) placed a burning bag of dog poop on Rodney Howarth's front stoop, and rang the doorbell, hoping his father (whom we didn't like) would come out and stomp out the fire, which he did, thus covering his pants, the front hallway and, unfortunately, their cat, with poop.

Anyway, on Halloween afternoon, several of us decided to go bowling at the Livingston Lanes. Livingston was the town just north of Short Hills. It was Scott McQueen, "Spike" Hughes, George Freund, and myself. One of the mothers dropped us off, expecting us to be there for a couple of hours, and not anticipating our urgent call soon thereafter, asking to be picked up. Unlike the Howarth incident (which was premeditated and did not implicate Scott, Spike, or George), what caused the four of us to leave Livingston prematurely was totally innocent, albeit more destructive.

None of us was particularly good at bowling, except for Scott, who had both style, and his own bowling ball. Although secretly jealous, we all made fun of him, wondering why anyone would want his own bowling ball, since there were so many to choose from at the alley. Scott said because it was the perfect weight and the perfect fit for his fingers. Not too loose, not too tight—just right. And he had all the moves of a pro down pat. He would gently rock back and forth, cradle the ball in his hand, deposit it on the alley, smooth

31

as silk, within inches of the start line, and curve it right where it belonged.

George and I had a genuine lack of style. Likewise, but in a different way, Spike (tall, lanky, strong and resembling a stork or a pterodactyl) had a huge wingspan but zero finesse.

I never got a whole lot better at bowling than I was that day. I did once bowl a 217, and I was on a winning team at a law firm retreat in Williamsburg in 1978, when we were supposed to play golf and it rained. For that big win, I was awarded a bottle of Mad Dog 20/20, which I still have. One of my partners, Stephen Watts, also won a bottle of MD 20/20 for bowling the low score of 16. We then moved on to a lecture by a psychologist who handed out mood rings. Stephen's mood was blue, but not blue enough to try the MD.

Once, I was bowling with cousins in Florida and one of them let go of the ball on the backswing, sending it past the onlookers up into the lobby, smashing into the wheels of a baby carriage.

Anyway, Scott, Spike, George, and I all played lots of sports: baseball, football, basketball, hockey, soccer, tennis, and golf. Plus, we had good grades and were reasonably well behaved. Renaissance men. We weren't much into track and field, although we knew the concepts (some of which crept into Spike's bowling technique).

For instance, we knew that in the shot put, the athlete cradles a small cannon ball in the fingers of his dominant hand, spins around in a tight circle to build centrifugal force, and pushes the ball out from his shoulder, without spinning it. And we knew that in the discus, the athlete grabs the disc under his hand, spins around the same tight circle to build centrifugal force, and spins the disc outward. In both events, the device is propelled outward in a high arc.

In baseball, there were essentially five pitches available to young teenagers: fast ball, change up, curve, screwball, and sinker. Some pros and college players had the knuckler (thrown with the finger nails dug in but otherwise sort of like a shot put), and maybe the slider (which, if attempted by a teenager, would usually result in a bean ball). If thrown by a right-handed pitcher, the curve was spun with the thumb headed outward, aimed at a right-handed batter's left armpit and curved in over the plate, causing him to back away. The screwball, if thrown by a right-handed pitcher, was spun thumb-in and did the opposite of the curve, heading outside the plate but curving in at the last second. In other words, the screwball thrown by a right-handed pitcher was to a left-handed batter what the curve was to a right-handed batter. Some right-handed pitchers, like me, had a natural screwball (or so my coaches said), but hardly anyone could throw one on purpose with control, because the wrist action was unnatural and awkward.

In bowling, there were essentially the same five "pitches," except, as between the curve and the screwball, the latter was natural and the former awkward. The really strong bowlers who had no finesse could throw a fast ball aimed either dead center or a little off the one pin. Old people and little kids favored the change up, sometimes accomplished just by pushing the ball off the starting line with both hands and hoping it made it to the pins (this method often yielded higher scores than my fast ball approach). Right-handers with skill (like Scott) would fire the ball with a wicked counterclockwise spin, aiming it almost at the right gutter and watching it curve into the right edge of the one pin with enough spin to knock down all or most of the pins. Occasionally, a large, strong bowler would throw something of a sinker, where the ball sailed about six or seven feet before landing in the alley, but usually without a lot of noise. It was more like an airplane making a smooth landing on a runway in good weather.

If a right-hander was trying to make the ball curve right to left (like the pros did, and like Scott did), he twisted his thumb in. This was tricky. It took a lot of practice. But it was almost impossible for a right-handed bowler to throw what looked like a screwball, down the left side of the lane curving in. To our knowledge, no one had ever tried such a shot until Halloween in 1960 when Spike Hughes gave it a go.

We arrived at the Livingston Lanes at about 4:00 p.m. There were about twenty lanes, with the usual groupings of bowlers. An early team or two with their silk shirts with the names on the back. A couple of birthday parties. A few families, or at least mothers with their kids and their kids' friends. All out for a good time. All expecting to be left alone to hone their skills and/or have some good clean fun.

There was one clock in the Lanes. It was about twenty feet up on the wall just beyond the last lane on the right. A huge clock, about two feet in diameter, with a white face and massive black hands. There was a brass casing around the device, holding the glass in place. The clock was totally out of harm's way, visible to everyone in the building, and handy for all to rely on to complete their recreation and time their rides home. We were assigned to the last lane on the right, with the clock on the wall nearest us. Being so close to the wall, we had to strain our necks to look up and see it.

Again, Scott McQueen had his own bowling ball. The rest of us had to select among the publicly available balls, looking for those that fit our hands and were of the right weight. Some were as heavy as anvils, while others were almost as light as duck pin balls. The finger holes were of varying widths, and picking the one that was just right was sometimes a real challenge. George and I used the medium weight balls. Spike, even though he was the tallest amongst us, wanted a light one so he could "fire" it. He knew he had no finesse. Since he couldn't pitch the sweeping curve that Scott had mastered, he was determined to overpower the pins. He was so powerful that occasionally he threw a sinker, where the ball traveled up to a third the length of the lane before thumping down with a loud bang. Sometimes he would even hit the one pin on a bounce. He loved this, although the other bowlers made it clear they could do without the distraction. But because Spike's repertoire was exhausted with the fastball and sinker, and he had no action on the ball, he wanted to step up his game. He wanted to try the fast ball-sinker-screwball.

The light balls all looked the same, with the little red specks. Spike grabbed the wrong one. It turned out to be a bit too tight on his fingers.

Bound and determined to throw a power strike, and at the same time contemplating either a curve or a screwball (although he had the thumb-in/thumb-out thing backwards) in order to gain the torque power that Scott exhibited with ease, Spike started his approach a few feet farther back than normal. With fast, long strides that resembled an ostrich running from a lion, he charged the release line.

Now, the causes of what happened next are multiple and complex. As best I can tell, they were a combination of overaggressive charging, attempting the screwball, one or more fingers getting temporarily stuck in the ball, and confusion between bowling, shot putting, discus throwing, and, perhaps, even jai alai. Spike was out of control. We could tell something awful was about to happen, and we started backing up. Spike got to the line in a clumsy burst of speed, fired his arm in a curved position, caught his right foot with his left, spun like a drunken ballerina, turned 270-degrees, and threw the bowling ball like a discus. It took off as though shot from a catapult on a 90-degree angle east and a 70-degree angle toward the ceiling. The arc was perfect and could never be replicated. This huge, albeit light, red specked bowling ball traveled 20 feet up the wall. It was spinning as Spike had intended it to, but it was not curving.

THWAAPP! The ball hit the face of the clock dead square. The clock blew up. The ball crashed down on our lane, careened off the gutter and eventually took out four pins, evoking a round of applause. The glass rained over three alleys. The face of the clock, with the hands spinning, landed about ten feet down our alley, just missing Spike, who had done a somersault over the ball return. The big brass ring came down with a *BOING* and bounced from alley to alley like a hubcap after a car accident. All that was left on the wall was a group of tangled, colored wires.

Except for the sound of the bouncing brass ring and the tinkling of falling glass, all you could hear were kids and their parents coughing up root beer.

The guy who ran the bowling alley lost it. He came charging up to us, screaming, "YOU ASSHOLES! GET THE F___ OUT OF HERE AND DON'T EVER COME BACK! EVER! DO YOU UNDERSTAND THAT? EVER!!!"

We answered with our feet, leaving hurriedly and quietly, stopping only to call Mrs. Freund to come get us, as she lived in the part of Short Hills closest to the Livingston line.

That night, Johnny O'Reilly, a couple of others (probably Tony Intilli), and I went out for Halloween. We skipped Rodney Howarth's house (particularly after seeing the cat staring out the picture window).

Having been banned for life, I never returned to the Livingston Lanes. In fact, I do not recall ever returning to Livingston. A friend who lives near there, however, informs me that (a) the establishment has changed ownership; (b) the new name is the "Hanover Lanes"; (c) there has been an extensive upgrade of the facilities, including the clock; and (d) the ban is still in effect.

THE COMMISSIONER

While we generally enjoyed the organized sports activities and leagues managed by the adults around town, we were nuts about our informal, haphazard pick-up games. Our venues were largely determined by the measured generosity of the kind people who owned the suitable yards and small ponds, and could tolerate our goofy antics. This left out a few, like the Livingston Lanes.

Strangely, we rarely considered the several well-maintained school playing fields around town, or even the two principal town parks. These all seemed to represent the adult world, which we were inclined to keep at arm's length.

These town assets may have even required some kind of official sign-up, which would have called for way too much planning. Furthermore, several of our dads had volunteered to serve on the "Township Parks and Recreation Council," which was all the more reason to fly under that radar line. Indeed, we were beginning to see a pattern here: our dads, in varying combinations, would regularly appear in positions of local authority, while we would be looking for a considerably more relaxed supervisory style. A few dads were running the show over at Scout Troop 15, more were coaching Little League, and even some were teaching Sunday school at Christ Church. These guys had all signed on for some kind of saturation parenting, and we weren't able to hide from them anywhere.

We just wanted to be left alone to gather on short notice and play our sports beyond the shadow of adult supervision.

So hockey found a perfect home at Jencko's Pond along Lakeview Avenue, and was a deep winter favorite. The Twin Ponds over by the Short Hills Club and Stone's Pond were terrific alternatives. Each

of these ponds seemed to have a mysterious but well-discussed variable in freezing characteristics, as improbable as that now sounds: ice
just felt different on each pond. Depending on how well you skated,
you quickly found a favorite kind of pond ice, one that seemed to
support your own skating style. This was all ridiculous, of course.
Indeed, one of the gang on the "Short Hills Detroits" had a wonderfully unique skating style: he simply skated on the side of the skate
boot, with the steel blade itself never touching the ice. As a result,
he was remarkably indifferent to ice conditions, willing to slide—if
not really skate—on any surface, and probably thought our theory of
variable ice conditions idiotic.

Touch football games traveled the circuit, moving during the
fall from yard to yard across the entire town. Long, narrow side yards
were highly sought-after and surprisingly available, although land-
scaping suffered significant collateral damage in the wake of our football games, and we were lucky to get more than two or three games
out of a yard before being asked to move along.

And so it went, even to the lesser sports. Basketball nets would
occasionally appear, limited to paved driveways, and generally
restricted to games of "H-O-R-S-E" and free-throw contests. A bad-
minton net or two would pop up from time to time in various yards
during the summer. Bowling lived in a kind of twilight zone of kid-
adult interaction, as we needed an adult in the early years to get
us over to the Livingston Lanes, and other more serious problems
would eventually soil that venue.

All in all, however, we were happy with our choices. Although
we heard rumors that the really rich kids out in the farther reaches of
the county actually had their own ponies and would play a kind of
pick-up polo, that world was far removed, and these comparisons did
not trouble us at all. Season after season, we were able to find great
places for our favorite pick-up sports, and one even then we knew
was a true gift of small town life.

As luck would have it, that venue was right next door to my
house.

The Stevens family lived on Lakeview Avenue, in a large and
handsome dark brick home. I am sure it represented a certain kind

of desirable period architecture, with an imposing front veranda, a long paved driveway and a detached white clapboard two-car two-story garage. The four Stevens children likely, and with good reason, considered the home itself to be the gem of the property: lots of bedrooms, a huge living room, a dining room and even a bright and kid-friendly sunroom. Their basement—which was not the scary kind in most Jersey homes—featured an impossibly massive pool table: said to be "regulation," no one could figure out how this monster had gotten down the narrow stairs to the basement. But we figured at least it wasn't going anywhere else soon, and playing pool became our indoor sport of choice.

For the most part, however, we were yard and outdoor people, always on the lookout for suitable sports facilities, and the Stevens' home did not disappoint there. The paved driveway featured a very official-looking basketball net, complete with backboard. Bolted firmly to the garage, it offered us a virtually indestructible, first-class basketball court. Better yet, the large backyard was just about perfect for ball sports, with a distinctive green-shingled garage roof sloping gracefully in dead centerfield in a way that mimicked, in an imaginative stretch, the imposing geometry of the soon-to-be-history Polo Grounds, then still home to the Giants. We found our "warning track" in a row of nicely maintained rose bushes along the centerfield perimeter by the garage, as well as a kind of natural backstop cage in some high, somewhat tangled bushes at the other end of the yard. A row of tall, slender trees (maybe blue gums) created a tight but playable third base line, and several working herb gardens along the house on the right created a compact, but very desirable, right field line.

A couple of garden benches by the sunroom added a suggestion of limited stadium seating for the very occasional fan or two—usually a sister, or a bored, and only slightly curious, neighborhood girl. Every once in a while, however, a girl would show up who actually seemed interested in the game—or more likely, at least in one of the players. That hinted at strange new developments off the field, which were both novel to us and a bit unsettling.

Maybe best of all, the adult management at the house really liked kids—their own, of course, but also the neighborhood kids along with their buddies.

This was glorious. A dual-purpose (treble, really, if you counted the pool table) athletic facility with friendly ownership—and all of this next door to me and my buddy Suds Estes, and just a short bike ride for most of the Woodland Road Gang.

What could go wrong?

Well, in a major miscalculation, we opened the baseball season with a spirited pick-up *hardball* game, and one of the very first batters promptly sent a sizzling line drive right through one of the two garage windows, just left of dead centerfield. Not only did the glass shatter, but it brought most of the supporting wooden pane structure down along with it. To our credit, we stopped the game, confessed to the kind Mrs. Stevens, and offered to pay for the damage, although she let us off the hook. She even made us some nice cookies and, all in all, was both forgiving and gracious, although we thought for sure there would be no more games played at Stevens Field. Luckily, we were wrong, for Mrs. Stevens seemed to have an agenda of her own.

You see, she had a rather wonderful dilemma with her fourth child: her youngest, a little fella we called "Willy." Willy was some three or four years younger than most of us in the neighborhood and in the awkward, unfair but apparently universal logic of most neighborhoods, he was often shuffled off to the side of most of our activities—a kind of "boy-in-waiting." In neighborhoods everywhere, this nasty childhood logic had little to do with merit. Kind, always willing to jump in on the fun, and apparently reasonably content to await his admission to the big boy world, Willy was really a terrific kid.

Willy was also brilliant. Off-the-charts brilliant.

Indeed, word had spread around our neighborhood that he could recite in perfect order the American Presidents *by the age of six!* He was one of the first sent off to private school, supporting the rumor that even our top-flight public school system could not keep up with him.

This kid was way ahead of most of us, and clearly destined for greatness. But before greatness, his mom needed a way to get him involved with the older kids, "playing up."

And the answer was right in her backyard.

Why not deploy this precocious but clearly underused neighborhood asset?

Mrs. Stevens let us know that she was quite willing to let us use the field if we could somehow adjust our game to limit any further damage. And an even more important and tacit condition of returning play to Stevens Field was that Willy would participate in some way.

Clearly, brilliance ran deep within this family, and we quickly got the message.

So with a little nudge, we designated Willy the official-in-charge, our *de facto* Commissioner, and he quickly set out to limit the collateral damage which had threatened further play. In quick succession, he outlawed all forms of hardballs, softballs, and even tennis balls as "dangerous instrumentalities."

What was left was something called "Wiffle ball."

The sport became the official game of our happy backyard league. The Wiffle ball came in two sizes. One was pretty much the size of a regulation hardball. The other was the size of a softball, and both were made of plastic and riddled like Swiss cheese with small round holes. Unlike Swiss cheese, however, these holes were in a precise and uniform pattern, perfectly designed to create a ball which completely defied the laws of aerodynamics and the logic of trajectory science.

Its relationship to a real baseball was largely illusory, other than being round. At least for a few innings.

It did things no real baseball could ever do, and didn't do the things a real baseball should!

It made no difference whether the Wiffle ball was thrown by a pitcher or fielder, or hit by a batter. Skill, at least at first, played almost no role. The damn thing would simply dip, rise, fall, sail, pitch up—or down—speed up, slow down, or even briefly hang motionless in midair. It was all random and comedic choreography.

Even the catcher, on those rare occasions when he actually caught an incoming pitch, would actually prefer to *walk* the Wiffle ball back to the pitcher, rather than throw it.

It was hilarious, and a perfect haphazard antidote to the formalities of the adult-managed leagues, and it matched quite perfectly the generally off-kilter way we boys engaged our world. Deploying the Wiffle ball in the backyard posed no significant harm, except to our easily bruised egos. It was a perfect choice for Willy's first rule, and we were hooked.

Willy even developed a theory about the ball, that it had been developed by a subculture of major league pitchers who threw something called the "knuckleball." Our young Commissioner gave us the whole backstory, soon convincing us that this mysterious and often misunderstood fraternity was led by future Hall-of-Famer Hoyt Wilhelm, who around that time was hurling knuckleballs with considerable success for the Chicago White Sox. That attention to detail lent the whole thing an odd but undeniable credibility, and helped cement Willy's new stature as a kind of "made man," neighborhood-wise.

We started to call him, simply, "the Commissioner."

He had earned it. The Wiffle Ball League of Lakeview Avenue was up and running, and the senior management in the Stevens home was clearly pleased. Willy had full League employment, and this made Mrs. Stevens quite happy. We had agreed to reasonable rules to safeguard the homestead, significantly reducing the chances for any further damage to structures surrounding the field, and this made Mr. Stevens very happy. I am sure he was pretty proud of his young genius, too.

So the games began, in the late spring of our sixth grade. Throughout the spring and summer months, the Commissioner faithfully balanced rule and reason, and successfully arbitrated many an on-field dispute. This was no easy task, but Willy was the perfect man for the job. Our behavior in general was as erratic as the Wiffle ball itself. Inclined toward the hilarious, comfortable with the haphazard, and generally skeptical of authority, we played right into the Commissioner's hands. His hyper-developing mind, even at this young age, could find order in our self-created chaos. But most importantly—and this really threw us for a loop—he became the authority figure even though he was not an adult.

Amazing.

He had found nothing less than a kind of wormhole in the complex fabric of the kid-adult-authority universe. Certainly it was a bit weird, with the older boys petitioning this younger kid to maintain the good order of the League, but it all seemed to work. His ideas were creative, his judgment sound and his rules fair. Frankly, it all really did hint at greatness ahead.

Look at his record. When we started to actually hit the crazy Wiffle ball with our beloved regulation Little League bats, balls would often sail right out of the park, usually over the garage roof, which we had dubbed the "Green Monster of Lakeview Avenue" in deference to the one Boston fan amongst us. When we did recover those shots, we saw the contest between bat and Wiffle ball was not a fair one, nor was it sustainable.

The balls were falling apart.

Stress cracks began to appear regularly. New holes joined the old, and with a general yellowing of the balls (no one remembers why this happened) they really did start to look like Swiss cheese. A kind of nasty plastic fuzz erupted over the whole surface, which itself had become decidedly "out-of-round." All of this added to the fun, as a misshapen Wiffle ball only enhanced its aerodynamic mischief. As a result, the game was spinning out of control. Sloppy fielding, erratic pitching, and huge numbers of home runs soon contributed to ridiculous scores. And we were running out of balls, as they were now being pulverized on a regular basis.

This was just the kind of challenge made for our child prodigy Commissioner, and he came through again.

His new ruling—I think he called it something like the "Inventory Preservation Rule"—mandated that all right-handed batters bat lefty, and all left-handed batters bat righty. We had no natural switch hitters, a fact I am now sure he had carefully considered, so this was generally a brilliant innovation, as the number of home runs dropped dramatically, along with ball damage.

Unfortunately, this new rule had an unanticipated consequence: instead of sizzling home runs, the league saw a dramatic increase in impossibly high fly balls. Soon they too would drop to earth in significant distress, sporting new cracks. On one occasion, high above the field, one of the cracked Wiffle balls actually fell apart, sending several separate and distinct pieces of the ball back to the field. Adding much happy confusion, this also provided a wonderful chance for mischief, always an opportunity seized upon by our band. Several players, each holding part of the now disintegrated ball, claimed an out to end the inning.

This was precisely the kind of tomfoolery unacceptable to the League Commissioner.

Likely alone among anyone present, the Commissioner actually knew about, and understood, the "Infield Fly Rule." Adopted in the 1890s, this rule would later be called—in a perfectly apt phrase—a "technical remedy for sneaky behavior" that would not have been necessary when baseball was a "gentlemen's sport." The short version is this: the Infield Fly Rule prevents a fielder from intentionally misplaying an infield fly (normally a single out) and then turning a double play by throwing out runners anticipating an easily caught fly ball.

Our Commissioner was clearly committed to this idea of gentlemanly behavior, and he quickly came up with a new rule. He called it something like the "Infield Exploding Fly Rule." This new rule addressed the developing nonsense on the field about multiple balls in play occasioned by the exploding (and imploding) infield Wiffle ball flies. The genius was this: if at least one piece was sufficient to be considered a ball in any meaningful sense, it could be played. On the other hand, if the ball was effectively destroyed, *no* part of it was in play.

This new rule solved this narrow technical problem, but it was clear that our Wiffle balls were still being subjected to terrible abuse, and our inventory was running very low.

So the Commissioner had no choice but to move in an entirely new direction—a total ban on "real" bats. He had discovered that the Wiffle Company had added an official "Wiffle bat" to its product line, in both wooden and plastic models. They were impossibly thin, ridiculously light and awkwardly long, and nothing like the bats we were used to. And, unlike our favorite real bats, these strange imposters were not the neat "autographed editions" coming out of Louisville, like my favorite, the "Moose Skowron Autograph edition." These bats sported nothing more than a weak corporate stamp of the logo of the Wiffle Company.

The structural absurdity of these Wiffle bats, with no apparent connection to the real world of baseball, further confirmed our suspicion that the Wiffle Company was run by pitchers—pitchers who hated batters. With the League soon demanding we bat from the "wrong" side, with a bat designed to make us look truly stupid, we again struggled at the plate. Strikeouts were called "whiffs," although I think that phrase probably pre-dated Wiffle ball, and carried its own quirky spelling. It was a perfect phrase, as we were again struggling at the plate.

As goofy as we looked with reverse batting stances and knock-off bats, we all loved the fun, the field and our innovative Commissioner. Our reputation spread, and soon boys from outside the neighborhood would regularly ask to play in a league game. The smart ones quickly figured out that their chances of taking the field were greatly enhanced if they brought along some baseball cards to trade or, better yet, simply give to us in tribute. Our Commissioner was already a great card collector, and was well prepared to sniff out poor deals. He was particularly wary of those fellas who tried to pass off a damaged "flapper"—those cards clipped to the spokes of a bicycle—as the stuff of acceptable tribute or trade. Despite the Commissioner's impressive and ever-growing collection of cards, there was never any hint of slippery back-room card deals in return for favorable treatment.

Yes, our Commissioner was on top of all aspects of the game, and honest to boot.

This all went on for several summers. New games were invented, and rules changed, to fit the ebb and flow of interest and number of players. The League at one point actually banned gloves, then reversed field and required them, although somewhere along the line we had to wear our gloves on the wrong hand. At another point we added goofy "Derbies," including the legendary "Cute Girls Home Run Derby." The object was to hit a certain spot on the green garage roof with a precisely placed home run shot, within a set number of pitches. By then we had discovered girls, and we figured that if word got back to the ladies that "an admirer" had won a Lakeview Derby in her honor (say eight home runs out of twelve pitches), this would somehow be the magic ice-breaker in a developing puppy love. It never worked, but the attempts were great fun. And since it was not a sanctioned event, we could even go back to creaming the ball with our preferred batting stance and our favorite real bat. You see, the Commissioner refused to consider this variation official League play, viewing it more as an exhibition game. While short of banning the practice, he was rarely seen at any of our derbies.

For several joyous and carefree seasons, this was a center of our own timeless world.

We felt, but would not have been able to articulate, precisely what the great sports writer Roger Angell described in "The Interior Stadium" from his book *The Summer Game*:

> Within the ballpark, time moves differently, marked by no clock except the events of the game . . . Since baseball time is measured only by outs, all you have to do is succeed utterly; keep hitting, keep the rally alive, and you have defeated time. You remain forever young.

It doesn't really work out that way, of course, and one day the league was destined to end. Other interests intruded, participation lagged, and one day the Commissioner simply suspended further official League play. The goofy derbies held on a bit, since they only needed a pitcher and batter, but that soon faded away too.

No, we would not stay forever young.

But all of us who played in the League like to think its legacy lives on, and within a circle considerably wider than our neighborhood.

You see, Willy, the first and only Commissioner of the Lakeview Wiffle Ball League, never lost his boyish love of the game and all things baseball, nor did he lose his dedication to the spirit of fair play and good order he brought to the League. A graduate of Yale and the University of Pennsylvania School of Law, William Stanley Stevens spent a lifetime in service to the law he loved with success and joy until his untimely death in his sixtieth year.

But he is best and widely known for a singular remarkable achievement, captured in the tag line of his obituary header as it appeared in the *New York Times*:

WILLIAM S. STEVENS, 60, DIES; WROTE INFIELD FLY RULE NOTE

The *Times* went on to describe Mr. Stevens' "slyly humorous" law review note, written while a law student at Penn, to be nothing less than a "cultural revolution" in legal writing, after which "law reviews were never the same." Comparing the Infield Fly Rule to the common law, his law note became one of the most celebrated and imitated works in American legal history. Within a year of its publication in 1975, his article was generating scholarly commentaries, imitations (the *Times*' favorite seemed to be something called "The Infield Fly Rule and the Internal Revenue Service Code: An Even Further Aside") and even citations in judicial decisions. As the *Times* put it, "it made lawyers think about the law in a different way."

Changing the way an entire generation of lawyers think about the law is one mean legacy.

And here's what we particularly liked: Willy describes the Infield Fly Rule as a technical remedy for "sneaky behavior." In his view, baseball, in order to keep alive the gentlemanly spirit of the game, drafted rules (much like our common law) to enforce civil behavior. Like common law, he argued, the Infield Fly Rule developed bit by bit, with refinements and adjustments added to address new problems as they arose.

Yes, greatness did come to our Commissioner, and maybe—just maybe—it all began with our sneaky tomfoolery in the Lakeview Wiffle Ball League right there in Willy's backyard.

Within a few years of the publication of this famous law review note, Stevens Field would be nothing but a memory, ground to dust to make way for the ever-expanding interstate system and its connectors in Northern New Jersey.

If you find yourself, some pleasant summer day, driving along Route 24 just east of Exit 9B to Hobart Gap Road, glance to your right and listen very, very carefully. You may hear—or maybe you'll just want to hear—the joyous sounds of boyhood bliss echoing forever alongside the rose bushes and blue gums of old Stevens Field.

But know this: as you move on down the road, those sounds—even if only imagined in gentle reverie—will fade away entirely. As did our youth, and probably yours.

POOR BASTARD

The only organized sports teams we had outside of school and club swimming were in the Millburn Little League, which played at the White Oak Ridge Complex. Some of our fathers helped out.

I spent my first couple of years in the minors. One reason for this is that I may not have been as good as some of the guys in the majors (there were only four or maybe six major league teams for the whole town—I can remember only the Firemen, the PBA, the Hawks and the Orioles—they kept playing each other). I also happened to have missed the major league tryouts for two or three years in a row because our family went to Florida for a couple of weeks at just that time.

Anyway, in the minors, we just had T-shirts with the name of our team and hats with the right color. The guys in the majors wore full uniforms. I eventually made it to the majors for part of my last official Little League season (the year I turned twelve). I played briefly for the Orioles (which had green and white uniforms). The coach was Mr. Estes, whose son, Scott (later "Suds") was in my class and a good friend (and in whose basement he and I once built a world class race car out of old boards and other junk).

After Little League eligibility ran out, I played in the Tri-County League (which is like a Pony League or a Babe Ruth League in other areas). This league was not well organized. There were two teams from our town—the Millburn Millers and the Millburn Giants. I played for the Giants. Also, in ninth grade, I played third base and pitched for the Millburn Junior High School freshman team (I think that team was also known as the Millers, which made things a little confusing). Our Junior High coach was our science teacher, Bob

Babb. When he was absent, one of the fathers, Lou Hughes, would fill in. His son was Dave "Spike" Hughes. Spike acquired that name because he invariably slid into second base "spikes high." Mr. Hughes was a very good sport for helping out so much, and we all looked up to him.

I played so much baseball my freshman year that it seemed I was always in uniform.

Sometimes we would have a freshman game and a Tri-County game on the same day. We couldn't drive yet, so we'd ride our bikes or walk to the games and change uniforms in the woods. The school uniforms were in pretty good shape. The Giants' budget was meager, and the uniforms were so worn out that sometimes we'd wear the pants from our school uniforms (although the color was different), just to keep from showing our underwear.

Besides Mr. Hughes, other fathers helped out a lot. My father never coached, but he umpired. He wasn't all that good at umpiring. Even I yelled at him a few times, back before they invented the concept of treating umpires with a modicum of respect.

The Giants were coached over the years by at least two of the fathers. One was Billy and Bobby Jaeger's father, Bob Jaeger. Another was Scotty and Dusty McQueen's father, Bob McQueen. This story is mainly about him.

One day, the Giants were playing in Chatham Township, which was two or three towns away. (Some of the towns were so small that, even getting caught at all the traffic lights, you could drive through four of them in about ten minutes.) Mr. McQueen was at the helm. One of the other fathers (probably Mr. Jaeger) was also there, because the fathers had to drive us, and we couldn't all fit in one car (although fourteen or fifteen of us somehow fit into two cars). Mr. McQueen was an insurance executive—very straight-laced and serious.

Scotty McQueen was in my class. He had several nicknames. For reasons I can't explain, he was known at the time as "Wiener." I'm guessing at the spelling. We were never sure. A year or so later, our high school math teacher, Mr. Eikenberry, who sometimes struggled with names, pronounced Scotty's last name as "MoleQueen." From then on, Scotty was sometimes known as "Mole." He grew up to be a radio station magnate and a multi-millionaire.

But during the time in question, Wiener, or Mole, was a fourteen or fifteen-year-old playing on the Millburn Giants. He threw righty and batted lefty, with a beautiful roundhouse swing.

We had an evening game at Chatham Township High School field. They had just installed a new, state-of-the-art backstop—the kind that had the curved overhang protruding out toward the field, making it impossible (we thought) to foul a ball back behind home plate. The laws of physics wouldn't permit the ball to go up or backwards without staying in the cage. Perhaps this was to protect the cars in the parking lot aft of the field. The old backstops just had a screen in the back, maybe with a little bit of a lid, but you could still foul the ball back into the woods, or under a car, often thereby delaying the game for a while. The idea of this new backstop was that you couldn't foul one back behind it.

Anyway, I can't remember the count, or the score, or whether we had any men on base, but Wiener took a roundhouse cut at a sweeping curve. He made angled contact. The ball proceeded at about a 70-degree upward and outward angle as if it was going right to the pitcher.

But then the ball started to rise and go backwards, accelerating in a reverse parabolic arc. As it gained height and speed, it barely cleared the lip of the cage and sailed over and behind the backstop until we all lost sight of it. Then we heard it. *CURPLAMPH!!* A horrible sound. And not the sound that all boys have heard many times when a hard ball goes through a house window. That's usually a "*CLINK.*" A clean break. This, on the other hand, was a dull thud, kind of like a sledgehammer hitting a metal door.

Mr. McQueen probably had some concern about what he thought had just happened. But the ump had pulled out a new ball, and the pitcher was about to deliver again to Wiener. All Mr. McQueen said, under his breath and out of one side of his mouth, was, "Poor bastard."

We lost the game. I remember that because we usually lost, and also because I recall Mr. McQueen holding us on the field to give us a speech about how we should have done this, and we should have done that. Then we all walked in silence back to the parking lot, carrying our stuff, including the two bags full of bats and balls. There were only three or four cars left in the lot when we got there.

Then we saw it and realized that the "poor bastard" was Mr. McQueen himself. Wiener McQueen had smashed his own father's windshield. Smashed it to smithereens. Well, most of the glass was still attached to the frame, but it was all white, with radiant cracks in all directions. There was a tiny little hole in the middle, on the driver's side. When he saw this, Mr. McQueen said something else under his breath, but we couldn't quite make it out. Driving home was a real treat, with Mr. McQueen alternately looking out the side window and peering through the tiny hole in the windshield.

With the exception of Mr. McQueen, we all laughed about this for years, and included it in our repertoires of baseball stories. Particularly the sound of that windshield smashing in the distance.

Forty years later, my wife and I were visiting my father and stepmother in Florida. We learned that not only had Mr. and Mrs. McQueen moved into the same assisted living complex, but they were around that weekend, so my father invited them to join us for dinner. We caught up on the families and then I said to Mr. McQueen, "Remember that game in Chatham?" I proceeded to retell the entire story. At its conclusion, he looked at me with a blank, humorless stare. Being in his mid-eighties, he had either genuinely forgotten the incident, purposely erased it from his mind, or was still silently seething about being his own Poor Bastard all those decades ago.

MR. JAEGER, MR. JAEGER, BOBBY DON'T FEEL TOO GOOD!

Mr. Bill Jaeger, father to one of our classmates, reached into his closet, pulling out his favorite shoes for another hot summer day. They were just right for the occasion, which that day was coaching his son's struggling baseball team. A sturdy blue cloth-covered pair with a thick rubber base, these shoes allowed his feet to breathe but provided enough traction for the ballfield's early morning dewy grass. These were not the kind of dress lace-ups most men in town wore during the week, commuting to their jobs in New York City. As comfortable as they were, these shoes clearly signaled a whole new set of challenges.

No, the life of a Tri-County dad-coach was not an easy one. Particularly during this star-crossed season.

It was an unseasonably warm June day, and Mr. Jaeger liked coaching the team, part of something called the Tri-County League. This league, which drew teams from Morris, Essex, and Union counties, was the follow-up organization to Little League, although not nearly as well organized. It was not affiliated with any national structure, like the American Legion program in other areas, and seemed to be held together more by good luck and good will than anything else. Most of us had at least once traveled all the way to another town, or even county, just to find that the game had been canceled and that someone had forgotten to tell us. Sometimes there were no umpires, other times the field had another game, and still other times the opposing team never showed up. "No shows" were a little bit like "snow days" during the winter at school—a kind of free pass to loosen up, have some disorganized fun and not worry about another competitive game. It also allowed for a much longer trip to the Dairy Queen, an unspoken after-game league tradition.

This league played boys twelve through fifteen, and as any parent knows, this is the red danger zone of hormonal chaos and peak stupidity for boys. Of the teams in the league, Mr. Jaeger's seemed to draw a surprising number of nitwits from our gang, who were busy surging up and down along the stupid scale—mostly up. This would have made for an interesting season in any event. But our gang also had few talents or skills remotely useful to a baseball team. Among the few talented players were his two sons.

Small in stature, athletically skilled, and very bright, these two boys made their dad proud. And the boys were just as proud of their dad, who had spent hours guiding this team through a difficult season. The rest of his team shared few of these attributes, although they were all pretty good kids, loosely defined. At least when their hormones settled down a bit. But Coach liked these boys, and they him.

This lineup of misfits, and the misfiring structure of the league, tried his patience. Basic skills, like running, hitting, catching, and thinking were thinly distributed among our players. Frequently, only one or two of these skills were distributed to any particular player. Even uniform standards were a challenge for his team. While most of the time the ballplayers wore the correct jersey, the choice of pants to partner with the jersey appeared to be random and haphazard. Pretty much like the play of the team.

The regulation socks issued with the uniform disappeared by the third game. Some of the team wore sneakers. Some wore cleats as required by the Tri-County League. A kid showed up for one game in loafers, although I think Mr. Jaeger kept him on the bench to make a point.

During the game, hats were turned around backwards; others moved 10, 20, and 30-degrees off center as the innings progressed. The fun-loving outfielders claimed that the infielders' IQs could be measured by how many "degrees-off-center" their hats were, subtracting from ninety to set their intelligence levels (which were below average to start). Hence an infielder wearing his hat 20-degrees off center was said to have an IQ of seventy. One of our brighter outfielders contended, in a related hat theory, that these off-center, tilted hats also functioned as sundials. Infielders' comments about shadows cast by the first baseman implied that we were rapidly approaching 3:00 p.m. These "scientific observations" we felt were novel contributions to the study of human intelligence and time-telling.

The outfielders were busy making innovative improvements of their own to their uniforms. The most popular seemed to be putting dandelions, which grew around many of the league outfields, in the buttonholes of their jerseys. This was a most interesting addition by the outfielders, who were filling quiet time between sky gazing and comedic rushes for soon-to-be-dropped catches. All this went unnoticed, however, since unlike Little League, we never had any fans watching the games, other than those who had wandered into the stands by mistake. And it never took them more than half an inning to determine the level of play, and then slip away in search of the correct game, mumbling quietly to themselves.

As the season wore on and more and more fly balls were muffed by the outfielders, one of them came up with the theory that they all had been raised wrong since birth, and should switch from right-handed gloves to left-handed gloves, or vice versa. Two of the guys actually tried it out one mid-season game, swapping gloves for several innings. The truly remarkable (or unremarkable) thing about this experiment was that fielder performance went unchanged. Fly balls continued to bounce off gloves of every type no matter who was wearing them. Mr. Jaeger put a stop to this nonsense, fearing a perceived decline in his dignity and associated community reputation. And remember, he really was trying to shield his two sons from his team spiraling like an airplane out of control—rapidly increasing in speed and dramatically declining in team altitude and attitude.

As the losses mounted, already marginal player discipline deteriorated further. Wisecracks begat more wisecracks, errors begat more errors, and things started really spinning out of control. Mr. Jaeger endured it all, quietly insisting on some minimal level of decorum and dignity, and always demanding better sportsmanship. This was, after all, "*Tri-County ball*," something we remember he said with all the misplaced pride of a manager somewhere way down the minor leagues, like say Davenport, Iowa.

As frustration mounted, an incident at the mound late in the season summed up the sorry and disordered state of affairs. Winding up with a kind of reckless abandon, our pitcher let loose a wild pitch that sailed high into the backstop, where it stuck for a moment. Our catcher fumbled around the backstop, shaking the cage a bit until the ball fell to the ground. Finally retrieving the wild pitch, he trotted it back to the pitcher standing on the mound.

This is pretty much what pitchers and catchers do, and is usually routine.

Except this time, as our catcher handed the scuffed-up ball to the pitcher, the pitcher wound up with a round-house right punch and coldcocked the catcher in the stomach, apparently in retaliation for missing the wild pitch which had sailed about eight feet over his head.

No, this was not what General Abner Doubleday had in mind at all.

Mr. Jaeger could only look down at his comfortable and comforting blue shoes. He couldn't think of a single rational response to this incident, or any sane reason why he should continue coaching this team. Like all the dads who spent hours guiding us in Little League, Tri-County, church, or Boy Scouts, Mr. Jaeger worked hard all week, and maybe in a job that he really didn't like, just to give us a good start in life. For this they were too often rewarded with immaturity, ineptitude, and indifference. They offered us so much. We owed them so much. We gave them so little.

Not even a normal return of a baseball from a catcher to a pitcher.

Remarkably, the decking of our catcher (which soon became a Tri-County legend) was not the crowning insult of the season. That happened in our last game playing for the kind and patient Mr. Jaeger. After losing by another wide margin, our final indignity was to play a trick on him using our star troublemaker Bobby "The Duke" Ellington. For some reason, the adults knew the young Mr.

Ellington as "Bobby," while we boys assigned him the name "The Duke" because of his last name.

The Duke had a terrific and well-practiced talent for pulling his eyelids back over themselves, making it look like his eyes had rolled back into his head, and that he was undergoing some kind of seizure. When The Duke was really on his game, he would add a nice little moaning sound and describe symptoms that clearly indicated he was about to throw up. This wonderful performance had been deployed many times over the years, and each new instance of it seemed to outdo the previous one. The very best performances included a concoction of Coke and lemonade "vomit". And, yes, The Duke had manufactured a small quantity of this little visual aid during the last game, "just in case."

And what better case than the end of a terrible season, right?

The Duke recruited three or four co-conspirators, mostly players with off-kilter hats and multiple flowered buttonholes. Clearly the cream of this dynamic athletic powerhouse. Coach's two talented sons were shielded from this unholy conspiracy, of course. The Duke reminded his buddies that they should use his proper name for this little caper, and the game was on!

"Mr. Jaeger, Mr. Jaeger, Bobby don't feel too good!"

The poor English was always a nice touch, worth extra points, and "Bobby" had such a nice rhythm and even a kind of innocence, adding to the tableaux.

Mr. Jaeger, a good but frustrated coach, but a great and caring parent, turned quickly to deal with a potential crisis. He immediately saw The Duke's rolled eyes, clutched stomach and wobbly carriage, and instantly reached out to catch the boy's sagging shoulders.

As he did, the Duke spit the colored concoction of fake vomit onto Mr. Jaeger's blue cloth top shoes, so carefully selected that morning. It was so authentic that it was a little scary, even to those who were in on it.

But the whole team of misfits quickly broke into hysterics at this masterful performance. The Duke had outdone himself, again, our very own genius of great humor and unbridled mirth. The laughter seemed to wash away some of the hurt of a very frustrating season, at least as far as it went.

Which wasn't too far. When we looked up, the Coach was now quietly sitting in the first row of the vacant stands. He had his head down with both arms cupping his chin, staring down at his soaking, badly stained shoes, slowing shaking his head.

We will never know for sure what he was thinking that day, but it's a good bet that he was doing more than just examining his favorite and now-ruined blue shoes. Maybe he was contemplating his wasted time spent coaching us misfits or maybe even parts of his whole life.

He stood up, his dignity intact but his favorite blue shoes disgraced, disrespected, and heading to the dump: "The game's over, boys. The season is over. Go home."

He couldn't look at The Duke, and frankly we were all a bit ashamed at how this little trick turned out. Most of our misadventures were not planned, but were just the idiocy of youth in haphazard and random collision with normal standards of conduct. But this one had *premeditated* written all over it. We knew it. He knew it. And that seemed to make a difference, at least for a while.

We didn't know then what the real world was like for most of our dads, although having worked our way through decades, we have a much better idea now. It probably wasn't much fun, many days. But you never knew it from them.

Maybe what held it all together, at least for some of them, was the thrill they got from telling their colleagues about our comical capers the next week at the office, where everyone could commiserate and have a good laugh. Perhaps the other fathers had their "Dukes" too, even teams of wonderful misfits, and continued to form lifelong friendships. Or maybe they found themselves in a happy place, even for just a moment, thinking about their own youths, which made it all worth it.

If any of this was actually the case, and we hope it is, we would be very pleased indeed.

THE SHORT HILLS DETROITS

When most people think of Detroit, they think of the city in Michigan that looks *south* into Windsor, Ontario, Canada. What many folks don't know is that there are actually nine cities and towns named Detroit in the United States. What even fewer people remember (except for a handful of baby boomers) is that there were about a dozen Detroits inside the town of Short Hills, New Jersey from 1958 to 1962: The Short Hills Detroits.

This takes a while to explain.

In the late 1950s and early 1960s, the only organized sports in Short Hills, outside of school, were baseball and club swimming. That was it. No organized football, basketball, or soccer. Everything was *disorganized*. We played disorganized football in the field behind Christ Church and several other venues. We played disorganized basketball in the half court above the church annex and on many driveways and streets. And we played disorganized hockey on the local ponds.

Some of the ponds were established, such as South Pond and North Pond. South Pond was owned by a private club (to which none of us belonged) and required a badge signifying permission (which none of us had) to skate. The ice was usually smooth and reasonably good for hockey. But lots of girls figure skated there, and families took their little kids. We would sneak on, get kicked off, sneak back on, get kicked off again, and then move to the less desirable North Pond. It was public and the venue for most of our "serious" hockey.

But there were also some smaller ponds. One was "Jencko's Pond," which was actually in Jimmy Jencko's backyard, behind a fence. It was small but good. Other ponds cropped up here and there after major rainstorms. They were mainly low spots in the woods and construction ditches in areas where new houses were being built. We spent a lot of time on those ponds, as they were the closest to us. Of course, they were rough and irregularly shaped with no boundaries. They were perforated by rocks, roots and grass and were bordered by bushes and trees. This wasn't so bad, except that four out of five hard shots sent the pucks into the woods, sometimes forever.

With the short-term ponds, and even with the big ponds, we often got impatient with the concept of freezing. We sort of figured: first day of winter = hockey. But in New Jersey, it didn't work that way. Sometimes first day of winter = football with T-shirts. We never knew. So when it did get cold, we occasionally jumped the gun and skated on the ponds before they were fully frozen. This led to some interesting and dangerous situations, and it also cost us a lot of pucks.

There were other occasions where the ponds were solid, but the ice was bad. For instance, a few times it rained at just about 32-degrees, and the ice froze in such a way that the surface resembled bubble wrap. You could walk on it, and it would pop, but you couldn't skate on it. Of course, we did anyway, resulting in hockey games played in slow motion, with cracking and sputtering everywhere.

Today there are indoor rinks with Zambonis, which are machines that clean and resurface the ice, making the skating easier. We didn't have Zambonis. We just skated on the frozen bubble wrap, sticks, and rocks, and we tripped every few seconds.

I mentioned pucks. Perhaps the most important piece of hockey material, these are hard disks made of intense rubber. They are virtually indestructible. A puck would look the same just before and just after being run over by a tractor trailer, being shot out of a cannon, being chomped by a wood splitter, and, of course, colliding with a bright, white smile—which it did routinely. Just ask "Suds" Estes.

Comedian Don Rickles, just coming into his own at the time, seized upon the hockey puck's dense, impenetrable quality and used it to inform one of his best known catch phrases—he would insult someone by yelling, "YA HOCKEY PUCK!"

Today, every team has a bag full of pucks. We usually had one puck at each game, unless someone forgot to bring one, in which case he would have to ride home on his bike to get one. In the meantime, we would use a rock or a tennis ball, which was better than the frozen cow dung used for the earliest hockey pucks.

Tony "The Lesser" Intilli had a puck with a white circle on it that said "Bosco." We always assumed this referred to what was then our favorite chocolate syrup used in making chocolate milk and ice cream sundaes. At nostalgia.boscoworld.com, you can read the recent testimonial of a woman who also grew up in the 1950s just a few miles away from us in Newark, a woman who claims to have been "a good Catholic girl" and always assumed that St. Bosco was sainted for inventing Bosco. The syrup was also used as blood in the movie *Psycho*. Bosco's most famous fan was probably George Costanza of *Seinfeld* (who used it as his ATM code). But he *drank* Bosco; he didn't use it for slap shots and inadvertently removing teeth, like we did.

We thought Tony's Bosco was the world's greatest puck. Whenever it flew off the ice into the bushes, there would be a time out while most of the players looked for it. At the end of every game, Tony took it home with him. If he had to leave, and we hadn't found Bosco, and it was found later, someone would take it to his house. For all I know, he still has it.

A few of the other guys would try to label their pucks by getting white medical tape and writing their names on it. This didn't work all that well. If the tape was on the side of the puck, it would be smashed regularly with the stick. If it was on either flat face, it would wear off on either the ice or the bushes. I can remember one genius (I think it was either "Bulb" Watt or "Dibbie" Poppy) writing the word "Mine" on his. At best, this was a questionable form of identification.

Another important piece of equipment was the stick. Today, each player has multiple sticks made out of highly durable material. We each had one, made of wood. When it cracked, we taped it up. Sometimes we applied a splint or even wrapped it in aluminum foil in an attempt to prolong its life. A few were run over by cars when they fell off the handlebars of our bikes on the way to and from the ponds.

GILBERT E. "BUD" SCHILL, JR. AND JOHN W. "MAC" MACILROY AND ROBERT D. "ROB" HAMILTON III.

We didn't have nets at the goals, just two stones, or maybe a couple of crumpled up shirts. This led to a lot of arguments over whether the puck had, or had not, gone into the goal. This, in turn, led to a lot of checking (explained below).

And we didn't have much in the way of rules. In organized hockey, there is a thick rule book. Many of the rules are based on colored lines on the ice. We didn't have *any* lines on our ice, colored or otherwise, so the concepts of "offsides" and "icing" that are so important today meant nothing to us. And we had no penalties. Our only "rules" were to try to complete the game without getting kicked off the pond by irate parents or badge marshalls, to try to win, and to try not to get so banged up that we had to visit either the pediatrician, the dentist, or the orthodontist (all of whom made fortunes off our mishaps).

One of the important skills in hockey (probably more important than shooting, blocking, or checking), is stopping. Not one of the guys I played with ever mastered the technique. Good players could stop on a dime, with a flashy spray of shaved ice. It took each of our guys about 20 yards to stop once he decided to do so; and by the time he did stop, he had lost track of why he was trying to stop in the first place.

One of our regular players was James A. Basinger. When we started playing hockey, he was known as Jim. Eventually, he became known as Bay, which is how you pronounce the letter B in Spanish. Our diminutive Spanish teacher, Lena Marie Abbott, gave everyone a Spanish first name. His was Diego. She could never pronounce Basinger, so she referred to him as Diego B. Eventually, she, and the rest of us, and people who didn't even know him, called him Bay. Even our parents called him that. When he eventually got married, it took a while for his wife Donna to accept this, but she has.

Bay was a very good athlete, particularly at baseball and soccer; but he was the worst skater in eight worlds. In fact, he didn't really skate. He moved (sometime forward, often backward) on his inner ankles. After several years of playing hockey, Bay's skate blades were still razor sharp and in mint condition, as neither of them had ever really touched the ice. Bay also spent a good bit of each game in the bushes, where he landed when he couldn't stop. He became some-what the opposite of bow-legged, as his ankles got used to coasting on ice, flaring his feet out and away from each other. He eventually overcame this impediment to his posture and no longer walks funny. He now successfully leads his congregation as an Anglican minister in Virginia.

But during his hockey days, if it weren't for friction, you could place Bay at one end of the pond, give him a slight nudge, and he would travel the length of the pond and into the bushes unless he fell or crashed into something along the way. His preferred stopping mechanism was to careen into another player, trying to grab his shirt or belt. If he missed, or if his stopping target was uncooperative, he would turn and peel away in an angled direction with the help of centrifugal force. But remember, he wasn't using the blades, just the leather, so the friction was more severe, which kept him in the game longer than he would have had he actually been skating.

We seldom had the right number of players on the ice. That, of course, depends on how you defined "on the ice." For instance, sometimes we counted Bay, even though he was only randomly located *near* the ice.

I mentioned checking. This is where one player intentionally plows into another to get him away from the puck. According to the rules, the checkee must be "on the puck." Random checking is prohibited. In our hockey, most of the activity was unintentional checking, where one skater creamed another (often a teammate) due to the inability to stop. Our version of checking looked more like human bowling.

In contrast to today's well-heeled and well-equipped youth hockey organizations, with their carpooling and their rolling equip-ment bags and heated locker rooms, and with families eating pizza in the stands, we toted our stuff to the ponds on our handlebars, donned our gear in the bushes, and had no fans. (In fact, the only people who ever watched us were those insisting that we leave.) Our equipment consisted of a single, battered stick, skates and gloves. If we could buy long ski socks and put them on over our blue jeans, we did, but they were often different colors. No helmets, no pads, no uniforms.

That is, no uniforms until we decided we needed jerseys bearing the name of our team.

At night, from the elevation of Short Hills, we could see the lights of New York City. We all had favorite sports teams from various cities. But in hockey, we were all New York Rangers fans. During our era, the Rangers had star players such as Andy Bathgate, Harry Howell, Camille Henry, Eddie Shack, Gump Worsely, Rod Gilbert, Eddie Giacomin, and Vic Hadfield.

But we couldn't be the Rangers, because there was already a team in Short Hills with that name. Those Rangers, with their slick uniforms, were considerably better than we were, and besides, they had the name first. So we had to choose another one.

There were only five other teams in the NHL then: the Montreal Canadiens, Toronto Maple Leafs, Boston Bruins, Chicago Black Hawks, and Detroit Red Wings. Of those, most of us seemed to favor the Red Wings, which had such great players as Alex Delvecchio, Gordie Howe, and Terry Sawchuk. (Now there are thirty teams, including two in Florida.) Back then, if we couldn't be the Rangers, we wanted to be the Red Wings.

We knew full uniforms weren't in the cards, so we settled on all getting the same jerseys with the name of our new team on the front. We couldn't acquire the actual logo, which was a red, spoked tire with wings, so we went for the letters. Unfortunately, we put this task in the hands of the wrong person: Billy Fitzsimmons.

Billy was a great guy. Always smiling. Affable. And his mother was a very nice lady. So Billy and his mother became the uniform acquisition detail. But they were a little short on their attention to this detail. Actually, a lot short.

Although they blamed this on each other for months, the story we eventually got from Mrs. Fitzsimmons was that when they went into the sports store to order the letters to be sewn on the shirts, and the guy asked what letters they wanted on the jerseys, Billy was so excited that he just said, "Detroit!"

They waited for about a half hour for the letters to come back, which were contained in an individual bag for each player. Neither Billy nor his mother inspected the bags before paying for them (with our money), or distributing them to the players. Eventually, we all opened the bags and found that the letters didn't spell RED WINGS, but rather . . . DETROIT.

A few of us figured out this was wrong, but by the time we spoke up, others had already started sewing the letters on their jerseys. Some delegated this to their mothers, who didn't know what slant to use, or what side of the jerseys to use. Other lads did the sewing on their own. The kit didn't come with instructions.

The first reviews of our finished products were so bad that we were widely perceived as brain dead.

Mr. Fitzsimmons thought this was hilarious. Mrs. Fitzsimmons shrugged it off with a "Who cares?" accepting no responsibility for her son's (and her) carelessness.

Despite the screw up, we took a vote and decided we would just use the letters we had.

Thus were born the Short Hills Detroits.

We had resolved to put the letters on a slant from the right shoulder to the left hip. If this were done correctly, then a person looking straight at the player from the front should have seen

R
   E
      D
        W
          I
            N
              G
                S

With our new name, and although we didn't have the letter S to add at the end, the lettering should have been

```
    D
      E
        T
          R
            O
              I
                T
```

A few of the mothers ignored the slant, and created

```
    D    E    T    R    O    I    T
```

Other than being incongruous, this wouldn't have been too bad. But a couple of the mothers (or maybe it was the players who couldn't find their mothers—one of them, I believe, being Duke Ellington) created this masterpiece:

```
                            D
                          E
                        T
                      R
                    O
                  I
                T
```

This was hard on the eyes. The only way to read this without getting dizzy was to look in the mirror. One of the fellows, or his mother, got the lettering right in terms of longitude but wrong as to latitude:

But it got even worse. Without any clear directions from their sons, two or three mothers sewed the letters onto the backs of the jerseys. Those players, not wanting to appear to be backwards, often turned their jerseys around, which had the advantage of getting the letters to the front but the disadvantage of having the high part of the jerseys' collars against their chins.

Then there were the jerseys (over half of them) where, even if the letters were on the proper side, and even if they were on the right slant, they were not tightly sewn. A few of them seemed to have just a single thread down the middle of the letter, so that the thing flopped around on the surface of the jersey like the ears of a Bassett Hound.

We probably should have thrown all these jerseys, with the sometimes backwards and often flimsily sewn on letters spelling the wrong word across their fronts or backs, into a bonfire. But enough of the players either liked the new deal, or were so tired of screwing with it, that they reaffirmed their vote to use the new team name.

Although we referred to ourselves as the Detroits, our letters spelled only Detroit. So I guess we could have been the Short Hills Detroit, kind of like the Alabama Crimson Tide, the Tulane Green Wave, or the Miami Heat. But we pronounced our name in the plural, and a few guys even added an "S" at the end—in crayon. Either way, the name caught on. We were the talk of the town.

Earlier, I mentioned the outdoor ponds. At the very end of our hockey careers, the first indoor skating rink in the multi-county area was constructed—the South Mountain Arena. So we no longer had to rely exclusively on the ponds. But there was one huge problem with the arena. It was booked twenty-four hours a day, seven days a week. Ice ballet, family time, little kids' time, old peoples' time, and a little hockey time. But the only time a terrible team like the Detroits could get on the ice was after midnight on Saturdays (technically Sundays). So we did.

There weren't a whole lot of these occasions, because we were getting long in the tooth, about fifteen; but on several late Saturday nights, we arrived at the Arena at around 11:45 p.m. ready to go. Nobody cared about our games—including us. We had no fans. Sometimes we had no opponents. But in the words of Mrs. Fitzsimmons, "Who cares?" *We were the Detroits!* We had un-uniform jerseys with floppy letters on backwards. We had splinted sticks covered with duct tape and aluminum foil. We had mismatched socks over our blue jeans. We had limited skill. We had only a few hours before many of us had to be at Christ Church in Short Hills to carry the cross in Crucifers' Guild.

Those of us who did have to crucifer (if that is a verb) would arrive in church beat to hell—no sleep, walking with a limp, chipped teeth, bloody chins, matted hair, dirty foreheads, having been hit in the face with pucks and sticks and checked mercilessly, often by our own teammates. We were a mess.

For reasons I can't fully explain, the Short Hills Detroits gradually became identified with our Crucifers Guild. This was not totally logical, because a couple of the crucifers didn't even play hockey (although most did), and a couple who did play hockey were on the Rangers. In fact, among the Detroits were several Catholics (including Tony Intilli, Billy Fitzsimmons, and Jim Higgins). So only a fraction of the Detroits were Episcopalian, and only a fraction of the crucifers were Detroits. But somehow the identity emerged, at least in the minds of certain disapproving parishioners looking for someone to blame for their suffering in the church aisles at the hands of these lads. After all, although our hockey antics were not conducted on church property, the aftermath sometimes worked its way into our Sunday duties.

The Detroits were not sponsored by the Church. In fact, there was probably no organization in the world that would sponsor such a terrible sports team. Had we been looking for a sponsor, we probably would have had trouble getting even the Juvenile Detention Center to sign on.

My stepmother, Betty, had three sons (now my stepbrothers) who were crucifers at Christ Church after my group moved on. She became the adult in charge of the Guild. So she knew about our issues with the collection plates and the mite boxes, and with keeping the cross erect. I was not aware of this until she was in her eighties. We were in Florida, and I was talking with my father, and somehow the incident when Nils Ohlson put my father's hat on the pew behind him (so he would sit down on top of it, which he did) came up. My father referred to him as "that damned Johnny Ohlson." At which time my usually stoic and straight-laced stepmother, who was in the other room making a gin and tonic, muttered, "Those damned Detroits."

GOD BLESS YOU, HARRY CHITI, WHEREVER YOU ARE

As the ice thinned on our favorite ponds in the early spring, we packed away our hockey gear, carefully folded our Detroits or Rangers jerseys, or what was left of them, and turned our attention to baseball.

As a failing baseball player—my career Little League batting average was .081, and I couldn't catch a cold in center field—my attentions turned to baseball *cards*.

Baseball cards were important in ways big and small. Not just a welcome marker of the spring and summer to come, they were a reassuring sign of sequence and order in our small world. Already beginning to feel the seductive power of promise and possibility, we crafted our individual strategies to capture a certain star player's card, bag a rare one, or build a complete set. We would arrange, divide, stack, store, catalogue, manage, and preserve our collections in hundreds of ways, and even invent games.

This often involved lifting parts—dice and "spinners" mostly—from other games scattered around the house and adapting them to our own purposes. Like most things, this went too far, and I once built a baseball field, complete with colorful ads cut from *Life* and pasted on the outfield walls, on a good-sized cardboard box, flattened and painted green, with a brown infield and surprisingly straight white baselines. The idea was to lay the cardboard field out on the floor, turn on the television to WPIX Channel 11 for a Yankees game, plop the cards of the players onto the field, and move them around in synch with the real game. This wasn't as dumb an idea as it sounds, or maybe it was. The backs of our baseball cards had all sorts of statistics and personal squibs which even the learned Mel Allen, the television voice of the Yankees, didn't know, which added to the fun. I would carry my cardboard field over to Estes' house across the street or to Stevens' next door, and call it an away game.

Yeah, maybe a little dumb.

Baseball cards worked in the real world, too. They helped shape our Little League caps, propping up the front from the inside seam, and they turbocharged our bikes when attached by a clothespin to the rear wheel for that perfect "flap-flap-flap" sound—a sound no girls' bike could ever hope to make with their playing cards, which operated at a different pitch. Pretty good stuff, we all agreed, for a little piece of cardboard, although employing cards for these jobs quickly destroyed them.

Completely.

Our baseball cards were a terrific foundation for new friendships, strong glue for sustaining old ones, and another wellspring for misadventure, like the trouble one card caused on a warm spring day in 1958.

Harry Dominick Chiti was a burly journeyman catcher who played for a decade in the majors. He started out in the Yankee farm system, and got to the majors with the Cubs in the early 1950s. During our years of peak interest in baseball cards, he played for the Kansas City Athletics. For boys in New Jersey, the Athletics were really a footnote to the real action in New York, so Chiti was not a household name, and it didn't help that he was playing in a city that appeared to be in either Kansas or Missouri, or maybe both. It didn't take much to confuse us, and he might as well have been playing in Tibet for all we cared.

The first Chiti card which floated into most of our collections, without incident or much interest, was a 1956 Topps card, number 179. These Topps cards were quite elegant, even against today's standards, featuring a head shot along with an action background shot. They were more or less an improved version of the 1955 Topps series, which themselves were very nice, and Chiti's 1956 card had a terrific play-at-the-plate action shot which attracted a few, if passing, comments that year. The good folks at Topps had wisely let these action shots dominate the cards, tastefully pushing to the upper corner of each card a small-print banner with the player's name, position, and team name.

We really liked what Topps was doing.

Chiti spent the entire 1957 season with the Triple A team in Richmond, which at the time was still part of the Yankees' farm system, and Topps did not issue a Chiti card that year. The best-looking set issued at the time—I think it still is—the 1957 set offered 407 cards in a new, smaller vertical format. The series featured multiple-player combination cards, complete year-by-year player statistics, and some really beautiful staged action shots. Indeed, the 1957 Topps Mantle, card number 95, is often called the most beautiful of that era, with Mantle gracefully completing his trademark swing in Yankee Stadium. The whole card is done in deep and rich baseball colors—the sharp white Yankee pin-striped uniform contrasts against the green grass—and we went nuts over it. Once again, small print on the card face let us focus on the great action photography. Best of all, a huge number of the really beautiful action shots featured other Yankees, Giants and Dodgers players. With only thin evidence—that the Topps people were operating out of Brooklyn and could easily send their best photographer throughout the city—we boasted that these great shots were a gift from Topps to the boys in Jersey.

This was nonsense, but made our crowd particularly happy, and I still have some of our favorite cards, not all of which featured star players. Bud was a Dodgers guy, and he went wild over the great-looking cards of Pee Wee Reese, Duke Snider, and Roy Campanella. These guys were stars, but Topps was also generous with really great shots of some of the lesser Brooklyn players—cards like pitcher Don Bessent, and backup catcher Al Walker. Ted Hellman, the avid Giants fan in our crowd, pulled the beautiful card of the great Willie Mays, along with great shots of guys like Dusty Rhodes, and pitchers Al Worthington and Ruben Gomez.

And best of all, at least for those of us who were Bronx Bombers fans, some of the greatest baseball cards of Yankees players we had ever seen fell from pack after pack all that spring and summer. We went crazy over the action shots of Billy Martin, Jerry Coleman, and Gil McDougald and a couple of extraordinary combination cards, including the legendary last card in the set. That card features a couple of guys named Mantle and Berra, in an iconic shot taken on the steps of the Yankee dugout. Even our soccer players loved it, and these 1957 beauties just kept on coming all summer.

Topps had done it again.

We scrambled throughout the summer trying to collect the whole marvelous set. By late fall, with our shoeboxes full and cards carefully tucked away in our closets, we could hardly wait to see what the great Topps Company would do for us the next year.

It seemed an unusually long wait.

At last, in the early spring of 1958 as we were finishing up sixth grade, Topps issued its largest series yet. It was supposed to be 495 cards, but card number 145 has never been found—either never actually produced, or simply lifted after production. Topps was very vague about it all, an early mystery which may explain our later obsession with conspiracy theories.

As the early-release cards fell from our first wax packs of the season, we found a few things we liked: another vertical format, new *Sport Magazine All-Star* cards, and more combination pictures earned some early season praise. However, even the welcome return of Stan "the Man" Musial to the Topps stable (he had been absent from the Topps series for a number of years) failed to reverse a general and growing disappointment in the series as we bought more cards throughout the spring. In fact, this disappointment was quickly spreading like a virus through town, our own *Walking Dead*.

Frankly, it looked like Topps had let us down.

Our bill of particulars read something like this. The '58 cards suffered from a serious shortage of action shots, giving way to boring "face" cards. What few action shots did fall from our wax packs generally looked like they had been lifted from nice on-field photos, then poorly pasted on solid color backgrounds which, in themselves, drew from a strange rainbow of colors largely unknown to us. After weeks of opening wax packs, most of us had only three or four cards we really cared about—cool cards with good action shots and respectable primary background colors we actually recognized from our time in grade school art class, like red or black.

The best of a poor lot was the Orlando Cepeda rookie card. This card, number 343 in the 1958 series, featured a pretty neat action shot—a long stretching catch at first base—and a recognizable red background. The Giants had just betrayed our trust and decamped across the country to San Francisco, but we could barely see the new "SF" logo on his hat so we cut this rare '58 beauty some slack.

There were a few others. Charlie Neal was a popular Dodger shortstop, and his card was a clean action shot. But even a true Brooklyn fan had to stretch to give the card its due as the Dodgers, too, had left us for the West Coast. There may have even been a handful more of these "good" cards, but I can recall only two, and to the great delight of Wiener McQueen, these were cards of players on the Cincinnati Redlegs. The first one was of Wally Post, a solid outfielder we had heard of, and the second was one of a virtual unknown named Pete Whisenant. These two cards sported the rare but comforting black background, and even today look pretty good. Moreover, as we were assured by Topps on these cards, the Cincinnati ballclub had not moved, although they were now called the "Reds." That was a bit strange, but not as strange as the 1958 Topps edition as a whole now seemed to be.

Topps, it was alarmingly clear, had produced only a handful of cool action cards, and our collections were soon awash in a sea of crummy face cards.

Unbelievable.

All spring those dreaded face cards, never a favorite in any year, fell from pack to pack. Estes pulled a goofy Gary Geiger card, number 462, over here. McQueen pulled a stupid Ralph Lumenti card, number 369, over there. On and on they came until the last straw— Hughes pulled a face card of the great Mickey Mantle. Then someone pulled a face card of the great Ted Williams. Finally, and this was just too much even for Bud, out popped a face card of the great *Sandy Koufax!* It was so bad that Mickey Mantle's face card, number 150 in the series, didn't look much better than Morrie Martin's, card number 53.

Morrie Martin?

Good grief, things couldn't get much worse. So it went, day after day, and soon a strange new sense of bewilderment and disbelief had overtaken our merry band. We were shaken to the core. And, more worrisome yet, a kind of cynical, even blasphemous, new attitude was afoot. We found ourselves, alone or in groups, laughing at—no, *actually making fun of*—Topps Baseball Cards.

What was going on? What had happened to the comforting sense of order we had always found in the card world? What of the magic of possibility, and even brand loyalty? The natural sequence and progression of things had clearly gone atilt. Those '57 cards just a year earlier were real beauties, and weren't things always supposed to get *better*?

Just what the hell was going on?

So throughout the spring we rifled through our packs, disappointment following disappointment. Interest in trades and flips waned. Cards of favorite players—formerly spared certain cardboard deaths as "flappers" on our bikes—were being chewed up all over town.

Who cared? These '58's sucked.

We even started talking about girls.

Some of us continued to buy cards, hoping against hope for some mid-course correction by the captains at Topps—maybe some kind of alternative or parallel set that we would actually like.

So on one fateful Saturday, well into this tarnished spring, a few of us were gathered at a pleasant little neighborhood store called Haggett's. For many of us, this was the best place to buy cards, although most of the chain grocery stores also carried them, at least by mid-summer. Another small store—the Glenwood Sweet Shop—also sold cards but never seemed to stock enough and quickly fell out of favor.

Like other similar mom-and-pop operations which had sprung up near Lackawanna Railroad commuter stations across Northern New Jersey, Haggett's was a cross between a newspaper stand and a candy store, with a tidy lunch counter thrown in for good measure. On the end of an attractive block-long run of small stores, it had a kind of ersatz "Olde English" look, a sturdy stucco and beam style that was quite popular in our town, and enjoyed the favored location closest to the station, almost directly across the street. It was run by a quiet, but pleasant, man who lived above the store. We assumed he was Mr. Haggett himself, but we never really knew that for certain. He seemed to like us, or at least he tolerated us. He was definitely happy to sell us the newest series of cards, which he always seemed to have weeks before anyone else, but I rather doubt that our nickel baseball card pack purchases figured meaningfully into his retirement dreams. He also made a killer classic bologna sandwich—white Wonder Bread, heavy on the mayo—and he wore lots of long-sleeved plaid shirts in the winter and white short-sleeved shirts in the summer, black plants throughout the year, and a kind of perpetually tired look on his face. In any event, it all seemed to fit with his jet black hair, which I also remember as severely slicked back. I don't think he had spent more than ten minutes in the sun in his entire life.

Haggett's was simply a magical place, and we gathered there several times a week, and almost always on Saturday in the spring and summer.

And do we remember one remarkable Saturday in late May of that strange '58 year. "Suds" Estes was there, as the two of us had ridden our bikes over from Lakeview Avenue. "Spike" Hughes, who had wandered over from his home right across from our Glenwood School, was there, with maybe a few others passing through. It was a warm and sunny day, right about lunchtime. Maybe we had enough change in our pockets for a dozen packs of cards, or just one or two if we raided our card funds in favor of a magazine, or one of those killer bologna sandwiches and a glass of milk. Now this is important: diverting baseball card cash to another purpose (even for those great bologna sandwiches) would have been simply *unthinkable* in 1957, and suggests just how deep our disappointment in Topps had become.

Gathered outside the store, and opening a few Topps packs, we were treated to a sad parade of baseball card horrors. Out came face card after face card, each more ridiculous than the last. We pulled a Willard Schmidt, card number 214, who was staring into a kind of inner space, a Jim Finegan, card number 136, staring off into outer space, and a Dutch Dotterer, card number 396, who looked like he *came* from outer space.

But trouble really started when we pulled the card of one Gino Cimoli.

His card number, 286, closely tracked his batting average, although this was pure coincidence, and we should have been happy to pull his card—at least in a normal year. He played, after all, for a favorite team, and the back of his card told us that he was in fact "the big Dodger surprise of last season" by proving he could hit in the big leagues. Since people were constantly reminding us that "attitude counts," we found the cartoon squib on the back of the Cimoli card mildly amusing, if not a bit unsettling. Cimoli's "determined attitude" the prior season, Topps reminded us, "helped him attain regular status." We figured someone at Topps must have been in charge of inserting this kind of adult-driven message randomly into their cards, and even if no one knew what "regular status" meant, we were sure none of us had attained it, or anything close to it. The ideas of "regular" or status of any kind were simply foreign to us.

The real problem with the Cimoli card, however, rested in what should have been its strength. It was, after all, a rare action shot.

But there was a catch.

The folks at Topps had completely butchered the Cimoli shot, and the card was a mess. Looking closely, we found a very thin blue-green line between his body and the yucky solid yellow background. Remembering the crisp photography of last year's cards, we figured Topps had taken a great on-field photo, then lazily—and sloppily—lifted his body to fit the stupid 1958 format. This pasting job, a kind of primitive PhotoShopping, was a disaster. Some loony in the Pasting Department over at Topps had in fact actually *severed the bat* that Cimoli had been swinging when photographed.

Completely gone!

Disappeared into that sickly yellow background!

The shot was absurd, and even a bit disturbing. His arms, without the bat, did not even look human—distorted and performing some wholly unnatural act. It made no sense whatsoever.

Yes, the '58 Gino Cimoli finally did us in.

We went into hysterics. I was crying. Estes was doubled over. Hughes was on the ground, quickly joined by others as the Cimoli card passed from hand to hand. Soon everyone was laughing as only idiot twelve-year-old boys can. We were out of control.

This was way too much. The 1958 set had now become a veritable fun house of misprints, misfits and freaks! Good grief, we agreed, these cards—and this blasphemy had been lurking just below the surface for weeks—were just plain *SHITTY*.

We could hardly wait for the next card to fall from a pack.

And as fate would have it, Harry Dominick Chiti, burly journeyman catcher for the Kansas City Athletics, Topps 1958 face card number 119, was just that card. We lads were not particularly gifted in the art of clever word play, spelling, consonantal alliteration, or any of the many nuances, rhythms, and subtleties of the King's English. But our idiocy antenna were up and our social defenses down and when the Harry Dominick Chiti card fell into our hands we went nuts:

"IT'S A SHITTY HARRY SHITTY CARD!"

It was perfect.

The bold name lettering. The face card, complete with a cock-eyed Athletics hat at least two sizes too small for this big-boned fella. The way everything was rhyming and flowing off our tongues with a kind of poetic magic, the day had become musical, manic and all too glorious.

"SHITTY, SHITTY, SHITTY" our chant continued, each of us rolling the now priceless Harry Chiti card through our fingers and doubling over with laughter. Come on, we all felt, just how much more unbridled hilarity could the Topps House of Fun (formerly known to us as the Topps Baseball Card Company of Brooklyn, New York) possibly give us?

"SHITTY, SHITTY, SHITTY."

It just doesn't get any better.

"SHITTY, SHITTY, SHI—"

Oh no.

"Hey," and I pointed up the block, "Isn't that Mrs. Birmingham over there, and isn't she . . . my God, she's *GLARING AT US. SHE'S HEARD US! AND SHE'S HEADING OUR WAY!*"

Mrs. Harriett Birmingham was our sixth grade teacher. An older, kind, patient, and wonderfully dedicated woman, she was one of our favorite teachers, too. She lived right around the corner from Haggett's, on Woodland Road just a few blocks away. Out for a quick trip to the S & S Grocery, we guessed, on this lovely Saturday afternoon, she was clearly none too happy with her soon-to-graduate sixth graders, who had clearly slipped into some kind of convulsive, profanity-laced, and very public anti-social delirium. It was all a very sad spectacle. As best we could, we pulled ourselves together, and I actually think we were in pretty good shape by the time she reached us.

"Hello, boys." This with a cold stare, never seen before, even in our worst days in her classroom, where profanity simply did not live.

"Hello, Mrs. Birmingham."

"Boys, I certainly hope I just didn't hear what I thought I heard."

Ouch. This called for some very quick thinking, and someone had to save the day. Spike was too busy looking down at his feet, and Suds had already ducked into the store for cover, crouched behind the massive candy counter. This was strictly off-limits, but Suds had chosen to deal with Mr. Haggett, rather than our teacher.

"Oh no, Mrs. Birmingham. We're just laughing at this ridiculous card of some guy named Harry *CHITI. SEE? C - H - I - T - I.*"

I carefully proffered the shiny red, goofy face card with the bold name lettering in our defense, handing it to her with a feigned confidence that we would dodge a bullet. Few weaker defenses have ever been seen on American soil.

But this caper ended, all-in-all, rather well, as did so many of our misadventures.

Mrs. Harriett Birmingham, late of the Glenwood School and with no apparent interest whatsoever in baseball cards but a pretty keen sense of what young twelve year-old boys were all about, looked at the card for a moment—a very long moment—studying we could only hope that boldly printed name. Harry *CHITI.*

And then she handed the card back to me.

"You be good, now. And your friend hiding behind the candy counter, too. Keep it down. See you in class Monday."

And just like that, she turned and walked away, a bemused smile on her kind face, which said it all. We had pulled it off, with enough plausible deniability for everyone involved, and we were off the hook, once again.

We would soon move on to junior high school, where other things—many, many other things—would displace baseball cards in our lives. But with the Topps company's unsettling fall from grace that summer of 1958, disappointment was no longer a stranger, and we would soon struggle in many other ways to find order in an increasingly confusing world. With luck, maybe some us would never forget the magic of possibility we first learned in collecting our baseball cards, but somewhere along the way most of our cards were neglected, then forgotten. Finally, they just disappeared.

And that's the thing about our youth. It disappeared a piece at a time, when we weren't even looking, until it was just gone.

MISTER, I CAN'T EVEN SEE *YOU!*

There was an unsolved murder in 1831 on a farm in what is now Springfield Township, New Jersey, right next to the towns of Millburn and Summit. The victim was one Baltus Roll. The land eventually became a world-class golf course and took the name "Baltusrol." This very elite club has hosted the U.S. Open seven times, including in 1967, when Jack Nicklaus won his first of two championships there.

I was there for that tournament, along with my college fraternity brother Donald "Squeak" Harjes, his girlfriend (now wife) Peg, and one of their female friends they brought with them (whose name I do not recall). Squeak had called and asked that I go with them. Unfortunately, that was the very day I was to be delivering an engagement ring to the young lady who would become my first wife, and she knew the ring was coming that very day, as we had picked it out together. Which is why she was so surprised to get a phone call from her best friend, who was collecting tickets at the Open. She'd seen me enter with Squeak and the two other ladies, and had immediately excused herself and headed for the phone. This took some explaining all around.

But all this has nothing to do with the story, which takes place several years earlier, when I was about fifteen.

Back in the early 60s, adults were much more trusting of teenagers than they are today. Which helps explain how Woody Thompson, Jim "Bay" Basinger, Rob Hamilton, and I talked the caddy-master at Baltusrol Golf Club into taking us on as caddies. We didn't lie to him. We just took a few liberties with the facts, such as whether we had ever caddied before, which we hadn't. In fact, not only were we worthless as caddies, we were worthless at golf in general. But as official caddies, we would be allowed to play golf on Mondays ("Caddy Day"), which is the main reason we signed up to be caddies in the first place.

On Caddy Day, only the caddies were allowed to play. No members. This was the one day each week that the groundskeepers totally had their way with the course, and they didn't care if they made noise, ran mowing machines over our golf balls (or clubs), or otherwise messed up our game. Actually, we didn't have much of a "game." Some of the real caddies were pretty good. But Woody, Bay, Rob, and I stunk. Bay usually shot in the mid-140s. In one day, the four of us could easily create (and fail to properly fix) more divots on this world-class course than during the entire preceding week of play by hundreds of golfers who knew what they were doing. Plus, one time, I accidentally hit Rob in the ear with a 6-iron.

Actually, during the summer, I had a "real job," working as a cabinet-maker's apprentice for my father's millwork company in Newark, so I usually didn't caddy except on an occasional weekend, but I definitely took advantage of Caddy Day. Looking back, we were basically just there for Caddy Day and had no other useful involvement in the Baltusrol enterprise.

But despite this deception, Baltusrol became our "home course." Sometimes we even invited guests. That said, I often teed off at Canoe Brook Country Club, where I also didn't belong. I would arrive at the 10th tee, usually at the break of dawn, with George Freund, and perhaps Big Al Schultheis and Wiener McQueen, and play the back nine before the real golfers woke up. No one could quite figure out who we were when we came down the 18th fairway an hour ahead of the first foursome of members.

It wasn't until after we were in college that golf carts became popular. Before then, most golfers walked the course with their caddies, or, in some cases, carrying their own bags. Which is what I preferred to do when playing with my father at Essex County Country Club, where we actually did belong. But playing where we did belong, as opposed to faking being caddies or sneaking on illegally, sort of took the sport out of golf.

As a kid, I didn't like using caddies, because I didn't need them, but my father insisted that we should use them as much as we could, because they needed the tips, and because unless everyone used them, they couldn't make a living, and therefore elderly golfers who couldn't carry their own bags wouldn't be able to play golf. I suppose this made sense, although I never bought into the implied collateral rule that you should always use a valet service at a restaurant, because older people can't park their own cars. Some valets are really good, but I think most of them, at least in New Jersey and Florida, were, at the time, affiliated with the mob.

Anyway, at Baltusrol we were usually not selected to go out on the course with the good golfers. We really didn't belong. We didn't look like caddies. We were clean-cut high school kids, and therefore in the eyes of the real golfers, presumably incompetent. In our case, the presumption was accurate.

Even when Baltusrol wasn't hosting championships, really good golfers played there. Including Jimmy and Bobby Farrell, brothers who were both pros but lesser known than Nicklaus, Palmer, Hogan, and stars like that. Either they were members, or the two guys they were playing with were members. I can't recall. But the four of these scratch golfers arrived in the middle of a beautiful, sunny afternoon when the course was somewhat busy, and most of the competent caddies were already on duty. Inexplicably, Woody and I got assigned to go around with the Farrell boys. Neither of us was big enough to carry both of their bags, since they were enormous and had about forty-five clubs each. So I got assigned to one of them, and Woody to the other. The other two players lucked out and got a real caddy—a big, strapping, and very affable guy who knew exactly what he was doing. He was much cooler and considerably smarter than we were: he knew what he was doing, could spot the ball, read the greens, give advice on the right club, knew who putts when, and held the pin when appropriate without standing in the line of the putt. We couldn't do any of this stuff. Basically, all we were doing was walking around with a bag and getting in the way.

Bobby and Jimmy were long ball hitters. They would smack the ball and say to us, "Do you have it?" or "Got it?" Sometimes we would say, "Sure thing," or "Nice shot," or "That'll play," or "You'll like that one," or some other terminology we had picked up on. But usually we hadn't a clue where the ball was. We were losing balls even in plain sight on the fairway. And if we found one, it usually wasn't the one we were looking for, or it was the right one and we had just stepped on it.

A round that should have lasted about three-and-a-half hours was well into the fifth hour when darkness overcame us. We were only on about the 15th hole. One of the players hit a ball straight away and turned to the real caddy and asked, "Did you see that one?" The caddy, shaking his head slowly, looked at the guy and said, "Mister, I can't even see *you!*"

Some professional golfers have a good sense of humor. Like Mexican-American Lee Trevino, who, it is said, was out cutting his own lawn in Texas, with a T-shirt on and sweating profusely, when a woman pulled up to the curb and asked him what he charged to cut lawns. He reportedly said, "I don't charge the lady who lives here anything, but she does let me sleep with her." The driver pulled away in a huff.

Anyway, the two Farrell brothers displayed no sense of humor when they dismissed Woody and me. We couldn't see how much of a tip the real caddy got, but the two of us got about one-third the minimum wage (and, at that, we were admittedly overpaid). We walked home in the dark. Yet to this day, if either one of us says to the other, "Mister, I can't even see *you!*" we start crying with laughter. And everyone around us, as is "par for the course," thinks we're idiots.

EAT A *MAD*, NEWK

I've never been a more loyal fan of any sports team in my life than I was of the Brooklyn Dodgers in the 1950s. Branch Rickey had the guts and good business sense, in 1947, to add Jackie Robinson (No. 42) to the roster, followed closely by such other great black players as Dan Bankhead, Roy Campanella, Joe Black, Junior Gilliam, and—one of our favorites—Don Newcombe. As young boys, the significance of the integration of the Major Leagues may not have sunk in right away, but we gradually got it and, with the rest of America, benefitted greatly from it.

Born in 1926—just two towns away from us in Madison, New Jersey, and joining the Dodgers in 1949—Don Newcombe (nicknamed "Newk") was the first black pitcher to start a World Series game. In 1951, he was the first black pitcher to win twenty games in one season. In 1956, he was the first pitcher ever to win the National League MVP and the Cy Young Award in the same season. He batted .271 lifetime with fifteen home runs, and was sometimes even used as a pinch hitter.

We were never certain why this gentle giant's nickname ended in a "k" instead of a "c," although, looking back on it, it was probably just to make sure no one pronounced it with a soft "c." But whatever the spelling, he was one of our heroes.

Several of my friends and I loved going to Ebbets Field to see the Dodgers play, and we did so often in the early 50s—boys of summer watching the team that would become known as "The Boys of Summer." We were all, at least in spirit, members of Happy Felton's Knot Hole Gang.

GILBERT E. "BUD" SCHILL, JR. AND JOHN W. "MAC" MACILROY AND ROBERT D. "ROB" HAMILTON III.

Among my very best friends as a kid in Short Hills were Sherwood "Woody" Thompson, and his brothers Grove, Jr. (or "Chip") and Curtis (or "Coots"). Their parents were also very cool and were good friends with my parents.

The Thompson house was a hangout to many of us. On the way to school in the morning, several of us would routinely meet up there and wait while Woody went through his morning scavenger hunt of trying to find some clean clothes and something to eat—usually toaster waffles or ice cream. On summer days and weekends, we congregated there, too—usually either in the basement or in the attic, where Woody had set up a fake radio station and also where he kept his collection of a million 45s. Among the regular congregants were Rob Hamilton, Jim Basinger, Jim Higgins, and Greg Hoehl (pronounced Hale, not Hole, as most substitute teachers called him). Sometimes we hung out there even when Woody wasn't home. If our parents were looking for us and didn't know where we were (which was most of the time), they would check first at the Thompsons.

There were better football fields in town, such as the church field (which we used for serious football, using pads and helmets) and the field next to John Gorringe's house (where, each year, we held the Toilet Bowl), but Woody's front lawn was always good for an impromptu game. Since it was tiny and sloped down to a road, we played on our knees, usually in the mud, thus tearing the yard (and our pants) to shreds and turning it into a series of hopeless ruts—all without a word of protest from either of Woody's parents, Grace and Grove.

Then there was Wiffle ball. The Mecca for Wiffle ball was the backyard of Joanie and Willy Stevens' house on Lakeview. But we got in a lot of practice swings right there in Woody's garage. As did all boys our age, we constantly chattered on, calling balls and strikes as if we were play-by-play guys. Each one of us became a major leaguer when it was our turn to bat. "And up to the plate steps Roy Campanella, with Pee Wee Reese taking a lead off first. Campy looking to hit the long ball. Warren Spahn on the mound for the Braves. He looks at first and throws. Pee Wee is safe. Campy back in the box. Spahn sets and delivers. A fastball slightly outside, but Campy hits a rising liner.

It's going, going, gone! A two-run homer for Roy Campanella!" We became experts at sounding like announcers. But there was no such thing as a home run out of the Thompsons' garage, because any hit that started to rise was clipped by the top of the garage door and often ricocheted to strike one of us in the mouth, ear, or eye.

Another prime activity at the Thompsons' was reading *MAD* magazine. This nationwide craze began in 1952 as the comic book called *The MAD Reader*, which morphed into *MAD* magazine. Almost invariably, the cover featured Alfred E. Neuman, the goofy teenager with freckles, a missing tooth, and misaligned eyes, whose face was always shown in full, never in profile, wearing a devilish smile, but with apparently nothing but cat litter in his brain. Under the motto "What, me worry?" he repeatedly ran for President of the United States. We couldn't wait to get our hands on the latest issue of *MAD*, usually purchased at the Glenwood Sweet Shop. We loved reading the feature "Spy vs. Spy" and all the other zany stuff in *MAD*, written by the likes of Ernie Kovacs and Stan Freberg. Decades later, one of the major contributors to the magazine, Al Jaffee, declared in an interview that "*MAD* was designed to corrupt the minds of children. And...we succeeded."

One of the short-lived features of this periodical, which was admittedly stupid and yet struck us as funny, was the concept of eating the magazine. The phrase, "Eat a *MAD*" was featured for a few issues, and we began using it liberally. We were never too sure whether someone was supposed to eat a *Mad* to feel better, or to get over a problem, or because he or she was a jerk, or for some other reason. But we began to look at the act of eating a *MAD* as a cure for whatever problem ailed us. So if I had a cold, Woody would say, "Go home, take two aspirin, eat a *MAD*, and call me in the morning," or some such drivel. If a teacher had acted out of sorts one day, then on the way home from school we would opine that the teacher would probably be more understanding and helpful the next day if he or she would simply "eat a *MAD*" for breakfast. Of course, none of this made a lick of sense, but we laughed hysterically at our own wit—which seemed to us boundless.

GILBERT E. "BUD" SCHILL, JR. AND JOHN W. "MAC" MACILROY
AND ROBERT D. "ROB" HAMILTON III.

When we got to be about sixteen, we were allowed to go into New York on our own to see the Mets. But in the last couple of years the Dodgers were in Brooklyn—1956 and 1957—we were about eleven or twelve and couldn't go without a parent. Scotty Russell's dad took us at least once. I think Grove Thompson did, too. My father also made the trek once or twice. None of the mothers would touch this—except Grace. I don't think any of the other mothers had even *attended* a major league baseball game in their lives, let alone possessed the mettle required to escort a bunch of high-energy boys. Somewhat of a free spirit, and a material witness to, and participant in, many of our capers, Grace had nerves of steel.

So it was 1957. The last year of the Brooklyn Dodgers, before their move to Los Angeles. Pee Wee (No. 1) was still the captain. This was ten years after the pre-television event in which No. 1 put his arm around No. 42 near first base in front of a few thousand skeptical fans in Cincinnati, which helped change baseball and all professional sports forever.

Anyway, by 1957, Newk was an accepted star. And we went to see him pitch against the Phillies. I know Woody and I were there. Chip and Coots may have been. There were a couple of others, perhaps Greg Hoehl and/or Scotty Russell.

Before we were seated, and with Grace a few yards behind us, each of us boys ordered a hot dog from one of the vendors who was walking around with a heated container full of wrapped dogs. We each gave him a dollar. He handed hot dogs to the other guys, but not to me, claiming I hadn't yet paid him. I said I had. Grace came up from behind and said, "What's the problem here?" I explained. The vendor said, "The kid's trying to scam me." Grace said, "If he said he gave you the dollar, then he gave you the dollar." Annoyed, the guy pronounced, "Yous are interfering with my business here. Kid owes me a buck. No buck, no hot dog." I began to say, "I already gave you the buck, you moron," but Grace waived me off and started interrogating him about how much money and how much merchandise he started out with. Even at that young age, I could read his mind: "Who does this broad think she is?" She made him count both his money and his inventory, right in front of all of us. After this shakedown, and to borrow a phrase from my father, this clown "didn't know whether to shit or go blind." He handed over the hot dog, and we left him standing in a daze, with Grace referring to him under her breath as "an asshole."

She was fired up and ready to watch the game. She seemed genuinely excited to be there.

In today's ballparks, you might have access to twenty or more types of craft beer, numerous world-class wines, top-shelf mixed drinks, and full dinners in gourmet restaurants, and you can buy about forty different kinds of food, including barbeque, brisket, sushi, shrimp, and designer ice cream. Plus, you can watch the game on a big screen TV from the bar, in a cushioned seat with luxury surroundings.

In the 50s, your choices were peanuts, popcorn, Cracker Jack, hot dogs (if you had a buck), French fries, ice cream sandwiches, M&Ms, Coke, maybe 7-Up, and beer. (Ebbets Field had Schaefer, The Polo Grounds had Rheingold, and Yankee Stadium had Ballantine.) Vendors walked around selling this stuff.

At Ebbets Field there was only one guy you could understand clearly. He just kept yelling, "PEANUTS, POPCORN, CRACKER JACKS." His diction was good. Another guy sold beer. Except he called it "bee." In fact he mispronounced just about everything, including "your," "cold" and "here," yelling "GET YOU CO BEE HEE." We thought this was funny and started mimicking him. We even went up to him and asked if he wanted to buy a "co bee" from us. He was not amused.

But our favorite was the guy hawking scorecards for "a mere fifteen cents each." Two or three times a minute, holding the cards high up in the air, he would yell "SCORECARD!" Except, being in Brooklyn, it came out "SCAW COD!"

In 1955, the great baritone Tennessee Ernie Ford recorded the very popular hit "Sixteen Tons," bearing the famous lyrics:

You load sixteen tons, what do you get?
Another day older and deeper in debt.

"Ole Ern" would snap his fingers as he sang this. We all loved the song.

Well, for reasons that are difficult to explain, Woody and I, and Chip and Coots, and others, using the tune of "Sixteen Tons," would sing out, "You pay fifteen cents, and what do you get?" and try to time it so that right after that, the guy would yell "SCAW COD." If we got the timing just right, we gave each other a slap on the back. Unlike the humorless "bee" guy, the "scaw cod" guy sometimes even played along, as did some of the fans in the nearby seats. It was all very pleasing to the ear. This was big fun back in the 50s.

During all the vendor excitement, and with the fading euphoria of defeating the hot dog guy, we were all getting very much into the game. Phillies versus Dodgers. Ebbets Field. Last year in Brooklyn. Last chance to see Pee Wee, Gil Hodges, Duke Snider, Carl Furillo, Clem Labine, Carl Erskine, Don Bessent (one of the first pitchers to wear round spectacles, which Woody always emulated with Grace's reading glasses when he pitched), Gino Cimoli, Junior Gilliam, Sandy Amoros, Charlie Neal, Sal "The Barber" Maglie, and Newk in their Brooklyn uniforms. The Dodgers were pretty good that year, finishing third behind the Cardinals and the Braves, who went on to beat the Yankees in the World Series. The Phillies, with stars such as Don Cardwell, Turk Farrell, Robin Roberts, Stan Lopata, Curt Simmons, Chico Fernandez, and Richie Ashburn, finished fifth.

I forget what the score was, but it was tight—late in the game. Newk was behind on the batter and needed to get an out. He was trying to concentrate. We were on the first base side.

Now, Major League Baseball players were accustomed to hearing fans yell stuff at them. "You're a bum." "You can't pitch." "You need glasses." "Go back to Duluth." "Get an arm." "Hole in your glove?" "Be a hitter." I'm willing to bet, though, that never in the history of Major League Baseball, other than on this particular day, did any player hear a group of voices, four or five young boys and a woman, demanding that he "Eat a *MAD*"

I forget whose idea it was. But collectively, with Grace listening in, we decided we needed to get Newk to start throwing consistent strikes. So after a few scores of "Mow 'im down Newk," and "He's all yours, Newk," and after a moment of silence, all of us, including Grace, as loud as we could, yelled "EAT A *MAD*, NEWK!"

Out of the corner of my eye, I could see the "co bee" guy and the "scaw cod" guy looking at us like, "What the hell does that mean?" Gil Hodges, tending to first base, gave us the same look.

Newk probably was not a reader of "*MAD* magazine," and I can only wonder what he thought we were trying to get across. We were not even certain he heard us, although he seemed to flinch. He threw a strike. We yelled again. He threw another strike. He got that batter, and the next, and the Dodgers went on to win the game.

When we called out to Newk, we weren't making fun of him. We idolized him. We just didn't give a lot of careful thought to the potential repercussions of interrupting his focus. We were trying to help him. And we always congratulated ourselves for doing so. Grace was a big part of this win.

Later, on the way out of Ebbets Field, we saw the hot dog guy, but when he spotted us, he bolted in the other direction.

We discussed our multiple successes all the way home.

Newk went on to play for the Dodgers in Los Angeles, then the Reds, and finally the Indians. After some medical problems, he returned to baseball in a back office position with the Dodgers, getting to watch, at the age of eighty-seven, Harrison Ford perfecting the role of Branch Rickey during the filming of the movie *42*. In the words of President Obama, Newk "is someone who helped…America become what it is."

I may try to send Newk a copy of this story to see if he remembers our chant in 1957, but I doubt I'll get to ask him about that incident this side of the Pearly Gates. And if I don't get the opportunity in this lifetime, when I get to those Gates, I'll gather up Grace Thompson and go looking for Newk so we can find out if he if he ever ate a *MAD*.

YOU WIN SOME . . .

Our high school sports—and football in particular—were a big deal in town, and most of us couldn't wait to join in the fun.

Maybe we should have.

Pulling for the "Millers"—our nickname, likely a nod to the old paper mill in town, although some clown claimed we were named for a tiny moth-like parasite—was all done in a kind of understated way. A very upscale, good-taste suburban style. Nothing like those sports-crazed fans in West Texas, under stadium lights in a kind of Friday Night Football Frenzy. If those games looked like a traveling preacher's tent revival, ours were a little more reserved—everyone was looking for a proper balance in our sports, and a measured experience for all.

But it still had the magic of *promise* as we left the haphazard sports of our backyards and local ponds for the world of high school competition. And like most of our missteps, this all started rather gently, although the very first thing we discovered was troubling.

Despite years of practice in backyards across town, most of our athletic skills were not usable currency. All those hours at Jencko's pond—wearing our treasured and homegrown Detroits or Rangers uniforms and perfecting our hockey skills—were completely wasted as the school did not have a hockey team. So, too, our painful mastery of the aerodynamic mysteries of the Wiffle ball, equally irrelevant. The same with one-on-one basketball, and four-man touch football. There wasn't even a dodge ball team anywhere around. On and on it went, our eclectic inventory of athletic skills completely marginalized. Yes, our talents were hopelessly mismatched to the needs of the real world, in what was a pretty good preview of the larger world to come.

Why didn't anyone warn us?

Worse yet, we soon figured out that we would actually have to *try out* for these high school teams. Now this was not as alarming, or even as unusual, as it may seem, since the kids today, the "Trophy Generation," have apparently never actually had to fight for a place on a team, and they always win a trophy even if all they did during the season was stand around. We, on the other hand, were used to regular athletic humiliation and disappointment, and fighting for spots on lots of teams. From the time we first attempted to throw a ball in the schoolyard, or were asked to join a pick-up game in the backyard or tried out for Little League, we had all, at one time or another, been cut, fired, traded, demoted, repositioned, not picked, picked over, or picked on.

We didn't like it, but we knew we could handle it. It was just the way things worked.

The next thing we found out was this: even if you were pretty good at your chosen sport (and some in the class were), the very best you could hope for in the first year or two was earning a spot on a *junior* varsity squad. This was certainly the case for football, basketball, baseball, and soccer. Track, tennis, and golf seemed to have a more relaxed take on things and did not require similar apprenticeships.

But for most of us, this apprenticeship seemed to have more to do with the cruel logic of the high school pecking order than any real measure of athletic talent. It was a doubly cruel reality. At the bottom of the high school status ladder, we were focused on just two things: girls and sports.

On the first front, we were rather tentatively learning how to date. No more screwy "triple" dates, or dads driving us to the bowling lanes. We were trying to go on Real Grown-up Dates, and again we were terrified, generally making fools of ourselves. On the second front, many of us were soon beating our brains out on the junior varsity circuit of our various chosen sports, where a good game-day crowd might number in the teens, usually just a few parents. There was no glory here, no cool school jacket. That good stuff was all reserved for the older *varsity* boys, who were soon dating all our sophomore girls. Stealing them away, really.

Why didn't anybody warn us about these things?

This was an injustice, common to high school students everywhere. But it was, for us, compounded by the fact that our upperclassmen may have been the most talented athletes in school history. These guys were winners everywhere. Football, of course, soccer, basketball, tennis, golf...the works. Over by the track, Paul "Boomer" Beck had been burnishing his national legacy as one of the greatest scholastic coaches of his generation, winning championships year after year, and sending out star trackmen to top-flight colleges across the country. Scholarships were pouring in from all over the place, and there was even talk of an actual big league baseball scout hanging around at our school's baseball games.

We had landed in the land of athletic greatness.

We just forgot to bring much talent.

At the top of the ladder stood the football team. Our freshman year, when we were still housed over at the junior high school—and not eligible to participate on the high school teams—an injury-riddled varsity club had stitched together a very respectable winning season, marred only by a loss to Verona. The next year, as sophomores-now-in-residence, our school powered its way to a Conference championship, with a strong 4-0-1 conference record.

Our team that year had a huge line, which played both offense and defense, and these giants were *tough*. They looked like they had to shave three times a day, and were all business on the field. There was even some talk that their helmets had to be custom-made, just to fit their enormous skulls. Now, this was all before the time of manic weightlifting programs, and these guys were just naturally built this way. Our ends were fast and agile, and they just could not drop a pass. The offense was led by a talented junior class quarterback who was a natural leader and a great guy and who actually seemed to value the junior varsity contributions, which generally consisted of getting flattened, tackled, blocked, overrun, and outrun as the scrub team for the big guys during practice all week. We really weren't more than tackling dummies for these guys. At the end of each practice, and by some kind of unstated understanding, we rookies quietly checked each other for missing body parts.

As scrub reserves, we were permitted to wear our team football jerseys in the stands on game day. Some of us thought this a curious tradition, with a distinctively mixed message. Sure, it marked you as a member of the football team. But it also screamed to the world that you really weren't good enough to be on the football team that *actually played football*. Today, of course, all of this would go unnoticed as team jerseys are available for sale to all takers. At professional sporting events now, half the fans in attendance come wearing the jerseys of their favorite players.

Stuck in the stands as we were, it was still cool as a sophomore scrub to be even a remote part of that championship team, and we were just happy to trail along in the wake of the junior and senior stars. Yes, we worshipped them as if they were gods, even if they were gods who regularly stole away our ladies, the mere mortals we were. That was what those capricious Greek gods did, and we figured someday we too could ascend to that lofty perch, and then steal the girlfriends of the younger scrubs.

But any hint of ascension would have to wait at least another year, although some of us were making modest contributions to a couple of other teams during the winter and spring, and those crumbs kept us going.

Our efforts also earned a few of us invitations to the annual spring "All Sports Banquet," an evening honoring varsity athletes. Sponsored by the town's "Scholastic Boosters," we wondered if there was a parallel dinner honoring the scholars among us sponsored by the "Athletic Boosters." None of us ever got that invitation, but that's no indication that it didn't exist, and it seemed just another strange irony in a confusing world. The jock event was held in a swanky dinner club called the "Chanticleer," which then rested majestically atop a hill right next to the school property. The club is gone today, cleared to make way for a swanky townhouse development. Homes there are impossibly expensive, and the complex would be a great place for any of the school's coaches or teachers to live, should they ever win the lottery. Maybe they should go in together on a group ticket. It would make a great story if they won, as long as they didn't get all stupid about dividing up the loot, which always seems to happen in those multi-winner cases.

Dinner fare at the All Sports Banquet was the usual rubber chicken, as I recall, with one strange published menu item: "green and ripe olives." We figured this was actually code for martinis, as the event was packed with important town elders, some of whom would make brief remarks, and all of whom would expect an adult beverage or two.

We also had a featured speaker, in this case a professional football player. He was a field goal specialist, and a pretty good one at that, named Lee Grosscup. He played for the New York Giants and lived nearby, and he may even have done the honors for free, as those were more innocent days, certainly in professional sports. Grosscup was a great choice, with a wry and self-deprecating take on football typical of the guys who play on special teams.

We also had a magician for entertainment that evening, the father of one of our favorite Glenwood girls. He was a really good guy, and he seemed to turn up all the time around town in support of various community groups, dispensing magic at places like Boy Scout Troop 15, or at the local hospital. If it did in fact exist, I am sure he performed at the scholars' dinner, too. I always liked his daughter, a pretty redhead, but never asked her if her father had another *real* job, although I assumed he did. I think he billed out as "Orla the Great," but in keeping with the generally understated style of things in town it could have been just "Orla the Good." I do know that he was modestly presented in the evening program as simply "Magician." Look, he really seemed to have a good time with all this, but I hope he was getting a little more firepower from his day job title. We loved the guy, and if he was as good at whatever-he-was-during-business-hours as he was a magician, he deserved something less modest from his day job.

All in all, it was a great evening, and after the featured speaker and the magic, those of us who played football got pretty excited about the next season. We would be juniors, and we could expect some reprieve from the scrub team. However, many of the best players would return as seniors, and the room that night was filled with football talent and promise. It was also a bit sad as we said goodbye to some really outstanding graduating athletes, including my favorites: a couple of football co-captains named Boyd and Aldridge, and the co-captain of the track team, a runner named Robert Lee who had really helped a few of us out that first year on the team. Actually, his name was Robert *E.* Lee, which was really something, and he had a very commanding presence which helped him carry it off. I often wonder where they, and many of the other guys, are today, and if they remember this magical time as clearly as we do.

When late summer arrived, and the dreaded double practices started, it was clear that we were going to have one fine team again. Just a few weeks earlier Coach had sent out a mimeographed letter telling us to *"THINK BIG: GO 90."* The local press picked up on this, and after carefully explaining that this stood for nine wins and no defeats, as Coach had left out the important hyphen, we quickly had a consensus motto for the year. Our local once-a-week paper was gushing in its position-by-position pre-season analysis, finding the team stocked with "talent and depth." Even the Newark *Star-Ledger* joined in with a rave preview. Frankly, there was great buzz all over the state.

This was not exactly the kind of measured sports attention the town was used to, but it certainly was *glorious!* None of us juniors ever got named as the "talent" in these previews, but we all kind of thought of ourselves as the "depth." And that was good enough for us. In fact, we soon started to think of ourselves formally as *"The Depth."* We were part of a team that seemed destined for greatness, and *we* were soon stealing some of the incoming sophomore girls. Even a few of our own junior girls were back on the dating roster, as their older boyfriends had cut them loose when they went off to college.

In mid-September we opened the season with a solid home-field win over Livingston. This was followed by another home win over Rahway, a non-conference game. Next up was Summit. Summit was a perennial conference powerhouse, and a very special rivalry as that town was right next door. They were very good that year, too. Although we thought we had outplayed them, we lost that home game, as well as one of our superstars to a broken leg. Our head coach summed it up this way: "We got all the hits while they got all the runs."

It was a frustrating day, and a bit confusing: we did, however, cut the coach some slack on his curious baseball metaphor. As I said, we were all a bit dazed, and even beaten up.

We bounced back with a 20-0 win over Chatham the next week. Those of us deep in "The Depth" really liked how our local paper described the play in the last quarter. With our coach sending in the reserves, the Chatham team "seemed to encounter more trouble with the second and third strings than with the starters."

Yeah, we liked that. Thank you, Mr. Michael Rose, late of the Millburn-Short Hills *Item*. We will never forget you.

We next beat a strong Clifford-Scott team in another non-conference away game, on a playing field legendary for its rough shape and against an inner-city team known for its tough brand of play. This was the kind of matchup always aggravated by that "suburban conference thing." It was never much fun, and wasn't that day either. But we brought home our fifth victory.

We began November with a huge non-conference win, crushing Sommerville 48-13. This set a new Miller single game scoring record, and the buzz really started. The media called this a "tune-up" for our last two games, both against tough conference rivals. The season took on a magical feeling unlike anything we had ever experienced. For many of us, and I want to be careful not to channel the likes of "Rabbit" Angstrom in the John Updike novels, it didn't get much better than this, and probably never would. We juniors all saw a lot of playing time against Sommerville, and had actually *been a part of athletic history!* "The Depth," had guys playing quite a few quarters, and well. Terry O'Brien, Suds Estes, The Duke, and "Swede" Olson (who also carried a second nickname—"Nils"—which was a rare and envied coup) all looked especially good, with solid play from quite a few others. I remember Rob got in, and guys like Hellman, Morgan, Higgins, Saboti, Hohnstine, and Happel also joined in the fun on the field, and they too played tough and well, and I have probably left out a few others. Yes, we really felt part of this great team, and we had gotten to play before a packed home crowd. One of The Depth even scored the final touchdown, which set the record. Yes, The Depth had come out of the shadows, and we felt wonderful.

Following this tremendous game against Sommerville, and as we entered the colder days of November, we saw a slight change during practice. Still demanding and tough, the coaches seemed to encourage a little more fun, and less punishing contact. Clearly, the coaches were pleased, the team tight, the wins coming. Bob Lilley, our amazing quarterback, team leader, and my personal hero (whom I would follow to college in a year), even persuaded us all to wear funny little red plaid caps called "Tam-O-Shanters" during warm-ups. Kids actually came out to the practice field to watch us in these funny caps, and share in this...*phenomenon*. We all knew this was special. No one, not even the school slackers, seemed to resent our goofy caps, which were now by the law of the high school jungle *only to be worn by football players*. Not only was a second consecutive conference championship very likely, but maybe even a state championship.

We next beat Verona 13-7, on their field. Verona had an exceptional team, and was looking like the team to beat in the coming years. This was a tough game, and we juniors saw only limited action, consigned once again to being mostly benchwarmers. It didn't matter. We were on the ride of a lifetime, our very own "Miller Time."

And there it was. Heading into the final game, the traditional Thanksgiving Day rivalry with the Madison Dodgers, we were just one win away from the greatest season in our school's history. This would be an away game for our team, a fact which caused us some concern. Although they were entering the Turkey Day Classic with an uneven 4-3 record, Madison had a nasty little habit of playing way above their record in this particular rivalry, which began in 1933. This caused even more concern.

Our town had by now completely forgotten all about this measured balance thing, and simply went nuts. Pictures of the football team dominated merchants' windows up and down Main Street, and some of us seem to remember something about special celebratory sales, with absolutely no connection to football, popping up all over town. Everyone got caught up in the fun, even if you were just a suburban housewife gobbling up these special discounts who had no clue what the fuss was all about.

Word got around, and it may even be true, that the great local Millburn Deli—legendary town hangout for generations of students—was planning some terrific game day discounts. Understand this. The Deli looms larger in our collective memories than any sandwich shop should, but for good reason. It made, and still makes, the best deli sandwich in the world, something called a "Sloppy Joe." It's not the messy hamburger kind of thing popular in the Midwest, but an amazing three-decker sandwich. No matter who else tries to copy this masterpiece, it just doesn't compare. We are still convinced there is a secret ingredient, which may have something to do with the brine they use to cure their coleslaw, and the whole operation may be one of the most successful small businesses in the country. (If you have never tried one of these beauties, do so before you die. They will ship anywhere in the world.) We loved the place so much that we let it slide that these great discounts, never before seen, were for sandwiches bought on Thanksgiving game day only. The football team couldn't eat that kind of thing on game day, but it all added to the fun.

Game day arrived, a crisp November Thanksgiving day. Our coaches, sensing history in the making, and well aware of the media all over the place, had convinced us to cool it with the goofy caps that day, although we had all worn them one last time during our light workout on Wednesday afternoon. We were all business that day, and the coaches were both classy and right: we would conduct ourselves with dignity, like the champions we fully expected to be. Players reported to the field for this late-morning game a little earlier than usual, particularly the seniors, and we all suited up just a little more carefully than usual.

This could be it!

The equipment managers were going crazy all morning checking on cleats and face masks and pads and who knows what else. Even The Depth went a little overboard about equipment. Games, we told the equipment boys, had been lost on account of one broken cleat. Once the coaches calmed us all down, we took to the athletic bus for the short ride to the nearby town.

Then the magic began.

When we got to Madison, the stands were packed, and the field was surrounded by standing-room-only fans from both towns. It was a zoo, but I did catch a glimpse of a cute sophomore I'd had my eye on.

Madison kicked off, our senior-heavy offense took the field, and we began a methodical march into football history. We couldn't do anything wrong, but neither could our opponents. It was quickly shaping up to be a hard-fought and balanced match. The seniors, as usual, were carrying the day. We took a lead into the locker room at half-time, and all of the coaches got pretty choked up during that last chalk-talk of the season. We all did.

The second half opened with a Madison score. But the outcome was no longer in doubt. We were on our way to the best season in school history, another conference championship and, we thought, probably a state championship.

Sometime after two in the afternoon on that marvelous Thanksgiving Day, time on the scoreboard clock ran out, and we had won by a convincing score of 28-14. We were declared conference champs on the spot, although we would still have to wait a few weeks for the sportswriters and coaches to vote to see whether we would be named divisional state champions, which they did.

It was just about the best moment of our lives, and when we boarded the bus which would take us back to our home field to shower and hand in our equipment, we put on our goofy caps. The coaches just smiled.

Of course, although we didn't really understand this yet, sooner or later we all pay a price for these magnificent, almost transcendent, moments.

The gods can take your women, and they can take your spirit too.

You see, time doesn't stop at the moment of triumph. There is always another day, another month and another year.

There certainly was for us.

AND YOU LOSE SOME

Even in the glow of winning the state football crown our junior year, there were a few troublesome undercurrents in the substantial media coverage. Subtle things, probably not even noticed by anyone but the juniors. Mostly, it was talk of how difficult it would be to repeat our success with the graduation of an exceptional class of athletes, and a largely untested group of seniors coming up next season.

Everyone was just waiting for the other cleat to drop.

We were very aware of this, as not a single junior had gotten enough playing time to earn his football letter. But we had played on a state champion team, and a few of us were very close to lettering, damn it, and that had to count for *something*.

So most of us simply enjoyed our championship and nurtured our friendships, which have continued to this day. We played other sports and navigated a surprisingly gentle passage through the rest of our junior year. Indeed, if I had to pick one school year as my favorite, this year would be probably win it. I even took one of the prettiest cheerleaders to the junior prom. Hey, I know that sounds kind of shallow, but I mean she was really, really hot.

Then suddenly it was June. We said goodbye to our senior friends, and happily took up the mantle as the new seniors. Less willingly, I said goodbye to the really, really hot cheerleader, who had gotten back together with her older boyfriend. Anyway, football was just around the corner, and this was a happy time, even if it looked like we were sailing into a disaster of Titanic proportions.

We had our mouth-guards and other equipment fitted at the end of August, and got ready to start double sessions on the first day of September. Things went south pretty quickly. It was hot. We were not in top shape. And injuries were exploding all over the place—knees blown out, collar bones snapped, ankles sprained. This was not good news for a team that had lost every one of its twenty-eight lettermen, and was beginning the season with limited experience. The local paper drilled away on this point—the "untested seniors." We quickly figured this was newspaper code for "these guys will stink." Unrelenting, it hurt, like a bad day at my dentist who had decided Novocaine was not an important part of a twentieth century dental practice.

"WE'RE DESTITUTE," our coach told one reporter, scanning the roster of players both healthy and injured.

"A roster," the reporter helpfully pointed out, "of generally unfamiliar names."

Yeah, like the guys who had been sitting up in the stands for the last two years with the stupid scrubs' football jerseys.

Thinking better of his choice of words, Coach backed off a bit. He was not a mean guy, and he figured some of us might even read the papers, so he added that we were simply "green" and would play "representative football."

Yeah, he knew we sucked.

But at least a new, far more realistic motto was born: "Green but Growing."

Like a staph infection, or a choking ocean algae.

We limped into a couple of preseason scrimmages, and even convincingly beat a pretty good Roselle team, which despite some rumors over the years was not a private middle school brought over from Pennsylvania. Whatever the case, we would face our away opener against Livingston on the last Saturday of September, ready or not.

Mostly not.

"Sort of like David against Goliath," our coach helpfully told the local paper, adding that their front line players weighed in at around 220, and our guys, "normal" for high school ball, around 180. Yeah, and their guys were *naked* when weighed, we heard, and ours were in full gear.

So our season opened, and all the Livingston linemen were fully clothed when they took the field, adding still more to their considerable weight advantage. They really were huge, but we actually drew first blood, scoring on a nice fullback sweep around the left end early in the first quarter. The extra point went wide, but we were sitting on a 6-0 lead. That held until Livingston scored with sixteen seconds left in the second quarter, and they converted the extra point.

We headed into halftime with a pretty good feeling, down by just a point. All coaches are pretty skilled at halftime pep talks, and ours certainly were. They had us actually believing we were on our way to a win. In fact, we were statistically outplaying our opponents, and we charged into the second half full of fight and hope.

Lots of it, in fact.

The only thing missing were those things called talent and depth, which had been our friends just a year ago.

Following a scoreless third quarter, things got messy indeed. Livingston scored on a short flip pass, after a long seventy yard drive late in the fourth quarter, and converted the extra point. Now trailing 14-6 late in the game, we drove some forty yards, all the way to the two-yard line. With a touchdown and a two-point conversion, we could tie the game. But on a broken halfback sweep, we lost a yard, and time ran out.

And with it some of the magic of football.

We were beat up, pissed off and only one game into the season.

Our next game was against a Newark school at home. We dropped that one 26-14. Down two.

Summit, a perennial powerhouse sitting atop the conference, shut us out the next week, 27-0. At least we weren't at home, and the traveling fans had started to thin. I think my girlfriend said she missed the game because she had a headache.

We were back at home for the next game, against Chatham. Despite our early lead and some decent play, Chatham bounced back to a 21-12 victory. The stands were looking a bit empty at home, too. This time my girlfriend said she had to wallpaper her bedroom. She was usually full of school spirit and one of the most popular girls in our class, although we later found out that our school custodian kept a picture of her in his utility closet, and that was creepy. Her brother had been an exceptional player on good teams a few years earlier, and was a star on the Cornell football team.

I really think that she just couldn't bear to watch this awful display week after week, so I never called her out on this. Other players were also reporting strange excuses which seemed to prevent their girlfriends from making our games. My favorite came from a younger player, a rather slow reserve lineman, who told me his girlfriend needed to wash her hair every Saturday afternoon.

At least he would have another chance next year.

Frankly, if we didn't have to be on the bench when we weren't on the field, *we* wouldn't have wanted to watch this mess either. We had no choice. The guys who spent most of the game on the field may have had it a bit easier, in a sense, although it's a stretch. The entire team performance on the field was usually deteriorating, week after week, on a kind of *macro* level, with multiple and simultaneous displays of fumbles, dropped passes, missed blocks, blown coverages, weak tackles, and many other horrors marking our every play. We were not a team undone by just a single screw-up, or even two. Rather, almost anyone on the team could easily make a truly comedic mess of any play, any time. On the bench, not to mention the stands, you could see these individual displays of ineptitude as a hopeless and wide-screen masterpiece. Like watching the new "Todd-O-Rama" cinemascope at our favorite movie theater up the road in Morristown, they had a wide-screen picture of *everything* happening on the field.

The guys on the field, on the other hand, were limited to a kind of individual *micro*-environment.

Within seconds of the snap, our linemen were usually face-down in the turf with a few hundred pounds of opposing player on top of them, our ends upended somewhere near the line and our backfield smothered by the rest of the opposition. None of these players could see anything much beyond their own facemask. They were crushed into the turf and generally oblivious to all the other disasters around them, unable to see it all, just the little football dramas on their own tiny patch of the gridiron. This tender mercy, which did not really make up for the physical beating the field guys were taking, only went so far. When a penalty was called, usually against us, and the refs were busy sorting it all out, the players on the field just couldn't help but look up and notice the scoreboard, which told the whole sad truth.

Caldwell was next, and that game just about did us in. In a matchup of weak teams, we looked pretty good. Playing away, we again scored first and actually held the lead for three quarters until disaster struck. A safety late in the fourth quarter led to a Caldwell touchdown and conversion to win the game 15-14. We totaled 293 yards on offense, to their 271.

This just isn't fair!

Down the drain went our hopes for a first victory.

Come on football gods, a single point? We said we'd give up the sophomore girls!

Those neat pictures of the team and even individual players that would normally pop up in merchants' storefront windows all over town about this time, well, they just didn't pop. Most of us stopped going to Main Street, not wanting to face these good people who had been reduced to placing faded merchandise and old posters for the Papermill Playhouse in their storefront windows.

We even stopped going to the Deli for our cherished Sloppy Joe sandwiches, not wanting to risk running into boosters or the parents of the seniors from last year's championship team. It was unbearable. Even as kids, we had some sense—call it misplaced hope—that when you have to pay the price, there's at least going to be a discount figured in there somewhere, or maybe just easy credit terms. Something to re-balance the scales, but this season shattered the idea.

Maybe that was what this season was supposed to be all about.

In quick and merciless succession, we lost to Clifford Scott, Sommerville, and Verona. We were the walking wounded. By then, in that wonderful tradition where the cheerleaders from each school cross the field to cheer before the other side, there was talk that our cheerleaders *weren't coming back*. The coaches faced an impossible task, but did their best to keep us afloat with more dignity than we probably deserved. A few reporters dug into the statistics and figured out that we really shouldn't be as bad as we were: in the first eight games, the number of first downs which separated the winning team (them, all of them) and the losing team (us, always) was only one. Actually, that's not bad. And it turns out that despite all the carnage, we also had a pretty good quarterback who had completed fifty percent of his passes. But what it all came down to as we limped toward our final game, the annual Thanksgiving Day Classic, against a strong Madison team at home on November 28, 1963, was that we sucked. After our loss to Verona on the 16th of November, we faced almost two weeks of long, cold and dark Jersey November practices.

We had no idea how dark those weeks would become.

We just wanted the gridiron gods to balance the account. *Hadn't we already paid the price in full for last year's magnificent season?*

None of us will ever forget where we were on the 22nd of November that year. On a bright and sunny day in Dallas, Texas, just before noon, President John Fitzgerald Kennedy took a bullet to the throat and one to the head while riding in an open presidential car, and his death was confirmed about an hour later. I have seen that iconic and haunting tape of a shaken and subdued Walter Cronkite reading the AP release from CBS studios in New York many times since that terrible day, and it never fails to crush me. None of us saw the bulletin live that Friday afternoon, as we were just wrapping up the school day and there were few televisions in the school, although I recall that strange rumors had been swirling around school for about an hour about something in Texas. These were disjointed and inconsistent, and we headed to practice unaware of the tragedy.

I will forever remember this day as impossibly cold, with a bone-chilling wind and dark, dark clouds hanging low over the practice field, although I suspect I may have created this dismal backdrop in my mind's eye after the fact. Sometime around 3:30, our coaches called us together as a team, told us to take a knee, and broke the official news of the assassination.

The whole season really ended for us that day, imploding along with our innocence.

No one really knew what to do, about anything. And much of what followed in those days is a blur of strangely conflicting and surreal memories. And ever since, I've wondered if history is written not to tell its story to those who were *not* there, but to help those who *were*.

Maybe we immediately stopped the practice, although some of us remember finishing up drills, and we figured the season was over. Frankly, that would have suited most of us just fine, including the coaches.

Everything everywhere was in limbo.

Uncertainty and real fear were spreading, multiplying exponentially as the chaos and confusion and unbelievable events of the next several days unfolded, pulling an entire nation down into history's sickening vortex.

It felt like we were drowning.

As anyone who was around then will tell you, it was a very scary and overwhelming web of events. Everything seemed to flow together in a terrible choreography, although most of us have spliced together strangely inconsistent memories of those few days, over the years confusing timelines and live broadcasts and taped bulletins in our private archives of that history. But we agree on this. A few of us on the team had driven over to the home of two of our best friends, a couple of twin girls in our class, on Sunday. We had just walked into their home at the very moment Jack Ruby shot Oswald in the Dallas jail, live on television. And I remember the twins' dad—a wonderful guy, a very successful executive and a sturdy Navy veteran—just staring at the screen in utter disbelief, saying over and over, "Just what the hell is happening?" *"Just what the hell is happening?"*

Exactly.

For the very first time I realized that the adults didn't have a much better handle on things than we did, and that was very scary.

And just a year ago, we were on the top of the world.

But the world can break your spirit.

And you may never get to balance your account.

In those sad days, we were all the walking wounded, and I don't mean just the players on a bad, beaten, and beaten-up team in a small town in Northern New Jersey. But as we all seemed to do, and still do, we pushed on. In homes, and schools, and offices, and churches across the country, we started to pull ourselves together.

Even on the practice field, after we buried a President.

It wasn't easy.

But the final game day arrived, not cancelled as we had expected, without much fanfare of course, and no joy. Thanksgiving had always been a great occasion, even if we had to dress for dinner, without the commercial stress of the Christmas Holidays just around the corner. And everyone in town loved the traditional Turkey Day football classic.

Just not this year.

We went through all the motions, reporting to the field early for the 11:00 o'clock kickoff, which had been moved to Saturday rather than Thursday, donning our pads and all the rest of a practiced ritual. Unlike the year before, nobody seemed particularly concerned about broken cleats or tired pads, and how such trivia can ruin a championship season, and the equipment managers weren't busy at all.

We knew they couldn't do anything about our broken spirits, of course, and that's all that really mattered by then.

The pre-game pep talk is an art form, even in a moldy locker room under outdated football stands in New Jersey, at the end of a terrible season. To their great credit, each of our coaches delivered a beauty. It was surprisingly upbeat but not phony, and balanced as those things often are not, given the larger realities afoot that week. No one was kidding anyone here, but it all boiled down to this: we had picked ourselves up after every game and every practice week after week, and kept coming back for more.

We were not quitters.

If you know sports, that's a pretty big deal. And it seems now they may have been talking in a larger metaphor that week, although they would have likely been uncomfortable if anyone said that. But it worked, whatever it meant, and we took the field with a kind of hope. Misplaced, of course, as Madison was bringing one of the best teams in the state, but enough to keep us going, at least for the next, and final, three hours of our football lives.

Come on fickle gods, haven't we finished paying the price yet?

Maybe we weren't the only people asking that sort of question during those dark days.

But the stadium was full of home town loyalists, and Madison fans were all over the place too. I looked around and actually did see my girlfriend, who had promised to come to the final game, her room wallpapering project over. I even saw the younger lineman nod to a girl I didn't know, who looked like she actually did need to wash her hair. There really is not much to say about the game, other than it quickly became a blowout.

No, we were not quitters.

Just really bad football players. Madison had an impossibly fast fullback, who would go on to play at Alabama. He may have gained two hundred yards just in the first half, and maybe more. I can probably look up his actual performance that day, but I am really afraid that it could actually have been more. The Madison defense was huge, tough, and hungry, and our running backs were cycling in and out with injuries both big and small. We ended the half down by a score of something like 38-6, and retreated into the locker room for the halftime chalk talk. We were pretty much out of gas, plays, players, and hope.

But we weren't quitters.

No, but we weren't idiots either.

Well, we really were, most of the time, but just not here. And things were still all atilt in the larger world, everything off course by a few degrees. So when the head coach started to wrap up his halftime talk by assuring us that, "Yes, we can still win this game," something snapped. From the edge of the encircled players, and most of us today agree it was the battered, bruised, and broken fullback who let it out, came an anguished cry. Others say it was one of our linemen, and one buddy of mine still claims it was the assistant equipment manager. As I said, we were all pretty broken. But let's be honest. We were all thinking the same thing, but I'm attributing this particular cry to the fullback:

"THAT'S JUST BULLSHIT."

But he wasn't finished.

"WE'LL BE LUCKY IF ANY OF US ARE STILL ALIVE IN ANOTHER HOUR," he screamed out, exploding with a season of pent-up pain, frustration and humiliation.

"When will this just end?" he finished, with his voice now trailing off to a mere whisper. This was a broken man. And he had lost his really, really hot cheerleader too.

At least it sounded like he was still planning to hang in there for the scheduled duration of the season. As the coach had said, none of us were quitters, although some of us do recall one of the assistant coaches nodding to the trainer, just in case the fullback, or any of the other players on the bubble, started to rip off his pads, prematurely. This may have even been in the contingency planning book for troubled teams: wrap a broken running back, and any other player on the edge, in athletic tape, and then chain him to a locker. Anything to keep every player in uniform until the end of the season, just a lousy hour away.

Then just like that, the outburst was over.

But a funny thing happened. Coach kind of cracked a smile. So did one of the assistants. We were all trying to read the signals here, but we soon realized this:

The air had finally been cleared.

Coach wrapped it up, and I remember something like this, although others have different memories:

"Boys, this year's been a bitch. Not just for you, you know. The season will be over soon. And let's face it, I don't think any of you seniors will ever play another minute of football in your lives after today."

No surprise there, Coach.

"So just go out there, play as hard as you can, and try to have some fun. You don't know it now, but you guys have built something more important than any record of wins and loses. We call it character. Never forget that."

And you know, we haven't.

This was not Knute Rockne here, but it worked, and no one had to be wrapped in athletic tape or chained to a locker, and we all took to the field for the second half. Where we continued, of course, to get whooped. We lost 48-12, but everyone was still alive at the end of the game, and our impossibly terrible season was over. Just like Coach had promised.

In the late spring of our senior year, we had another traditional "All Sports Banquet" where we celebrated some of our other athletic successes. Not much reference to football, of course. Back again at the "Chanticleer," our dinner menu featured "boned breast of capon," which set off Higgs, or maybe it was The Duke, on a mildly off-color but entertaining frolic and detour about boobs, a subject of growing interest and much curiosity. The adults were still sending that coded message about martinis, as we saw a repeat of the "ripe and green olives" item on the menu. All the coaches were there, of course. After our disaster of a football season, along with some other mildly disappointing team performances in the winter and spring, everyone thought the Boosters should have opted for an open bar, and just let it all hang out.

It would have been a kind gesture.

The printed program called for two speakers that year, a former Davis Cup captain and a ballplayer from the New York Mets, named Tracy Stallard. The Mets were a lousy team then, so it made some sense, and he might have been a lot of fun. Most of us just don't remember him at all, so maybe he was a no-show.

Also a no-show was our favorite magician, Orla the Great. We learned later he had gotten a last-minute call from Overlook Hospital to share a little of his joyful performance with a very sick young boy, who needed all the magic in the world. Yes, Orla the Great was the best.

We just wished he had been around for most of the games of our final football season, pulling a few needed touchdowns out of his magic hat.

RUSTY, THE WONDER DOG OF ESSEX COUNTY

Only two things could rival our love of all things sport: our neighborhood dogs, and our neighborhood friends. They all kind of went together. Some neighborhoods were particularly well known for great pairings of boys and their dogs. A few were even legendary, both boy and dog, bringing exceptional credit and comfort to their families.

My dog was not of this kind. Probably not me either.

His name, at least his first name, was Rusty.

This cute little brown and white puppy was purchased with the understanding that he had something called *papers*. This didn't mean anything at all to me at the time, since I was eight. But the dog was an English springer spaniel, and this was apparently important, at least in some circles.

My parents decided where I would be shipped off to camp for half the summer based wholly on haphazard conversations at cocktail parties around town, after the second or third martini at that. Yet they had done *months* of research—like in the town library—and maybe even made a few discreet inquiries to the town's Animal Control guy, trying to figure out what kind of dog would be a good match for our family, as well as any special breed quirks. After all this, they decided on a springer spaniel, which they were cautioned to buy only with a testament of good, even noble, English breeding.

A "purebred," I remember them saying, and one with proper breeding "papers."

I just wanted a dog who would play catch and fetch.

Clearly, they had been hanging around a new circle of friends, as most of the dogs around the homes I visited were just lovable mutts.

My parents would sometimes get carried away with all things English, so it was not surprising they decided a springer spaniel would be the perfect family dog. I am sure they were doing their best to find a good dog, and maybe even one bred from a line which could be traced back centuries—perhaps even to a sturdy and loyal spaniel standing at the side of his baron at Runnymede, nuzzling his master's leg at the signing of the Magna Carta.

Cautioned to buy only a dog with papers, no one, however, had clued them in that springer spaniels were bird-hunting dogs. This was quite unfortunate, as our backyard was postage-stamp suburban. A robin or two flew around, but certainly no pheasant or quail, and my dad couldn't even shoot a cap gun. About this time—I still think of it as the high point of The English Period around my house—my dad had also bought a tweedy, and very English, sport coat, along with a matching driver's cap. He would wear this goofy ensemble while raking leaves, or driving our second-hand Oldsmobile. Maybe it helped him think it was a Rolls.

These kinds of inexplicable behaviors popped up without warning in suburbia, quiet clues suggesting a looming mismatch between dreams and reality, and they were always ignored at domestic peril.

So on a pleasant early fall evening, we poured into the not-a-Rolls family car, and drove a short distance to a modest home in the neighboring town of Springfield where, in a cramped kitchen, we were introduced to a new litter of tiny brown and white springer spaniel puppies.

While my parents and the seller-breeder were busily reviewing these papers—and it is safe to assume my parents, despite their research, had no clue whatsoever whether these documents were even authentic, or how some guy raising these puppies in a corner of his kitchen could possibly be a legitimate "breeder"—I was far more interested in watching this cute little puppy busy chewing up *his* papers. These papers, at least it seemed to me, were of more immediate importance: old newspapers carefully placed in the room for this puppy's "business." But I could see that the pup just wanted to clear a nice little spot so he could take a dump on his own terms—on the bare floor—which he soon did. A prodigious dump at that, and he seemed to look at me with a goofy smile, and a very satisfied look indeed.

A conspiratorial look, you might even say.

I fell in love with the little rascal right then and there, a bond which I hoped was forever. Forever, of course, is the stuff of eight-year-old boys.

The "papers" did eventually pass muster with my parents, no surprise there. We were told that a "dog with papers" would require a first name, a second name and a kind of "hailing port." So on the spot we named him "Rusty" (me, and an obvious color-coded choice) "Hunter" (this from the breeder-seller, an alarming clue missed by everyone else in the room) "of Essex" (no argument there, as he would live with us in New Jersey's Essex County).

Everyone seemed pleased, although I was sure I would never reveal the dog's three names to any of my buddies, most of whom had mutts with only one name, and often just one syllable.

A tidy little sum of money changed hands, and off we went with this slightly perplexed but adorable new addition to our family. Yes, we had ourselves a dog of impeccable breeding, "to the manor well born" and all of that.

At least on paper.

But from the first night at home, we knew the dog wasn't quite right. Lovable, spirited, and already utterly essential to my boyhood happiness, yes. But he was completely untrainable, and soon to prove himself worse than that.

He peed in his water dish, and drank from the toilet bowl.

He played with his blanket-bed, and slept on his favorite toy—an overstuffed teddy bear he had lifted from my sister's room.

He cowered at friendly faces, and went into spasms of happiness at the first approach of complete strangers.

He ate shoes for lunch without gastric distress, pulling for reasons completely unknown only top-of-the-line, Sunday's best black lace-ups from my father's closet. And for snacks he preferred my fleet of balsa-wood ship models which I had crafted with painstaking effort, which he also digested without problem.

He ralphed, of course, his puppy chow at dinner, dog food purchased at an absurd mark-up from that clown breeder-seller in Springfield, in a year-long puppy chow contract deal virtually unbreakable, like a contract with your phone company.

No, we had not bought a purebred.

We had bought a *poorbred.*

By that time we suspected the poor dog's papers were forged anyway, and we had been taken to the cleaners by the man who was clearly "all seller, no breeder" and the undisputed East Coast champion of the puppy-chow up-sell.

Soon, to our further dismay, the dog took to bolting out of our yard, heading to points unknown, and things really started to spin out of control.

Those electric collars were yet to be invented, and no one ever put up a chain-link fence which, by unspoken agreement, would have ruined the whole feel of the town. Of course, if you traveled just a few miles east, fences sprouted all over the place, marking the tidy and quite inviting little backyards of Maplewood and the Oranges, where a dog could enjoy just enough freedom, without undue family drama. The cluttered backyards as you approached Newark were a different story, and if you have seen the opening credits for *The Sopranos* you have taken this journey in reverse: Tony Soprano ends the sequence by pulling into his slice of suburban remove—no chain-link fence there—and it was all filmed within a few miles of our town.

So we quickly rigged up a truly goofy contraption, which we thought would give the dog a little exercise, but keep him in a yard without a fence. Retrofitting the backyard aluminum clothes-line pole with all sorts of doubled-up leashes, we created something that looked a bit like a large beach umbrella, but with its radiating spokes flipped up by a wind, and the cover gone. The whole thing was supposed to be able to rotate 360-degrees around a base which was anchored securely into the ground.

It never worked that way, of course. Failing completely, the contraption looked worse than any fence ever could.

Rusty quickly figured how much fun it could be to get the thing to exceed what you could think of as its rated spin speed—which was pretty much the gentle nudge of a suburban mother hanging up the drying, or at best a stiff breeze—by racing around in a tight circle. Almost nothing good came of this. He would nearly strangle himself when clothes lines and leash tie-ins and spokes got all mixed up, or he would bend the central supporting aluminum pole almost to the point of breaking, or—and I think this was his real game—he would delight at the sight of a few drying clothes spinning off into the dirt rut he had created running around our contraption, which after only a few days looked like those mysterious crop-circles which began showing up in England. This experiment lasted just over a month, when we took the whole battered and bent clothes line thing down, and bought our first electric dryer.

So the only boundaries my dog would know would be self-imposed ones, or those we could teach through applied discipline and suitable training.

That left us out.

Since it was quite clear that Rusty was incapable of absorbing anything related to the ideas of "boundary" or "discipline," we soon placed all our hopes on an identification tag worn around his collar. This was a key part of the town's dog licensing requirements, and a pretty good idea at that. We complied, the good citizens we were, with a nifty little tag which simply said "Rusty: DR-9-4827." That was our phone number, and it would soon prove quite helpful.

For you see, Rusty became a world-class wanderer.

He was clearly not of the tradition of the noble dogs steadfastly astride their great baron masters at Runnymede. Rusty hailed from lesser nobility. If you know the great writer George MacDonald Fraser, you have probably met the type in his *Flashman* series, centering on one Harry Paget Flashman. "Flashy" is a much beloved and highly celebrated British Victorian rake—the faithless husband to the lovely Lady Elspeth, and a soldier of dubious courage and certain moral deficiency. Fraser himself conceded this knave to be a total discredit to the English line, truly a "scoundrel, amorist and self-confessed poltroon" of the first order whose legendary misadventures marked what he dismissed as a wholly scandalous and haphazard life.

Yes, the very model of our own English scalawag.

Like Flashy himself, Rusty's misadventures were soon the stuff of legend, although not of the fictional kind.

Rusty was a rounder, you see, and quick to please. At first, he seemed content to broadcast this prowess by humping, with distressing frequency, and total abandon, any human leg around. These journeys of self-discovery did not satisfy the poor lad, as we had rules about that sort of thing, and would quickly bat him off, so he soon moved on to a stable of various stuffed animals. Most disturbing, I once found the dog romancing a freckle-faced, red-haired, wooden Howdy Doody ventriloquist dummy, which he had found buried in my closet.

My mother wanted to throw the dummy away, and probably the dog, too.

But Rusty soon had bigger game in mind, and began taking mysterious little trips. Disappearing acts, really. Often, in fact, he would take off and be gone for days. On Rusty's early jaunts, we would get calls from folks throughout the town who had enjoyed random moments of canine delight with our wandering and highly entertaining dog, phone calls alerting us to encounters we soon started to call "Rusty Sightings." Sometimes the dog would even hang around with these nice people long enough for us to come get him. Had *YouTube* been around then, Rusty would have been an overnight sensation.

His absences, however, eventually grew longer, and the phone calls fewer. We all started to think Rusty might actually have found a complete alternative universe somewhere out there in Greater Jersey. Maybe in up-scale Morris County, where he had adopted another family of significantly deeper pockets and was trying out a different, more affluent lifestyle, like all those housewives on cable shows, who are always busy "marrying up." Look, we all worried about the dog, and it was quite comforting to think some nice people up in Bernardsville were taking good care of the rascal on his little vacations from us, a bit like the story, years later, of Mr. Charles Kuralt, the beloved host of the CBS show *On the Road*. It turns out the well-traveled Mr. Kuralt had maintained for years two complete and separate families, discovered only after his death: one in New York, and the other, as I recall, in Montana. The Montana clan was dubbed his "shadow family."

Both Kuralt and Rusty were lovable, that I will concede. And I read somewhere that the shadow Kuralt family was aware of the original, like an understudy to the star in a Broadway play. That could explain why that nice family in Bernardsville never called us up. They must have cherished every borrowed moment with Rusty, who had clearly cleaned up his act for them. I just hope nobody up there had a Howdy Doody dummy, and everybody had lots of dress shoes.

When he would return from the tasteful and very fashionable Morris County, northwest of town—where English tweed jackets and driving hats did not look absurd—he always looked at the top of his game. He was groomed and well-fed, happy to see us, but always sporting a slightly vague look. You may remember years later some sad pop song that talked about "smoke in your eyes from a distant fire." That would fit. We were always ready to welcome Rusty back, of course, and the quiet gentility he had picked up out there made his re-entry into our lives quite pleasant. Maybe they put something in the Morris County water supply.

Anyway, this gentility would quickly wear off and was usually followed by a more troublesome choice of destination.

If Bernardsville was host to a kind of transformed Rusty as "good dog," his other frolics were another kind of Rusty entirely. On these trips, Rusty the "bad dog" headed toward a very different kind of experience, more edgy and urban Union County than fashionable, good taste rural Morris County.

For Bernardsville, think rolling hills and tailored estates, Izod and J. Press, and cordovan penny loafers. For Newark and even Union County, southeast of town, think pizza joints and parking lots, leather jackets and pointed black shoes, and old brick buildings of questionable virtue. On that *Sopranos* credit thing, you may remember the shot of the pizza house. It's in Union.

Rusty's return from the edgier urban counties evidenced a life in those parts of wild abandon and total debauchery, with no residual signs of another loving alternate family *there*.

Rusty would look like he had been on a two-week bender, a disgrace to his breed.

His coat was matted and filthy, his eyes unfocused and bloodshot. He was exhausted—no doubt from entertaining some stable of willing partners—and he looked like he had not had a decent meal during the entire time of his detour. He smelled, I swear, of cheap whiskey and painted women.

I even feared he had been taken into a motorcycle gang.

My mother, on the other hand, just feared he had picked up some dreaded disease.

Through it all, I just loved the little rascal without condition, and I forgave his misdeeds and every transgression. I could even overlook his presumptively divided domestic loyalties. I too might have been tempted by a very upscale Bernardsville adoption, and I had convinced myself that his gang affiliation in Union County was not wholly voluntary.

But all did not end well, at least for me. Maybe Rusty, too.

Rusty Hunter of Essex (and, it would seem, of Morris, Union, and God only knows where else in New Jersey) would be with us for just a few short years. Sometime during my second year at summer camp, the management at home had enough of the little rascal's antics, as well as a real worry that his rakish good luck would eventually run out, and he would come to a nasty end on some Jersey highway.

So they schemed to write the little fella out of my life.

Rusty would "go to the country." On a kind of permanent vacation, I remember them saying. To a place where he could frolic and romp and roam, in the manner of his presumptive life in Bernardsville, it was suggested. This would be a place where he would enjoy a life of boundless adventure and lessen his chances of getting squashed. He would, in short, be put in a position to regain his noble bearings, and reform his wanton ways. There was also some talk about how the glue and paint—it was actually called "dope"—from the dog's balsa wood ship model snacks had screwed up his mind, although no one seemed to be concerned about what the paint and glue fumes could be doing to *me*.

Of course, I wasn't eating my ship models, or for that matter, my father's dress shoes.

In any event, I thought that even a gentle transfer of ownership and up-market lifestyle for the dog was total rubbish, although it was presented, with significant validity, as preferable to the apparent alternatives: squished on some road, or "put down."

So Rusty did leave our home one sunny August afternoon, in my eleventh year and his third, in the back of a nice-looking station wagon. It was a "country-suburban" model, the kind you might remember from those days with an attractive wood siding, real wood at that. I have strained my memory for more detail, the comforting kind that would suggest this was a chariot-of-choice for dogs heading to some true canine paradise, something like handsome gold lettering for the "Happy Pasture Farm of West Simsbury, Connecticut." Yes, something like that would have worked just fine.

In any event, that's the story I have chosen to believe from that very first, sad day in the late summer of 1957, after which I never saw the dog again.

Later—and truth be known, for longer than was healthy—I would think about a blood line of goofy and completely lovable brown and white spaniels somewhere up in the Connecticut Valley known for a preference for black Sunday's best shoes and balsa wood model ships.

None of this, of course, helped that day. I was barely holding back the tears, having locked myself away in our impossibly little den, really an alcove maybe six foot square which could barely hold three people and our old Sylvania black-and-white console television. The room faced our driveway where all this was playing out, and I wanted no part in any of it. I pulled the shades, and flipped on the television. The movie "Robinson Crusoe" was playing, the early one starring Dan O'Herlihy.

As Rusty left my life, rolling down our short gravel driveway, the last scene was playing. The camera turns away from Robinson, who is slumped wearily in a rowboat finally come for his rescue, and then slowly pans back to the desolate island he has shared for years with his faithful dog.

The dog is not with him, and the movie ends with a last sad look at this lonely island, with the fading sounds of a barking dog.

All hearts get broken, of course. And there has to be a first time. That August afternoon, in the summer of 1957, was mine.

SCHOOLED

MAD has been a chronicler of American life unlike any other publication. In fact, I would argue that you can use this book as the text for teaching 20th Century American history—providing, of course, you were being home-schooled by circus clowns.

- John Ficarra, Editor, in introduction to *MAD for Decades*

PLEASE, MRS. PENALTY, NOT THE FAULKNER

Either the British biologist Thomas Henry Huxley (known as "Darwin's Bulldog"), or someone else, once theorized that if you were to put an infinite number of monkeys in front of an infinite number of typewriters for an infinite period of time, eventually they would write a Shakespearean sonnet. My friends and I weren't monkeys (we were goofballs), there were only about thirty of us in our junior high school typing class, and we took the course for only one semester. So, we didn't have a chance to produce anything of Shakespearean quality. But after fifty-five years, three of us somehow managed to write this book.

In my adult life, I've informally polled hundreds of people to learn what I already knew, and that is that one of the most valuable courses any of us ever took in school was typing. Okay, learning to read, speak, and count were pretty important. I didn't mean to belittle those skills, which do come in handy. But without typing, I'd be screwed.

At Millburn Junior High School in the late 50s, our faculty had the foresight to know how important it would become for all of us to have this skill. How they knew that is a mystery. At the time, the world's only computers were the size of a room, we did math on a slide rule, and there was no Internet.

Our first typing teacher, Miss Quibedeaux (name changed here), was young and pretty, probably right out of college, and seemed sort of flirtatious. And she may have been, because several weeks after the semester opened, we were told she left town suddenly "for Hollywood." We figured her sudden departure had more to do with a pregnancy test than a screen test, but the transition opened the door for our new substitute teacher, Mrs. Faulkner.

As was the case with most of our teachers, Mrs. Faulkner was a very decent person who valiantly tried her best to teach us something important. Actually, she was terrific, which is why this book is error-free (except for any typos made by the editor), and also why I'm embarrassed by what we did to her on two occasions.

Although electronic typewriters were just entering the marketplace, the machines in our class were purely manual. There was a mechanical arm that went up and smacked the ink ribbon against the paper, which you had to feed page by page. There was only one font and one color (black). Wite-Out had just been invented, but it looked awful, and if you typed over Wite-Out (which you had to dab on with a tiny brush and then let dry), it appeared as though you had mounted the letter atop a splotch of plaster. You couldn't just make a copy of the splotched version, because the modern copy machine had not yet been invented. There were also secret erasers that were supposed to be able to remove an errant letter, but invariably they caused a huge smudge, if not a hole in the paper. So if you were typing something important and made a mistake, you started over.

The force of the arm hitting the ribbon depended on the force of the finger hitting the letter key. If you tapped the key too gently, you might get a hit on the paper, but it would be more gray than black. If you hit the key too hard, the image on the paper could be too dark. If you were inconsistent, you could get a mix, so that "See the dog run" might come out as "**See the dog ru**n." Accordingly, Mrs. Faulkner encouraged a nice, even, firm but not overbearing touch.

The keys were not labeled. The whole point was for us to memorize where they were. We accomplished this by keeping our eyes focused on a large poster in the front of the room, which displayed the keys. In the beginning, I would type stuff like, "Aaarh$g)m8sprl#!" My classmates were no better. For instance, if we were supposed to type, "It is now 1958," the line might read, "Ir uz nou 1498."

After a while, we got a feel for where the important keys were; although we—or at least I—always had trouble hitting the Z without peeking, and I doubt any of us had enough skill to hit the numbers correctly without hunting for them. (I still can't do that.) Fortunately, we didn't have to memorize where "Page Up," "Page Down," "Control," "Alt," "Delete," "Insert," or similar keys were, because they hadn't yet been invented. To move the paper up or down in 1958 and 1959, we had to turn knobs on both sides of the typewriter and hope the paper didn't go in crooked.

Speaking of which, all of us had a problem as we approached the end of the page. If we stopped paying attention, we would type right off the paper and start banging the arms against the ribbon and the barren backing bar, with the paper falling on an angle over the top and onto the floor in front, where it couldn't be retrieved without the assistance of a student in the next row, who may or may not be inclined to help. Also, if we did get the paper back, it might be sporting a footprint. To prevent this type of accident, we would have to take a ruler and draw a very light pencil line toward the end of each blank page, so we could spot it as we approached the bottom. Of course, later we had to erase the line without smudging either the pencil mark or the fresh ink on the page. This drill led to some very messy work. Shakespeare probably rendered his manuscripts more neatly and quickly using a quill pen by candlelight.

Once we mastered the basics, we were expected to type passages from the typing books. These were 8½" x 14" notebooks with flip-tops—and we placed them on a portable metal stand so that they stood at about an 80-degree angle.

The typing room was on the second story of our building. There was no air conditioning. On nice days, the windows were open. Also on nice days, we wanted to be outside. So we devised a scheme to get out there.

I say *we* devised the scheme. It is possible, though, and even likely, that we learned this scheme from the folks in the grade ahead of us. But even if we didn't devise it, we perfected it. Once, when Mrs. Faulkner wasn't looking, several of us put our metal stands on the windowsills and opened the windows real wide, so that the breeze came into the room. We then sneaked back to our desks. Mrs. Faulkner, who had her back to us while writing on the blackboard, didn't see the maneuver, but she started to feel the breeze. She looked back at the class and said, "Will someone please shut the windows?" We jumped up, shut the windows, and by doing so, propelled all the metal book stands down into the courtyard below. To her credit, Mrs. Faulkner didn't lose her temper. She just told a couple of us to go down and retrieve the metal stands, which we did, taking our time to do so. Given her nonchalant reaction, my suspicion is that we *did* learn this trick from the prior semester's class, and maybe even that Mrs. Faulkner knew it was coming and let us get away with it.

But she didn't see our next trick coming. And I'm pretty sure we invented this one.

Today, when you hit the "H" button on a computer, an "H" magically appears on your screen. During the period 1958-60, you needed that "H" arm to smack the ribbon. Eventually, some genius in our class figured out that if you took a nice, sharp, new pencil, with a flat-ended eraser at the end, and carefully lodged the eraser against the "H" arm, and the front of the pencil in the notch where the arm hit the ribbon, and pounded the heck out of the "H" button, the pencil would fly straight forward for quite some distance, at sufficient speed, and with a perfect arc.

So we devised a plan. It was intricate enough that we had to practice it, which we did by sneaking in after school a time or two when Mrs. Faulkner wasn't in the typing room. When we had all the nuances down pat, we decided to go for it.

We waited for Mrs. Faulkner to take to the blackboard.

Our scheme took a lot of concentration and coordination. It required about a dozen boys (the girls declined to cooperate in our clever caper) to quietly and gradually shift their mortar-like typewriters on their desks at slight angles so that those on the outside aisles were pointed toward the center of the blackboard. Those fellows sitting in the middle of the room had perfect sightlines and thus didn't need to shift. Each of us got Mrs. Faulkner in our crosshairs. Small combat smiles crossed our faces. The first day we lined up the typewriters, she never went to the blackboard, so, before we left the room for the day, we had to restore our typewriters to their original positions, pointing straight ahead. But the next day, she made a move to the blackboard. Without a word, and using only hand signals, we re-aimed our weapons toward the target. At the moment her chalk hit the board, roughly twelve index fingers whacked their respective "H" keys and all those pencils were launched.

The result was mixed. Some of the erasers slipped off the firing pin, causing the pencil to just tilt over into the guts of the typewriter. For one shooter, the pencil somehow flipped, hitting him point-first inside his left nostril. Some of the pencils were propelled into the backs of the heads of the students in front of the marksmen. Some went toward Mrs. Faulkner, but petered out and were declared duds. One clattered off the blackboard, falling noisily to the floor. But about six of the pencils hit their mark. At least sort of. Two lodged very nicely in Mrs. Faulkner's hair bun. Two hit the back of her blouse. And a couple nailed her in the rear end.

By the time she turned around, we were all concentrating on our work, seemingly oblivious to the bombardment. No one pointed any fingers at the perpetrators. She couldn't prove who we were by counting pencils, because we didn't all start off with the same amount. It was the perfect crime.

But we didn't repeat it. We just savored the moment, which became the talk of the school. Those of us who were thinking of eventually writing books made mental notes.

No one got detention, but Mrs. Faulkner did declare that if we pulled another stunt like that, she might impose "The Penalty." No one had the nerve to ask her what "The Penalty" was. We speculated it would involve coming in after school and writing "I will not bombard Mrs. Faulkner with pencils" ten thousand times on the blackboard. But again, we never found out.

For some reason, this veiled threat led many of us, for a few days, to occasionally blurt out, to each other but not to her, "Please, Mrs. Faulkner, not *the penalty*." This quickly morphed into "Please, Mrs. Penalty, not the Faulkner." This, of course, is stupid, which you probably thought when you read the title of this story. But as the

"Blue-Collar Tour" comedian Ron White is wont to say, "You can't fix stupid."

Fortunately, most of our teachers were like Mrs. Faulkner. They took things in stride. We behaved most of the time, and we were generally good students, so we were given some leeway. The harshest thing any of the teachers ever said was uttered by Mr. Rooney, who, when annoyed with a remark made by Kenny Washburn, retorted, "Swallow yourself, Washburn."

Other gentle educators included our Modern European History teacher, Miss Passoth, who was up at the blackboard with her back to us, when Kenny Sikes sneaked up behind her and outlined her body on the blackboard with a water pistol. She froze for so long that she never even figured out who did it. And she didn't ask. When she turned around, she pretended nothing had happened.

These were good times.

One last thing about the issue of pressure on the typewriter keys. Every once in a while now, my cat Ella takes a nap on my laptop keyboard. Sometimes she dreams and her muscle and paw movements result in edits to my documents such as "qqqqqqqqqqqqq]]]]]]]]]]]]." She has, however, managed to type out two Shakespearean sonnets.

SINKING THE *BISMARK*

No, the life of a substitute teacher was not easy, at least around our gang. Adding insult to injury was the fact that a substitute's troubles weren't even confined to school hours. This was especially vexing to our beleaguered substitute typing teacher, the remarkably patient Mrs. Faulkner. You now know her as Mrs. Penalty. One February day of our eighth grade year her troubles lasted long after the last bell, late into the evening in fact.

Usually our good humor and quickness to laugh off minor misdeeds served us well, and we frequently deployed these defenses with a kind of embarrassing earnestness. This seemed to work, particularly with our substitute teachers, and sometimes even with our parents. While a little laughter was good, something awful lurked just below the surface. That something was The Giggles, and no one was really safe.

It has likely happened to every kid, and is a first and rather terrifying sign that we are never really in complete control of *anything*. This was particularly true of our tribe of fun-loving boys: the girls, naturally, seemed far less likely to tip over the laughter boat. Eighth grade seems to be peak season for The Giggles, just about everywhere. In that one year alone, I can remember four or five times I sailed right off the edge, and it was almost always at just the wrong time, the wrong place and in the company of Suds Estes. There was a terrible case of The Giggles which broke out, for absolutely no reason, in Church School during the lesson, and another spectacular outbreak in geometry class, although I distinctly remember that Suds brought that one on by introducing his soon-to-be-famous "pencil through his head" trick, and I still go nuts when I see him eyeing a pencil, as I know exactly what he is thinking.

These episodes tapered off by ninth grade, but after a long period of dormancy and relative quiet, they have recently resurfaced.

I blame both Bud and Rob, and the writing of this book. Indeed, our wives refused to join us when we began our "organic writing sessions," where we quickly fell into hysterical idiocy. We also worked up a pretty good appetite while doubled over in laughter. That's weird, I know. But with our usual poor judgment, we would soon find ourselves dining out. Unable to dial things down in public—no surprise there—we now know many of the managers of the popular mid-priced chain eateries in our three towns. In at least one memorable case—a stuffy private club—we were actually asked to enjoy our dessert elsewhere, although the request was made with a professional elegance. Frankly, we had to agree with the call, but I soon decided that the club was just not a good fit, and subsequently un-joined.

Anyway, the very worst case of The Giggles that eighth grade year brought together the unlikely collision of a British-made movie, Mrs. Penalty, the manager of the local movie house, dozens of innocent by-standing (by-*sitting?*) movie patrons, me, and my sidekick Suds. It wasn't pretty.

Going to the movies was usually a safe thing, and actually encouraged by our parents, who could count on knowing exactly where we were and what we were doing for a good two or three hours. Millburn sported a perfectly respectable movie theater for the younger crowd, and that's where our parents would usually deposit us. I don't think we cared that it lacked the newer, larger screens, or technologies then coming on the scene; it seemed to get most first-run movies and a few Saturday morning serials. The popcorn was also very good. In just a few years—by the time we started driving, when popcorn was not the primary thing on our girl-crazy minds—we found a new favorite theater, the much larger one in Morristown. It was called the "Community Theater", with the promise of something quite special. In addition to this fancy name, it had an impressive lobby, all of which seemed to suggest to our dates that they were something special too. In one of those crazy teenage universals, if you meet anyone from that time and place in Jersey, they all understand why we called these trips to Morristown "going to the Taj Mahal." You see, right next to the theater was a very unusual building. Just one story, and built of dark-gray stone, it had strange, slit-like windows with ornate grillwork and an elongated reflecting pool, at least as I remember it. (Maybe it was just a bloated lily-pad pool, actually fairly common around the area.) It was all quite mysterious—even *romantic*—although that strange building may simply have been some sort of municipal utility building, or maybe even a mausoleum, which wouldn't have been very romantic at all.

But in February of 1960, on a chilly Friday night, Suds and I were certainly not thinking about romance. We were thinking about a war movie. The British had just released *The Sinking of the Bismarck*, a very serious and somber black and white movie telling the story of the ill-fated German World War II battleship *Bismarck*, and centering on the sea duel between the German ship and HMS *Hood*. Remember, in 1960 the Brits were not far removed from the horrors of the London Blitz, and the movie is not particularly sympathetic to the German cause, although many critics claim it is fairly balanced and generally historically accurate. The movie, directed by Lewis Gilbert, has a largely British cast, completely unknown to us. We did, however, know a bit about the battle, and would learn even more months after the movie was released, when a singer named Johnny Horton recorded a pop song about the *Bismarck*. We just wanted to see a neat sea battle on the big screen, and root for the good guys.

It isn't a long movie—just over ninety minutes—and mixes historical newsreel footage with staged sets and model ships. Reviews of the movie were favorable at the time, and the film has apparently held up well over the years. Some critics even praised the special effects, mostly ships blowing up.

Soon into the movie, Suds and I were not buying any of it. We weren't critics, but the whole thing looked goofy.

For starters, we began laughing at the dialogue, which seemed stuffy on both sides, as well as the accents. One critic years later made reference to a very poor Churchill imitation in the movie, so maybe we weren't so far off here. Suds had been to the Admiral Farragut Camp for Boys several years earlier, and I was counting on him to clue me in on all the nautical talk and terminology. But he just kept shaking his head whenever I glanced over at him for an explanation. He was having a tough time with those accents, too, and I doubt they spent a lot of time at his camp on German battleship specs.

We did buy into the newsreel footage of the launch of the *Bismarck,* but once the action shifted to the obvious wooden models of the warships, floating in some kind of ocean simulation tank, we started to lose it. The really goofy thing about this was that the model scenes were considered pretty advanced for the times.

Suds even started whispering to me that we could do a better job staging this sea duel with the many model ships I had built over the years, and suggested we do just that in the spring on a small pond in the neighborhood. He had forgotten that most of my balsa wood Navy fleet had been eaten by my ex-dog Rusty a few summers earlier, so I countered by suggesting we could stage a submarine duel using the tiny model submarines we had purchased from the good people at Kellogg's in Battle Creek, Michigan. Our defense budget was thin, but all it took to get one of these beauties was a box top from some cereal, along with a dime carefully taped to the box top in a precise and secure crisscrossed pattern. A primitive little gray plastic submarine would soon arrive by mail, along with instructions telling how the new submariner could make the vessel dive, and hopefully resurface, using either baking soda or baking powder. The instructions were specific and did not offer this as a choice, of course: the physics of the thing only worked with one of these two common household products, but none of us could ever remember which one of the two it was. I know I lost many a sub, dooming them to sink to the bottom of the pond fueled with the wrong substance. And to this day, should I stumble upon one of these beauties, there is only an even chance that I will pull the correct fuel out of the cupboard. At this moment I think the right call is baking soda. But I could be wrong.

Of course, while we were drifting off on these detours, and our discussions becoming sillier and louder, nearby movie patrons were growing impatient with our silliness. The crowd, less two, was absolutely riveted to the screen as the movie moved toward the climactic final scenes. At the very moment that some character on the screen—I remember him as a doomed sailor on the *Hood*—shouted the ubiquitous *"Matey"* to one of his shipmates, the patron right behind us decided he'd had enough. Deploying a little movie flourish, and with a curious mix of humor and lost patience, he leaned over us and said:

"PIPE DOWN, MATEYS!"

"Mateys?"

That did it.

The Giggles, which had been building up for almost an hour, rose to the surface like one of those properly fueled Kellogg's submarines. We pointed to each other, mouthing the word "Mateys," and lost all control. The more we tried to stop laughing, the more we *couldn't* stop. Honestly, we tried to focus on the screen, but the balsa ships provided no help there. Each salvo splashing into the model ocean tank brought us closer to ruin, and every new British phrase just added to our hysteria. Estes even suddenly remembered that my fleet had been eaten by my dog, and threw that embarrassment back my way.

At least we weren't in church.

The guy right behind us had lost all patience by now, and did what should have been done long before: he left to find the manager, who was probably also the guy running the film, and maybe the popcorn guy too. Before another balsa wood ship model took another hit, we were being escorted out of the theater, walking the perp walk. We trudged up the entire length of the theater aisle, past the noticeably unsympathetic stares of an almost full house, poorly suppressing The Giggles the whole time.

Most of our friends' parents were not big Friday night moviegoers, and we figured this little display of teenage idiocy was being witnessed solely by strangers, a lucky break.

"So it *was* you two creating all that fuss down there."

This came from a shadowy figure, sounding just like Mrs. Penalty. As our eyes focused, we saw that it was indeed our beleaguered substitute typing teacher, and she was pointing toward the front of the theater, shaking her head.

We didn't know that her husband was a real movie nut, and a bit of a British history buff to boot. But there they were, both sitting far back in the theater, right on the aisle, now watching the two of us doing the perp walk, being booted out of the movie house and maybe even facing another institutional ban.

The theater was dark, of course, but Mrs. Penalty had sharp eyes, like all substitute teachers, always attuned to the new mischief which tended to follow them around. That is unfair, and substitute pay stinks, but it is a universal fact. Substitute teachers can be as unhappy as dentists, who I once read are the unhappiest of all professionals.

Mrs. Penalty, however, didn't look nearly as pissed off as her movie-loving husband, who was probably lamenting that he'd have to come back and see the movie again without disturbance, preferably on a school night when idiot teenagers were not loosed on the community, but home polishing their typing skills.

We were just praying that *he* wouldn't throw us another one of those goofy British phrases.

Mrs. Penalty's jurisdiction, we figured, didn't extend to the theater, although we were sure we hadn't heard the last of this. Our escort urged us on, out the door and into a chilly night. We killed about half an hour hanging around Main Street in town, the chill helping The Giggles run their course. One of our parents came on schedule to retrieve us, around nine o'clock. Counting on the likelihood that our disgraced exit was not observed by anyone else who knew us, and that a substitute teacher outside her jurisdiction and off the clock would probably not call our parents, we played it cool.

When asked how we enjoyed the movie, we just replied that it was pretty predictable, and that the *Bismarck* sank at the end.

We only assumed that was the case, taking our cue from the title of the movie and our general understanding of the facts, as we hadn't seen the last part of the movie. So in history class on Monday we made sure to ask the teacher how it all ended for the German ship just in case someone, maybe a parent, would probe for a little better accounting of the movie. This was a somewhat surprising question, as we were then studying the Spanish-American War. But our history teacher was always pleased when we showed *any* interest in history, even if we were off the timeline by decades, or even centuries. He gave a spirited and quite captivating accounting of the battle, although we later figured that he had simply seen the movie over the weekend, too. Fortunately, there was no sign he had seen our perp walk. Maybe he had caught the flick up in Morristown, or somewhere in the Oranges. By the time he finished his riveting recap, we were very sorry that we had not seen the end of the movie, even with the balsa wood ships.

With The Giggles having quietly returned to wherever they hide for most of their lives in young boys, our parents sensed nothing amiss. The manager, or maybe it was just the popcorn guy, had issued no permanent ban, and we would return to the scene of that crime many times in our lives, often making it through the entire movie. Even Mrs. Penalty, in class Monday, just shook her head when we walked in.

We had dodged another bullet.

Yes, there was some public humiliation, but no serious reputational damage, although I still feel The Giggles threatening even today when I hear some distinctive and slightly goofy British phrase at the movies. I then want to dial up my buddy Estes just to see where it could go, but these days I take that "no cell phone" rule seriously, and so far I have resisted the urge to call, but it's been close a few times.

You know, that's the great thing about friends, and laughter, and stories remembered from afar: you just never know when something will trigger a warm memory. Especially one that requires the stifling of hysterical and irrational laughter.

MR. BARKLE LOSES IT

We could, and often did, screw things up when we were handed off to other adults in charge of things outside of school, and they were also remarkably patient and forgiving in the face of our perpetual goofiness.

In short, we rarely saw many adults really lose it, although there were some pretty close calls. There was, however, one very notable exception, and he was to be found nowhere near our usual haunts, and was neither coach nor scout leader. He didn't teach at Glenwood, or in Church School, and he didn't sell us baseball cards or model planes.

No, sir. We met him when we were conscripted, *en masse,* by our mothers and shipped off one Friday afternoon in our sixth grade year to something called "dancing school." His name was "Mr. Barkle." We never knew his first name, although he was rumored to have one, and his little Friday afternoon business was called, simply, "The Barkle School of Dance." Like an itinerant preacher, he did not seem to have any kind of permanent home base, although he may have maintained an actual dance studio somewhere—maybe one for older folks, kind of like an Arthur Murray franchise studio, somewhere in the Oranges.

For all we knew or cared, he may actually have been the real Arthur Murray.

There was also competition in our town for developing dance talent, as unlikely as that all now seems. Each was housed in one of two members-only social clubs.

Mr. Barkle gathered his charges at a swanky, very "old Short Hills" club, named quite smartly "The Short Hills Club." Charming, in a shake-shingle and brick kind of way common to towns throughout the area, it seemed a bit stuffy, at least for our money, which was not much as we were a bunch of twelve year-olds. Founded in 1875, it deserved its reputation as a very upscale club, really the nicest in the area—excellent tennis courts, paddle tennis platforms, a beautiful dining room and other classy amenities. But most of this was strictly off limits to the dance students, whose parents were often not members, so this all mostly rumor.

The part of the club we were allowed to see was very well furnished, although I was always afraid to sit on any of the chairs. Delicate, and a bit pretentious, they were no match for our boyish roughhousing. Other delicate things were lying around, and I was generally terrified of the place even though its message was one of calm gentility. It was like going to your grandparents' house, or even the formal living room in your own home: you didn't touch anything, and you would prefer to be almost anywhere else.

The principal rival to Mr. Barkle's program was another Friday afternoon operation, housed in the "Racquets Club." This club had a wonderfully distinctive look, a tall and imposing brick structure, like a medieval castle. We were not far off the mark: the noted architect Stanford White is said to have designed the building—which opened as the "Music Hall" on March 27, 1880—to resemble a chateau in Angers, a small and picturesque town in Brittany, France.

This chateau sat directly across from the train station.

Ironically, the building was once home to the Short Hills Club, and it hosted the first services of our Christ Church in 1882. Sadly, this wonderful landmark building was destroyed by fire in 1978, and was replaced by a new club building. This time around the Racquets Club upgraded its facilities, adding an Olympic-sized pool, improved tennis courts and other first-rate amenities, although I think most people really missed that medieval castle/chateau look.

My folks had been members briefly, sometime in the early 1950s, and I hung out there, mostly at the little two-lane bowling alley in the basement. This was a purist's dream, as pins were spotted by hand. I just don't remember how it all worked, but I think we followed our bowling balls down the alley, and set our own pins. This was slow work, and we were lucky to bowl four or five frames, tops, before we got bored.

The overall feel was rather funky, certainly not stuffy, and a place where you could even have fun. The second floor, reached by a spectacular semi-circular stairway, blossomed into a huge high-ceilinged great room, with a worn but usually polished oak floor. A small stage, which was a holdover from the building's earliest days when it functioned as a kind of all-purpose social, entertainment and community center, gave the room both dignity and a sense of purpose, although I never saw anyone perform anything on it.

The castle/chateau was the Friday afternoon destination of another crowd of kids, whose parents had entrusted their children's ballroom dancing preparation to a nice lady named Miss Chaliffe. She, like Mr. Barkle, enjoyed a fine reputation around town, and her classes were also well attended. Indeed, her operation was at the time the latest in a tradition which, according to the local Historical Society, dated back as far as 1889, when a Mr. Walter ran a dancing school every Wednesday afternoon and evening in the building during the winter. The old *Short Hills News Item* once quoted Mr. Walter as saying, "The art of dancing is an innocent and delightful amusement; it improves deportment, refines the manner, and develops ease and grace of motion."

This was just the kind of miracle our parents were hoping for, and signed us up without hesitation.

Although none—and I mean none—of the lessons stuck, I am sure that both Mr. Barkle and Miss Chaliffe were talented ballroom dancers, as well as competent and committed teachers, and each seemed to command extraordinary loyalty from parents all over town, although such loyalty was probably mostly about neighborhood carpooling convenience. Whatever our parents paid for this part of our education—in a touching but misplaced hope that our "deportments would be improved" and "our manners refined"—it was wasted money, and a spectacularly poor investment in our future.

So I headed off to Mr. Barkle and the stuffy club with three other kids from the neighborhood when Friday dancing classes started, midway through sixth grade. Suds Estes, thank God, had been conscripted along with our two favorite neighborhood girls—Liz from across the street, and Joanie who lived right next door. A number of our friends who had been plucked from our gang and sent to private day schools in the area were also enrolled, so we could again goof around with these good friends we really missed. That may have been the only good thing about the whole show.

Everything about this conscripted servitude challenged our developing world view, much like the draft would years later.

Just dressing for dancing school was weird, and clearly a very different experience for the boys than it was for the girls. The girls arrived completely put together, while we boys were still struggling with shirttails, loose neckties, buttons that had gone missing in the few minutes we had carpooled to the school, and mismatched socks. It was clear from the start that we weren't even on the same playing field. Giving the impression that they had actually dressed hours earlier, the girls may have secretly met for tea or punch somewhere before class, where some kind and matronly older woman gave them all a kind of "heads up" for what lay ahead. They just looked so *confident*, arriving in crinkly dresses with an enveloping air of calm. We boys, on the other hand, looked as if we had just been pulled off the backyard with barely time to dress on the way. This was no illusion: we squeezed at least a little touch football or basketball into our dancing school pre-game preparations, but we usually did remember to shower.

We weren't animals, you know.

All of this did not go unnoticed by Mr. Barkle. Tall, white-haired, and always dressed in a starched white shirt, subdued tie, black lace-ups shined to Marine Corps standards, and a no-nonsense game-day face, he was nothing less than elegant, and clearly a gentlemen of the old order.

He just didn't smile much.

Frankly, we were terrified of him.

Our mothers, on the other hand, seemed to go all gooey over him, particularly when they took turns as a roving squad of hostess-chaperones. They seemed determined to match this guy's sense of style, looking like they were going into the city for an elegant night at the 21 Club. These mothers-on-duty would sign us in, and when they weren't chatting up Mr. Elegance, they would try to help the boys finally complete their dressing—like an offstage manager adjusting a character's costume before he entered stage left.

They knew that none of us, without that help, would pass muster with Mr. Barkle.

Remarkably, even with those last minute adjustments, many of us would begin to decay on the short walk to the ballroom. Sometimes it was a kind of spontaneous combustion, but usually the less formal look was pushed along by one or another buddy yanking on a shirt, or messing with a tie. These mothers should have taken a cue from our beloved game of football and positioned a field judge at the threshold to drop a flag, sending us back ten yards for a re-do. This would have helped to defuse Mr. Barkle's evident and ever-growing frustration with the whole show before it boiled over, which of course it eventually did.

As in most of our misadventures, we just never knew when that flashpoint would come. But we quickly learned that the little mistakes set the stage, like the quieter performers who open for the big acts—the real show.

This was the case at the stuffy dance school.

Over the years, I have heard vague and unconfirmed reports of better success at the other dancing school. But how anyone could have thought that our band of pranksters would actually be able to learn to dance is the biggest mystery of all.

Horses, maybe even walruses, would have been better dance students.

Our dancing school experiment went on for two years, although we never advanced from basic to intermediate steps. It was more like repeating a grade in regular school, and the whole thing was a terrible misdirection of parental funds. If the idea was to equip us to dance our way to success, it failed.

Completely. At least for me, singing lessons would have been a better bet, and I can't carry a tune in a lunch bucket.

Nothing made sense until we finally figured out there was a hidden agenda, one far beyond the narrow technical matter of dance steps. These Friday afternoons were really about the larger lessons of something called "the social graces." Our parents may have even negotiated a secret treaty for this instruction. The girls caught on intuitively so their parents likely never even knew about these secret agreements, which may have even cost a little extra. Certainly Mr. Barkle had some neat marketing materials to push this, maybe a little trifold with "before" and "after" pictures of twelve- and thirteen-year-old boys, like an orthodontist, or even those dreaded private military schools all over the South where we were sure a few of us would end up.

Had even one person clued *us* in, disaster may have been averted. After all, although we didn't see the foxtrot as critical to our successful entry into the real world, we all had some vague sense that we would someday have to clean up our acts. A few social graces, willingly learned and polished on those Friday afternoons, would have come in quite handy. We might have even enjoyed our several hours with the girls, and lowered Mr. Barkle's frustration level.

Of course, none of that happened, and I fear we truly broke Mr. Barkle one Friday afternoon.

Here's what I remember.

During the first part of any lesson, we were assigned a partner. I think it may have been by height. Mr. Barkle was joined by his partner, one of the mothers-on-duty, and they would demonstrate the dance. Actually, they were trying to *teach us* the dance, although most of us never made that connection.

"Glide. One, Two, Three. Glide. One, Two, Three."

This may have been a waltz, or a foxtrot, or just about anything else.

I still don't know, and for that reason chose to elope and marry on the top of a mountain on Maui largely to avoid the dreaded First Marital Dance, a humiliating ritual even for good dancers. As it turned out, my understanding bride still insisted we have "our first married dance," and we did. It was one of those short metronomic glides on the worn floor in a breezy waterfront bar in the charming village of Lahaina, a few miles down the mountain, and three hours into the marital adventure. Even three or four rum punches in, I still looked like a wounded gazelle. A *happy* wounded gazelle, at least, because it was a very special day.

But long before that pleasant evening on Maui, I was living in panic those Friday dancing school afternoons, as Mr. Barkle would call on two students to showcase their mastery of the day's lesson. Session after session the poor man would watch these sorry show-and-tell performances, only to be completely unhinged when the rest of the students would join these poor kids on the dance floor, dancing with neither skill, grace nor joy. It was painful to watch.

Morale plummeted along with discipline, already thinly capitalized.

As we headed toward our release date, things were starting to go off the rails. Boys were coming in late (from the playing fields, of course), and falling to a new low in sartorial mischief. Two of the boys, aware of the very strict "no gum" rule, skillfully launched a new game: they would move their jaws up and down to *simulate* chewing of the gum. This little gem really annoyed Mr. Barkle, which just added to the fun: these guys were sure they would not get thrown out of dancing school for attempted gum chewing, and they were right.

Several of the boys had also figured out a way to roll out one of the club's windows, a trick not available until the club had opened them for the pleasant Jersey spring. Their escape was short-lived, returned to class by one of the groundskeepers who was pulling a little extra green as a bounty hunter, although such exchange was handled discreetly. Some even say Mr. Barkle cracked a smile at this nonsense, but I doubt it.

As the classes limped into spring, even Mr. Barkle seemed to grow a bit testy with *his* dance partner, and didn't look like he was enjoying his practiced foxtrots either.

On a Friday in late May—and in a tired and broken voice, a sure sign that we were nearing the end of a tough dancing school season—Mr. Barkle announced a "boys' choice" dance. This was a semi-routine exercise, which had come off without a hitch a few times during the winter, the downside usually just the spectacular misjudgment of who would dance with whom. I don't remember if the girls were under strict orders to accept, with grace, every invitation to dance, but I think they were at least strongly encouraged to accept the first dance offer presented. This wasn't the real world yet, and we weren't asking anyone for her hand in marriage, so the first boy to ask a girl would generally get the nod. This put some premium, of course, to get there fast, crossing the dance floor over to the girls' seats.

This time, it just didn't work out very well.

One boy (tentatively), then two or three (more assuredly), and finally a virtual mob of boys raced across the dance floor in a frenzied attempt to be the first one to ask our very own carpool mate, Joanie, to dance. Joanie was enjoying a fabulous sixth grade run: a charter member of our exclusive neighborhood Yogi Bear Club, Grande Dame of the Wiffle Ball Circuit, and the apparent Belle of the Barkle School of Dance.

How she viewed all this attention I may never know.

What I do know, however, is this: the ten or twelve boys who had joined this stampede quickly collided with one another, smashing into chairs both occupied and vacant, and eventually crashed and fell into a kind of flailing heap before the reigning Belle of the Ball. At that magic moment, the stuffy club more closely resembled a rugby scrum than a dancing school, and we had become a part of dancing school legend, at least along the East Coast. While all sorts of wild rumors would later surface about "the stampede," no one was actually crushed to death that afternoon. In some versions of the story, somebody in the pile actually still uttered a boys' choice invitation, but I believe that also to be a myth. That one girl fainted—one of the girls from private school, groomed to avoid this sort of behavior—is a more believable detail which soon surfaced, but I cannot vouch for that one either.

We had reached flashpoint.

Mr. Barkle exploded in a rage. Having already abandoned all hope of teaching us how to dance, it was now clear that we had failed to learn even rudimentary social graces. In fact, packs of wild animals on the Serengeti possessed better social skills, and honored more social norms, than this gang. Frankly, it was a very low point for all.

Charged with the task of teaching us the finer points of social interaction, Mr. Barkle had barely missed presiding over a mass-casualty event on his own dance floor.

"Improving deportment?"

"Refining manners?"

Poor Mr. Walter must have been rolling over in his grave. The mothers-on-duty were aghast, and even Mr. Barkle's partner was quite visibly shaken, although she was never really in the line of fire. A few chairs were smashed, but they were not the delicate ones, just those white wooden folding chairs the club used for weddings. The girls were none too happy either, as they generally enjoyed their time at dancing school and it was clear that this Friday's edition was over.

In all fairness, the dance floor was always a bit slippery, and the soles of our shoes were not well worn. At least that was the party line we all used to excuse this disaster. With just a couple more sessions left, we really did try to shape up a bit: while we knew we couldn't really ever learn to dance, we figured we could at least try to act like we were aware of the basic norms of society.

The "boys' choice" option was removed from the playbook, and I remember no further stampedes. We were finished with the whole thing, and our rookie year was over, and none too soon. Stampede behavior was clearly not the lofty goal our parents had set for us, and hardly the stuff of that thing called "social graces." Mr. Barkle eventually recovered, and was able to continue his good work for years to come. We showed up for a second season, and many of us were on a kind of secret double probation, like those fun-loving idiots in *Animal House*. This cut into the fun, but kept the whole operation quite tame. Mr. Barkle for years continued to guide generations of young boys to great and graceful ballroom dancing success.

Just not us.

In the early 1990s, my wife and I attended a swanky business conference at the elegant Broadmoor Hotel in Colorado Springs. As is usually the case in this sort of event, this three-day conference kicked off with a fancy evening cocktail reception. We joined our group of some thirty executives and their spouses on the hotel's expansive outdoor deck, which faced Cheyenne Mountain. This was a business group new to the both of us, so we were making every effort to meet as many people as possible. One of the women, even from a distance, looked vaguely familiar. We circled around, and I could tell she was trying to place my face too.

Finally I broke from the pack and made a beeline over to her.

Well, that did it, apparently jogging her memory.

"Weren't you part of that stampede crowd at the Barkle Dancing School? We even danced together once or twice."

Yes, she was one of a handful of dancing school girls who had decamped to private school at an early age. She was also Bud's cousin, and all of us had been in kindergarten together, the three of us actually walking into our first day of school holding hands. She was a very pretty girl then, and time had been kind to her. I enjoyed our brief visit, although we both quickly dropped any further reference to our Friday afternoons with Mr. Barkle. I never saw her again.

But the stampede disaster did provide one valuable life lesson. Most of us never wear new shoes without first scuffing the hell out of them.

FIRST DATE

We all knew that it had to happen sooner or later. We also knew that once it did, our lives would be changed forever. Sometime in the mid-season of our first year in junior high school, when we were newly-minted teenagers, we started to notice girls.

We had noticed, of course, that girls were *around* before then. And unlike some of our buddies who had been dispatched to all-boy private schools, we had girls all around us at Glenwood. Smart, and also quite mysterious, they were usually interested in things we weren't, and never seemed to get into our goofy kind of trouble.

Each gave the other a wide berth, an unspoken détente which seemed to work out for everybody for years.

Until it just didn't.

It all started to come undone when our town merged three neighborhood elementary schools into one consolidated seventh grade. Suddenly, there were lots of new faces, and our world—carefully constructed of baseball and hockey, Wiffle ball and sports cards, bike adventures and other all-boy idiocy, was all about to change. Collisions of the tectonic plates went more smoothly.

And no one seemed interested in telling us how to rig for any of it.

No one.

As we learned years later, nature had played a very cruel joke on our merry band. While all around us girls were maturing at warp speed, we boys had clearly stalled out somewhere in the early fifth grade, and would remain there for most of our lives. Someone should have let us in on this cruel irony.

So they came, that first wave of these new people from other elementary schools, beyond the limited radius of our bike travels.

The first months were filled with fumbling attempts to make new friends, including meeting the new girls, but I kept to the program. Pushed along by things I did not yet understand, and swimming against the currents like those struggling salmon, it suddenly seemed a good idea to ask a girl on a date.

The First Date Ritual in our town operated under very strict, if unwritten, guidelines. Dates had to be double, limited to three hours, and involve some kind of daytime activity, although picnics were out, as well as walking deep into the Arboretum, a lovely woods not far from our old Glenwood School. Only parents could drive the kids, and older brothers or sisters were barred even as observers.

This left bowling and roller skating as the serious contenders.

Skating held the terror of actually touching a girl, either by choice or in collision, so bowling was the clear first date choice, and it wasn't a bad one. Most kids—including the girls—had been to a few bowling birthday parties by seventh grade. Although four of our buddies had been banned for life from the Livingston Lanes, other lanes near town were unsullied by our idiocy, and would welcome our business. Clean and family-friendly, except on Tuesday evenings when the league bowlers would show up, Florham Park was a particularly nice place to bowl. It had no extradition treaty with the Livingston Lanes, and apparently not much contact with them at all, even at the Bowling Lanes Owners Association of New Jersey (there must have had one), so they never learned of the lifetime ban.

Florham Park became my go-to dating venue, along with many of my buddies.

And a delightful girl, whom I will call Lynne, agreed to an actual date, late in February. Cute then, and a knockout today, she makes it to every one of our class reunions, and always looks like she has just stepped out of a John Cheever story: very upscale Greenwich, refined, quite regal—in that cool Greenwich way—and impeccably dressed. She actually lives just outside of Atlanta, adding an irresistible Southern charm and even a championship golf swing to her many charms.

Every time I see Lynne, it makes this memory more painful.

Lynne, on script, agreed to a Saturday morning bowling date. Billed as a double date under the existing rules, I asked Wiener McQueen to ask out Lynne's friend Donna. Wiener came up with the marvelous idea that we nudge the whole operation to a kind of *triple* date. We were sure that a large supporting cast would help us get through this. Three boys, two girls seemed about right, if a little unbalanced.

So we recruited "Spike" Hughes, and he was in.

Spike and Wiener then asked out Miss Donna, in unison. She accepted this strange version of a double date with good humor, Lynne having greased the way.

As the three of us boys tried to sort out this now strangely unbalanced date, our parents were principally concerned that we learn the proper way for a gentleman to introduce himself to a young lady's parents, although they were also a bit confused about who was on what date with whom.

Frankly, we all were.

So we decided that at least two of us would present ourselves at each of the girls' homes. Actually, it was agreed that *only* two would go to the door. After all, we didn't want to look like a posse.

Once we had the lineup figured out, we practiced the whole introductions drill. In fact, we drew it all out much like one of the plays we were then learning at Saturday morning basketball at the junior high school gym, and it went like this. My father would pick us up immediately after basketball practice, in time to arrive at Lynne's front door promptly at eleven o'clock on Saturday morning. She lived close to the school, so this part was easy. Hughes and I would do the honors there. My father would then drive us to Donna's home, somewhere off Old Short Hills Road, where McQueen and Hughes would do the honors. Assuming neither of the ladies backed out, he would drop the five of us off at the bowling lanes, and pick us up mid-afternoon, carefully keeping us to the three-hour rule.

As Saturday approached, we weren't sure any of this was a good idea. But we had the players sorted out, we had carefully rehearsed separate introductions for the MacIlroy-Hughes battery at Lynne's and the Hughes-McQueen battery at Donna's, and we were ready to get into the dating game.

What could go wrong?

For starters, we didn't have time to take showers after basketball practice, a very strenuous one at that. So on our very first date, we stank. We had worked up a peculiar mixture of first-date nervous sweat, athletic sweat, sneaker stink, gym odor, and locker room musk. Each smell alone would have been distasteful to our dates. In combination, it was nothing less than disgusting, and maybe even toxic. We had also just discovered the manly ritual of dousing our faces with a men's cologne called English Leather, which just added to the problem, as the product had not been tested under these extreme conditions.

Next, despite hours of rehearsal, we hopelessly screwed up the "meet the parents" script. In my own defense, I think I actually remembered the right lines. I just lost the bigger picture, or what I later learned was something called "situational awareness."

"Good morning," I carefully said to Lynne's parents, a strikingly handsome couple who had cheerfully greeted me at their front door. "My name is John, and this is my friend David Hughes."

Oops.

Just then, Lynne began descending the stairs, smiling and looking wonderful. Everything seemed on track, except that Hughes had called an audible, and I had failed to notice that he had pulled himself from the line-up, and standing in the foyer behind me was young Mr. McQueen. At least I didn't introduce him as "the Wiener." What was particularly absurd about this whole mix-up was the fact that Spike was already a tall six-footer, and Wiener barely topped out at five feet. It was impossible for anyone with a brain to mix them up, but I had. My first pitch in the dating game went high and wide.

"Hi, John. Hi, Scott. Where's David?"

What a disaster. No one would ever believe anyone could be this stupid and socially incompetent, even on a first date. This would be all over school, probably by the end of second period Monday.

I would never have another date!

But Lynne's parents were a gracious sort, and seemed to take this confusion in gentle stride, even as I blithered and stammered away, turning a vivid shade of crimson. Mercifully, young Mr. McQueen quickly recovered the fumble, and presented himself very nicely indeed. *His* mind was still intact, and he was quite sure that he knew who he was. Both parents, I am sure, still thought I was an idiot, and were certainly hoping that Lynne would have the good sense to focus her attention on the competent half of her double date, or maybe even the other fella still in the car. Even as a complete unknown, the Third Man on this "double date" was a far better choice.

By the time Lynne joined in on all the fun and we had correctly sorted out the players, everyone had started to notice those awful odors. That actually helped. We were a very unpleasant presence in what was a well-scrubbed, tidy, and fine-smelling home, and were to be removed as quickly as possible. Had that not been the case, I think Lynne's parents would have asked me to take a competency test, which I would certainly have failed. With enough teenage angst, awkwardness, confusion, and even strange odors for one suburban morning, we were politely ushered out the door.

So began that first date, and with it a remarkably checkered romantic life. Not unlike so very, very many dates which lay ahead, I was indeed enjoying the company of a very attractive and delightful girl, clearly above my pay-grade, while she was already counting the minutes until the whole thing ended. The Hughes-McQueen script at Donna's house went much more smoothly, and we all had a good time at the bowling center, all things considered. The smelly bowling shoes which the shoe guy had issued to the girls seemed to level the playing field odor-wise, at least a little bit, although both girls wisely kept their distance on the bench seat behind the racks.

Lynne's dad figured my father could find his way back to their home, so the chances were pretty good he would see his delightful daughter again. (He had, however, never seen the shoe guy.) Not surprisingly, during the course of the date, Lynne had given very clear indications that I should expect no further outings, even in novel dating combinations. It was all done with a kind of classy Greenwich-style decorum, and Lynne and I never went out again.

We did, however, enjoy many laughs and a pleasant friendship through our school years, and I always enjoy seeing her at our class reunions, and yes, she remembers the date.

I've just never asked if she ever still goes bowling, and she never asks if I still use English Leather.

THE DANCING BEAR'S CARNIVAL SURPRISE

With neither skill nor interest following us as we exited from our dancing schools a few years earlier, we were terrified to learn that we would be expected to go to real dances in high school. We figured this too would not end well, and we were right.

Like most high schools, ours had several dances throughout the year. Everyone at least thought they *should* go, and I have talked to maybe six or seven people in my entire life who actually had fun at these dances. Mismatched dates and broken romances were just the start of the emotional carnage, with larger institutional failures lurking behind some unfortunate choice made by someone on one of the planning committees. Indeed, you can make the case that *all* of the choices made by the various planning committees for these events are unfortunate, beginning with the fact that these dances are almost always staged in a school gym or cafeteria, at least until senior year when things usually move off-site to minor up-grade, like a mid-price local hotel. These are not evenings in Paris, even though the hands-down winner in choice of dance name seemed to be "April in Paris," at least in New Jersey. This unimaginative handle was, and, may still be, true for dances across the country, even if the event rocked its way into May or June.

It might even be fun to try this.

Go anywhere, find a crowd of complete strangers, and work the crowd with this opening line:

"Didn't I see you about a century ago at our freshman prom, that awful 'April in Paris' thing?"

You'll be a hit, I bet, with about half the people, who may never figure out you were no where near *their* magical evening in Paris. It's all about the same nonsense, everywhere.

We slogged through our share. "April in Paris" (yeah, I know) as freshmen, something also imaginatively called the "Soph Hop" the next year—a tame event marked only by the refreshingly stupid appearance of one couple in an outfit perfect for a "Sock Hop"—and even an unauthorized crash of the dance sponsored by the class ahead of us, which was really just a taste of that sophisticated experience until we were politely given the boot. With clearly stunted imaginations in our crowd, we were surprised when our class Junior Prom Committee actually hatched a clever and promising name for the event.

"Carnival."

Not "The Carnival," or "Carnival Nights," or even "April in a Carnival."

Just "Carnival," like *"Animal House"* a few years later.

And just like that movie, our Junior Prom danced into something of a legend, even without John Belushi. But we did have our very own larger-than-life character, a good-natured and rather beefy football player nicknamed "The Dancing Bear." Only slightly less crazy than Buluschi, Bear had been left largely on the sidelines of anything to do with the school, except football. That seemed to work for everybody, until for reasons still unclear, Bear suddenly got all goofy about school spirit and made his case about working with one of the prom planning committees. His pitch was effective, and genuine—there was even talk that Bear had a kind of "inner Bear" ready to blossom—and he was drafted by the usually low-risk, no-brainer Refreshment Committee. Since we were allowed to serve only snacks and punch, and Bear had joined the Chef's Club, everyone figured he could work his way through this new school spirit thing without doing something crazy. He could nurture the new "Inner Bear" and even add a little needed weight to his thin list of extracurricular activities, Chef's Club carrying no credibility at all with the folks in the school guidance office, and football not much more. The Committee did back Bear off one of his ideas, that he personally patrol the parking lot and bust the ass of anyone sipping those stronger refreshments which were rumored to be in the parking lot during our dances. One of the Student Council types on the committee reminded Bear that parking lot control was someone else's responsibility, outside the scope of the Refreshment Committee's limited charter. This guy—a strict constructionist, and now a hard-core Republican—was right on, and Bear settled down until his next idea.

Things might have been very different if that Student Council guy had talked him out of this one too.

The Dancing Bear, you see, knew someone who knew someone else who ran a boardwalk concession down the Jersey Shore and who could bring a bunch of cotton-candy-making machines as a themed-rich refreshment surprise of the evening.

Everyone loved the idea. Even the future Republican. And no one in adult authority saw much downside risk, so the cotton candy machines were a go.

No one had ever seen The Dancing Bear so happy.

Bear—who was known for mostly delivering excuses—promised to deliver four machines, one for each corner of the gym. The machines themselves were kind of small aluminum things, he said, but they were housed in marvelous wagons standing about five-feet tall, each in a classic cherry-red and yellow livery, with white spoked wooden wheels. They looked like miniature Conestoga wagons, with the owner's name carefully applied in funky letters I would still describe as *circus-carnival-wild west*. Best of all, the whole deal was free. When the Decorations Committee saw these pictures, they decided to shelve another color scheme and went with matching red and yellow streamers.

"The Full Carnival," they called it.

Word slipped out that The Dancing Bear had scored a coup, but the planning committees had taken a blood oath to keep it all a surprise, so no one really knew what to expect.

With red and yellow streamers transforming the gym into a fair imitation of a carnival tent—along the way violating about a thousand sections of the local fire code—and four magnificent cotton-candy wagons spooling up in each corner of the gym, prom goers arrived that Saturday night in October of 1962 to something special, and a beaming Dancing Bear.

Curiously, the Dress Committee had opted out of formal attire, so most people arrived in what today would be called "business casual," except with ties for the boys, and no slacks for the girls. This would prove to be the second bad decision by a prom committee, although we didn't know that just yet. You see, formal attire, although it seemed to transform us into stuffy people we didn't know, did seem to cut the usual level of boyish idiocy. If we really didn't know how to act like adults, we at least looked like them. It didn't help much, but did dampen some of the nonsense. By the same measure, dialing down the dress code only dialed up the idiocy. That's why no one gets to go to a prom called "April in Togas," at least until college.

Things did, however, begin pretty well.

Even, it was said later by the survivors, the evening at first seemed *magical*.

But "magical" is a funny thing, and legend has it all starting out as an accident, a runaway cotton-candy machine going nuts and spewing a sticky pink lava into a small crowd of gawkers, more an incident of mild curiosity than a global catastrophe. Things, however, quickly took a spirited turn like those wedding videos when the groom and bride start smashing pieces of wedding cake into each other's adoring face, and then things go south, wedding cake insanity spreading like the zombie apocalypse throughout the room.

Pink cotton-candy, and a little blue stuff too, soon gooed up everyone and everything in sight, and The Dancing Bear's Carnival Surprise ruined the whole night.

His gooey pink cotton-candy was just too much fun, particularly for the "happy" crowd who had joined the unfolding disaster after a little pre-game in the parking lot.

Whether trying to have fun with the sticky stuff, or just trying to avoid it, we were all doomed to have at least *some* close encounter of the cotton-candy kind.

The Refreshment Committee had also come up with a couple of snow cone machines, also decked out in happy carnival colors. While they did not malfunction, the little white paper cones did, adding to the mess. Snow cones were not Bear's idea, but he was already crushed by the disaster and never again volunteered for a dance committee. He even quietly quit Chef's Club, which was usually a safe harbor for most of the goofballs in the school, and a last refuge for the socially wounded. He did, however, continue to play tough football, a blessing. His wafer-thin school activity transcript ("Varsity football, 1,2,3, Chef's Club 2, Junior Prom Refreshment Committee, 2") was no barrier to a small college football scholarship which came his way late in our senior year, much to the relief of the guidance office.

Coulrophobia—the fear of clowns—is a recognized phobia. My sister has it. And since our little cotton-candy disaster, I hate that shit, and avoid places that may sell it, like the circus. So there is no chance that I will force her to see the circus should she be visiting my little island when some circus comes to town, which is highly unlikely anyway. This also works out for my Nebraska-born wife, who has dialed her clown phobia up a bit to include the whole circus too, elephants in particular. You see, on our second date, I took her to the opera Aida, performed in Omaha, Nebraska at the Ak-Sar-Ben Arena, where we both were nearly crushed to death by an elephant who had charged out of the famous procession scene.

Yes.

Nearly killed by an elephant at an opera in Omaha.

Only quick and last-minute thinking by one of the elephant handlers saved us both from an embarrassingly ridiculous way to shuffle off our mortal coils.

Who knows? Maybe surprises, and even disasters, are just the currency of life experiences, from operas in Omaha to Junior Proms in New Jersey, warning us that reality rarely meets expectation—not just in our early years, but long afterwards too.

But I did learn two important things that night: elephant breath is awful, and Ak-Sar-Ben is Nebraska spelled backwards.

WHAT WAS THAT AGAIN, COACH?

Coaches had it easy, at least compared to the regular teachers. After all, coaches could walk around campus all day in comfortable, loose-fitting athletic warm-up suits and cool sneakers, wearing those necklace whistles to boot. These clothing and accessory privileges seemed to piss off other teachers, and I suspect this tension really spilled over the top at the quarterly "in-service" all-faculty meetings with the Superintendent and Board of Education, unless the coaches all decided to upscale their garb, which I doubt.

Coaches could also count on keeping all verbal instructions to, and communications with, their student-athletes to the native tongue, which avoided all kinds of frustration of the type happening over in the foreign languages classes. Best of all, coaches got to regularly throw things at students, a practice strictly forbidden in virtually all settings, save the athletic field.

Coaches had, at least during regular school hours, a pretty good lifestyle.

On the other hand, our coaches carried burdens not shared with the purely academic faculty. They spent long afternoons, some evenings, and many Saturdays actually coaching. With talented athletes, this could be very rewarding and maybe even fun. But not so much when the athletic talent is scant, as it often proved to be among our crowd, especially in our early years. Moreover, coaches usually worked under the spotlight. Even in a community known for carefully balancing its sports program, team performances were regularly out in the open, always covered by the often heartless media, and followed by some fans with a rabid intensity.

The contrast with what went on quietly inside the classroom was dramatic.

Think about it. Every day, students were dangling participles and mixing metaphors in English classes all over the place. Nines were being miscarried every day and theorems tangled in math classes. Things, very important things like the famous PSSC ripple tank, were dropped routinely over in the physics lab, and major events in human history were randomly reshuffled in chronological chaos over in history class. Students were daily relocating towns, cities, famous landmarks, and even whole countries on world maps in geography class. This was a daily symphony of screw-ups, across the academic landscape.

But no one ever heard about *these* disasters.

Over on the athletic fields, by contrast, and outside the academic fortress, every fumble, dropped pass, missed goal, missed serve, missed return, missed putt, missed basket, and missed play was right there for anyone to see. And that was just practice. Dial it all up a notch on game day, and everyone was watching. So maybe our coaches didn't have it so good after all.

Indeed, our coaches were also burdened with one particularly stressful extra-curricular charge. They were the go-to candidates for teaching something called "Health Class." This mysterious tutorial cropped up only twice for us during our high school years.

The first time was in ninth grade. Boys and girls were split into different sections: one section was taught to the boys by the freshman football coach, the other by the girls' gym teacher. I have no idea how today's Boards of Education deal with the new voice of those students with sexual identity issues, or even if anyone teaches "Health Class" anymore, as a lot of these topics seem to be regularly on display on cable, and in a more entertaining fashion. But those sensitivities were nowhere evident in our day, so off we went to begin our separate understandings of all things human-body.

Well, not all things, as it turned out, at least until the second installment, later in our senior year.

Freshman year, the whole course lasted about ten weeks, one day a week. It was very PG, and completely avoided any of the really interesting stuff—like just about everything we were beginning to want to know about girls. The classroom had a kind of "pull-down, life-size, see-through" poster of the male body, which someone cleverly nicknamed "Adam." Adam was vaguely anatomically correct, we were able to confirm, but there was no sign of an "Eve" poster, although we were sure the girls had one in their section. That was a major disappointment, but the whole class was designed to be pretty non-threatening. The male body poster made several brief appearances before disappearing back into its protective shell, but it did give us a marginally better idea of what was going on deep inside our bodies, which too often seemed a distant cousin.

But a lot of the class focused on what was happening on the surface, mostly pimples, facial hair and the art of shaving. These were not distant relatives, so a lot of our time was spent on good hygiene practices—supposedly a good defense against those dreaded pimples. When a good washing didn't do the job—which was most of the time—we plastered Clearasil all over our faces, along the way ensuring a rich retirement for Dick Clark. We also got some needed shaving tips, and a bizarre discussion about *tapeworm,* although I think it was a subject introduced by some wiseass student rather than the coach. Since that strange detour, I have been terrified of tapeworm, although I can never remember if it comes from eating undercooked pork or walking around barefoot. Wormy diseases were not really in the coach's playbook.

At least I did learn to shave with both skill and regularity, even if I am slipping a bit now. I take lots of showers, although I still keep a small tube of untinted "adult" Clearasil hidden in the back reaches of my medicine cabinet, just in case. I don't walk around barefoot, even in my own living room. And I will eat a pork chop only if it's charred to a cinder, and nothing but beef barbeque, even in North Carolina.

The next installation of our class was called "Senior Health," another ten-week course in our final year, where things took a welcome turn, even if the girls were still barred. Our varsity football coach, a good guy I will just call "Coach," seemed reluctantly willing to get into the more *practical* stuff, but in class he stayed close to a Board-approved script with only a little more detail about bodies, both male and female. With a surprisingly light touch for a tough-hearted coach, he gave us a gentle introduction to the things happening at the horizon of most of our dating lives. The use of the word "sex" was off-limits, along with other words which were orbiting the whole mess in the football locker room. The course enjoyed a kind of tasteful camouflage, hiding under some fuzzy name such as "The Reproductive Arts." This gentle euphemism would have fit right in with the way things were talked about in our town, and maybe people thought it really had something to do with art.

No one should have been too alarmed in any case: it was all surprisingly dull, and a little too mechanical. Frankly, few of us had much experience at the further reaches of this thing called sex anyway. We pretty much hung around second base, give or take a steal or two.

But Coach made up for this with some great practical dating tips during class, as well as his offer to talk to the boys after school about "other things." Which would, of course, be condoms, and some bizarre method having to do with "rhythm." This was all a hypothetical thing in my case, and would remain so throughout high school, so I never asked for that private tutorial. It turns out it really wasn't too complicated a thing to figure out on my own, eventually.

But Coach was in top form when he outlined a game plan for dating, which was, of course, related to that sex thing, but easier to talk about in class. He would have to walk a fine line here, too, and he became the go-to guy on all things girls and dating, even if by default. He had figured out that few of us were getting any kind of "guidance" on these things at home, and most of us were hitting that playing field without a clue.

We didn't know the rules, or even if there *were* rules.

And worst of all, we were engaging an opposing team whose players all seemed completely in control of *their* games. The girls not only knew the rules, they *made* the rules. Coach knew that this mismatch would be part of our lives forever, but he didn't have the heart to let us in on that cosmic cruelty. He really just wanted to level the playing field a bit, and give us a kind of dating game plan.

Like any good football coach would, he broke it down into a defensive plan, and an offensive one.

His defensive strategy was the easier one for us to understand. The key concept was "the bimbo." Coach was the first to introduce this word to us, and he really nailed it. While he would not name names, Coach deployed something we quickly named The Bimbo Defense to steer us away from troublesome territory, girl-wise. Our tony suburban school in the early 60s was a time and place of very tame dating standards. A little "making out" was all right, and the "good girls" would be sure to keep things well under control. But even in the virgin forest of our school, there dwelled a few of the more adventuresome ladies. There were girls who, by whispered word of mouth, seemed to enjoy the boys more fully, but all that may have been just talk, and didn't seem to set off too many alarms. Except for Coach, who was the first person any of us heard use the term "bimbo," deploying the word one Tuesday night at our Varsity Club meeting which served for a time as an *ad hoc* version of one of those previously offered "post-school-hours" supplemental sessions.

"Nothing but trouble, boys, those bimbos," he cautioned, as he vaguely pointed a finger toward the world outside the Varsity Club meeting room. No names, of course, but we knew he was thinking not only of those dangerous ladies lurking over in the next county, and in the city, *but even some right here in our own school.*

We got the point.

His other strategy, his offensive game plan, was seemingly based on his personal list of desirable qualities in a mate. While we just wanted to get into the game, with maybe a couple of dates and a shot at a great partner for the Varsity Club Dance, Coach was thinking way ahead. This probably explains why he always led off with his all-time preferred characteristic in a mate, which we thought was pretty weird, at least at the time.

"Good breeding stock," he would intone. "Very important, boys."

Much to our amusement, he would then go on about child-bearing hips, the fleeting looks of youth, compatible personalities, homemaking skills, and even the importance of a good family health history. Frankly, his list was pretty far removed from what we had in mind as our ideal, which probably veered dangerously close to "the bimbo." I have also wondered if the girls, over in their section of Senior Health, were also being urged toward a comparable set of desirable qualities in a mate. That idea still scares me even now, and probably would have terrified all of us then had we thought about it.

Coach also had two other gems of dating advice. The first was a somewhat obsessive insistence that we scrutinize the mothers of our prospective dates—who might eventually become lifetime mates, which were then pretty much exclusively called *wives*, at least in the boys' class.

"Take a good look at their mothers, boys," he would remind us. "Yes, there's your future."

That seemed to have some logic, after what we had learned about genetics in class, but this counsel posed some practical problems. Mostly, we would have about two minutes to check out these moms when we went on dates—like when we picked our dates up at their homes. By that time, in the very act of asking a girl out, we were already well along that sequential dating path, choice-wise, and often already so smitten that we were unwilling to look at reality anyway. Also, we figured our dates, even in those brief two minutes, expected our attention to be focused on *them*, and not their mothers. A dad was usually there too, and we also figured he wouldn't much appreciate our checking out his wife, particularly if we started with weird sidelong glances at her childbearing hips and questions about her health. Maybe we could have found some other, more neutral, territory to really study the moms, like church or in the stands at sporting events. Rarely did we make sound choices, but this was one: this mom thing seemed very, very creepy, and this whole idea went absolutely nowhere, pretty much like most of our young dating lives. We probably backed off a bit too far: I even got into the strange habit of barely even glancing at the mothers of my dates, which just made me look stupid.

The other thing Coach often talked about was something he called "The Woo." The very first time we heard him say this phrase, we thought he was simply going to introduce us to some new female body part, which had been hidden from us, or maybe he was just introducing a new code word for some part we already knew something about.

We were all ears.

But it was soon obvious that this was a far more complex thing, something called "romancing." It was never clear whether he was talking about deploying this concept to get a date, or to move things along during a date, or whether this was a tip for the later stages of dating, or even after marriage. But it clearly was some kind of key to the whole thing, somewhere along the line, so important that this hulking and no-nonsense former Little All-American tight end would talk of the importance of manners, and courtesies, and even the remarkable power of flowers to ease the way in relationships. He seemed to be suggesting that this was the best method to power our way to happy and fulfilling relationships with the very best girls, not only in our school, but in the wider world beyond.

As our buddy Don Hohnstine has reminded me, we cut Coach no slack on this at the time. After one of The Woo Talks, when we left class we would gleefully dash down the hallway with what became known as "The Woo Chant," pumping our arms up and down like we were steam locomotives and shouting "Woo. Woo. *WOO!*" This kind of sophomoric display—we were seniors, no less—guaranteed that we rarely got a date at all, much less one that would demand even a basic understanding of the higher romantic skills.

Like I have said many times, we were idiots, and would have been considerably better served—not just in high school, but in important relationships years later—if we had paid a little more attention to Coach's faith in the power of The Woo. But I do know this: flowers work, at least some of the time.

AT LEAST *SHE* HAD FUN

Trouble followed our football coach just about everywhere our senior year. Even into the usually calm waters of his Varsity Club.

The Varsity Club had few responsibilities, and Coach encouraged the Club toward a kind of benign self-management, which should have been fairly risk-free. Of course, it wasn't, as things turned out.

We elected some good guys to run the show, at least at the top of the ticket. Chick Chandler served as president, and he went on to become a beloved coach a couple towns away before an untimely death. Billy Jaeger, a talented multi-sport athlete who had survived the antics of his dad's Tri-County baseball team, was a solid and responsible vice-president. We remember a position called the sergeant-at-arms, an inexplicable slot as we did not maintain any kind of armory, but nobody can remember anyone who actually held that position, or why. We also had a couple of other officers, and that's where the trouble started.

Suds Estes was a consensus-choice to serve as secretary-treasurer—he could read, write, and add, even if trig was causing him some problems. No alarms yet. But the last office was an appointed position, and new to the club. It was, in fact, kind of an audible called at the line of scrimmage by Coach, and I held it—the position of "club chaplain." I now think Coach thought I would be a good balance to my buddy Suds, figuring I could borrow a little of the Episcopal Good Will I was enjoying as a Crucifer at Christ Church to keep things on track at the club.

It should have been a brilliant call, that borrowed good will informing better conduct at our weekly meetings, held in the same room as Senior Health.

And it did, for a while.

A "while" was two months in this case, when Suds and I were given an important assignment in support of the only real thing the club did during the year—holding something called, imaginatively, "The Varsity Club Dance." Like most high schools, there were various class-sponsored dances throughout the year, but this one was unique. It never had a theme name, just "The Varsity Club Dance." Most of these dances were a disappointment, of course, as we all fumbled our way through everything connected with them: bad dates, no dates, broken hearts, and spectacularly bad choices in attire, and these are just the humiliations at the top of the list. Some were institutional disasters, as you also may know.

With this track record, by the time we were seniors the bar had been set pretty low for our dance.

Maybe that's why Suds and I were appointed the Two-Man Entertainment Committee. Since Suds was treasurer, and the really big expense was always the band, there was some logic behind the choice. Maybe Coach was counting on me to spread more of that Episcopal good will.

Logic aside, it turned out to be a spectacularly bad choice.

Essentially, we took this assignment as an open invitation to drive all over Northern New Jersey checking out local dance bands in order to sign one up for the dance. There were limited places to find bands willing to play these high school gigs, and the way we looked at the possibilities, they came down to only two: bars and private girls' schools.

That still left lots of places to visit, many with the promise of a cold beer or two and others with the distinct possibility of meeting those mysterious girls who had been well-hidden from our view at fancy private girls' schools. While we both knew the band deal would eventually be sealed by Estes the money man, we quickly discovered that having a chaplain along could help get us into schools, particu-

larly the ones run by nuns and other clergy. So we decided to play it
up a bit, donning jackets and ties for all of these scouting trips.

Years later, one of our buddies, who had been a painfully slow
reserve guard on the football squad but a notably serious crucifer,
told us that he'd heard I had actually carried my *Episcopal Book of
Common Prayer* on all of our scouting trips, including the bars.
Although I wanted to push this, it was a wholly groundless detail.

"Come on," we said with the pious indignation we knew he
would like, "you think we'd bring the *Book of Common Prayer* into a
bar?"

But we had discovered that most of the girls' schools seemed to
have some significant relationship with a church, or at least seemed
to be very pious operations. This was obviously true for a couple
of Catholic schools high on our prospect list, and just the kind of
discovered reality that could, considering our goofy ways, push us to
questionable choices.

So it is not surprising that Suds and I both have a vague memory that I may have deployed a small Crucifers Cross, or at least
a Crucifer's lapel, on a couple of trips, particularly to the Catholic
schools. Some of us had run into serious cross trouble over at Christ
Church, and this was a very tender subject. For the sake of our Eternal
Souls, I hope that we're wrong about this.

With or without such pious props, we spent the first week or
two driving around to various schools and introducing ourselves to
those in charge. Coach was generous about writing chits that excused
us from class, so that we could launch these missions in the early
afternoons.

These were surprisingly successful trips.

We were clean-cut varsity men, which helped, from a town
which enjoyed a gentle reputation. We were dressed in jackets and
ties and, well, we were just so earnest. Suds and I were also world-
class bullshitters, so we soon had over a half dozen solid admissions
to upcoming dances.

Frankly, we were *magnificent*.

We even had one suggestion to consider the priesthood (that
during a very pleasant chat at a Catholic school), and someone even

offered to write each of us a letter of recommendation for college. No, make that a great recommendation.

We now think we misunderstood both gestures, and were getting dangerously sure of ourselves. Cocky, if you will.

And that's when the trouble usually began.

The first tiny cloud was the growing displeasure expressed by our respective girlfriends at our growing out-of-town social calendar and dance card. We had indeed forgotten to get *four* tickets to these dances, an oversight quickly brought to our attention.

"Choose one, and only one, girls' school where you may preview the band, or the poop will hit the paddles." Their tone was unmistakable, and the message clear.

Even today, Suds and I take full responsibility for the catastrophe that followed. But in our defense, had we not been backed into this corner—and had we been able to preview even three or four bands—we might have avoided the looming disaster. With only one preview slot now allowed under our new constraints, we picked the very tony Miss Beard School for Girls for our visit, not far away in East Orange. Over the years, Beard had taken some very nice girls from town, and we thought this a very responsible choice. So that's where we went, one Friday night in early November of 1963, armed with a small cash retainer to get our band.

The dance was noticeably classier than most we had attended, reminding us of our days in dancing school at the elegant Short Hills Club. Held in a richly paneled ballroom, which was clearly never used as a gym, everything was a cut above, and Coach's hand-picked envoys stepped up their game, too. We actually could have passed as gentlemen, suggesting we may have picked up some of the social graces from poor Mr. Barkle after all.

We were on a tight leash, so we got right to it, carefully listening to the band. With five guys, they were a little loud. But the songs were the popular ones, well within the mainstream, and these guys *ROCKED*. While they didn't look like they had just shopped at our tweedy, upscale local clothing stores—Root's in Summit or Martin Eastman in Millburn, the two shops favored by the preppy set, or even Mr. E's which pushed a slightly more urban look—they all wore jackets and ties. This was a generally accepted code for respectability, certainly among bands, and was just the kind of thing Coach would notice. Their haircuts were maybe a little inner-city rough but, all in all, these guys seemed to have been a sound choice for the classy Beard School. They also seemed to be sober, which was something else Coach would appreciate.

What I am about to say is very important to our defense: neither of us remembers seeing *any kind of name* on the band's bass drum. Also, no one seemed to refer to them as anything but "that great band." We were all having fun, and Suds and I were even making some new friends among the Beard ladies, with a few promised invitations to visit their homes down the Shore in the summer. With all the fun, this little no-band-name detail seemed unimportant, a detail of no possible consequence.

We had no idea what we were doing, of course, but if these guys were good enough for the fashionable, good taste Beard School, they were good enough for us. We signed them up on the spot, with only a handshake and a modest cash engagement retainer. Suds says I even blessed the happy transaction, with a promise of some kind of contract to follow, and then we were out of there. We had done our job, and we were very pleased with ourselves.

No, this was one we never saw coming.

We reported back to Coach, and told him we had a band "from the very classy Beard School." This may have been a sloppy turn of phrase at best, and even a bit misleading, because we both had a feeling that Coach thought we had signed up a classy little band of well-scrubbed and well-mannered *actual Beard ladies* for our dance. But he seemed happy, so we let it slide.

"I knew I could count on you two guys." That was high praise in coach-speak, and we were very proud of ourselves.

Yeah, Coach was very happy indeed.

That was when we should have really started to worry.

Our job was done, and some of the other committees were soon stepping up their games as the evening of the dance approached. As you might guess, the committee with the worst job was the "Decorations Committee." It was also the largest, filled with about twenty completely unimaginative varsity jocks. As I mentioned earlier, unlike the other school dances during the year, the Varsity Club Dance never had a "theme name." This was a particularly cruel irony as the already uninspired committee didn't even have an obvious clue to guide them in *some* direction. Even a minimalist approach would have helped, like a couple of mildly appropriate posters taped to a wall: some travel posters, old game-day sports posters, or even a nice gallery of "Most Wanted by the FBI" mug shot posters from the Post Office. Yes, that would have been cool, and not such a far-fetched possibility either. You see, as we had heard for years, although it was never confirmed, a former Postmaster General of the United States actually lived in town, and he (if he existed) might have enjoyed helping us out here.

Without a single idea, the committee punted, the usual option for most of the club's jocks, even if they were not football players. They simply moved the whole show from the gym into the school cafeteria. Apparently they thought an undecorated cafeteria was a better deal than an undecorated gym, and they may have had a point. At least it would smell better, unless the day's lunch special had been particularly awful. With a much lower ceiling than the gym, the cafeteria was also a more *intimate* setting. This could have been a good thing.

It wasn't, as things turned out.

Unfortunate rumblings about the pathetic failure of the overcrowded but under-talented Decorations Committee seemed to taper off, however, as the word got around that the Two-Man Entertainment Committee had really come through, signing up this "very cool band from the Beard School." Apparently, Coach was not the only one thinking a classy chick band would be enough style for the night, even in a cafeteria that had all the charm of an empty airline terminal at a second-market airport at 2:30 in the morning, or a medium-security prison.

At least, we all joked, we wouldn't have to worry about a riot.

As the Friday of the big dance approached, Coach dedicated the regular Tuesday club meeting that week to a pre-dance chalk talk. It was moving, really, reminding us of the importance of the romantic touch, and The Woo. He worried that some of the socially less-gifted jocks had struggled to get dates, although he was not willing to actually arrange dates for these date-less boys—a beefy lineman or two on the football team, a couple of promising but still awkward and too-tall basketball players and the equipment manager on the soccer team. But he did tell them to keep trying and not give up, like coaches always do, even as the clock runs out.

"If all else fails," Coach said, suggesting actual limits to the power of The Woo, "you boys without dates come anyway."

This was not only a kind suggestion, but it proved to be an important one, although no one knew it at the time.

Friday arrived, and after class the useless Decorations Committee moved the dining tables out of the cafeteria. For most dances at the school, actual decorations had to be set up, and this pre-dance ritual would take two or three hours. Our committee finished it up in about twenty minutes, giving them all a chance to swing over to the Millburn Deli for the afternoon snack of choice, at least among the varsity men: a hard roll, with butter and Russian dressing, and a quart of their fabulous sweet iced tea, brewed with a recipe as guarded as that of Coca-Cola.

They had left the cafeteria as dance-prepared as it could be. Cleared of all tables, at least it didn't smell like stale spaghetti or those Friday fish sticks.

Coach went home to change into a coat and tie, which was a once-a-year deal for him. The varsity men went home to change into their coats and ties as well, as required by Coach. Suds and I had decided to double date, choosing my car for the occasion. A well-worn but sturdy four door white 1957 Chevrolet, my car was already on its fifth or sixth owner before my dad bought it for a couple hundred bucks off a lot somewhere along Route 22, in the middle of my junior year. I had mixed feelings when everyone started calling it the *White Trash*, but it seemed to be a term of endearment, as many high school nicknames are, even if they don't sound endearing. Anyway, it fit, and a lot of folks were sad when my father sold it years later for about twenty-five dollars to a hard-working but very poor laborer from Newark, who said in broken English that it was his first car, and that he would probably keep it forever.

I hope he did, because the current classic car guides put the value of this 1957 Chevy at about $43,000. I wonder what it will be worth when forever arrives.

Anyway, the very bright possible future for the laborer from Newark was unknown to the Two-Man Entertainment Committee as we rode once again into the night. And, as it would soon turn out, into school legend.

We picked up our girls in the *Trash*, getting to the dance about half an hour early, just before 7:30. We had agreed to meet the band and help them set up. This had further impressed Coach, who was clearly pleased that he had chosen us for this important committee.

We knew one thing all along, of course, but it only became immediately clear to everyone else—and Coach in particular, who walked in a few minutes later—that the band were not *really* Beard Girls. As I said, we had not been eager to correct this misconception, particularly since our buddies on the Decorations Committee were counting on some classy and good looking Beard Girls to add some much needed sparkle to the cafeteria, a sparkle those empty airline terminals could surely use as well. Suds and I just didn't have the heart to disappointment them in advance.

We were a little surprised, however, to see that the five band guys had decidedly loosened up their profile, which had been pretty tight at Beard: maybe they just looked better in a dark-paneled and quite elegant private school setting than an empty school cafeteria.

Way better.

These guys showed up in a style familiar to you if you have seen the Broadway musical *Jersey Boys*. We called it "hoody" back then, with lots of black leather clothing and alarmingly tight pants. It looked like these guys had just walked in after spending the afternoon on a corner in the less desirable part of Irvington, and then forgotten to shower and change for the evening. This was not a style favored by many in charge around our school. Of more immediate concern, it was a style which drove Coach absolutely crazy.

While this was even mildly troubling to the Two-Man Entertainment Committee, things looked under control as the band set up with a reassuring professional detachment on the stage at the front of the cafeteria, which was raised just slightly, maybe a foot or so off the cafeteria floor. We were completely clueless how any band should set up, so it didn't strike us as strange that the band still had not posted their name on a standing placard somewhere on the stage, or even plastered their name on the drum. This was apparently what bands did, but nothing seemed amiss to us. I mean, there didn't seem to be any pyrotechnics or other dangerous weaponry up there, and nothing in the band's behavior set off alarms—other than that hoody dress thing—even if they weren't very friendly.

The band was ready to go at eight o'clock sharp, just as the cafeteria filled up with beaming varsity men, and the dance began right on time, just as Coach wanted it.

Things started off well enough.

The turnout was good, and most of the varsity guys had eventually gotten dates. There were some truly amazing matchups, with even hugely popular girls arriving with the more date-challenged boys. This was the one dance where the usual social rules were suspended, with the really cute girls, in a burst of school spirit and a gentle nod to the jocks, accepting dates unacceptable any other time. Yes indeed, Coach seemed very pleased with these social successes: the dance was filling up with good girls of strong breeding stock, with hardly a bimbo in tow.

To be sure, the band did seem a bit loud, having apparently calibrated their sound to a gym-sized room, and not a low-ceilinged cafeteria. But the crowd was soon into it, even the socially awkward varsity men with dates way beyond their pay grade. As things turned out, it has always been important to us to remember just how *happy* these varsity men seemed in the early part of the evening. Things rocked along through the first, and longer, set without trouble, although by 9:30 the band had gotten very, very loud indeed, and seemed to be veering off into some decidedly less mainstream songs. Estes and I were paying some attention to this, as any competent and alert Two-Man Entertainment Committee should, although no one else seemed to notice, maybe due to the fact that they were going deaf by then anyway.

Except for Coach, who seemingly had no such hearing problems, and had caught a whiff of trouble too. He called us over.

"Boys, how about talking to these clowns at the break about lowering the volume for the final set, and maybe cooling it with some of those weird songs?"

It was hard to hear Coach, so we cupped our ears in the universal semaphore for "talk louder." Had we known what was just around the corner, we would have signaled the universal sign for "we surrender," right then and there.

"TELL THESE CLOWNS THEY'RE TOO LOUD, AND THE SONGS TOO WEIRD."

"Got it, Coach," and we kind of nodded in genuine agreement.

"AND WHAT THE HELL IS THE NAME OF THIS BAND ANYWAY?" Coach added, already looking to put this group on something like today's "no-fly list."

The Two-Man Entertainment Committee shrugged but quickly went to work, and came up with a plan. We agreed to ask these guys, in a kind of "varsity-men-to-hood-aw-shucks-way," if they wouldn't mind toning the whole performance down a bit, both volume and song selection. We could have avoided some later unpleasantness if we had just stopped there.

But we didn't, of course.

When we grabbed the lead singer at the break, and tossed out the aw-shucks requests, we added another suggestion.

"Since we kind of forgot to ask your name," I piously suggested, "why don't you weave it into the performance, you know, with a real *flourish!*"

There were really only two or three things wrong with this approach. First, hoods hated that varsity men "aw-shucks" stuff, even from the most earnest of jocks. Second, even had they been willing to make an exception for the very earnest Two-Man Entertainment Committee—it was, after all, carrying some of that pious good will—the word "flourish" had really set the lead singer off. We just didn't know it yet, although as it rolled off my tongue that night it did seem a bit much—more SAT than *Jersey Boys* language, which we would soon learn a bit more about. And finally, no self-respecting Jersey band *ever* ceded ground to anyone about song selection.

We knew nothing of these realities, of course, as the lead guy kind of nodded and left to join his bandmates, who had all repaired to their van in the parking lot for a little refreshment.

Pleased with our mission, Suds and I rejoined our dates and buddies. Our hearing had returned for the most part, and we were delighted to learn that this roomful of jocks—and maybe a few of their dates—were having a good time. A few of the varsity men who had dated over their pay grade were struggling a bit, and we even heard that several of the more mismatched couples had already thrown in the towel and left the party. This was not wholly unexpected, as there was always talk around the Varsity Club Dance that some of the very popular girls always planned it that way, hoping to catch up with their usual boyfriends for a late-night after-date date, when the clock ran down on those special dating rules.

We reported to Coach that everything was in order, although we still did not know the name of the band. We wanted to be surprised with that flourish thing as well.

So while we enjoyed this quiet band-break time, the band itself was apparently enjoying large quantities of adult beverages. The bandleader was also, we now think, whipping his drummer and three sidemen into a booze-fueled frenzy about stupid jocks and earnest spoiled varsity bullshitters, and a coach who was getting ready to ban them anyway. At least this guy was perceptive, and no one said hoods were stupid. We think this was the likely bottom line over in the van:

"*F____ 'em.*" A useful hood phrase, with little ambiguity.

"We'll play what and how we want to, and if these stupid varsity men want to know who we are with a FLOURISH, we'll show them who we are with FLOURISH!" We still picture this in our minds as a very varsity coach-like rallying pep talk.

"THESE STUPID JOCKS WILL NEVER FORGET THIS BAND, OR THIS BAND'S NAME!"

After a break that seemed a bit longer than it should have been, the band returned and the music started up again. But even after the first song, it was clear that they were actually spooling *up* the volume, and starting to act a little crazy. A couple more songs into the set, now at truly dangerous decibel levels, the Two-Man Entertainment Committee started to really worry. The singer was slurring his words at the borderline of incomprehensibility as he leaned over the stage at increasingly dangerous angles.

That whole *flourish* idea was quickly beginning to prove a very, very questionable suggestion. We just didn't have time to stop what we were sure was the coming train wreck.

The band cranked up its fourth song, and immediately exchanged glassy-eyed glances among themselves, as menacing as those silent eye-to-eye signals in a commando unit just before an ambush. Before we knew it, at about 10:40, the lead singer began jumping up and down like a crazed madman, shouting at the top of his impossibly magnified voice:

"HEY, VARSITY MEN! YOU HAVE BEEN LISTENING TO THE MUSIC OF *THE SCREAMING ORGASMS!* YOU IDIOT JOCKS, NEVER FORGET US, *THE SCREAMING ORGASMS!*"

Good God!

The name of this band was the *SCREAMING ORGASMS?*

And the Two-Man Entertainment Committee had completely overlooked this little detail!

Well, the band was right about one thing. The Two-Man Entertainment Committee was not likely to forget them, nor would almost anyone else within a thirty-mile radius, as amps started blowing up, the drummer began smashing his drums into smithereens and the three sidemen jumped into the crowd, smashing their guitars on the lip of the short one-foot stage while wildly gyrating in a kind of intoxicated stupor, terrifying everyone on the floor. But mostly terrifying Coach.

They say that after a disaster, people often suffer from something called hysterical or traumatic amnesia, unable to remember things clearly, or even at all, because the brain simply can't cope. The Two-Man Entertainment Committee fit that bill, and we were certain our coping days were over. What we do remember is disjointed and even inconsistent, but seems to follow a general pattern. All I could think about were the lucky varsity guys who had left early and would likely be spared any connection with this fiasco. There is some agreement that Coach, who had been a very fleet-footed Little All-American tight end in college, sprinted for the lead singer, pulling along several date-less linemen with him. The three sidemen went down, each under a huge tackle, and the coach collared the lead singer, pinning him against the cafeteria wall. Some say that even the smallest varsity man there, the equipment manager on the soccer team, rushed up on the stage and clocked the drummer with a hard right, permanently quashing the idea that equipment managers shouldn't really get their varsity letters. Good for him, if the story is true.

It all settled down pretty quickly. Coach turned the lead singer over to someone else, told the tacklers to ease up, and sent for the Two-Man Entertainment Committee.

"You two idiots found these Screaming *ORGANISMS* at the Miss Beard's School for Girls?"

"ORGANISMS!"

Coach had not grasped, it appeared, the most scandalous part of the disaster, the band's actual name. I mean, *orgasm* was one of those words that Coach couldn't even use in our Senior Health class.

All we could do was nod, and lower our heads in the universal sign for total surrender. I don't know what semaphore we would have had to employ if Coach had caught the band's real name. Maybe the one for self-immolation.

Anyway, the dance was over, obviously. The Two-Man Entertainment Committee still had a lot of explaining to do, mostly the following week in fun places like the principal's office. In a great move, bullshit-wise, we both quickly agreed with Coach's idea that a list of "questionable entertainment" be developed. He said he would make sure the very first band on the list would be the "*Screaming Organisms*," and we again nodded in enthusiastic agreement.

Things like this are always more fun for the kids than the adults-in-charge, and the story of the great Varsity Club Dance Disaster soon took its place among the legendary misadventures of the Short Hills youth. A couple of the usually date-less linemen told the guys in the club that all in all it was the best three-quarters of a date they had ever had. One, an underclassman we barely knew who had brought an attractive date we didn't know at all and had stayed for the chaos, actually told us that his date said it was the *greatest night of her life*.

Well, at least *someone* appreciated the hard work of the Two-Man Entertainment Committee. We figured she was an adrenalin junkie, and we soon decided to spread the rumor that she was a Miss Beard Girl.

It only seemed fitting, after all.

As this disaster slid into the history books, it soon became known around school as *"A Night to Remember,"* lifting the title from the book by Mr. Walter Lord. Our dance was the first varsity production to earn a theme name, albeit posthumously. Probably the last.

Mr. Lord describes in harrowing detail the sinking of the *Titanic*. That doomed ship—Rob's grandmother survived the sinking as a young girl—slipped below the cold North Atlantic that tragic April night in 1912, just two hours and forty minutes after striking an iceberg. This was exactly the same amount of time it took for this legendary Varsity Club Dance to go down too. But no one would ever confuse the brave, doomed musicians who rode *Titanic* to their cold grave with the disgraced band that sunk our dance decades later.

Yes, Coach would have liked *that* band.

And there is no evidence whatsoever to support the wild rumor attached to this story that *The Screaming Orgasms* actually made a follow-up appearance at our school, never having been properly identified on Coach's no-fly list.

THE CAMDEN KID

By now, you may have guessed a few important things about our youth. Most important was this: despite all our frolics, detours, and misadventures, we were at heart good boys, if not model citizens. But our faults were many.

We were certainly not "thinking globally," nor were we thinking much about the years ahead. Usually, in fact, the boys in our merry band were barely thinking about the *minutes* ahead.

Most of us had rarely been anywhere terribly sophisticated. Maybe a few of us had been early exiles to summer camp, but that would hardly qualify. A trip to Roy's Hobby Shop in the town of Summit, right next door, was a big deal.

This gentle remove from most things serious in the world outside was broken only by a very few things.

The Korean War perhaps should have shaken us up, but it went largely unnoticed by young boys of the time. About all we knew was Ted Williams had flown jets in Korea, but this fact was learned from the back of his baseball card. We all remember something called "duck and cover drills," our school's defense against a Soviet thermonuclear attack on New York City, about seventeen miles away as the neutrons fly. Fortunately, we really didn't realize the utter futility of the whole thing, and we just thought folding our bodies under our desks a fun little break from the usual school day routine. This breezy approach to matters atomic would all change, of course, in a very few years. At the time of the 1962 Cuban missile crisis—the day before the critical blockade showdown, I think—the *New York Times* published a front-page map showing the predicted effects of a nuclear strike on the city and surrounding suburbs, in easy-to-understand concentric circles. We were toast, well within the inner circle of death, and no one did their homework that October night.

There was, however, one important exception to all this benign remove—something called the "field trip." This was a clever invention deployed to introduce us to a taste of the real world, and we could count on a few of these each year throughout our days at the Glenwood School. These field trips were carefully scripted excursions, parceled out in short and measured doses, as the Board of Education clearly didn't want us to see *too much* of the real world yet. We were still in our bubble, and didn't know that much of the rest of the world, even then, was a mess.

So field trips were carefully vetted, and intended to show us a kind of "world lite." No trips to the inner cities of Jersey City or Newark, although those would have involved minimal planning— just a quick drive down Springfield Avenue, and we could have been back right after lunch. (Kids today go to Honduras to rebuild dams, so go figure.) Our Boy Scout leaders did once bring a bit of Newark to us—a broken-down former professional boxer to give us boxing lessons. Pushing forty, he showed up at a troop meeting one evening in boxing shorts and a fabulous bright red boxing robe—which in large gold letters told us he was "Solly"—and he smelled of whiskey. We loved it. We quickly figured he was at least half whiskey-drunk, and maybe a little more punch-drunk than that. And his name may not even have been Solly, as we usually screwed up names like we screwed up everything else, and I may be mixing his name up with Solly Hemus, a second baseman then playing for the Phillies. But his demonstration was a big hit—even if he lost his balance on a few upper jabs, and his rope-skipping was a little iffy—and we learned that night to call him a pugilist, a little touch that seemed to please him enormously. The leaders apparently were willing to overlook most of his flaws, and he was signed up on the spot to teach scouts the finer points of the boxing game, although I don't think there was a "merit badge" as part of the deal. About a dozen of us enjoyed Tuesday evenings with our own, and usually sober, pugilist, perfecting upper jabs and the curiously interesting art of skipping rope, a staple of training. We met in the Fellowhip Hall of Christ

Church, and "Duke" Ellington became his best student. But the elders whisked this poor man away a couple of months later, before The Duke grew too attached to him. As I said, everyone wanted to keep us safely in the bubble, and not much else was ever imported from the real world.

We went, instead, on field trips to tame places like museums, or maybe a dairy or animal farm in Southern Monmouth County. No demonstrations of artificial insemination, please.

At the management level, there seemed to be a general belief that these excursions should be educational, the sights not unduly alarming and the "takeaways" of some benefit to our development.

Many of us, on the other hand, returned from these trips with no measurable increase in knowledge, and we were often quite disturbed by what we had seen, or more likely, what we had done. Solly had been a better bet, as at least I mastered a mean left jab. The only takeaways from the field trips I can remember were the terse little notes I was often instructed to give to my parents upon my return to home base, something Solly would never have done.

We went on dozens of field trips, sometimes in a regular yellow school bus, and sometimes in a fancier charter bus with real seats, and sometimes a bathroom. The charter bus trips were big deals, and the best was our trip to some bizarre museum in Philadelphia, in fifth grade. There may have been more to it than I remember—which was mostly a giant model of the human heart. A static model, it was huge—large enough for kids to walk through. It didn't beat, thank God, no fake blood pumping through it as we all walked around, in and through it. The whole thing was scary enough, even at perpetual rest. A kind of living heart would have been terrifying, at least for me, and I would likely have spent the rest of my days hearing strange sounds from my own chest that didn't match the well-working Philadelphia model. I wasn't keen on learning too much about any part of our bodies, as I figured it was just more stuff to worry about, like those disturbing concentric atomic attack circles.

I was buddied up with either Suds Estes or Spike Hughes. I think Estes. He was more like a brother, actually, and would become my best friend and remains so today. As much as we goofed on each other, in Philadelphia that day he kindly talked me through my aversion to all things body, and off we went on a rather dizzying frolic through the various chambers of the heart. It was so much fun, we returned to the model after eating our lunches, which had been carefully and lovingly made by our moms and brought along.

Instructional signs along the model experience explained how the heart works: the muscular ventricular chambers propel blood out of the heart and the two atria—left and right—hold the blood returning to the heart, and *just at the right moment,* they empty into the right and left ventricles. All about timing, it seems.

We couldn't really slide down, crawl into, or play with things like the model mitral or aortic valves, like you can do on the playground equipment at most McDonald's today. It was more like a trip through the Guggenheim Museum, where we also once visited and walked round and round the perimeter, and couldn't play with anything there either.

On second thought, maybe the Philadelphia Heart was not as well planned out as the Guggenheim.

You see, some other kid, with a little tag on his shirt telling everyone his name and that *his* class field trip originated in Camden, found the whole vertiginous experience simply too much. After chowing down on *his* mom's homemade sandwich he *promptly ralphed*—AT JUST THE RIGHT MOMENT—emptying his lunch into the left ventricle of the Philadelphia heart!

Yep, it's all about timing. Maybe someone should have posted a warning to wait at least an hour after eating before entering the heart, like around town swimming pools.

Fabulous!

That kid from Camden made the whole trip worthwhile.

Neither Estes nor Hughes claims any memory of this. Perhaps they were in a different chamber of the heart at the time, or had broken away entirely in search of the Bowman Baseball Card Company, which we knew was located in Philadelphia. They have never come clean. In any case, our little brains back then had room for only one big thing surrounding any experience. Naturally, whatever important or worthwhile educational ideas learned at the start of the journey through the Philadelphia Heart were quickly displaced to make room for the clearly bigger event—the ralphing kid from Camden.

That night at supper I had a little explaining to do, having earned once again one of those awkward notes, to be delivered to my parents. You see, on the bus back home, my teacher had asked me what I learned on the trip. So I said that stupid kids from Camden eat tuna fish for lunch. Like I said, only one thing per trip would stick, and I wasn't trying to be a smartass.

THE GREAT RIPPLE TANK DISASTER

If you've seen John Hodgman, you've seen Johnny Weir. John Hodgman is a comedian who became very popular on the Daily Show, and on the Apple "Get a Mac" TV commercials, and who has written extensively on the history of hobos. Although he is about two generations behind Johnny Weir, he is the spitting image. His voice is the same, as well as his facial expression, which displays a constant faint smile, as though he's thinking something funny but trying to be serious.

Johnny Weir was my physics teacher senior year at Millburn High School. He was a good teacher and a good person who never lost his temper, which is why I've always felt so bad about what we did to him.

This was the only school adult to whom we referred by his first name. When addressing him directly, it was "Mr. Weir," but for some reason, we felt entitled, when talking amongst ourselves, to refer to him as "Johnny." My recollection is that we had inherited this right from the students who preceded us. We meant no disrespect. In fact, we really liked him a lot. To us, he was a ready source of humor.

I just didn't quite get physics. Part of it was the method of testing. Everything was multiple choice. The answer was either (a), (b), (c), (d), or (e). There was no in-between. One of the reasons I think I've done okay as a lawyer is that my brain doesn't work in that black-or-white way. Sometimes I see things in shades, and after asking a few questions, the answer may change. I tried this methodology out in physics, but it didn't pay off. Whoever wrote the tests (and it wasn't Johnny, because they were preprinted) must have thought only in cubby holes. In grading, Johnny obviously didn't pay attention when I wrote things in the margin, such as "It depends on ___," or "(b) if ___, but (c) if ___," which worked quite well during the two full days of essays when I took the bar exam in 1971 (the year John Hodgman was born). If, in the eyes of the physics test writer, the answer was (d), you got blanked on that question if you put down anything else.

There was one curious thing, though, about these tests. The writer must have loved symmetry, because it turned out that if you used the same letter for every answer (in other words, if you filled in (c) for all 30 or so questions), you would get a C for a grade. Bobby (The Duke) Ellington figured this out when he missed the first test, came in the next day, hadn't studied, was sent to the back of the room to take the test, handed it in two minutes later having answered every question with choice (c), and got a C. From then on, he would be "sick" on every test day, arrive the next day, and get a two-minute C. Johnny always turned red when this happened. The Duke always had a Cheshire cat grin. We all came to expect this. I never missed a class, studied my ass off, devoted fifty-five minutes to every test, and didn't do a whole lot better than The Duke.

There was a tradition at MHS that the two seniors with the highest cumulative grades over the past three years would carry the flags at the beginning of assemblies (during the Pledge of Allegiance) and then, at the end of the assembly, march first out of the auditorium and stand opposite the main doors in the hallway until everyone had exited and headed off to their next classes. Maybe this tradition was limited to the boys, since there were two boys and two girls all of whom up till then had straight A's. Anyway, for the 1963-64 school year, the flag bearers were Bob deVeer and me. The girls with straight A's up to that point were deVeer's girlfriend, Laura Calhoun, and Donna Cross, who was not my girlfriend but was a very nice person.

Much of our physics class was taught through experiments, and Johnny was genuinely excited about all of them. He loved to tell us about them in advance. He knew we could learn more if we appreciated what we were doing. He wanted us to genuinely enjoy the class.

A ripple tank is a large flat pan with raised sides and several pieces of attendant apparatus that, together (and used properly) helps to teach fluid mechanics (in particular, circular waves, plane waves, refraction, diffraction, and so on). We didn't know what any of this meant, although we did have some grasp of the basics, i.e., (a) if you drop a stone in a pond, the waves go out in concentric circles; (b) if you twirl your finger around in a circle, you create a whirlpool; and (c) if you push water away, the nearby water moves away with it, and then, if it hits a barrier, it bounces back. But we knew all this from our childhood bathtub days. We also knew that you could skip a rock on calm water and ride waves in the ocean if you got in the right position. What we didn't know (and couldn't, at the age of seventeen, figure out) was how anyone would measure any of these phenomena or, more importantly, why. We were about to find out the *how*; the *why* never quite sank in.

By the way, instinctively, we also knew to be careful when carrying any container filled with liquid, because we might spill it. Remembering this a few weeks later might have come in handy.

During one of the classes early in the semester, Johnny Weir made a little speech to us that went sort of like this: "In a couple of weeks, we're going to have a really interesting experiment using what is known as a 'ripple tank.' I'll explain more soon. But I wanted to warn you now about something important. We will be filling the ripple tanks with water. When we're done with the experiment, the only way to empty the tank is to siphon it into a bucket, using a rubber tube. It will take five to seven minutes to siphon your tank before you can pick it up—totally empty—and carry it across the room, where you'll be stacking it with the other empty tanks next to the sink. So you have to finish your experiments in plenty of time to do this. Don't ever, *ever* try to carry a full ripple tank across the room. You can't do it. It's impossible. *Impossible!* Can't be done. Ever. So don't even think about it. I just want to be sure there's never any misunderstanding about that aspect of this really fun experiment." He was trying to be serious, but you could tell he was enjoying this lecture, picturing what might happen if anyone were stupid enough to try to carry a full tank. He was looking out at a bunch of blank stares.

A couple of weeks later, right after finishing an experiment on what happens when you freeze rubber, Johnny launched into a reprise of his warning about the ripple tanks, which he said would arrive in a couple of weeks. "Remember, you *must* siphon. Do not try to pick these up until they are totally empty. Promise me you will not even try." The Duke missed that two-minute speech because he was in the back of the room getting a C on the test from the day before. But his missing the speech had no effect on the disaster to come. That was purely deVeer and me.

At least two more times, Johnny warned us about the ripple tank experiment. For some reason, the idea of spilling water warranted more face time than the dangers of spilling acid, or getting electrocuted—both of which should have been real concerns with this crowd.

Looking back, I've often wondered how easy it would have been to invent a ripple tank with a screw-in plug that could be removed to empty the tank. We had already sent men into space and were only five years from the first moonwalk, so this emptying mechanism should not have been too hard to figure out. If you look on the Internet, you'll see that today ripple tanks even come on stands with oscillating paddles and cameras attached. I don't see any plugs, but I'll bet they're there. Our tanks were just large rectangular slabs we placed on tables. They were about one-and-a-half by three feet, and had walls about an inch high. You filled them with water by pouring it in with a watering can or jar. Perhaps the act of siphoning itself was part of the lesson in fluid mechanics. If you stick a rubber hose in a container of fluid (water, gasoline, whatever) and suck on it until just before the fluid enters your mouth, and even if you drape the tube over the higher lip of the container, yet if you angle it down over the side, the water will drain down and out.

I don't remember whether our physics class was always right before assembly period. I think it was not, because otherwise part of this story wouldn't fit. There must have been a slight scheduling change that day that placed our physics class just before the assembly.

I also don't remember if we always had the same experiment partners in physics class, or if we mixed and matched. Sometimes we may have been in threesomes. At least on the day in question, my experiment partner was Bob deVeer.

So deVeer and I launched into our ripple tank experiments, measuring waves, whirlpools, and concentric circles, and dutifully recording the results in some kind of journal, to be prettied up later with notes, charts, and graphs. I'm not sure whether we were slow in our experiments, just got so interested that we lost track of time, or were fooling around too much. I do recall that several times, we looked up at the clock, remembering that we would need to wind up early, put on our ties, and bolt for the auditorium to get in place with the flags before any of the classes let out.

It got to be about seven minutes before the bell, but we had only two minutes before we had to leave for the auditorium. We didn't have the five to seven minutes Johnny had insisted we reserve to siphon the ripple tanks. Others in the class, like Lynn Stottlemeyer, were beginning to siphon. When we pulled out the siphon hoses, we were already in a losing proposition. We got that picture after about thirty seconds. So we did the only thing we could do. We carefully nudged the ripple tank to the edge of our lab table, which was, unfortunately, on the other side of the room from the sink. Even this slight movement caused some spillage. (My socks would remain wet throughout the next hour.)

Then we did the unthinkable. We slowly lifted the ripple tank, each of us holding one end. No one saw us at first, and we looked at each other with approval. We thought, *We can do this*. We took a step. A ripple ensued. We compensated by lifting one end. This caused a larger counter-ripple, which we fixed by creating yet a larger one, and so on. By this time, a silence had grown over the room which, for some reason, Johnny didn't seem to perceive. Everyone froze. The only movement was Johnny (with his back to us) cleaning something in the large metal sink, and deVeer and I taking our third set of steps, which resulted in higher waves and more compensation. There were at least ten steps to go on our precarious and doomed trek toward the sink.

It all went by so quickly that it's hard to recall the details. But I think I remember the following: (a) a strong look of disapproval from

Lynn Stottlemeyer, who stopped siphoning; (b) The Duke laughing and siphoning at the same time, which caused him to breathe in water, which in turn exited in a stream through his nose (which fit the theme of fluid mechanics but no one took the time to measure); and (c) hearing, simultaneously, someone yelling "Don't do it," someone yelling "Bonzai," and someone else saying something like "You guys are so screwed."

Picture in your mind the instant when Gertie and E.T. first saw each other in the closet. That was the look on Johnny Weir's face as he heard the shuffling of feet, turned from the sink and saw our panicked expressions about four feet away, juggling, and at a frenetic pace, a teeter-tottering ripple tank looking more like a pinwheel, with several gallons of by then uncontained water headed right for his head.

Johnny didn't actually fall into the sink when we reached him, because it was too high and his center of gravity was too low. Had the lip of the sink been a few inches lower, he would have been sitting in it. But he did get drenched. Other than our socks—from a minute earlier—we didn't get a drop on us, nor did we witness the aftermath, which involved the school custodian. In unison, we gave a hurried, "We're so sorry, but we've got to go."

Now, I can't remember whether Johnny knew why we had to go. I would think he did because we probably needed permission to leave early for the assembly. But what makes me think he didn't know, or that it hadn't sunk in, was the look in his eyes when, about an hour later, he filed out of the auditorium and saw the two of us standing there in the hallway, with our ties on, holding the flags. I could read his mind while he was processing this data point: "These two imbeciles couldn't follow a simple instruction that I repeated at least four times. They almost killed me, and my pockets are still filled with water. And yet they're at the top of their class?"

Bob deVeer (who was smarter than I was anyway), got an A in physics. I got a B. I've always considered it to be a charity B, because I probably deserved an L.

Since both Donna Cross and I got one B that semester, we became co-salutatorians, with deVeer and Laura Calhoun as the co-valedictorians. The four of us all made speeches at the football stadium during the graduation ceremony. I don't remember if Johnny Weir was present, but then it's tough to remember that level of detail after half a century.

SHIT, WE FORGOT THE EGGS

I was in Millburn Junior High School for four years. Our grade school, Glenwood, was out of room and kicked the sixth graders into the junior high, with the real junior high kids in grades seven through nine. Millburn High School was grades ten through twelve.

Starting in seventh grade, we all had an "activity" class, packed in with our academic courses. I took Mechanical Drawing in seventh grade, Wood Shop in eighth grade, and, of all things, Chefs' Club in ninth grade. Chefs' Club was not Home Ec. It was cooking for guys. The girls had Home Ec, and some were serious about it. The Chefs' Club guys were a joke.

In retrospect, I'm glad I took Mechanical Drawing, because it helped me later when I became a part-time draftsman. Wood Shop I didn't much need, because I was "raised" during summers and vacations by a group of European cabinet-makers. Now, I wish that when I got to high school, I had taken Auto Mechanics, because the only particular skill I have with cars is parallel parking.

So I took Chefs' Club in ninth grade. My partners were Terry O'Brien and Bobby ("The Duke") Ellington. We weren't bad people, but we were bad at cooking, and totally irresponsible. The Duke, though, was particularly out of control.

On the last class of the year, we were supposed to be making coffee cake. We screwed around for most of the hour, and much of the time were cleaning stuff up, because we had made such a mess. There was flour everywhere, including in our hair, up our noses, and in our pants cuffs. It was getting close to the bell, and we had to line the waste can and finish wiping the counter. We never even got to sample our own coffee cake. One reason for that, in addition to

192

being in a hurry, was that Terry looked over and said, "Shit, we forgot the eggs." There they were. All three of them. Still sitting on the counter, not even cracked.

To this day, that coffee cake is being used as a ball-peen hammer at the Millburn Junior High School.

Anyway, we needed to line the waste can. This might seem like a routine exercise, except that with The Duke, nothing was routine. He had a plan that involved the cooking teacher, Mrs. Kellerman. He sent me into the closet where the newspapers were piled up, and he engaged the sweet Mrs. K. in conversation near the closet door. In a pre-planned move, I exited the closet in a rush, opening the door real hard. The Duke put his foot down solid so the door would bang into it, making a loud noise, and he pretended to be hit in the face. He screamed and fell to the floor. This alone would have been sort of funny in context, but, for reasons no one could explain, The Duke had developed the skill of turning his eyelids inside out. After feigning being smashed in the face, and on the way down, he performed this trick with his eyelids. He rolled face up on the floor as though he were dead, with his eyes open—except you could see only half of his eyeballs, because his inside-out eyelids were folded on top of them. Mrs. Kellerman passed out on top of The Duke, and we had to use about a pint of water to revive her, before running out the door to get to English, where we were continuing to learn to diagram sentences.

We didn't see much of Mrs. Kellerman after that and suspect she spent much of her time in therapy.

I can't remember which year in high school (perhaps senior year) I took Chefs' Club again. I have no recollection of how good we were with eggs, but I do remember that my partners and I were as irresponsible as my ninth grade group. My teammates were Jay Schwartz and Bob Kimmke. Both were worthless. While I had the advantage of having trained with Mrs. Kellerman, Terry, and The Duke, these two guys were novices, and it showed.

They say that cooking is an art, and baking is a science. Although baked Alaska has the word "baked" in it, I'm not sure if it qualifies as real baking. Regardless, in our case, the scientific experiment went bad. We were the first, and hopefully the last, cooking team to ever blow up a baked Alaska.

If you enter Millburn High School through the main entrance, go up to the first hallway, take a right, enter room 112 (right across from what was Mr. Eikenberry's math room), take five steps, then look up, you will still, to this day, see the remains of a baked Alaska stuck to the popcorn-type ceiling. After half a century, you may have to squint to see it, but it's there.

GOT A TIP?

The plasma membrane is an important biological structure which separates what's inside a living cell from its external environment. It is semi-permeable, and seems to be a very good idea.

Something like that existed in our high school.

Our teachers and coaches were inclined, and probably encouraged, to limit off-the-clock contact with students, generally keeping their "other" lives hidden from view. This, too, was a good idea. But occasionally we would bump into a teacher outside the bubble, and these meetings were awkward, even weird. And sometimes these encounters could be very interesting, like an out-of-body experience, but without leaving New Jersey.

This was certainly the case for Suds Estes, who breached that membrane late in the spring of our junior year in a chance meeting with one of our favorite teachers. Let's call him "Coach Lou."

A popular junior varsity baseball and soccer coach, Coach Lou carried a few extra pounds, as well as a permanent five-o'clock shadow, like Richard Nixon. He had been a steady catcher on his college baseball team, and Coach reminded us of another of our favorite catchers, Harry Dominic Chiti, a journeyman major leaguer who had played for a while on the Kansas City Athletics, although we were never sure if the Athletics were from Kansas City, Kansas, or Kansas City, Missouri. Both men were strong-armed, quick with a bullet throw to second base, of unfailing good cheer, and looked to be a bit older than their late-thirties. Curiously, neither could ever find a baseball hat that fit.

Coach Lou also carried extra duty as the school's "driver education instructor." He would daily pour himself into the passenger side of our student driver car—a dark blue four-door Ford without the trimmings—and hand the keys over to some goofy sixteen-year-old who had never even been allowed anywhere near the prized family Buick, except in the back seat where he could fidget and even roam in those days before seatbelts.

But after a few "chalk talk" pointers in class, Coach Lou would hand the keys to some walking-and-soon-to-be-driving student teenage hazard, send the rookie driver two or three times around the school parking lot "just to get the feel," and then unleash him onto the car-choked and legendary highway system of Northern New Jersey, which was—and still is—populated by some of the world's worst drivers, drivers who operated their vehicles as if they were on crack even before crack was invented. This all assumed that the rookie had not creamed into some poor teacher's car on the lot, although the seasoned faculty had long ago figured out the loop, and parked strategically.

We were sure Coach Lou's life insurance premiums topped those of skydivers, and hoped he got hazardous duty pay.

These driver's ed cars did not have seatbelts—these lifesaving restraints were a good idea whose time had not yet come. Nor were the cars outfitted with dual controls, an even better idea whose time had come and had actually been deployed, so we heard, in fleet cars in several nearby towns. But in our town, if the student-driver went crazy or panicked or just wanted to do stupid things to impress some cheerleader or jock in the back seat, the instructor had to lean over, grab the only steering wheel and hope to correct the car's course before it plowed everyone into oblivion—oblivion-by-teenage driver a stupid theme for a bunch of pop songs at the time, like *Teen Angel*. Maybe these songs were written by moonlighting driver's ed teachers.

Of course, we just hoped that Coach's strong arm would come in handy, and he could over-power the idiot student driver in time to avoid pop-song disaster.

One of our buddies, and I'm pretty sure it was "The Duke," wasn't so happy with all this. He insisted that there had to be a "big bean bag balloon-y thing" which would pop out of the dashboard and cushion the collisions we all figured were coming, but we just told him his idea was nuts. "No way," we all said, "Just can't be done."

You know, we always underestimated The Duke.

And, as you have learned, we were mostly idiots, usually missing the boat and remarkably blind to the mid-century promise of automotive innovation. We could, though, tell you any car's make just from its tail-lights, and who sang those oblivion songs.

Coach Lou, on the other hand, was a man grounded in reality, and a man who knew how to read the odds, which were never very good for anyone on a Jersey highway, or for junior varsity misfits either. So he quickly developed a lighter touch—sticking to the roads less traveled—and he would often guide the student driver to a neat little pizza shop not far from the school for what he called "parallel parking instruction." This was curious. Although this route kept us largely out of harm's way, and the pizza joint did have a large and inviting private parking lot, the lot was *head-in parking only*. But everyone played along, and "the Pizza Run" became a rite of passage. It was loved by all, even if nobody learned how to parallel park. But we did learn a great deal about pizza, since Coach Lou turned out to be a True Renaissance Man of New Jersey Pizza. Yes, that man loved his pizza.

Coach Lou also loved playing the trotters down at the Freehold Race Track in Southern New Jersey.

We stumbled upon this exotic fact late in our junior year, but not because Coach Lou steered a group of student-drivers toward the track one day for "extended highway practice." No, this little gem was presented to our gang by Suds Estes, who himself had a little secret. After getting his license that spring—along with a battered old VW for a couple of hundred bucks—Suds would also take his own occasional trip to play the ponies at Monmouth or the trotters at Freehold.

On one of his secretive jaunts in the late spring of our junior year, Suds literally bumped into Coach Lou at a Freehold two-dollar bet window. After that disquieting moment when the student-teacher membrane broke, he did what any seasoned gambler would do:

He asked Coach if he had any "tips."

When teacher meets student in the real world, all the rules seem to change. But our man Suds had an innocent charm, and could ask just about anything of anybody with limited downside risk. Really, he could bullshit with the best of them, even at a racetrack. So with this simple but engaging opening, Suds had pierced that unseen wall separating student and teacher, and these two now entered into a kind of undocumented partnership. They were undercapitalized, of course, but dreaming big.

Yes, these two scallywags were literally off to the races.

And into legend as well, although we think Coach Lou let this story slumber more quietly around the faculty lounge.

With mixed results in the first couple of races, Coach Lou kept the dream alive with his talk of the big payout on the late afternoon exacta. In telling the tale, Suds had to bring most of us along slowly with the track lingo, and the exacta was one of those exotic bets which required you to pick the exact one-two finish to win. A highlight of any day at the races, a winning exacta could pay handsomely. It all sounded impossibly cool, particularly to the uninitiated. Which was just about every one of us, except Suds.

The only secret trips most of us had been taking since the rest of us got our driver's licenses were over a monster bridge linking the great state of New Jersey to the largely unheralded land of Staten Island. Staten Island was a neat place for lots of reasons, but the only one of any real interest to us at the time was the relaxed view a couple of saloons over there took of the New York drinking age, a very accommodating eighteen. When asked if we seventeen-year-olds could show a license proving we could drink, we usually just pointed outside through a smoky saloon window to the battered yellow New Jersey license *plate* on one of our cars, a gesture which seemed to pass muster. But most of the time no one even asked, and we learned a little bit about our neighboring state, and lots about beer.

Although we thought of ourselves as quite worldly, "real men" on the Island, none of our new saloon buddies ever talked about horse-racing, although most of them looked like they had surely lost a few bets somewhere along the line. And none of our goofy school field trips had deposited us anywhere near a horse track or, for that matter, any other place associated with the gambling arts, slow horses, fast women, or cheap whiskey, which eliminated Atlantic City from contention for the senior trip, and that would prove to be a great disappointment. So Suds had to bring us along slowly in sharing his track adventure.

Here's how it went.

Back at the track that spring day in our junior year, the ponies were indeed running pretty well for the new partnership. Figuring Coach Lou—he was an adult, after all, and a coach—knew what he was doing, Suds was soon following his new mentor's betting strategies and choices, with modest shared success.

That's what partners do, and they were having a good time doing it.

The weather was fine—one of those magic Jersey spring days that trick you into forgetting about the killer Jersey humidity soon to come—and the crowd spirited. Our partners had even found a very nice pizza vendor, somewhere under the grandstand, who met, if just barely, the high standards developed on the Pizza Run. Suds still swears Coach Lou wouldn't buy him a beer but, as I said, he had a charm that could disarm an army. So the no beer thing is probably bullshit. I mean, we had nicknamed him "Suds" a year earlier, and I doubt he would have tolerated an afternoon at the track without a brew.

Coach Lou was biding his time until the big race, when he could bet his exacta and hope for a huge payout. And that's exactly what the partners did. Coach studied the racing form, cross-checking it against the dailies in the *Atlantic City Courier,* or maybe the *New York Post.* And Suds studied Coach.

This was all taking a little longer than it should have, and Suds, a very cool customer and usually unflappable, was getting worried that they could miss the bet.

"Coach," our junior partner gently pushed, "What're we gonna do?"

"We're gonna clean up, that's what we're gonna do," Coach Lou boomed with an unwavering confidence, folding up all the racing sheets and dailies covered with his notes, which by then looked as cluttered, and even magical, as a Persian cuneiform tablet, cuneiform writing having been one of the few things any of us remembered from sixth grade, other than the eight weeks we seemed to spend on Eli Whitney's invention of the cotton gin.

"This is the one we've been waiting for. I'm putting fifty dollars on number 5, 'Model Man,' to win, and ten dollars on an exacta—5-3. The horse is showing as a thirty-to-one long shot, which will give us a huge payout."

"I'm in, Coach."

This guy's a *genius,* our young gambler thought, and he's got guts going with this long shot. And we were talking some big bucks here, certainly for Suds and probably for Coach with his junior varsity coach pay, even with the little extra bump from the driver's ed gig.

So our partners raced to the betting windows. Coach went with his fifty dollars on Model Man to win and a ten dollar 5-3 exacta. Suds emptied his pockets for a more modest five on the horse, and just a two-dollar 5-3 exacta, placing his bets with maybe a minute to spare.

Our hopeful partners quickly made it back to the rails.

And then they were off—the horses, that is, which I believe is how the track announcers phrase it. Some eight magnificent trotters in colorful silks, with the partners tightly focused on Model Man, who had, in the end, gone off as something like a thirty-five-to-one long shot. Suds still claims that Model Man sprinted from the gate to take a ten-length lead at the half-mile pole. By the time this beauty hit the stretch, he was twenty lengths ahead of the field, and then he thundered across the finish line a full ten seconds before the two horses which were neck to neck in a fight for second place.

What a pick! And better yet, one of the two horses in that fight for second place was . . . YES!

Their exacta pick, number 3, "Galloping Gal."

But it was a photo finish, and our partners just stared at each other for what seemed forever.

"Ladies and gentlemen," then boomed the track announcer, "Galloping Gal, horse number 3, is declared the second place winner."

THE EXACTA WAS COMPLETE!

Model Man paid seventy-two dollars to win for a two dollar ticket, and the 5-3 exacta paid *three-hundred twenty dollars for a two dollar ticket!*

Suds figured that Coach's two bets yielded him a payout equal to about four months salary, even if you figured in the driver's ed gig, and Suds' winnings had effectively tripled his entire net worth, even if you figured in the few prized baseball cards he had kept from my flipping and trading clutches a few years earlier, including a very nice 1957 Topps Mantle, and even a slightly battered '56 Harry Chiti wearing another hat that just didn't fit. Suds swears to this day that Coach Lou even wanted to adopt him on the spot, and bring him to the track all summer long as his good luck charm.

"I've never won this stupid exacta before!" Coach shouted to the small crowd which had gathered around them, rustling Suds' hair like a proud father. "Not one damn time."

WHAT?

Suds flinched, in shock.

One member of the gathered crowd asked Coach Lou his "secret," which I understand is bad form, even at a track in New Jersey.

"Pure genius, really," replied the very happy Coach in an unguarded moment. "My old girlfriend lived at 5 Maple Avenue, over in Teaneck. Model Man was horse number 5, so that one seemed a no-brainer," continued Coach, dialing it all down a bit.

NO BRAINER?

What was all that Persian cuneiform writing about?

"And the second horse was just about as easy," Coach went on. "Galloping Gal wore number 3, and that old girlfriend was the youngest of three sisters. Quite a gal, she was."

Coach was a horse-picking genius all right. And with a flourish Coach dropped the last "secret."

"The horses were also wearing my favorite two colors, a nice crimson on the one, a handsome gold on the other. I got a couple of over-stuffed deep-crimson easy chairs back home, with gold trim. That did it for me. I just knew I had a big winner."

JUST KNEW?

Coach had won this thing as a *lover* and a *decorator?* The big bet had been riding on street addresses of lost loves and the color palate of over-stuffed living room chairs?

And then an uncharitable thought crossed Suds' now worldly mind. Maybe this idea of piercing that teacher-student wall wasn't such a good thing after all, and maybe some things *should* be left a mystery.

The crowd soon grew. Everyone loves a winner, and one tired guy, who had joined in the fun and looked like he was getting ready to ask Coach for a loan, piped up, "You're a lucky guy, you know?"

"LUCKY?" roared Coach, again dialing it up. "You think I'm *lucky?* I've been coming down to this track for years. I'm nowhere near breaking even. And almost twenty years of driving around as a driver's ed teacher with a carload of idiot teenagers. This is a lucky guy?"

Turning to the wide-eyed Mr. Estes, he dialed it down. "These Jersey highways, well, you know, maybe I am a little lucky at that . . ."

The tired guy backed off, as it was clear Coach wasn't lending out money today.

By the time the partnership collected their winnings, the formula for the win seemed pretty unimportant, although Suds was sure by then that he would challenge any move by Coach toward adoption.

Screw his damn addresses and colors, was what Suds was thinking as they continued their celebration at a roadhouse just a few miles from the track. But this is what he actually said:

"Got any tips, *here,* Coach?"

Yes, Suds could sometimes play dangerously close to the edge. But Coach missed the gentle jab, his head still swimming in the glory of the day, the quiet memory of a lost love and maybe a martini or two. Or perhaps he was just a really good guy, like most of the adults we would know throughout our young lives, and had figured it all out.

"Go for the cowboy-cut sirloin."

This Coach Lou said with a broad smile, and maybe, although Suds to this day isn't sure, with a wink, which seemed to say just how funny and wonderful and crazy and unpredictable life can be, all mixed up with favorite colors and lost loves and maybe even the disappointments of a life lived in the shadows of varsity coaches and stuck in a driver's ed car facing daily near-death experiences in Northern New Jersey, but also with the promise of some very, very good days too, when we all beat the odds.

SUDS CUTS IT CLOSE

Economics has been called the "dismal science." And that may be the case if you are studying the global recessionary impact of a sovereign debt crisis during the Panic of 1890 at the London School of Economics, or trying to balance the federal budget, or maybe just your own checkbook. But not for a couple of us who met economics for the first time in a senior high school class, taught by our backfield football coach. Let's call him Coach Artie.

Only two or three years out of a local college, he had been a scrappy and fleet-footed halfback and a varsity tennis player. He joined our high school football staff our sophomore year, and took over the tennis program our junior year. Single, impossibly handsome, and always dressed in a cool collegiate-casual kind of way, he would often turn up at school functions with a date just a few years older than we were. These dates rarely made more than one or two repeat appearances, although one young lady had a good run our senior year, showing up for tennis practice the entire season and at our graduation. The tennis team really liked her, and took their practices up a notch when she visited. Maybe Coach later married her. We don't know, but we hope so.

Yes, Coach lived cool, and everyone loved him, and we just didn't think of him as a *real* adult.

Maybe that was the problem. Not for us, but for whoever decided that the handsome new guy on the block was having way too much fun and should therefore be handed the job of teaching economics. And not just any economics section, but economics for the less-motivated among us, the kind of students who were not likely to see an appointment to the Federal Reserve in their future, and maybe not even a job as teller in the local Jersey State Bank & Trust. This was clearly not a choice assignment and seemed by default destined to fall to a rookie.

Suds Estes and I ended up in this class by default too. You see, after clowning our way through three years of French, we landed our senior year in something called "Advanced French," taught by a Madame Something-or-Other. We had heard that she couldn't even speak English.

This was disquieting.

Neither of us was advancing very well in anything, much less a foreign language. So we entered her classroom that September of 1963 on high alert, sensing doom. Gently closing the classroom door on our first day, Madame turned to the class—Suds still swears she looked right at the two of us, sitting in a far corner of the room, which suddenly seemed very small—and said, "*Mes amis, vous ne parlez pas Anglais en ma classe. Rien. Jamais. Comprendez?*"

No English? *Never?*

We were doomed.

Early in our language studies Suds and I had perfected the art of deploying English standbys to fill those many awkward gaps in our French vocabulary—the unknown *le bateau* becoming *la boat,* for example. Or maybe it was *le boat.* We just figured that adding those strange gender-changing "le" and "la" articles, along with a wink just to let everyone know we weren't planning on joining the Foreign Service, or even the French Foreign Legion, would get us through the day. And it usually did, until we arrived in Madame's little slice of all things French.

We had mastered one or two phrases, of course, and within seconds of Madame's challenge, Suds and I decided to use them. We headed for the door, which luckily was not locked, turning only to wish our remaining classmates *"bon chance, et au revoir."* Out we went and directly to our guidance counselor to figure out how we could fill this newly-created gap in our schedules. The only thing open at that time slot was Coach Artie's Economics for Slugs. The guidance counselor didn't exactly call it that, although he did make it clear that this class would not be a hit with any of the colleges on our wish lists, which he had pulled out of some file which always seemed within his reach, wherever we ran into him.

Weird.

Reluctantly assigning us to the class on the spot, the guidance counselor wished *us* good luck this time, and in English, and we left his office.

With little guidance but at least a full class schedule, we happily bounded into Coach's class. He looked very happy to see us, and after our brush with certain academic death over at Advanced French, nothing in his economics class looked anything remotely like "advanced," or even "dismal," to us.

Au contraire.

It was a damned lifeboat.

And not only had we sailed away from those treacherous French shores, in this class Suds and I were positively gifted. Geniuses, really. Everything was taught in our native tongue, the material was basic, and the homework light. And Coach would often engage the two of us—the only football players in the class—in lengthy sidebar sports talk while most of the class worked on assignments actually connected to the study of economics. We didn't really learn much about economics, but we did learn a lot about football and what is was like being a cool single guy and dating really great-looking girls and being in the real world. We both took economics again in college—where we were to learn what that "dismal science" thing was really all about. It was too bad not all economics classes could be like Coach Artie's Economics for Slugs.

Our detour with Coach did give us two adventures, though, both strangely connected.

At the end of our enjoyable senior year in Coach's class, we faced a final exam. By that time, both Suds and I had received college acceptances, much to the relief of our guidance counselor and, by rumor, to the surprise of Madame Something-or-Other, who caught us in the hall one day and instead of ratting us out said something in French, which we thought was congratulatory, but we have never really been sure. Anyway, we had read the fine print on our college letters, that thing about final admission hinging on satisfactory final grades. But like graduating seniors everywhere, we kind of blew that off, so we were quite relaxed about our final exams that spring.

Whenever any of us chose the relaxed standard, trouble usually ensued. And no one could do *relaxed* better than our man Suds.

Our economics exam was scheduled for an afternoon slot, beginning at one o'clock sharp. We woke to a spectacular early June Tuesday—not a cloud in the sky, high in the low eighties, and just the kind of day you would want to go down the Shore. But we couldn't, of course, what with that exam looming on the mid-day horizon. But Suds figured it was still a good morning to find at least a little sun, and maybe a swim at the local town pool which had just opened for the summer. I took a pass on the sun-and-swim, deciding a little more reading about economics would be a good idea, and even a few of those old football plays, just in case Coach was going to have a little fun and slip us a gridiron question or two.

Coach had reminded us to be sure to bring our textbooks to the exam as a kind of admission ticket, so I figured my last minute studying would help me remember that detail too.

I showed up in the exam room a little before 1:00, handed Coach my textbook, and sat down, saving a seat for my buddy. Suds hadn't showed up at 1:00, or 1:10, or even 1:15 when Coach finally had to hand out the exams. It was only an hour exam, so time was ticking, and we were already well into the test. This was more than a little unsettling. But at about 1:40, and down the school driveway just outside the open windows of our exam room, came a distinctive roar. Most of us knew the sound of his car—a beat-up VW bug, with an engine that sounded like a sick lawnmower, relieved that Suds was finally here.

Well, not yet actually taking-the-exam-here, but close.

Relief, however, soon turned to astonishment as we watched him pull smartly into the only available parking place this exam day, the one marked:

RESERVED FOR PRINCIPAL

Yeah, this was Suds at his best: top down on his faithful VW Bug, radio blaring, parked in the alpha space, and a mere twenty-five minutes remaining to finish a one-hour exam.

Some claim they could even smell the Coppertone, and see that his hair was still wet. But this was the truly amazing thing: just as he opened his car door, he hesitated, then *SAT BACK DOWN*. He reached over to his radio and suddenly turned the volume up. The distinctive sounds of the Ronettes singing "Be My Baby" drifted into the classroom.

OH NO, I remember thinking.

We all loved this song that spring—released just months before, it had climbed to number two on the Billboard Top 100—but for Suds it was simply the greatest song ever recorded. He had talked about that song for his funeral, should he cash in early, and certainly at his wedding, whenever that would be. We all vaguely pledged to see the Ronettes in person, someday.

"Be My Baby" is not a long song—two minutes, forty-one seconds—and it's kind of corny. But when your buddy is already late for an exam and parked in the principal's spot, it seems like an eternity. At least it did to those of us who were already comfortably into our exam that day. Bopping away with the top down and the radio volume up, enjoying his song once again to its very last notes, Suds had clearly gone to another happy place that afternoon. And into legend, of course.

We just hoped he had remembered to bring his textbook. Which, when he finally shut the bopping down, turned the radio off and raced into the classroom, he hadn't.

NO BOOK?

Even at warp speed, I knew it was twenty minutes minimum to his house and back to retrieve the book, leaving him about ten minutes to show Coach his stuff on the exam. But as I said, Suds was one cool customer. When Coach Artie said "Get the book" and Suds just kind of grinned, I knew a legend was about to be born.

"No sweat, Coach. It's just around the corner in my locker."

SUDS HAD NOT TAKEN THE BOOK HOME TO STUDY!
"I'll be right back."

Yes, this was a relaxed standard, all right, and I feared the worst, what with that fine print stuff from the colleges and all. And just to seal the legend, he asked Coach how that great girlfriend of his was doing, and "maybe we can all hit a few tennis balls later today." Suds returned as promised in less than a minute, with a textbook that looked almost untouched, as he hadn't taken the book out of his school locker for *months.*

I have always wondered what frolic and detour he might have found on that fifty-second roundtrip to his locker if he had an iPod then, just to plug in a couple more verses.

I have never asked Suds his grade in Coach Artie's class. He must have done a masterful job in about ten minutes, and we both went off to college in the fall as planned, all courses passed and that fine print on our college admissions no longer dangling over our heads.

During college, I always remembered that promise to see the Ronettes in person. It took almost seven years from that June test day, but I finally did. Living at home for a brief period before graduate school, sometime during the summer of 1971, I learned that the Ronettes were playing a gig at a bowling alley bar, not far from home, their days of number one hits behind them. I called Suds, of course, to join me. With a new baby at home, he had to pass. But I could tell he was happy I remembered the pledge.

"Those Ronettes," he said. "They're still the greatest." I know he was thinking about the legend of the Economics for Slugs final exam, and we both laughed.

So on a rainy Friday night a few days later I drove alone to an alarmingly depressing bowling alley bar, somewhere around Wayne, I think, the kind with those awful blue-white lights which made your clothes do strange things—showing all your lint, spotlighting your dandruff—and repainting your teeth as well. I bought a couple of drinks for a young lady who was sitting next to me. She was dressed neck to thigh in a striking silver lamé hot pants thing, and I soon discovered she was about seven feet tall. Those two drinks I bought her were maybe her eleventh and twelfth of the evening, and I soon began to question just what I was doing with my life. But I stayed long enough to hear those Ronettes belt it out, and I can tell you even in their lesser years, in a crummy bowling alley bar in Jersey, they still did one hell of a job with "Be My Baby."

And should you ever give Suds Estes a call on his smart phone, know he will be smiling, as his ring-tone plays "Be My Baby" and probably always will. Yeah, that Suds is a legend, and loyal too.

LESS THAN DIVINE INTERVENTIONS

A boy is the only thing God can use to make a man.

- The Reverend Herbert Cooper,
overheard in our church

THE GREAT COLLECTION PLATE DISASTER

Laird Schoeber was diminutive. But he was a much bigger deal than the rest of us, as we "looked up to him" and unanimously elected him President of the Crucifer's Guild at Christ Church in Short Hills.

The crucifers were in the nature of acolytes, altar boys and such. The word "crucifer" means cross-bearer. There are crucifers used in several Christian churches, including Episcopalian (which we were), Anglican, Lutheran, and Catholic. Today they include girls; back in the early 60s, it was a guy thing. Had girls been involved, there might have been less mischief, and thus less ridicule from the girls toward the guys who so often messed everything up.

After being initiated by memorizing the Apostles Creed, the Nicene Creed, and about six other important pieces of Episcopalian literature, and practicing endless ceremonial duties, we began to take on minor, crucifer-type functions, pretty much bundled into the category of standing around. Eventually, we were made responsible for lighting the candles. This we did with a long brass instrument that looked kind of like a fireplace poker. It had two alternate ends to it: one was a wick, which you lit in the hallway before approaching the altar; the other was a cup that you used at the end of the service to snuff out the candles. All this sounds easy, but back then, it was a mother, because these were real candles, they were up high and far away, and the wicks would get bent. If you couldn't get one lit, you weren't allowed to climb up on the altar and fix the wick, because the congregation was either already seated or filing in, and you were the only part of the show in motion, so everyone was staring at you. When the candle wouldn't light, you had two choices: leave it unlit (which we sometimes did, to the dismay of the minister), or, long distance, try to use the snuffing cup to scoop some wax out of the tip of the candle, or smack the candle so some wax spilled out, so you could lift the wick up just a tad with the edge of the cup and then try to light it. Invariably, when we did this, the wick on the lighting instrument would lose its flame, and we would have to retreat to the hallway and come back in, causing a delay in the opening of the service. Plus sometimes the candles were left in the leaning position during the service. Eventually, we learned to come in early, climb up on the altar, and fix the candlewicks well before the service started.

The candle lighting pole (I don't know if it had a more religious sounding name) was almost as long as Laird was high. Plus, Laird's arms were very short, so there was no way he could reach the altar candles without a stepladder. Accordingly, he had a permanent bye on lighting the candles.

Anyway, after perfecting how to walk in and out, and how to light the candles, we eventually assumed responsibility for carrying the crosses in and out of church during the processional and the recessional. These were meant to be very serious ceremonies. In the small services, there might be only one cross. In the large ones, there would be three. But the sole cross in the smaller services, and the middle cross in the large services, was enormous. It must have been seven feet high (which made it twice as high as Laird), and it probably weighed fifty pounds. Some of the young crucifers couldn't even hold it the right way—elbows out and staring straight ahead. We looked like the guards at Buckingham Palace. No way Laird could carry the big cross, or even the little ones.

Which is why we shouldn't have let him carry the collection plates. I say "we," but remember, Laird was President of the Guild. He was in charge. He did what he wanted to do and gave us our assignments, which he posted on the board in the crucifers' dressing room. He was smart enough not to assign himself candle-lighting or cross-carrying duty.

The other players in the church ceremonies, in addition to the choir, were the ushers. At the time, as with the crucifers, all ushers were men. My father, and many of my friends' fathers (such as Messrs. MacIlroy and Hamilton), were in the mix. Some of them, including my father, doubled as Sunday school teachers. We treated them as poorly as we did our scoutmasters. Such as the time my father stood up in the pew to sing a hymn, and Nils Ohlson, who was sitting behind him, gently moved my father's brand new stiff-brimmed brown businessman's hat directly behind my father, so that when he sat down, he crushed it. It made almost a snapping sound, as though he were sitting on a box of saltines. This was just before a prayer, and I could tell my father was praying for lightning to strike Nils at the earliest possible moment.

Nils' full name was either Nils John Ohlson or John Nils Ohlson. We called him Johnny until he was about fifteen; then it became Nils. My father knew him as Johnny. Young Master Ohlson was also co-responsible with Big Al Schultheis for an incident that took place about a half hour after the hat caper, in which they loosened the screws in the legs of the folding table in the Sunday school room, so that when my father came in and placed his Bible on the table, it collapsed.

When my father was about eighty-one, living in Florida, he and I were going over the old days. My wife Ginger was there. My stepmother Betty was in the other room, although you could tell she was sort of listening, since she was giggling. My father suddenly remembered the hat incident and muttered, "That damn Johnny Olsen. He purposely caused me to squish my brand new hat."

The ushers' duties included getting people seated and then taking up the collection. For full services, there were usually six ushers and six collection plates, all made of heavy brass or copper. Empty, the six plates together weighed almost as much as Laird did.

The collection started with the minister carrying the six empty plates, in a stack, down from the altar, across about thirty feet in front of the choir boxes (which were on both sides of the platform), to a spot where there were two steps leading down to the main part of the church at the congregation level. He would stop at the top of the platform, just in front of the communion rail, and the six ushers would approach him, each taking one empty plate. So far, so good.

The minister was Herb Cooper. He was a big guy. Sometimes we affectionately referred to him as "Fat Herb." He and his wife, Kay, and my parents, were good friends. We occasionally visited them at their second and third homes in Florida and Rhode Island. Eventually Woody Thompson dated their daughter Joannie. One time, Woody was with me in Florida, and we went to visit the Coopers with my parents. Herb offered each of us a beer, even though we were only about sixteen. Some years later, Herb officiated at my first wedding. There was a timing snag, as he and the best man had trouble locating me when the ceremony was about to start, since I was in his study reading a new *Sports Illustrated* article on Roberto Clemente.

Anyway, back in the 60s, a lot of parishioners put coins in the collection plates. I think they had just invented collection envelopes, in which people could insert paper money without anyone being able to see how much. As we got older, and if we were in the church proper and not on duty as crucifers, we would put in a dollar bill. But many people threw in their loose change. Everyone had quarters, but back then, there were a lot of silver half dollars in circulation. With hundreds of people at some services, the plates got real heavy, real fast. When filled, any three of them weighed as much as Laird. In other words, if you put three of them on one end of a seesaw and Laird on the other, the seesaw would reach equipoise.

So the ushers would take the empty collection plates and pass them back and forth across the aisles until the collection hymn ended, then they would come forward, in unison, and present the plates either just before, or just after, the Doxology. I can't remember the exact order.

At the right time, each usher would hand his plate to the crucifer whose job it was to accept the plates and then turn and hand them to Herb for a blessing on the way to the altar. The plates were stacked one on top of another in the outstretched hands of the crucifer.

For reasons I cannot, to this day, explain, Laird appointed himself the collection plate guy on this particular Sunday. The rest of us were off in the wings. Sometimes we would abandon the wings to go outside to throw a football around. But we stayed close this time in order to see how Laird would handle the collection plates. The wait was well worth it.

Each of the six ushers handed a plate to Laird. Remember, there were a lot of half dollars and quarters on these plates. After about twenty seconds, Laird found himself holding six full plates, which, together, weighed much more than he did. He was supposed to turn gently, face Herb and hand him the plates. He sort of did that.

Imagine trying to lift the front end of a station wagon in the air while a friend retrieves a baseball from underneath. You couldn't do it. But somehow Laird, perhaps exponentially strengthened by an adrenalin rush, kept his act together. With a huge bead of sweat on his brow (which we could see from thirty feet away), and his face turning purple, Laird rotated 180-degrees to face Fat Herb, who was two steps up. By this time, Laird was going into muscle spasms and had shrunk by at least another inch. By the look on his face, he was saying to himself, "This is not destined to go well."

If Nils Ohlson, or Johnny Mac, or Big Al Schultheis had had plate duty, there would have been no problem. But in Laird's hands, the bottom of the bottom plate was only about a foot off the lower floor when Herb reached out, but Herb was two steps up and twice Laird's height. Herb's left hand somehow got to the bottom of the bottom plate, but his right hand only made it to the bottom of the next-to-the-bottom plate.

I've watched this over and over in my mind, in slow motion, over the years. It was awful. The corner of the first plate dropped down on top of Herb's left foot, at which time he dropped the other five plates on both of his and Laird's feet. At which time he fell down on top of Laird.

You could see Herb's lips moving as he tumbled down the stairs. Laird reported later that while on the way down, Herb uttered a few words that he probably hadn't said since he was in the Navy, pre-divinity school.

All six plates rolled forward, and all those half dollars and quarters rolled down through the aisles, with dollar bills floating in the air. This was a solemn occasion gone awry. Laird was squished. Little kids got up and started scooping up the money, about two-thirds of which was returned to the plates. This event was the talk of the church—until the great cross disaster and the great mite box disaster.

THE GREAT CROSS DISASTER

We weren't bad people. We were just bad at doing certain things. Such as crucifering. All Episcopal churches have someone carrying at least one cross in and out during the processional and recessional. In some small churches, and if you wanted to, you could carry the cross with one hand, since the wooden pole is the thickness of a pool cue. And during the service, you can post the cross in a receptacle that resembles an umbrella stand.

But not at Christ Church in Short Hills, where the cross we carried in and out was huge. It was tough to carry correctly, even with both hands. It was about seven feet high with a wooden staff as thick as the business end of Ted Kluszewski's bat. Riveted to the top of the staff was a solid brass cross with a heavy round base and the wingspan of an owl. During the service, it had to be secured by a special locking mechanism.

On this particular Sunday, cross duty fell to Jeff Noe. During the processional, he walked in behind Rev. Herb Cooper, carrying the cross, with his left hand gripping the pole at his waist, his right elbow horizontal to the floor, and his right hand next to his chin. Woody Thompson and I were the sidemen, walking with our hands clasped in front of us.

At the end of the processional, Jeff placed the cross in its special spot, which was on the far end of the choir box, on the left, about six feet from the communion rail. In order to keep the cross steady, you would put the bottom of the pole in a little cup bolted to the floor, but would then hold the pole steady against the outside of the choir box with a brass latch that would sling over and clasp around the wooden staff of the cross, to keep it upright. The latch was in turn secured by poking a cotter pin through a hole drilled in each piece of the latch. Jeff did that, piously, as he, and all of us, had done so many times before, without incident. Although none of the parishioners could see the latch, they could see the top half of the pole and cross and thus had faith that the huge device was safely strapped in for the service. The routine was foolproof.

Jeff, Woody, and I had nothing to do for a few minutes, so we went off behind the choir box and into an alcove, out of sight of the congregation. Sometimes during a hiatus like this, we would play a few hands of cards. But I don't think we did on this particular day, because of the events that so quickly followed.

We were only a few feet behind the choir and right under the organ pipes—during a hymn the sound could be deafening. And the first one was. Until it all stopped, as Rev. Herb Cooper got ready for a reading at the top of the stairs, down near the pulpit, about twenty yards away. You've heard the phrase "So quiet you could hear a pin drop"? For a moment, that's how quiet it was; and then that's precisely what we heard—a pin drop. Inexplicably, the pin holding the latch that was holding the cross in place slid free, dropped, made a tiny "clink" and swung free as a bird, with nothing holding the latch together. Only Jeff, Woody, and I noticed this. For us, the world stood still.

The following transpired over the course of about twenty seconds: all three of us started doing the Army crawl (alternating our swinging elbows on the rug) toward the cross, keeping our heads down so none of the parishioners could see us (we were hidden by the back of the choir section). Our style was good, but our speed was poor, particularly since all three of us were crawling down the same narrow hallway and kept getting in each other's way, kind of like the marching band as it clumped together into a brick wall toward the end of the parade in the movie *Animal House*. Woody and I were better crawlers; Jeff was in front of us, and we kept pushing up against his feet. We were all whispering, and there may or may not have been a hushed "Damn it" or two. If only one of us had attempted the rescue, we may have pulled it off. But the clumping doomed us.

We could only imagine what went through the minds of the two or three choir members who were on the far edge of the choir box closest to us as they looked down and saw the three of us fumbling toward the cross. Their unrest may have contributed to the instability of the cross, which, for the past few seconds, and with the cotter pin dangling, had been held erect only by the force of inertia. Even a choir member breathing in the direction of the cross could have freed it. Something did.

Remember, the rest of the choir, and all the parishioners, could see only the top of the cross, but not the loosened latch, or the cotter pin, or us. What they did see, though, at the very end of this twenty-second period, was a single hand coming up over the tip of the choir box, trying, unsuccessfully, to stuff the cotter pin back into its loop. They also saw the cross start to shake, as Jeff's hand fondled the latch. It may have even looked to the congregation as though he were undoing the latch. Actually, within a couple of seconds, that same hand was muffling a "Shit!"

Because the unthinkable happened. Despite our best efforts, the huge staff shook free of its bonds and descended toward the communion rail. Jeff's hand was impotent to stop the catastrophe. The massive cross came down with a *"WHOOSH,"* smashed into the communion rail with a huge, dull *"CLANG,"* bounced about two feet in the air, came down again, and settled on the rail, bent beyond recognition. The lower prong of the cross (the one heading south, riveted to the pole) took the brunt of the crash and was severely dented, but the other three prongs (north, east, and west) were wrapped around the communion rail and each other. The entire mechanism was in the shape of a garden tool with all three points of the cross curved forward in the digging position. Another image that comes to mind is the talons of an osprey.

Jeff was too rattled to do anything but exhibit rattling, so Woody and I, together, and still out of sight of the masses, twisted the pole from the bottom so that the bent prongs of the cross turned upward. We then proceeded to drag it off the rail, across the rug, and back behind the choir box. This event did not go unnoticed by the crowd, although most of them probably did not fully appreciate what they were witnessing.

About twenty minutes after the mishap, Herb, also a little rattled, was serving communion—at the exact spot where the cross smashed into the rail. If the cotter pin had waited until then to wiggle loose, the woman who was taking communion would have been decapitated. We weren't in a position to see the look on her face as she first spotted the large gash in the communion rail which, for several weeks before it was repaired, would cause many parishioners to wonder.

After retrieving the mangled cross, we took it out through the side door, laid it on the huge, flat-topped rock out back where we often sat to tie our shoes after playing football, picked up a medium sized rock and started pounding on the cross as though it were a horse shoe on an anvil. Although the claws straightened out a bit, the cross was, for all intents and purposes, history. Fearing a lynching, we didn't put it back on the stand. We hid ourselves and the cross in the hallway until the end of the service.

Herb wasn't too clear about what had transpired—until the recessional, during which Jeff, who had recovered somewhat but was still shaking, carried the cross down the center aisle with Woody and me on either side, our hands clasped in front of us and staring straight ahead. The expressions on our faces were as reverent as we could muster. The damaged cross looked like a large hand that had been deformed through years of palsy. The clergy and most of the parishioners were disgusted, although we did spot a few off-duty crucifer's who thought the situation hilarious. Several of them met us back in the Crucifers' Room after the service for an insiders' postmortem.

The next week, the church purchased a shiny new cross.

My father owned a millwork company, and since he and Herb were friends, my father routinely donated free woodworking to the church. So, if asked, my father probably would have fixed the communion rail as a favor. But here, he didn't wait to be asked. There was no doubt about his commitment, as his son had by then been fully implicated in what became known as "The great cross disaster."

It turned out there was nothing really wrong with the cotter pin. The whole episode was attributed to "user error."

THE GREAT MITE BOX DISASTER

In the late 50s and early 60s, a nickel was a big deal. With one of them, you could go to Haggett's and buy a Snickers bar, or a pack of bubble gum with Topps baseball cards. With a dime, you could buy a Vanilla Coke. So nickels and dimes were important to kids back then. That's why we were asked to "give them up" for Lent. To sacrifice and deprive ourselves for forty days and forty nights.

A mite box is a small cardboard container which is used to collect coins for charitable purposes. At Christ Church in Short Hills, mite boxes were handed out to all the children at the beginning of Lent. You could fold up the box and turn it into a little bank. The children were encouraged to put their small change into the boxes. One of the main events on Easter Sunday was the presentation of the mite boxes. Everyone looked forward to this, particularly the parents and grandparents. Some of the kids even did chores around the house to earn money to put in the mite boxes. They were proud to be part of this noble enterprise.

We all knew that nothing but positives would come out of this deprivation. The pooled contributions would go to the poor houses, or maybe to a local hospital. Some may have reimbursed the general fund for buying a new cross. We weren't too sure, but we knew some good would come from all these stored up coins.

As crucifers, we wore "cassocks"—not to be confused with "Cossacks" (marauding Ukrainians), although we were, in some respects, more dangerous, at least to the concept of peaceful worship. Cassocks were long black robes adorned with waist-length, rippled, white pullover blouses. (Some may have called them "cottas," but we didn't.) The robes were supposed to be ankle length, barely touching the shoes, with little or no break.

Remember, this was the early 60s, when most boys wore white socks. Black socks were for nerds. We hadn't even learned how cool it was to wear no socks, a practice which worked its way into our later dress code. We were under strict orders to wear dark socks, and we sometimes did that, but we usually had white socks on underneath them. We took off the dark socks as soon as we could, often even before the service started. The cassocks were supposed to be long enough to hide whatever socks we were wearing, so it shouldn't have really mattered.

All of these garments were hand-me-downs. None of them fit particularly well, especially the diminutive Laird Schoeber's, which had to be stitched up to remove a couple of feet of material.

We stored the cassocks in a closet in the Crucifers' Room, which was just a few feet from one of the side doors to the Sanctuary. We pretty much had our way with that room, and used it not only to don our church garb, but also to tell stories about recent events—stories that we often had to interrupt if the adult who had oversight over the crucifers happened to walk in. I've polled several of the former crucifers (now, of course, at least seventy and short on memory), and no one can seem to recall the name of the poor "man of the church" who had domain over us, or even much what he looked like. Actually, we basically paid him no attention, even when he accompanied us on our annual outing.

Speaking of which, one year we all boarded a bus to Madison Square Garden to see the New York Rangers play the Toronto Maple Leafs. The highlight of the game turned out to be what was to become known as "the second greatest hockey fight in world history." We never knew what the greatest was, but we did learn we had witnessed the second greatest. During this fight, everyone hit everyone else. Some players even hit their own teammates. Skaters who were not punching were jumping up and down on the other players' gloves and breaking their sticks. All six players on each team received the maximum six-minute penalty. Everyone was taken off the ice. This could have resulted in a canceled game. But the ref (there was only one of them in a position to make this call, as the other had been cold cocked and removed, unconscious, from the ice by the two apologetic coaches) decided to let three skaters on the ice for each team, to then be switched with the other three from each team, causing twelve minutes of hockey to be played with only three from each team on the ice. Of course, one of the players on each team had to tend the goal, which made the rest of the ice pretty much two on two. All things said, this was a great show.

I can't remember who won the game. I do remember that Duke Ellington kept throwing Cracker Jacks down on top of a guy several rows in front of us, and when the guy turned around, The Duke and Robby Ill kept pointing at our minister, Rev. Herb Cooper, who was sitting in the row in front of us and came close to being punched out.

Big Al Schultheis was always an excellent source of humor. Like the time he was fifteen or sixteen and some kind of bad wanted a job to earn some "real money." He finally landed a high-paying gig at the Esso station on the north side of Millburn Avenue, near the Lionel Train store. He was so proud. Unfortunately, on his first day of work, Al left the pump handle in the gas tank of a car as it drove away, thus ripping the handle from the pump, busting the gas cap, and spilling gas all over the station and into the road. Al spent the better part of the summer working for free, to pay off this mishap.

But he still loved cars. He was always going to the drag races in Flemington. And he liberally used drag racing terminology, such as "hemi" and "cam." Most of the rest of us had no idea what he was talking about, although we always listened intently. Actually, Al may have learned some of those terms in auto mechanics shop. For those of us in Chefs' Club, our terminology was limited to "whisking" and "rendering."

But none of this has much to do with this story, which relates to one particular Easter Sunday service in approximately 1963.

Everyone looked forward to the Easter service, which was ripe with tradition and ceremony. Parents encouraged their kids to fill their mite boxes. The Sunday school classes held practice rounds, to be sure everything would go smoothly. Everyone was taught the engineering concepts of piling the mite boxes on top of one another, box by box, row by row, to build a structure that eventually took the shape of either a house or a church, or maybe a giant mite box. And it was built right there on the floor, in front of the center aisle. The little kids practiced this over and over, to make sure that when the time came on Easter Sunday, everything would go smoothly. The event was not unlike the opening ceremony at the Olympics. It was much anticipated.

Even families that usually didn't come to church would come on Easter, so there were many more kids than usual. Sunday school classes were suspended so that the mite box ceremony could go forward in the church proper, with everyone watching.

The little girls were all dressed in pastels, some with hats. The boys all wore ties and even had to shine their shoes. The mothers, fathers, and the grandparents were so proud, all with their hands clasped. They took a lot of pictures. Cell phones had not yet been invented, so real cameras were in play. Everyone was excited about this important event. It was Easter Sunday. Mite box day.

I think we had five crucifers that day, but three of them were either up near the altar or temporarily outside playing football. The up-front squad in the church was just Big Al and me. I can't remember exactly why, but Al was stationed toward the center of the stairs leading up to the choir area, precisely where Herb Cooper had landed on Laird. I was off to the side, about where I was when Laird went down. Al must have been up there to make sure nothing went wrong with the mite boxes—although everything did.

I mentioned the Crucifers' Room. Well, on Easter morning, Al and I entered the room together. We were both a little late and in kind of a rush to suit up and get in the queue. I had pulled my cassock and blouse off their hangar, and Al suddenly had a funny look on his face. "Damn," he said, "my outfit's still at the cleaners." He then reminded me that a week or two earlier, his cassock and blouse had been soiled playing football, and he had discerned that the church patrons (other than the off-duty crucifers) wouldn't understand the mud stains on his garb, so either he or his mother had taken the entire outfit to the cleaners. Unfortunately, no one had picked it up. "No sweat," I said. "Borrow one." He agreed. He reached randomly into the closet and pulled one out, but it was Laird's. In unison, we both said, "This won't work." So Al reached in again until he got a bigger one. Al was kind of full figured. Not quite as much as The Duke, but he couldn't wear a real skinny cassock like Woody Thompson's. As we were running out of time, he chose Nils Ohlson's robes. In retrospect, this was a grievous error.

Nils was about five or six inches taller than Big Al. In order to walk around in the borrowed cassock, Al had to sort of scrunch up the sides of the garment a bit to keep from stepping on it. A few minutes later, he was doing this off and on while in full view of the parishioners, who were all hyped up for the big ceremony. From the side, I noticed the garment issue and hand signaled Al to be careful, but he was too caught up in the drama of the event to notice me.

There was either a special hymn sung by the choir, or special organ music that played, as the children came forward with their offerings. They were in two single file lines formed in the center aisle. The adults could never have pulled this off, because of the agility needed to squat, lean, and reach as these kids did. They knew exactly what they were doing. They had been taught to gently place the mite boxes in a more or less symmetrical pattern, securing them in rows north, south, east, and west, and one atop another. Gingerly, and with enormous pride, and glancing back to their parents and grandparents for approval, they built this structure out of the mite boxes that they had so dutifully filled during Lent, with the nickels and dimes, and occasional quarters, they had secured.

Al got out on the steps just above where the mite boxes had been arranged. I was never certain exactly why he suddenly turned. Perhaps Herb had said something to him. Perhaps it was part of the planned choreography. In any event, he turned. But to do so, he had to shuffle his feet. This is where things went awfully wrong.

Imagine you've just spent hours building a house of cards, carefully balancing them, one on another, and one against another, until you used all fifty-two from the deck. Meticulously placing each in a delicate position. Hoping no one sneezes. And just as you're admiring your handiwork, an anvil falls out of the sky and lands on the house of cards, crushing it flat. That's what it looked like when Big

Al fell backward, spread eagle, into the mite boxes. Actually, he did a reverse swan drive, waving his arms as though he were trying to fly.

The mite box castle exploded. Unfortunately, virtually none of the kids had put any dollar bills into the mite boxes, so this wasn't like landing on a mattress. It was more like landing on a rock pile. Out of the maybe sixty or seventy mite boxes, there were only one or two left intact. The others went everywhere, and all the coins sprayed out onto the nearby parishioners, or otherwise rolled down the aisle.

In isolation, this would have been a remarkable occurrence, had many of these same people not witnessed "The Great Collection Plate Disaster" only a few weeks earlier.

From the look on his face, it was clear that Herb remembered that recent event, because after he went and got some collection plates, he was very cautious approaching the stairs. Anyway, he got the plates down to the scene of the mayhem to try to recoup as much of the money as practicable. It's impossible to know how much of the change that was scooped up off the floor made it back into charitable channels, as opposed to back into the pockets of those who had foregone Snickers, Topps gum and cards, and Vanilla Cokes.

Al recovered, and I think later that day, he went to Flemington to relax. He continued to blame the incident on his mother, for not going to the cleaners.

But to this day, there are still people who, when they first think of Christ Church in Short Hills, picture the center aisle covered with sprawled out people and loose change.

MORE MISADVENTURES

. . . in other parts of the world, you don't even show up at someone's house unless you are invited.

- Joel Stein, *Time Magazine,*
February 10, 2014

THE HOMESICKS

"It's all about fun."

That was the word around our homes in the spring of 1956 as many of our parents figured a little time apart for many in the Glenwood gang would be in order, and they discovered even modest family budgets could spring for something called "camp," at least in some form. We were nine and ten years old, just hitting the pre-summer stride of our usual idiocy. Summer promised too many idle days of high mischief, and was just around the corner. Shipping us out would be a clever defensive play, with most of us going in different directions and our neighborhoods given a rest from our usual nonsense.

There was only one problem.

Most of us didn't want to go away to camp. I mean, we were pretty much "all about fun" around home base anyway. So parents had to really ramp up their pitch, although very few of them had actually been to camp when they were kids. They were selling a fantasy, cobbled from random conversations with other non-camper parents and what they would learn from some camp brochures, which all looked about the same. Clueless, my parents painted the idea of camp as a kind of glorious extended field trip, but without the teachers and the threat of those nasty notes sent home. I remember my parents came home from a little mid-winter dinner party at Johnny Stedman's, all fired up about a small camp in upper New York called Chenango. The Stedmans' pitch sealed the deal for my exile that summer. And that was that. No pre-exile inspection trip, and I don't remember anyone even looking at a brochure, although Chenango was thinly capitalized and may not have had one.

Curiously, I also don't remember seeing Johnny Stedman at Chenango that summer. Maybe his parents were just investors.

But I eventually bought into the pitch too, one of many kids in our gang who disappeared that summer into camp.

Suds Estes was shipped off to the "Admiral Farragut Camp," down the Jersey Shore. This was a bizarre choice, as he had never shown any interest in boating, sailing, or joining anyone's navy. I think the management over at his house just wanted us separated somehow, somewhere. Like my parents, Estes' folks had probably picked up some loose cocktail talk about this Farragut camp. Since it was pretty close to home, but far from Chenango, it simply fit the bill, at least for his parents.

He hated it.

Starched white uniforms, formations, drills—it was all modeled on boot camp, and the next summer he found a much happier home at a camp "O-At-Ka" ("Our Aim Is To Achieve") buried deep in the Maine woods, and far from anybody's navy.

Wiener McQueen got a lucky draw and was shipped to a baseball camp run by the great Ted Williams, although Williams was pretty busy in those days actually playing baseball and I now wonder how regularly any of those boys actually saw him. Perhaps the campers were hauled to Fenway once or twice in the season for some face time, a distinct possibility since Wiener returned from camp and generously gifted me with a signed Williams' baseball. Even better, he gave me a small, perfectly squared piece of paper signed with a personal "To John, Ted Williams." I still have this gem today, safely secured in a Pro-Mold two-piece, snap design and archival safe clear plastic holder, kept in my safe deposit box. Thanks again, Wiener.

Willy Stevens, taking a brief leave from his duties as Commissioner of our Lakeview Wiffle Ball League, went off to a "Camp Wonsonnett" somewhere in Connecticut, and a camp "Men-E-Tonk-A" captured a few boys from town.

A number of local boys found themselves enlisted in a tony sailing camp called "Monomoy" on Cape Cod. I would join them for my third and last year of camp. I never really did learn, however, to sail that summer, although our buddy Bob deVeer quickly mastered the lessons and later in his life became a skilled yachtsman who sailed both competitively and for adventure. I know Bob made several successful ocean crossings over the last years. I couldn't sail across the camp's marked course without major disasters and screw-ups, assuming I could even rig the damn boat, something else I never mastered. But I did hit a monster triple on the camp's baseball field, only to be stranded on third base when the game was called for supper. I remember this for several reasons. I had been batting about .081 back home in Little League, with significantly more promise than performance on the field. Even at that young age, I was clearly already in the twilight of a very mediocre baseball career. In fact, the word going around the Glenwood gang was that I had not scored a single run during the entire Little League season. They were only half right: I didn't score a single run the year before either. At Monomoy, with our best hitter at the plate, no outs, and the shadows clearly bothering the pitcher, I had actually sparked a rally with my monster triple. So when the counselor-umpire called the game, leaving me on third base, I was sure that my best shot to actually score a run had just evaporated into the early evening and I would *never* know what it felt like to cross home plate.

I was right.

These little dramas were playing out at camps all over the place. Stories of summer triumph and tragedy at some camp that sounded like "Nishkaboga," although I might be confusing this with a river which also sounds something like this near my wife's childhood home in Iowa. Still other stories would reach us of misadventures among the boys sent for shorter stints at the local Boy Scout camp. Bud was part of that crowd. Although he had been skating on very thin ice over at Troop 15, he seemed to enjoy a very healthy run at one such scout camp, "Ken Etiwa Pek." One of the Boy Scout tales reaching our outpost attained near-legendary status, as you will soon learn.

Most of our camps had a few things in common. They all had an iconic archway entrance welcoming kids to their new summer home, with a hand-carved or hand-painted wooden sign hanging over the archway. I know this because everyone would return from camp with a brochure or postcard or even a snapshot of happy campers at the front entrance. Remarkably, every sign looked like it had been made by other kids as some rainy-day craft activity a year or two earlier, with one notable exception. Estes reported back that the Admiral Farragut Camp had opted for a slightly more imposing front gate of old ship cannons, crossed swords and a highly polished brass ship's bell. The whole set-up seemed to be more about discipline than fun, and I would have gone AWOL right then and there.

Taken together, these entrances were cleverly intended to let us know we were leaving the real world behind and entering the special world of camp. Sure, it was a bit staged, and I think Farragut over-played its hand, but it all worked. So, for a time beginning in the mid-50s a fortunate number of us came to enjoy this great experience.

We swam, played softball, volleyball, and enjoyed games of "hide-the-flag" in the evenings. On stormy nights, we went on a boys-only adventure, something called a "snipe hunt." During the day we learned how to shoot arrows at the archery range and we learned to shoot rifles at the rifle range. At night, back in the tents with lights out, we were learning most of all to "shoot the shit."

Looking back, that might have been the most useful acquired skill of all.

Many of the boys' camps had a girls' operation next door, tied together in some kind of ownership linkage. My Chenango did, but I can't remember its name. A deep gorge, about twenty feet deep, sep-arated the boys' tents from a log cabin chow hall, where the girls also ate. We crossed a shaky wooden bridge to get to the chow hall, and that was the only time we ever saw the girls, at least up close. But we didn't sit with them, as a couple of long serving tables kept us apart like the DMZ which had just been created in Korea. Things never got out of hand, and the DMZ held. I guess management could have blown our spindly bridge if it had.

This separation extended down to the shore of our shared lake, the magnificent spring-fed Lake Otsego, which had been carved out by the glaciers some ten thousand years ago. As camp lakes go, it was alarmingly deep—two hundred feet at one point—and rumored to host a kind of Loch Ness monster. One kid during my second year actually claimed he saw it late one night. But he was always making stupid shit up, although people still talk about sightings of a monster in Lake Champlain, not far away. Who knows: maybe we should have cut the kid some slack. Camp legend also had Lake Otsego plunging to a depth of "over a thousand feet" at its deepest point, which the counselors claimed was just beyond the buoys and rope which marked the limit of the camp's supervised swimming area. More bullshit, of course, but it did spook us into staying close to shore, and made their lifeguarding duties easier.

Someone had also rolled a good sized boulder on to the beach to mark the boys' and girls' boundaries of our small, separate rocky beaches. There were exotic tales that some of the older girl counselors would go skinny-dipping early in the morning, with remarkable details a bit above my pay grade. This drove the counselors on our side of the DMZ crazy, and me too. None of us, however, ever saw skinny-dipping girl counselors, although one kid from Elmira claimed he actually did see the lake monster one night, and skinny-dipping girls one morning. But his details were stupid, and his stories quickly dismissed, both more triumph of hope over reality.

Curiously, almost every teenage movie ever made about camp had a skinny-dipping bit, all very PG-13 at that. I am now sure those Hollywood types logged, at best, a few hours in day camp, and were just up-selling the whole thing to boost the box office. And maybe the camp owners were in on this deal too. One exception was Disney's crack at the genre, *The Parent Trap*. Disney created a great fake camp—Camp Inch—where Haley Mills meets Haley Mills, and everyone seemed to keep their clothes on.

With skinny-dipping off the table, we did have one closer encounter with the girls. A square dance held in the chow hall, it was a disaster—as bad as dancing school—and everyone was glad the DMZ was breached only that evening.

But camp was generally wonderful, and most of us are sad to have seen many of them disappear over the years, although I think Estes would be very happy to learn that Farragut fell. (My guess is its bones are still there, converted into a classified Homeland Security Training Facility.) There are many reasons for these closings, I guess, and some of them may make sense. I know that I have looked for two of my camps, actually walking the sites. Chenango is gone completely, with barely a hint of the marvelous place it had been. Monomoy has been scaled back to the point that I could not recognize much of my past there either, although I really wanted to find that third base bag. They have added a day camp option, and sliced the sleep-away sessions—which they call "Campers A-Way" sessions—into shorter segments. I just hooked up into their alumni group—thanks, Nancy Garran—after being missing-in-action from their alumni roster for over fifty years. Most of the people I now read about in the camp's classy Alumni Newsletter look like they turned out very, very well. In most of the newsletter photos, alumni are happily marrying and remarrying, and having babies and grandbabies, and getting fabulous promotions and retiring, and going to reunions in snappy blazers all over the place. Even the dreaded "Passings" section is tastefully done, lives of alumni told well, and gently. There just aren't that many photos of alumni actually *sailing*, so maybe I wasn't the only one challenged by that acquired taste.

I do, however, have a couple of cool ties with sailboats on them, and I had hoped to be able to send in a nice little photo of my own sporting that classy, very Cape Cod look. I had in mind a very specific shot of my inking a multi-million book deal with a big-deal publisher—indeed, the *very big-deal* publisher who was also a camp alum, and prominently featured in the Newsletter. This whole "old camp tie" thing is fun that way, and quite a few marriages, at least, seem to have started with this connection, so why not a book? I sent a note to the publisher, along with another unsolicited manuscript summary and a little happy talk of the great days on the Cape of our youth, although we were not at the camp at the same time. I thought it all masterful, and I did indeed get a quick and impressively personal reply, which is way more than our other book queries were earning. Now, I am no stranger to rejection—and this publishing house did pass—but their rejection was thoughtful, pretty much on target and done with exceptional grace. But it was still a rejection, although our agent called it a "good rejection," something we haven't really pressed him on because it sounds rather impressive, and takes the sting away.

I had even picked out one of my cool sailboat ties for the photo, and a snappy double-breasted blazer. Maybe if enough people buy our book, I'll still get to send one of those happy photos to the news-letter too.

I suspect others have taken to these nostalgic re-connections. We all should.

And not many years ago, a friend from Monomoy sent me a picture he had found, showing a group of us young boys sitting around—you guessed it—a real campfire pit. We were all dressed the same, in white T-shirts and khakis, and it looked like everyone had just gotten the same impossibly short haircut from some circuit-rid-ing camp barber. He asked me if I could pick us out of that group of twenty or so happy campers, but I couldn't. The picture, which wasn't very good to begin with, had faded terribly over time, as has our eyesight. It could have even been a stock photo from one of those Hollywood movies.

The whole thing should have been a disappointment.

It wasn't, though, because the photo was solid proof of a magi-cal time and place, and I was touched that a friend would remember it all as fondly as I did, and remember me too.

The adults, in the end and all operating off the same script, had been on target after all. Camp really was fun, although I did miss my dog, the Glenwood gang, and even my family. And luckily for me, none of that ever reached the dreaded stage of something called "homesickness," a strange disease, which swept away a few of our camp buddies before their enlistment was up.

We called these poor kids "The Homesicks," and camp was not so much fun for them.

At the time we figured it was the homesick camper who pulled the plug on himself, but I now suspect that camp management looked at this illness as a kind of dreaded contagion, culling The Homesicks from the herd before the disease spread like Ebola, or whatever is wiping out the good people of earth in all these zombie apocalypse shows today. Clearly, if it hit and the homesick virus got out of hand, our already thinly capitalized camp operations would be in serious trouble. Most camps, when we started to compare notes, had a similar protocol, and the same kind of antenna for developing trouble. If some kid started to whine about "really missing mom's cooking," phase one would kick in, a kind of DEFCON One. The camp cooks upgraded the chow for a day or two, throwing a little extra peanut butter and jelly into the mix and scratching the chipped-beef-on-toast, known throughout the camp world—and most armies—as "shit-on-a-shingle." If his grumbling continued, the counselors backed off a bit from the usual ribbing, and gave the kid a little more personal camp care, maybe a little extra time on the rifle range or a day off from making his bed. By DEFCON Two, a discreet call was made home to the parents, who hopefully hadn't forgotten who he was. None of us remembers a parent just dropping in to give the kid a little support, like visiting rights in a medium security prison, or even a parent showing up to actually repatriate the child. No, it all went down like this. We returned to our tents from afternoon activities, and saw the camper's bed stripped down, his clothes trunk gone, and his name off the tent roster board. Yeah, DEFCON Three.

It was all very sad and creepy, much like the scene in every war movie when everybody's favorite airman—and he is always the good-hearted Irish kid from the Bronx—doesn't return from his mission. Usually we liked the homesick kid, and missed him. We were, however, all secretly relieved he had gotten the Homesickness and not us, so we felt guilty too, a kind of survivor's guilt. We also wondered if there may have been a kind of halfway house camp somewhere nearby, jointly owned by all the local camps, with a few more comforts of home—better pillows, maybe, blankets which weren't scratchy army surplus, an upgrade from our outhouse and better food more like Mom's—where the Homesicks could be rehabilitated and even returned to base camp, cured and ready to rejoin the whole adventure. This idea was prompted by the disappearance of a particularly popular, but unhappy, camper, and we really wanted him to come back. But neither he, nor any of the other Homesicks, were ever seen again.

Although a couple of boys insisted that it was just a failure of that half-way house treatment plan, most of us concluded that the halfway camp simply didn't exist, and we cut our losses and accepted the departure of our friends.

I wonder how all this would play out today, what with cell phones and helicopter parenting and all the rest. Even if the kids were supposed to surrender their cell phones. I mean, the whole point of camp was to *get away*, right? But maybe cell-phones keep kids so linked to their mother-ships—a kind of electronic vaccine which keeps the Homesickness at bay—that nobody gets homesick today, even if kids go away to camp anymore.

SON, I'D BE HAPPY TO

In the summer of 1956, shipped out to Camp Chenago, I spent almost a month a few miles outside the village of Cooperstown, in the low rolling hills of the Chenango Valley in upper New York State. It turned out to be a great choice, even if I was known as a "half-summer" camper. This was a compromise between going to local "day camp" or "full summer," and carried a touch of stigma, and a couple kids called us "half-asses." I was used to worse, and a little ribbing did not spoil a magical time.

And Half-Summers certainly did not carry the stigma of the dreaded "Day Campers."

At day camp, all anyone did was work for hours each day on a woven, stranded plastic lanyard, until their heads exploded, and that was that. Few kids logged more than a week of this nonsense. I tried day camp once, around fourth or fifth grade, when it was held at the Glenwood School, under the old wooden bike shed that is no longer there. I made it three days until discharge, and never finished my lanyard. But I left with my head intact, if not a bit disillusioned.

The full summer deal, on the other hand, could stretch out eight or even nine weeks, which seemed to be a very long time to a ten-year-old. There had even been quiet talk in day camp that the parents of one kid in town shipped him off for one of those nine-week enlistments at "sleep-away" camp in June, and had *completely forgotten* about him by late August. This was typical day-camp nonsense—rumor clearly designed to push the local experience as a safer alternative—although the family which was usually mentioned had eight kids, and the kid a real jerk, so maybe there was something to it.

I wasn't worried that my parents would pull that stunt, and I knew they would be pushing the budget at four weeks. So four weeks would be my camp experience, running from late June through late July.

To the surprise of everyone, I was a reasonably dedicated and well-adjusted camper. Something in the water, I guess, around Cooperstown. Or maybe they doctored the chow with a mild drug, like the Army was doing about this time on unsuspecting volunteers at some creepy secret research base in Maryland, or maybe Nevada.

In any event, my Camp Chenango was a great fit, and I never caught the dreaded homesickness virus, or even a cold. Small, rustic, and all-boy, my new four-week summer home was a heavy canvas tent resting on a wooden platform, raised three or four feet off the ground. Twelve boys were assigned to a tent, and there were ten tents resting rather tentatively on a wooded slope leading to a rocky beach along the shoreline of Lake Otsego. A deep gorge, as you now know, separated us from a log cabin activity center and chow hall. This gorge was a kind of unspoken DMZ. We shared half the chow hall with a girls' camp next door, but even there we were separated by the food serving tables.

It all worked.

Camp management had recruited a quieter mix of personalities, at least as compared to the Glenwood gang. With a few notable exceptions, the boys of Camp Chenango sailed through our days in the woods with surprisingly few screw-ups and demonstrably reduced boyhood idiocy.

The secret to all of this—the dangled carrot—was the possibility of a weekly trip to the Baseball Hall of Fame, as long as you were on your "good behavior." As a result, I was a "Good Behavior" each of my four weeks, and each Saturday morning trip was magnificent—the Hall itself, of course, and more baseball cards any of us had ever seen.

But a big part of the mystique of the whole Cooperstown experience was Doubleday Field.

I remember it as closely adjoining the Hall, although it is actually a block or so away. It was quaint, and in need of a little paint. My guess is it still is. Opened in 1920, a wooden grandstand was added in 1924, which in turn was replaced by steel and concrete in 1939. It sported a handsome brick main entrance, and a seating capacity of around nine thousand. I remember thinking it looked absolutely nothing at all like the few major league fields any of us had ever seen, either in person or in pictures. It had, however, all the right body parts: a tidy infield, a nicely groomed outfield, inviting but ancient seats behind the backstop, and rows of bleacher seats along the base lines and framing the outfield. On most days, the gates were open and you could just walk in, grab a seat, and dream everything baseball.

Despite the magic of the day, I was mildly disappointed the first time I saw the field, which looms large—if improbably—in baseball mythology. But my disappointment was fleeting, because I knew one thing:

This was the birthplace of baseball!

This was the stuff of unchallenged legend, passed down from generation to generation by anyone who'd ever picked up a ball or a glove or a bat, and there were few young boys anywhere, or any men either, who wouldn't swear that General Abner Doubleday invented the game right there in 1854. We would later learn, of course, that this Doubleday stuff was nonsense, but it didn't matter. This place was fantastic.

Although we "Half-Summers" took a little ribbing, at least I had chosen the right half. One of the benefits of Chenango in the first session was the tradition of attending the "Hall of Fame Game," which then was part of the ceremonies for new inductees into the Hall of Fame. This annual game began in the 1920s as an Old Timers' Game, and in 1940 the Major League owners agreed to send two teams to Cooperstown to play in a mid-summer exhibition game to honor the new inductees into the Hall. In the early days, one team was picked from each league, and this was the only interleague play, at least until the World Series. At some point, the interleague tradition for the Hall of Fame game was lost, interest seemed to wane, and in early 2008, Major League Baseball announced that the final Hall of Fame Game would be played on the 16th of June. The Chicago

Cubs and San Diego Padres were scheduled, but the game was canceled due to rain, never rescheduled, and that was that. Doubleday still hosts amateur and American Legion games, along with popular fantasy camps during the summer.

But back in the 1950s, the game was such a big deal that any camper could go, even if he was not a Good Behavior. I went to the Hall of Fame Game twice.

The inductees into the Hall my first year included the great Detroit player Hank Greenberg. Mr. Greenberg was certainly not pleased that year, as the Giants beat the Tigers 11-10 in twelve innings. I was a bit overwhelmed, and I didn't even try to bag an autograph, which was possible, if you knew what you were doing. In 1956, I was clueless.

1957 was a different story.

I had watched veteran campers come back with all sorts of wonderful stories that first year, and I was determined to get into the Hall of Fame Game autograph action the next year. Most seemed to have *actually talked* to a real major leaguer, and quite a few had bagged those coveted autographs. This was the real deal, but it clearly called for some serious tactical planning.

So on July 22, 1957, as soon as I jumped off the camp bus which had lumbered us into town for the game, I made a beeline for . . . the Hotel Otesaga. You see, the obvious play was to hang around the field and engage a player or two during pre-game warm-ups. The whole set-up was kind of loose and fun, and this was generally a successful strategy. But the rumor around camp that year was that players from both teams were staying at this grand old hotel just a few blocks from Doubleday. If you got there early enough and picked them out of the crowd in their civvies as they were relaxing before reporting to the Field—usually on the rear veranda overlooking Lake Otsego—you would likely get an autograph or two.

That, I decided, was the way to go.

I raced to the hotel, only to find it awash in fans, tourists, baseball writers, baseball players (somewhere, I assumed), scouts (wouldn't you think?), and tire salesmen from Akron. I am not completely sure about this, but I recall picking up some story that the hotel, which should have merely been at full capacity, screwed up and also booked some kind of tire convention. Or maybe this crowd from Akron had just come to watch the game, too. Whatever the reason, the place was a madhouse. Overloaded, and its usual quiet gentility in tatters, I was crushed. Everyone was confused, some were pissed off, the situation was spinning out of control and *I just wanted a lousy autograph!*

And not just *any* autograph.

I had already determined that I was going to bag an autograph of the great Stan "The Man" Musial.

For reasons that remain unclear, Mr. Musial had not appeared on a Topps baseball card for a number of years. He had not surfaced in any of our wax packs that year, and we were sure his absence was again a given for 1957, and we were right. In the back of my eleven-year-old mind, as muddled as it was, I thought I might even ask him about that business, but only after getting his autograph. This was heady stuff, and would have been a legendary scoop for the Glenwood gang back home.

But the plan crumbled quickly.

I could barely move through the crowd and, worst of all, I didn't have any real idea what "the Man" looked like, as I didn't own a single Musial baseball card. I did know he wore the number 6 on his Cardinal uniform, and I could have easily spotted his very unique batting stance, which was legendary. But since the players were not walking around the hotel in uniform, nor spontaneously breaking into batting stances, I was done. Crushed again.

I couldn't tell a ballplayer from a tire salesman, and the whole place was a zoo.

So I retreated back to the center of town, which was just about as crazy. But I had my ticket to the game, a bleacher seat somewhere in the outfield. It was still too early to enter the field, as these games started around one or two in the afternoon. I just walked the town with the crowd, and I am sure I bought a couple of wax packs of Topps baseball cards. Maybe I was still hoping to pull a Musial that year.

I wandered into Doubleday in time to see warm-ups, as that was my fallback plan for an autograph, and easily found my seat in left-center field, low and close to the grass. These were the cheaper seats, but great for our gang, and I was happy to rejoin the other campers. Left-center field was exactly 336 feet from home plate. I looked it up. In many major league stadiums, this would have been disappointing. Far from most of the action, most major league outfielders never talked to the fans. This may have been a major league rule, or at least some unwritten understanding. Also, an outfielder, on average, makes about three plays a game, leading some baseball wit to suggest that they should actually buy a ticket to the game. But at Doubleday, none of this was a problem that July day.

Real Major League players were lollygagging all over the place, within easy reach if you leaned just a bit over the short outfield fence, and everyone was talking to everyone.

It all had the feel of a neighborhood pick-up game. Even, in a stretch, like our Wiffle ball games. A bunch of Cardinal players were joking around with White Sox guys in left-center, pitchers from both teams were tossing the ball around and I even spotted Musial staging his unmistakable batting stance over by the Cardinal dugout. Kids were leaning over the fence everywhere, talking to players, and even the umpires were joining in the fun. It was wonderful, and beyond just promising.

I knew that I could get an autograph, and I did that magical afternoon.

At first, I was a little disappointed in whose it was, although such disappointment would eventually turn out to be quite misplaced. But remember this: I had reached for the moon with Musial that day, and failed. But one of the White Sox players hanging around left-center seemed approachable, clearly enjoying the whole relaxed show and not overly interested in outfield warm-ups, particularly since he was wearing a catcher's mitt.

In those days players did not wear their names on the backs of their uniforms, so I took my program, scanned the roster and found a name to match his number, 28. I had never heard of the guy, but eagerly leaned over the fence and made my play.

"Hey, Mr. Battey, how about signing an autograph?"

I was new to this autograph business, and hoped this was proper form. But I wasn't sure.

Mr. Battey had signed a big league contract in 1953 as a teenager growing up in the Watts section of Los Angeles, and had spent his early few years mostly in the minors, struggling at the plate. But on this July day in Cooperstown, he looked like one very happy fella, wearing that major league White Sox uniform. It looked fairly new, and was—he had just joined the team for another crack at the big leagues. He would stay with the club through August, when he was shipped back down to the minors, only to be recalled to the major leagues again in September.

So he would wind up having a pretty interesting year in 1957, with a few ups and downs. As would I, and most of my friends.

Yes, he was just a backup catcher, but he had come a long way from his first and noticeably uneven few years as a pro. He spent his first year with the Colorado Springs Sky Sox of the Single-A Western League. Playing in twenty-six games, he hit just .158 and was demoted to the Waterloo White Hawks, a team in the Iowa League. With regular play, his batting improved and in 1955 he was promoted to the Triple-A Charleston Senators. Some solid hitting down there again caught the eye of management, and he finally made it to the majors in September, only to return to another minor league team as the 1956 season opened. Still struggling at the plate—something I knew all about—he was playing well defensively, and the White Sox brought him back up. He played in four games with Chicago in 1956, and was with them on opening day in 1957.

So we found ourselves—both of us boys, really, one a struggling and largely unknown Major Leaguer from Watts, and the other a struggling Little Leaguer from suburban New Jersey—forgetting all our troubles on this glorious Hall of Fame Game Day. Soaking up the magic of Cooperstown on a day when all things seemed possible, we were quietly edging toward our chance-but-happy meeting along the left-center field fence of Doubleday Field in the early afternoon on the 22nd day of July, 1957.

Yes, we both must have been thinking, it sure is a mighty fine thing, this great game of baseball. Battey looked right up at me hanging over the fence with my pen and program, and hope.

"Son, I'd be happy to."

I will never forget his grin, which was as wide as the distance he had traveled from a scruffy sandlot in Watts to the very birthplace of baseball. And that was it. I would bag my autograph after all, even if it wasn't Musial. I'm sure few fans caught our brief exchange, and they wouldn't have cared anyway. I may have been the only fan to ask for his autograph that day, although I hope I'm wrong about that too.

He signed, that grin never leaving, and my new hero trotted off toward the infield, and his baseball future. I wonder if he had any idea that day just how bright that future would be. You see, Earl Jesse Battey, Jr. had not caught his stride, not just yet.

I don't know if he played in the game, but since it was an exhibition most managers liked to play a lot of reserves, so he probably did. Although there is likely some box score in a dusty recess of the Hall, I prefer just to think he got in a few good innings, and maybe even sparked a rally on the way to the Sox's lopsided 13-4 win that day. Anyway, that's how I want to remember it, so I won't be rifling through any archives soon.

Like most of the gang back at Glenwood, I was a Yankee fan, and after I tucked away my Battey autograph that summer, I paid only casual attention to his career, and then for just a very few years. I am sorry now that I didn't watch more closely.

Traded from the White Sox to the Senators in 1960, he stayed with that organization, which decamped to Minneapolis as the Minnesota Twins in 1961, until he retired in 1967. But what a career he had in Minnesota. A three-time Gold Glove winner, he was an All-Star in four or five seasons, even winning the most All-Star votes for an American League player for the 1965 game. Some say his play was the major reason the Twins won the American League pennant that year, and he finished strong in the league's MVP voting.

That was all in the future, of course, and no one really does know how his game will play out.

But I had my first big league autograph, and that would at least earn a nod from the boys back in the neighborhood, even if no one had heard of Earl Battey just yet. I mean, what kind of autograph was my buddy Suds Estes likely to bring back from the Admiral Farragut camp?

Later that summer Wiener McQueen would return from his camp, a Ted Williams baseball camp no less, and share with us a bunch of great Williams stuff, which was very impressive indeed. Somewhere along the line, someone in the Glenwood gang probably did bag a Musial autograph, and maybe a Yankee great or two on some sports banquet circuit in our later years.

But I would always have my Earl Battey.

I was not thinking about this in the summer of 1957, but it seems to me that two of the best descriptions of what America is all about, or at least used to be all about in our youth, have come from a couple of Frenchmen. You have certainly heard of the first, Alexis deToqueville. His *Democracy in America,* published in two volumes in 1835 and 1840, is a masterful essay, but it took him hundreds of pages to figure us out.

But you may not have heard of the second, a French-born historian named Jacques Barzun, and he nailed it in just a paragraph in an essay he wrote sometime in the 1950s called *God's Country and Mine.*

"Whoever wants to know the heart and mind of America," he said, "had simply better learn baseball."

With penetrating clarity, he described important American values and virtues that rest at the core of the game of baseball, a game he came to love—daring and judgment, accuracy and speed, a practiced eye and hefty arm, a mind able to react to the unexpected, a bundling of talents and the willingness to work together. I think the game for him was nothing less than magic.

Yes, he nailed it.

But he cautioned the newcomer to learn the game gently, perhaps by watching a game in some small town.

Maybe Jacques Barzun was even sitting by chance in a quaint stadium in the center of a tiny village in upper New York State, waiting for an exhibition game of no real importance on a hot July day in 1957. If he was, and he had looked toward the left-center field fence and listened in at just the right time, he would have witnessed some of that magic, in a place and time when all things seemed possible.

"Son, I'd be happy to."

SON OF A HITCH

There's a special place in heaven for the fathers of our youth, who did so many things, and gave so much of their time to help us and our friends mature and become productive adults. Many of the fathers were members of The Greatest Generation. They fought for their country; they provided for their families; they put in thousands of extra hours to encourage and help their offspring to become useful members of society. That's why it's so hard to explain what we put them through.

Among the greats was Mac's dad. Mr. MacIlroy was one of the scoutmasters of Boy Scout Troop 15, which was headquartered at Christ Church in Short Hills. Mac was no more respectful of the fathers (including his own) than the rest of us were. Also in our troop were Scott Estes, Terry O'Brien, Bob deVeer, Duke Ellington, Billy Fitszimmons, Tony Intilli, Woody Thompson, and others. Each was a mess. We entered Boy Scouts at eleven and exited at fourteen, so there wasn't a lot of maturing accomplished.

Troop 15 was organized into patrols. Each patrol had some kind of animal name. There were the usual suspects, such as the Wolf Patrol, Bear Patrol, Lion Patrol, Tiger Patrol, Hawk Patrol, Cobra Patrol, and such. Silhouettes of these animals were sewn with thick black thread into round shoulder patches with a black edge and a red interior to provide a contrast to the image of the mascot. These patches, as well as corresponding flags and other paraphernalia, could be purchased at any of the major department stores (such as Bamberger's and B. Altman) in the Boy Scout department.

By the second year, some of us were bored with these routine patrol mascots. It was either Woody or Tony who got the idea of experimenting with new mascots unrecognized by the Boy Scouts of America. We were not sufficiently skilled (nor were any of our mothers, had we chosen to ask them, which we didn't) to create our own patches from scratch. So we bought some off-the-shelf Cobra patches and, with a pair of tweezers and a needle (and, as I recall, an eyeglass repair kit), started removing the head and the tail from one of the patches, leaving only the curved, tube-like body. After the prototype was perfected, we went into mass production for the eight or so members of the patrol. Each patch took about an hour. I think I remember Woody Thompson's mother, Grace (who would go on to help us with future underground activities, including skipping school, and with a particularly satisfying frolic at Ebbet's Field) doing the brunt of the labor on the flag. We put a lot of work into this transformation.

There was a patrol roll call toward the beginning of each troop meeting, during which someone (either the patrol leader or a designee) had to step forward and "report in" for each patrol. Then the scoutmasters would solemnly file past, just to let everyone know they were ready for action. One scout would dip the flag and announce the name of the patrol, followed by the entire patrol yelling out a motto, such as, for the Lion Patrol, "Ready to roar," or, for the Wolf Patrol, "Ready to howl," or drivel like that. I think Woody was our spokesperson for this particular gig.

As we entered the meeting hall, no one had noticed the changes in our shoulder patches—we'd kept turning so that our shoulders would be out of view of the scoutmasters, and even the other scouts. We wanted our new mascot to be a surprise. Of course, we kept the flag tucked out of sight until the right moment.

That moment came early in the meeting, as the scoutmasters were rounding the bend, going from patrol to patrol, and heading for ours. Anticipating what was to come, and while trying to stand at attention, we were internalizing our hysteria. Tony Intilli had snot coming down over his upper lip.

Messrs. MacIlroy and Conchar approached. Woody stepped out. He dipped the flag, which was hard to see as it was bobbing up and down, but I recall Mr. Conchar looking at it sort of cockeyed.

We turned our shoulders out toward the center of the room so every-one could see them, as Woody declared: "Leech Patrol," and we all yelled *"WE SUCK!"* This was the last time we were allowed to express that particular motto, and in fact we were forbidden from discussing it even among ourselves. But we were heroes to the other patrols.

To this day, over half a century later, I sometimes wake up in the middle of the night from a dream about the look on Mr. MacIlroy's face. His skin was normally somewhat pale from all the time he spent riding the Erie Lackawanna train back and forth every day to New York City. But over about three-and-a-half seconds, the color of his face changed as though someone had pulled a cork from the top of his head and poured in a quart of cranberry juice.

All the fathers were disgusted, their lack of approval "leeching" into the next event, which was the knot-tying relay.

As maturing scouts, there were a bunch of things we were sup-posed to know how to do but couldn't quite get the hang of. We couldn't start a fire with flint or by rubbing sticks together, although we became quite proficient at putting out a fire by standing over it and peeing on it. We couldn't really cook, other than canned beans, and even there, it took a couple of misfires before we learned you had to take the top off before putting the can in the fire. And our tents were so poorly constructed that the strongest of them would not have withstood a baby's sneeze.

The only occasion I can remember ever going on an outdoor camping trip in Boy Scouts where it didn't rain the whole time was the time we arrived in the woods just as a snow storm started, although being cooped up in a wobbly tent for many hours in a heavy snowfall with one or two other adolescents, particularly after eating a can of beans, did provide the opportunity to perfect the art of farting.

There are several kinds of knots using the word "hitch." The half hitch is a simple overhand knot, where the working end of a line is brought over and under the standing part. This is not to be confused with the old cowboy movies, where the rider jumps off his horse and just loops the reigns over the hitching post, which I can't believe any horse would fall for. Anyway, the half hitch is insecure on its own, but is strengthened when used with a timber hitch to help stabilize a load in the direction of a pull. There's also such a thing as a two half hitch, a double half hitch (which may be the same thing), a clove hitch, and a taut line hitch. And at least back in the late 50s, Boy Scouts were expected to be able to tie all of these hitches. Neither Woody nor I, nor any of the other Leech Patrol members, ever learned any of the hitches nor, for that matter, the bowline or the sheet bend (which we were also supposed to know). Combined, our repertoire was the square knot (which we sometimes muffed) and the bow (which wasn't in the Scouting Manual but did come in handy when tying our sneakers and wrapping Christmas presents). The rest of these knots were of no value to us. It was our view that anyone who could do them was just showing off.

Anyway, right after the opening ceremonies on the first night of the second year (we were about thirteen), and just after we had unceremoniously announced our new patrol name, there was to be a knot-tying relay. Each patrol would line up and send its members the length of the auditorium, touch the wall on the other side, run back and have to tie whatever knot the scoutmaster yelled out. There were a couple of vertical and horizontal poles mounted on wooden stands for use in knot-tying. Each of us was supposed to know every knot, so the scoutmasters felt free to yell out any one of them. The scout would come panting up, tie the knot, wait for approval, and then fall away and sit down while the next patrol member took off for the far wall to repeat the loop and tie a new knot.

I think we led off with Billy Fitzsimmons. He raced to the far wall, returned, and the scoutmaster yelled "square knot," which was a blessing for Billy, since that's the only one he had practiced. The rest of our hearts fell, as we all knew that none of us would be able to tie any other kind. The square knot had been used up. I was in the queue for the anticipated third leg of the race. Ahead of me in the second slot was Woody, who knew full well, while running, that he wasn't going to get a bye with a square knot, but rather would be forced to tie some knot—probably a hitch of some sort—about which he was clueless.

Woody came back from the far wall, ran up to the tying post, and started a mad fury of loops and turns. Mr. Conchar looked down at him and suggested he may need the help of a fellow patrol member, and stared at me. I came over and started looping, twisting, and pulling. By the time we were done, we had used up all the rope, and there was a huge multi-layered kink on top, covering about eleven loops, and the ends were frayed. It took about ten minutes to undo this beehive, thus effectively ending our patrol's participation in the relay.

During the confusion, Mr. MacIlroy rushed over. He was already fuming over the Leech Patrol incident. Only half the blood had drained from his face. He looked down at Woody and asked, as calmly as he could, "What, son, may I ask is that?" Woody looked up and told him it was a "son of a hitch." The two of us were banned from the next two Troop meetings.

Mac, having also earned himself a brief suspension by renaming his patrol the "Cuckoo Patrol," soon opted for an early retirement from all things Scouting. He got into sailing instead and, decades later, went on to become the Commodore of a yacht club in Hilton Head, from which he and I and our wives almost got ejected a couple of years ago for laughing so loudly about this story at the dinner table that we disrupted the other guests. (Actually, our wives were not laughing.)

I'LL HAVE A MANHATTAN

In the famous 1851 painting by Emanuel Leutze, George Washington and a contingent of his Continental Army are shown crossing the Delaware River on Christmas night, 1776. Two of them, including Washington, are standing at the bow, and another soldier is holding a large American flag affixed to a short pole. Washington and his platoon are depicted traversing the icy waters between Pennsylvania and Trenton, New Jersey. Insufficiently clothed, they would go on to reach land, walk through snow, and surprise and defeat a sizeable group of Hessian troops who were reportedly into the holiday sauce.

Our group of marauders didn't cross at Trenton; we traversed the corner of New York, New Jersey, and Pennsylvania and landed at the town of Delaware Water Gap, Pennsylvania, near the Poconos. It wasn't winter; it was early summer. We didn't have ten in a boat; we had seven boats, each with a crew of two. Except for Nils Ohlson, none of us stood. We didn't have a large American flag on a very short pole; we had a tiny yellow flag on a very long pole. We didn't capture anyone, but we evaded capture. We didn't shoot at anyone, but we deserved to be shot. We didn't encounter any ice on the water, but we had ten pounds of it in the beer canoe. And some of our group were most definitely into the sauce.

It was June of 1963, and we were all rising seniors at Millburn High School. Our "thought leader," Nils, decided we should take a two-day, two-night canoe trip down the Delaware. Experience the outdoors. Camp out. Commune with nature.

As the jumping off point for our nature trip, we chose Port Jervis, New York, which is an old railroad town perched on the Delaware and Neversink Rivers. It borders both Pennsylvania and

New Jersey. In 2008, *Budget Travel* magazine named Port Jervis one of America's "Coolest Small Towns." In 1963, it was way short of cool. Essentially, it was a dump, but (a) since it was technically in New York, eighteen year-olds could legally drink there; (b) sixteen and seventeen year-olds posing as eighteen year-olds could get away with drinking there; and (c) it was a town from which one could canoe to the scenic Delaware Water Gap in Pennsylvania, which is a deep cut in the Appalachian Mountains through which the scenic river flows. To our unwary parents, only (c) sank in.

Speaking of our parents, this was the last phase of the Ozzie and Harriett and June and Ward Cleaver era. JFK was flourishing in the third year of his presidency. We were part of Camelot. Life was simpler and less dangerous than now. Our parents trusted us. We were allowed to hitchhike, take the bus into New York City to ballgames, play hockey without helmets, skip school and go to the beach, shoot BB guns at each other, set off fireworks at will, fabricate howitzers out of old swing set parts, drive our parents' cars (if we were seventeen, which I wasn't yet), and stay out until all hours without question. There was very little supervision. Most of us were good students, and none of us did anything all that bad.

The notable exception to this standard of lax discipline was Mrs. MacIlroy. She had been scammed one too many times with bogus itineraries, and she therefore banned her son, Mac, from the adventure. But there were no questions asked when the rest of us told our parents we were going up to Port Jervis to canoe down to the Gap. None of the boys with licenses wanted to drive because then there would be no way to retrieve their cars after the journey south. So a few of the parents agreed to tote us and our gear to Port Jervis and pick us up two days later at our destination.

I don't recall any of our parents, either at home or during the ride up, even asking where we were going to spend the night. I guess they assumed (as we did) that we were going to camp out along the river. Our plan was burdened by rampant ignorance and universally poor reconnaissance on multiple levels. Perhaps most importantly, the Weather Channel had not yet been invented, so we had no clue there was a huge thunderstorm about to hit as our parents drove off.

All that said, if the movie *Deliverance* had come out before this trip, and had the Ozzies and Harrietts and June and Ward Cleavers of our lives seen it, none of us would have set out on this excursion in the first place. But fortunately for us, the movie didn't come out until 1972. So our parents weren't at home worrying about shotguns, bows and arrows, inbred locals, or dueling banjos. None of those things entered into our particular equation anyway. But other things did. And what our parents should have been worrying about was underage drinking, vomiting, paddling under the influence, shooting the rapids and going over waterfalls without helmets, violent river crashes, breaking and entering, larceny, violation of noise ordinances, sleep deprivation, and the mass destruction of an entire fleet of canoes. But I'm getting ahead of myself.

Upon arrival in Port Jervis at about 6 p.m., we found the canoes lined up on the edge of town, along the riverbank. We were on our own.

We were looking at a night of camping out and discussed making a bonfire (probably illegal in the river park). We had no food to cook, no water to drink, and no tents to sleep in, but we did have sleeping bags. Those of us who were veterans of Boy Scout camping trips were at ease. Others were less so. But we were all a little unnerved by the ominous sound of thunder in the distance.

And then the skies opened up.

To the extent we could hear each other through the thunder and the driving rain (which was the consistency of buckshot), we developed a plan to look for shelter in town. When the first bolt of lightning hit one of the nearby trees, we ran for cover. To some of us, this was less important than finding a bar. So we split up. One contingent scouted for a bar while the other group sought any roof whatsoever, whether situated over a bar or not.

I was part of the shelter contingent. One of us spotted the open door of a two-story gas station. Actually, the gas station was on the first floor, and the second floor was a Knights of Columbus lodge.

I have no idea why the gas station guys agreed to let us spend the night upstairs. Maybe we paid them a few bucks. Maybe they had no authority to lend out the lodge and didn't care. Maybe they just felt sorry for the seven or so drowned rats they were staring at, laden with drenched sleeping bags. They certainly would never have comped us at the lodge had they known about the other seven who were currently populating the bar.

On an acceptability/hospitality scale of one to ten, with ten being the highest and equivalent to a seedy U.S. Route 1 motel, the lodge hall was a two. It was one narrow flight up a set of rickety stairs from the gas station. Although not immediately evident to the naked eye, the floor was slanted, east to west (i.e., if you placed a marble on the east side, it would roll to the west side, or if you poured liquid on the east side, it would flow to the west side). No marbles crossed the room that night, but a considerable volume of liquid did.

The one bathroom was filthy. In the main room, there was a desk and two or three folding chairs. The two windows were stuck shut. There was no air circulation. But there was a roof, causing us to say, in unison, "We're golden!"

We headed out to find the bar brigade, in the pouring rain, thunder and lightning.

The bar was a dive. Of course, we didn't have a lot of experience with dives, because we were either sixteen or seventeen. The legal drinking age in both New Jersey and Pennsylvania was twenty-one. So just a few hundred yards from us, across the two state lines, even the eighteen year-olds could not legally drink.

The bartender had developed a scientifically reliable method for determining whether his customers were of age. Declining to inspect drivers' licenses (which, back then, could easily be altered), his practice was to ask: "You boys are old enough to drink, aren't you?" If the customer nodded up and down, or muttered anything that didn't sound like an unqualified *no*, he was served.

Despite the number of young boys in town that evening, there was apparently no police surveillance. For if the constabulary had been paying attention, there would have been multiple youthful detainees who, on the way out, bumped into the door jam, stepped on each other's feet (causing sneakers to come off), laughed uncontrollably, zigzagged across the street as though trying to evade an alligator, barfed on the curb, and eventually fell through the doorway of the gas station.

Ambling, sashaying, and sauntering are alternate terms for walking in a leisurely way. All three are sometimes used to describe a person who is approaching a bar for a drink, as in "he sashayed up to the bar." Teenagers who have never had alcohol are not real convincing at either ambling, sashaying, or sauntering. But Rob Hamilton did all three, as he nonchalantly lodged his elbow on the stand-up bar and uttered, "I'll have a Manhattan." The expression on his face was not dissimilar to the elaborately confident look we often saw on Barney Fife (Don Knotts) when he was about to do or say something he knew nothing about.

Rob started a tab. What happened next wasn't pretty.

When interviewed fifty years later, Rob conceded that at the time of the Port Jervis caper, (a) he had never had a "real drink;" (b) he had never even tasted a Manhattan; and (c) he didn't know what a Manhattan was. He had just heard some adults order this cocktail, and he might have even known what it looked like, but he had no idea what was in it or how powerful it could be.

Although Rob was sixteen, the bartender didn't ask for ID or even ask his age—at least not yet. He mixed the Manhattan. Rob took a hardy swallow. Although he tried to look nonchalant and confident, anyone paying attention (which did not include the bartender) might have noticed that he appeared as though he had just taken a gulp of varnish (which is about what a Manhattan looks like). No longer attracted to this particular admixture of spirits, but embarrassed to say so, Rob downed the Manhattan and asked for a gin and tonic. This was a defective decision on multiple fronts, made even more questionable by his next one, which was to order a rum and Coke. Somewhere between the first and third drinks (he finished all of them), he was asked the litmus test question whether he was old enough to drink, and since he didn't (and perhaps couldn't) answer in the negative, he continued to inflate his tab.

Similar scenes transpired with most members of the dive bar contingent until they all eventually gravitated toward their lodging for the night. Maybe they thought they were going to have beds. Rather, they shared the slanted floor.

A couple of us who'd had little or nothing to drink, and had gotten acceptable grades in physics, noticed the pitch in the floor and, accordingly, bunked up against the east wall. Everyone else slept downstream.

It's bad enough to hear someone throw up in a nearby bathroom, even with the door closed. But it's really disgusting when the sick person is only a few feet away, and there's nothing to throw up in, and there are no mops, and there is no air, and you have to spend the whole night there because it is storming outside.

The worst scene was one of the fellows who was looking for a waste can or something to wretch in, and all he could find was a desk drawer, which took the full brunt of his noisily disgorged upchuck. This left an unattractive sight for one of the other guys who, the next morning, opened the drawer to figure out why it was dripping.

This all sounds pretty bad; and it was. But actually only about three of the guys threw up.

The next morning was beautiful. Bright sunshine. Crisp air. Perfect. The canoe adventure was about to begin.

No one was much interested in breakfast.

The day started with an argument among the heaviest drinkers as to which way we were supposed to go on the river. This issue was resolved by the others, who noted that the river was flowing only one way, so that must be the direction in which to point the canoes. This bit of arcane naval science was the only guidance we had in deciding to go left (we were on the New York side) toward the Water Gap. We had no map. We didn't know the distance. We didn't know how many days it would really take us to get there. The planning had been bare bones.

Someone conned a grocery store clerk into selling him a couple of cases of beer to go with the sandwiches and bags of ice he bought.

We were off. No sleep; no breakfast; no skill; no map; no timetable; no plan; no clue. And no cell phones. This was 1963.

One of Pennsylvania State University's most famous graduates is Fred Waring, who was a musician, bandleader, and radio and TV personality for decades. Known as "America's Singing Master" and "The Man Who Taught America How to Sing," among his most famous songs was "I Scream, You Scream, We All Scream for Ice Cream," recorded in 1927. His band was known as "Fred Waring and His Pennsylvanians." Mr. Waring also funded the development of the electric blender, which was later known as "The Waring Blender."

None of which really matters here, except that, during the first day, we came across a beautiful golf course on the Pennsylvania side of the river. We beached our canoes next to a steep embankment leading up to the course, which, it turned out, was part of an exclusive resort owned by Mr. Waring. There was a big sign with his name on it facing out to the river and advertising that he and the Pennsylvanians were appearing there. (Why they felt the need to announce that to the people on the river was unclear, but they did.)

Nils was determined to get into Penn State, but he couldn't have known of Fred Waring's popularity there. Had he known of Mr. Waring's sway at Penn State, Nils probably would not have led a raiding party (consisting of himself and Jim Higgins) up the hill and onto the golf course to purloin the flag from the picturesque 16th hole. For reasons known only to himself, Nils had to have that flag as a status symbol for his canoe. He and Higgs reached the top of the cliff, scurried to the green (the way John Belushi scurried around sororities in the movie *Animal House* fifteen years later), grabbed the flag, ran across the green and the edge of the course, and slid down the embankment to the awaiting fleet.

Because of the angle, we couldn't see everything perfectly. But the scene of those two guys up on the green was reminiscent of the famous photo at Iwo Jima. But instead of four heroes planting a flag on a hill, two miscreant high school kids were removing one. Plus, in the background, there were four very angry golfers running down the fairway, screaming and shaking their fists and golf clubs as the thieves made their getaway.

The theft complete, the flotilla proceeded downriver with the flagship vessel in the lead. On more than one occasion, however, Nils (unlike George Washington) proved how tough it is to stand up in a waterborne canoe while holding a flag.

Skipping over a few details, suffice it to say that, collectively, we proved the following:

— When one aluminum canoe crashes headlong into the side of another at full speed, the dent in the target canoe does not cure itself.

— Some money and most knapsacks float.

— The flotation lifespan of ice is brief.

— Sleeping bags take a long time to dry out.

— Going over a steep vertical waterfall in a canoe is not a good idea.

— When the bow of a canoe is stuck nose down in rocks and mud and the entire boat is vertical, it's hard to stay in it.

— Standing up in a canoe, with or without a flag, is a substandard practice.

— Although it's easy to pee standing next to a golf course green, it's really tough to do so from a moving canoe.

— If there are no large rocks barring the way, it's almost as fast to run the rapids sideways as it is either bow first or stern first.

— Wet stuff stays wet when either it continually rains or you repeatedly capsize.

— Wet clothes are uncomfortable to wear, particularly in the wind.

— Watches that are not waterproof don't work too well after several minutes submerged under water.

— Sleeping on a bare concrete floor is painful.

Speaking of which, it occurred to us at around 8 p.m. that we would need to either camp out somewhere or find shelter again. Since our shelter choice had worked out so well the night before, we began scouting out opportunities. This quest was hastened by the onslaught of another thunderstorm. We passed a local hot dog stand and grabbed dinner. Before long, we spotted some riverfront houses and sneaked into someone's garage, which became our bunkhouse for the night. Having evolved into a mature group of travelers, no one threw up, and we didn't make much of a mess. But it was tough sleeping on that concrete floor on top of soaked sleeping bags. There may have been a light switch, but if there was, we didn't dare flick it, because that would have alerted the residents to the fact that we had commandeered their garage. (Perhaps they figured this out the next morning if they looked inside their garbage cans.) Someone muttered something like, "At least we had lights at the damned lodge." But we quickly fell asleep, thinking about how much of our stuff was slowly making its way to the Atlantic Ocean.

We drifted into the Water Gap—long past the time our canoes were due back—sometime during the second afternoon. We could tell we were late from the position of the sun. How late we couldn't surmise, as none of our watches worked. We could also tell we were long overdue from the expression on the face of the proprietor of the canoe rental company, who had apparently been waiting for hours. He was so relieved to see us, and to count seven canoes, and so distracted by the golf flag, that he didn't make an immediate inspection of the boats (one of which was in the shape of a W). Three of our fathers were there to drive us home. My father was one of them, although he wasn't the one who had to put up with the flagpole in the car. As we drove away, I remember looking through the rear window of his station wagon and seeing the canoe guy, staring at his gnarled, gashed, scraped, and misshapen boats, shaking his head back and forth as though attending the funeral of a loved one.

Today, Chamberlain Canoes offers a three-day overnight canoe adventure from Port Jervis to the Delaware Water Gap. "Fun, nature, and relaxation await you." With all our diversions and mishaps, how we made it in two days remains a mystery. Chamberlain advertises that it has been operating for thirty years. Apparently, it is one of the successors to the business of the fellow whose ruination we surely contributed to over fifty years ago.

The night we returned home, I dreamed that the canoe guy had gone to a local bar, ordered a Manhattan, and decided to chuck it all and move to California to become an avocado farmer.

FAT JACK D' MAZZO AND THE FANTABULOUS FART-A-PHONE

When you tell people you're from New Jersey, they usually ask, "What exit?" That's because many people spend their limited time in the state just driving up and down the Turnpike or Parkway.

Neither road goes anywhere near Newton, which is just north of Lake Hopatcong, just east of the Pennsylvania state line, a little south of Port Jervis, New York, and has the same latitude as Stamford, Connecticut. Newton is in the Kittatinny Valley on the edge of Great Slate Mountain, and it is the county seat of Sussex County (the New Jersey county with the highest number of dairy cows from 1850 to 1950, boasting "more cows than people").

Between 1937 and 1972, there was a summer camp nearby, known as "Camp Ken Etiwa Pec," operated by the Orange Mountain Council of the Boy Scouts of America. With others from Boy Scout Troop 15 in Short Hills, I attended Camp Ken Etiwa Pec for four years, between 1957 and 1960. It was a hoot.

It was hard to accept that this place was in New Jersey. No highways, no muffler shops, no pizza joints, no oil tanks, no shopping centers. Just woods, hills, and a fairly large lake. It could have been Vermont or Minnesota for all you could tell by looking at it. Very rustic and teeming with wildlife.

For some reason, summer camps back then always used Indian names. Earlier, at YMCA camp in the town of Summit, at the age of nine, I had been a member of the Inca Tribe. Our tribe leader, Carl, had a lisp and was always yelling "Hey, Incuths!" Once, I heard him refer to one of the other counselors as an "athhole."

Anyway, Camp Ken Etiwa Pec was divided into "units," each with an Indian name. There were at least the Cherokee, Iroquois, Apache, Seneca, Seminole, and Muncie Units. The Troop 15 guys were in the Muncie Unit. At first, we complained of being relegated to a unit with such an unferocious name. We couldn't figure out why we weren't the Mohicans, Chippewas, Ojibwas, Kiowas, or such. None of us had ever heard of the Muncies.

It turns out the town of Muncie, Indiana was named after the Muncie tribe of the Delaware Nation that inhabited the White River region of central Indiana. But even if we had known that, we wouldn't have cared. It was a weenie name.

So upon arrival our first year, we figured we were doomed to be the weenie tribe. It didn't turn out that way, though. We ruled.

That's because even though we weren't all that good at crafts, and despite a notable handicap in the skill of knot-tying, we had good athletes, and athletics were a large factor in who ruled. Being Indians, we didn't get in a lot of softball or football, but we did compete in running, hiking, boxing, horseshoes, fishing (casting into inner tubes), archery, target shooting with .22s, rowing, canoeing, and swimming.

We wiped up in the water sports. For some reason, we had several campers who were particularly good swimmers. Each year, there was a contest to win the "All American Water Boy" award. This required the contestants to swim across the lake, get into a rowboat and row back, switch into a canoe and cross again, and then swim back again. We usually had good results, and I happened to win the individual award each of my last two years. (Whoever set this up the first year I entered was a moron, because at the end of the race, all the canoes wound up on the far side of the lake, so the rowers had to go back across and tow them back. We eventually fixed this, properly sequencing swimming and boating so that at the end, everything was where it belonged.)

Boy Scout camp was not without its dangers. One morning I woke up in a sleeping bag face to face with a three-foot-long coiled rattlesnake. As anyone would have done, I pulled the zipper shut and yelled until a counselor gave me the all-clear. Some of the hiking trails were a little much, with roots and rocks everywhere. One time I tumbled down a hill, took a big puncture under my kneecap, and spent a couple of hours in Newton Hospital getting stitched up. Then there was the danger of pinkeye (which several campers seemed always to have). Underwear fungi and athlete's foot were rampant. And although I wasn't too bad at boxing, once I did take a punch directly in the throat, which sent me to the ropes.

And there was the danger of eating the food. Of course, the place where we ate was called the "mess hall," and it was usually a mess. There was always a barrel into which we had to scrape the swill from our plates. We understood the swill was then carted off to a nearby pig farm, although we were never convinced it wasn't recycled into casseroles. We eventually began referring to the mess hall as the *swill hall*. Although the "bug juice" (similar to Kool-Aid) we drank was probably not made from bugs, the many bugs in attendance seemed to drink a lot of it.

Another danger was heatstroke. Granted, this was New Jersey, not South Carolina, but it could get mighty hot out there when we weren't in the lake. Zero air conditioning 24/7. And each day, at least once, we had to stand at attention in the open area, under the sun, while the flag was raised or lowered, announcements were made, awards were handed out, and our uniforms got inspected.

Following Alaska by seven months, Hawaii became a state on Friday, August 21, 1959. There continued to be buzz about Puerto Rico, D.C., and Guam, but with fifty as a good round number, statehood action ended on that day. During an hour-long statehood celebration, we had to stand at attention in the bright sun, each of us drenched. Two guys went down for the count.

Just going to the bathroom was dangerous. Except for in the nature lodge (where we occasionally went to watch a snake swallow a bird), there was no plumbing. Each unit had a strategically placed latrine. The Muncie two-holer was about 100 yards up a steep, rocky hill often populated by snakes. This wasn't so bad during the day, but it was a mother at night.

Fortunately, as young teenagers, we had pretty good bladder control. Also, there was the failsafe of being able to pee in the woods, even out in back of the platforms on which the tents were mounted. This sometimes caused odor problems, but they were worth avoiding the walk up the hill. If you did pee in the woods, you had to be sure the Camp Director's wife (Mrs. Camp Director), or daughter (Harriet), the only females we ever encountered, didn't see you.

Pooping was another story. For that, unless we were near the Nature Lodge (about a half mile from our unit), we had to use the latrine, up the hill. Throughout the day, we would strategize our bowel movements to try to avoid having to go up the hill in the dark. This usually worked, although the aftermath of eating in the swill hall led to some issues for some of us on some nights.

Speaking of the latrine, we didn't call it that. That's what guys in the Army called it. In the Navy, it was the head. In England, the loo. In other contexts, the can, outhouse, privy, and throne. At Camp Ken Etiwa Pec, it was the looie. Actually, we weren't sure whether it was spelled "looie" or "louie." Either way, it was pronounced the same (loo-eee).

Which helps explain how hilarious it was when, during our second summer, we were joined by two brothers about a year apart. Their last name was Paper. One can only wonder what their parents were thinking when they named their sons Henry and Louis, nicknamed by the parents Hanky and Louie, and, by us, Hankypaper and Louiepaper. Not Hanky Paper and Louie Paper. There were no spaces—no pauses in the pronunciation. The accent was on the first syllable. *Hanky*paper and *Lou*iepaper (as in snot rag and toilet tissue).

How parents do this sometimes amazes me. A guy named Hack U. Stephenson wound up as the head surgeon at the Virginia State Penitentiary. I was once appointed to sue him on behalf of an inmate whose thumb he had cut off unnecessarily. Then there were twins born a few years ago in Petersburg, Virginia, who, somewhat hastily, and perhaps as the result of either attractive or unattractive hospital food, or too much drugs, were given the first names "*Orange*Jello" and "*Lemon*Jello" (with the accent, in each case, on the second syllable).

In addition to the perils of going to the looie at night, and all these other aforementioned dangers, there was poison ivy. We got it all the time. Half the campers were walking around with it between their fingers. A few people had it in the cracks of their rear ends, the result of not being close enough to the looie when they had to poop, and carelessly letting their hands graze the poison ivy while pulling up skunk cabbage to substitute for looie paper.

But we had one fellow, Jerry Shereschevsky, who repeatedly boasted immunity to poison ivy. "I've never had it and never will." He would rub the leaves around in his fingers and never come down with the rash. We gave Jerry a bad time about a lot of his traits (including the fact that he always snorted when he laughed, and when he peed off the back of his tent, he usually got half of it on his pants and the tent platform). So to show us how cool he was, he ate some poison ivy. This was the last we saw of Jerry. Within about a half hour, he was in an ambulance on the way to Newton Hospital, where we understood he was treated well into the next school year with poison ivy in all his organs—including stomach, bladder, spleen, lungs, and eyeballs.

One final danger was the lifesaving instructor, at least until he was neutralized.

I think his name was Guy. He was one of three counselors assigned to the waterfront, which consisted of the lake, a bunch of canoes and row boats, a complex of aluminum docks that formed a walking area, a shallow swimming area for the guys who were still learning, a deeper racing area for the good swimmers, and the very deep part of the lake for boating and learning lifesaving skills.

We were all into earning merit badges. After achieving canoeing and rowing, I signed up for lifesaving, which I figured was a gimme, as I had already been crowned the "All American Water Boy." Guy apparently knew this, so he decided to give me a bad time. I was about thirteen, and he was about eighteen and quite a bit taller and heavier than I was.

After passing the swimming, diving, and breath-holding parts of the training, and after a couple of sessions of "rescuing" other scouts by swimming out to them, grabbing them across the chest and chin, and bringing them back to the dock, I figured I was golden. I was treading water with my back to the dock, facing out into the lake. Without warning, Guy jumped off the dock, landed on my shoulders, and dragged me down about thirteen feet under water. I had no air, while he had plenty. He probably thought this was hilarious.

I didn't make a habit of fighting with guys much older and larger than I was, but I was both pissed and desperate.

First, I dropped my right hand down behind me and grabbed his privates. As he winced, I got one hand on his shoulder and twisted my body around just enough to bury my knee in the same place. It's hard to make your knee go real fast when you're under water, particularly when you're being strangled, but it can be made to work if you have the right angle and a neck to pull on. Anyway, that's when he took in all the water. He stayed down. I went up.

The other lifeguards didn't see what had transpired under the surface, but they probably figured it out, since I walked up the ladder and left, while Guy couldn't climb up the ladder. The other guys had to pull him up onto the dock, where he assumed the prone position with his hands cupped over the front of his bathing suit while his buddies started pumping water out of him. When they finally realized what had happened, and after they were pretty sure Guy was going to make it, they started laughing. But that didn't keep Guy, upon revival, from ejecting me from the lifesaving class. I probably could have appealed, but I had had it with him, so I flipped him the bird, which pretty much ended my quest to achieve this particular merit badge. I actually felt a bit benevolent for having afforded the other guys an opportunity to perform artificial respiration, as I could tell while leaving the venue they needed some practice anyway.

Guy tried not to ever again look me in the eye, but whenever I saw him, I purposely winked at him. He just turned his head, probably relieved that I hadn't reported him to the Camp Director for attempted murder.

When I first met Jack d'Mazzo, he was a twelve year-old lad from either South Orange, East Orange, West Orange, or maybe Verona, New Jersey. He was a bit rotund and affable, with a polite, understated way about him. He never blew his own horn. Except. . . well, I'll get to that.

By this stage in our lives, we had all learned, of course, that if you put your hand under your armpit and scrunched your arm down fast, you could make the sound of a fart. This became a daily activity, and we were always trying to make it louder and louder. We were also learning to make that sound by squeezing our hands together in a special way. This was hard, so we enjoyed it even more, spending many hours trying to perfect the trick. Some of us got so good at it that we even started to practice fart ventriloquism, where we could squeeze our hands together, aim the sound at someone else, and cause observers to believe the perpetrator was some innocent person across the room. This always got a lot of laughs. Except when we tried it out on our own parents.

There was a soft side of Camp Ken Etiwa Pec—a side that recognized the potential artistic skills of the campers. Each year I was there, the Camp Director hosted a talent contest. This was a big deal.

It's hard to find a young teenage boy with any artistic talent. Girls, yes. Brenda Lee, LeAnn Rimes, and Allison Krause were all about thirteen when they became stars. Boys that age, at least back then, might have been good at baseball, hunting, or bullshitting, but most (with the possible exception of Wayne Newton) were not good at any of the arts. There were, though, a few of these lads who had started to learn some form of entertainment, and some may have gone on to become great. There was a piano in the swill hall (usually covered with a tarp, to protect it from bug juice and the spoonfuls of apple butter we flung at each other), and a couple of guys could play it. There was a guy who could play the guitar, one who did magic tricks, a stand-up comedian, and a couple who could sing.

The talent show was usually at the end of the third two-week period each summer. We all had to be there, including the counselors and lifeguards. Even Mrs. Camp Director and Harriet were in attendance.

So one day we were sitting around in the Muncie Unit, practicing fart ventriloquism. Jack came by, showed us some improvements in technique he'd been working on, and then displayed how he'd taken the talent up several notches. We couldn't believe what he could do. He was an absolute fart virtuoso.

One of us said, "Why don't you enter the talent contest?" He said, "I don't have any talent." We all said, "Sure you do. This is great." "But I didn't sign up." "So what? You can apply for a late entry." "Okay, but one of you has to come with me to ask permission." So I went with him. We approached the counselor-in-charge and told him Jack wanted to enter the talent contest. "Well, what does he do?" "He plays an instrument." "What instrument?" "It's a secret." "He plays a secret instrument?" "He does, and you won't recognize it, and won't know what to say. So I had best introduce him." He relented and put Jack last on the line-up.

The night of the talent show came. We watched the piano player, the guitar player, the magician, the comedian, the singers, and the rest of them. They were all pretty good. The applause was polite.

It was Jack's turn. I walked up front, winking at Guy as I went past him. "Folks, you're really going to enjoy this. I give you Fat Jack d' Mazzo and the Fantabulous Fart-a-Phone." At which time the counselor/emcee started to shuffle. I could tell he was annoyed that we had tricked him into letting Jack enter the contest with such a bogus "talent."

Jack looked out at the crowd. He had brought no props. Everyone thought he was going to talk or sing. Slowly, he raised his left hand, exposing the web between his thumb and index finger. Palm down, he turned the web toward his mouth and started to blow on it, making it vibrate and thus farting "Melancholy Baby" just as smoothly as if it had come over the radio.

Few know this, but "Melancholy Baby" was first sung publicly by the great William Frawley (Fred Mertz on *I Love Lucy*). Later, famous versions came from Bing Crosby, Judy Garland, Ella Fitzgerald, Barbara Streisand, and The Monkees, and it was the favorite song of Sugar Kane (Marilyn Monroe) in the movie *Some Like It Hot*. Presumably, none of those folks ever got to hear the Fat Jack version, but they would have loved it, because he played it as clearly as Benny Goodman could have played it on the clarinet. In fact, Jack could even change, and mix, the tones, so that it sounded like a clarinet, then a trombone, then a sax, then a French horn. A virtual orchestra. There was even a hint of drums and a harp.

Anyway, the counselor/emcee's annoyance dissolved when he saw and heard what Jack was doing. Even Mr. and Mrs. Camp Director liked it. And Harriet was beside herself.

When he finished, and without saying another word or taking a bow, Jack put his instrument in his left pocket and his right hand in his right pocket and started to slump off the stage, probably figuring he had made a fool of himself. He was obviously surprised by the deafening round of applause and the standing ovation. Everyone was standing and chanting, "Fat Jack! Fat Jack! Fat Jack! More! More! More!" Jack did an encore of "I've Got Rhythm." It took a while for the crowd to calm down.

Fat Jack d'Mazzo and the Fantabulous Fart-a-Phone was the hands down winner of the 1959 Camp Ken Etiwa Pec talent show, even in the view of the other contestants.

The next year, the Paper boys and I asked Jack if we could audition to be his backup group, making fart noises with our hands. He declined. He went solo again (reprising his first two hits, and adding "Yes, We Have No Bananas"). He won for the second straight year.

I don't know what became of Jack. I do know he was working on perfecting "I Only Have Eyes For You," "Mack The Knife," "Oklahoma," "Love Letters in the Sand," the theme to *Rawhide*, "Wake Up Little Susie," "Purple People Eater," and a medley of Christmas favorites, including "The Chipmunk Song." The last time I remember talking with him, in the summer of 1960, we were encouraging him to interview for a job in the Skitch Henderson orchestra.

THIS IS NO FUN

Located well north of Albany, New York, and with ninety-nine miles of coastline, Raquette Lake is the largest natural lake in the Adirondacks. It's really a gorgeous spot with wilderness all around. Over a period of three summers in the early 1960s, it was my father's favorite place to take the family on vacation. This was supposed to be fun, and, in many ways, it was, although sometimes, for my father, it wasn't. His least satisfactory moments came in the form of golf, boating, and watching his children and their friends experience the thrill of flying in a sea plane. These types of events should have brought him pleasure, but they didn't always work out. Each year, at least one thing would happen that would rattle him.

For starters, my mother wasn't an outdoorsy person. Her father died when she was ten, so she had never gone camping, fishing, or boating. She was strictly an indoorsy person. So how it came to pass that my father conned her into doing three tours at Raquette Lake is a mystery.

My mother was the queen of drama. She had a way, when confronted with a situation that didn't sit quite right with her, of turning to my father (Gilbert), with her hands on her hips, and with an interjection that was half question and half exclamation, howling, "Gilly?!" (with the emphasis on the second syllable). Somehow, he was supposed to deal with whatever was eating at her, which was often impossible to discern, even after a full inquiry. This happened every few hours.

Each of the three years, I invited one of my great friends to go with us. The first year, it was Rob Hamilton. We were both about fourteen. Rob and I had then, and have now, a unique bond of humor. The same things make us laugh. To make them funnier to each other, sometimes we provide special accents to the words, and/or tilt our heads, and/or contort our faces in ways we remember others doing in the past.

It was a long ride to Raquette Lake—probably six or seven hours. Each year, somewhere south of Albany, we would stop for a picnic. I don't remember the details of each picnic, but I remember the first one as though it were yesterday.

We pulled off to a roadside picnic area. We had sandwiches and fruit and a cooler full of ice and, fortunately, grape soda.

Today, almost no one drinks grape soda. Although it is making a comeback, the only place you can usually find it is in specialty stores that sell vintage candy and gum, PEZ, wax bottles with colored sugar water inside—50s stuff. The original was Grape Nehi, which is what Radar O'Reilly lived on during the "M*A*S*H" years. As kids, we loved Grape Nehi. It became so popular that other manufacturers started to copy it. Even the local Short Hills grocery store chain—Shop Rite—came up with its own version. I think there were four or five Shop Rite grape sodas in our cooler at the roadside picnic area in upstate New York. If the product had been Nehi, we probably wouldn't have wasted so much of it.

For reasons I can't explain, other than teenage idiocy, Rob and I decided we would gross out my mother. Now, you have to understand that it didn't take much to gross out my mother, which was why we, and others, did it so routinely. She was an easy mark.

I think we devised our plan without even discussing it with one another. We communicated solely through facial expression. I recall that each of us took a huge mouthful of grape soda, feigned being sick to our stomachs at the same time, and staggered toward my mother, who was laying out the picnic table. There were two small trees near the table, about three feet apart. Wobbling, each of us approached a tree, grabbed onto it, hauled back, and unleashed the grape soda, much of it through our noses. It took minutes for the spray to settle.

After she finally closed her gaping mouth, and with her hands on her hips, all my mother could say, was "Gilly?!"

The picnic proceeded, although we heard about the incident for years.

After lunch, during which there was very little chatter, we proceeded to our destination.

FIRST SUMMER—GOLF

The campgrounds at Raquette Lake were owned by a family named the Lamphears. In fact, the family seemed to own much of the real estate up there, because the name was everywhere. Lamphear Road, Lamphear General Store, Lamphear Gas Emporium, and Lamphear Marina. The Lamphear name is still prominent in the area. For instance, the Lamphear Fishing Derby is held over a two-day period in the middle of May of each year.

Mr. Lamphear was probably around sixty—to us, ancient. We would see him interacting with his employees, all of whom, in his presence, were extremely deferential. "Yes sir, Mr. Lamphear." "No, sir, Mr. Lamphear." "Right away, Mr. Lamphear." For some reason, seeing these guys kowtow to Mr. Lamphear struck Rob and me as funny. We loved mimicking them.

My father had rented two little cabins. Actually, the one he, my mother, and sister stayed in was little. The one Rob and I stayed in (about twenty yards away) was the square root of tiny. It was so small that if you were to sit in a chair on one side, you could almost put your feet on the opposite wall. There were two single beds, which took up the whole place. The commode was outside. There was a puny screened-in porch that would accommodate only one person at a time. Only if you kept your arms at your sides could you turn around in it. But to us, this was high living. Our own house.

Early the first morning, a couple of the workers were coming down the trail for something or other on their way either to fix a boat, or put up a sign, or something. We heard them talking about their boss. At least twice, they referred to him as "Old Man Lamphear." For some reason, this tickled us. So we started using this phrase off and on. "There's Old Man Lamphear."

Perhaps because he was missing most of his teeth, one of the workers had trouble pronouncing the unflattering nickname he had for his boss. He puckered his mouth in such a way that neither the "l" nor the "d" in "Old" came out clearly. Ditto the "n" in "Man" or the "r" in Lamphear. Accordingly, he referred to our host as "Oh Ma Lamphea." That's the way Rob and I, puckering, have always uttered this phrase. To this day, if either of us just looks at the other and says "Oh Ma Lamphea," we both break out laughing, tears coming out of our eyes. We contort our faces when we say this. Our wives don't get it.

On about the third day of cloudy weather and not much to do and my mother staying indoors, my father decided it would be fun to play golf with Rob and me. And it *would* have been, if there had been a real golf course nearby. We never saw one. What we did find was a dusty torture palace designed to ruin the day of all who entered.

This was not a country club. It was a run-down, blue-collar public course. There was no pro shop—just a counter with a Coke machine and a rack of stale Nabs next to a cash register, where you paid your five bucks and picked up a scorecard and a pencil. If there was a driving range or a putting green, we didn't see them. We headed straight out to the links.

I can't remember if this was a par three course, or just a course with short holes. It looked easy. My father was sure to break ninety. He was ready for a good round.

But there was something about the place that struck all three of us as not quite right. Nothing was green. Everything was tan. Tan and hard.

On a normal course, you put a tee between your fingers, bend down, stick it in the ground, stand up, take a few practice swings, and hit your ball out onto a soft, green fairway. Here, unless you happened to bring a hammer, or carried a rock around with you (which each of us started doing), you couldn't get your tee into the ground. With or without a tee, you were looking at a tan landscape made up of hills, rocks, and craters. The "fairways," "roughs," and "greens" all looked pretty much the same, with slightly varying slants. It was like being on the moon.

Appearing confident, my father addressed the ball. He was very powerful. He used to be able to walk across a gym floor on his hands, and could really cream the ball. Unfortunately, this was not a course where you really wanted to cream the ball, because the harder you hit it, the harder it bounced and ricocheted from hill to rock to tree to hill to rock to nowhere. It was like playing pinball. There was no way to predict where the ball would end up. It would zing here and zang there. Sometimes it would go twice as far as it should, being reenergized by skipping off rocks. Other times, if the rocks were facing the wrong way, the ball would fly back, land *behind* the tee, and you'd find yourself "lying one" with more distance from your ball to the pin than when you started.

The scores started to mount up quickly. Instead of just "laying one up there," where it might land on semi-flat surface and roll toward the pin or the green, you had to play the ricochet.

Or your ball got stuck in a ground crevice just deep enough to hold it there—forever. On a normal golf course, you could hit behind your ball in the grass or dirt with an iron and lift the ball out, accompanied by a divot. Here, if you tried to hit behind the ball, either your club would skip over the ball, or it would stop dead where it first hit, thus numbing your hands and forearms and disfiguring your club. It was like trying to golf off a jagged rock. The ground was so hard that if you could crowbar out a piece of it, you could use it to cut diamonds.

The sand traps were essentially shale pits.

To make matters worse, you couldn't tell the greens from the fairways, except that on the former there were flags sticking up, usually slanted. The greens didn't seem to have borders. And they were so hard and slick that it was like trying to putt on an autopsy table. It could take one person fifteen minutes to nine-put a green.

Almost immediately, we started losing balls on the fairway. My dad started using phrases like "Son of a gun," which soon escalated to "Son of a bitch," and similar expletives. By the twelfth hole, he exhibited kind of a vacant stare as we aimlessly looked for another new ball he had lost. He looked down at the ground and muttered to no one in particular, "This is no fun."

We were rolling along at a pace of about 150 strokes each for the full eighteen holes, when my father spotted a chance at redemption. He was going to man-up and drive the thirteenth "green." This green was on the edge of the course, not too far from the parking lot. After abandoning his tee, he just set the ball on the ground and smacked it with a two-iron. The ball stayed low and sailed over the green toward the parking lot, which we couldn't quite see but knew was there.

Try to imagine the sound you would hear if you stood on the edge of your yard and drove a golf ball on a low line drive into the side door of your car. That's the sound we heard. My father just stared straight ahead, apparently not wanting to know exactly what had happened. But he had his son and his son's friend standing next to him. He couldn't walk away and avoid responsibility. With him on point, we walked over to the parking lot. It wasn't hard to find the late model luxury car. His ball had hit exactly in the middle of the chrome strip separating the door from the window. One-sixteenth of an inch higher and the ball would have gone through one window and out the other. One-sixteenth of an inch lower and the door would have looked as though it had been rammed by a rhino.

My father's next utterance was, "Is anybody hungry?" Or maybe it was, "Who wants to go fishing?" Either way, we left from the thirteenth fairway, dropped our scorecard into a garbage can on the way to the car, and headed back to the lake.

SECOND SUMMER—BOATING

Jim Higgins maintains that he does not remember spending a week with us the next summer at Raquette Lake. But for the sake of moving forward with the story, let's just say it was him.

By this second summer, our family was staying in a more upscale cabin on the other side of the lake. The bathroom was inside.

The cabin was near a marina where we could check out motorboats. By "we" I mean my father. He explained repeatedly to Higgs and me that the motorboats belonged to someone else (i.e., Old Man

Lamphear) and could be "dangerous to operate." Without meaning to do so, he proceeded to show us just how dangerous they could be.

My mother declared that we needed some groceries. My father could have driven to the grocery store. Instead, he told Higgs and me, "Wouldn't it be fun to go shopping in a boat?" Figuring we'd probably get to steer the boat, we both said, "Sure," even though we were having a pretty good time hanging out with some of the other teenagers. The store was across the lake and down a couple of miles. Off we went. A new adventure.

On the way back, I asked if Higgs and I could take turns steering. My father's response went something like this: "This is a very powerful machine, and there are a lot of unknown obstacles out here on the lake. I'm going to steer for a while until we get our bearings a little better. I'll give you guys a go when we're back in more familiar, and calmer, water."

With that, there was a loud *"CATHWAP,"* as the blade of the outboard motor crashed into a protruding rock, or maybe it was a stump. The back of the motor abruptly emerged out of the lake like a rising sailfish. With the propeller still spinning (but with one of its prongs exiting west like a Frisbee), the entire motor flipped over into the boat. The propeller crashed down into the grocery bags. Higgs went port; I went starboard; and my father dove for the bow. Then silence. We all pinched ourselves. No one was hurt. "Wow! That was a close call," my father said. "See? I told you this is dangerous." Nothing from Higgs or me on that comment. We started repackaging the partly damaged groceries.

Then it dawned on us that we were a couple of miles away from our cabin area. We had lost our exact bearings. We didn't know where any other rocks, or stumps, were, and oh, as I mentioned, the motor was totally inside the boat.

Although my father had led a company of engineers in WWII, he didn't really have any engineering skills. He had been a lumberjack, a carpenter, a cabinetmaker, and a candidate for a degree in architecture when he joined the army, lied about his eyesight and went to Officer Candidate School (OCS), and then to Europe. But a real engineer he was not, particularly in the mechanical sense. Higgs and I were fifteen and knew nothing about motors or engines (a knowledge level that has remained static, at least for me). But somehow, the three of us got the motor back to where it belonged, and through nothing short of a miracle, it started up—albeit at somewhat of a putter at first, particularly given the missing propeller blade. Having proved his steering prowess, my father took the wheel, stationing Higgs and me on the starboard and port sides to watch out for impediments—of which we saw none. In fact, the only impediment we perceived all week was the one we hit, and that was after the fact.

By this time, of course, no one back at the home front could figure out where we were. My mother had come down to the dock, because she was awaiting the arrival of the groceries. This is what she, and the others who had gathered to await our arrival, saw:

A boat with three very still males aboard was approaching, first at a slow speed. Then one of the males—Higgs—started waving his arms about. Another—it was me—started yelling. The driver—my father—exhibited a look of panic and had one hand over his head. It looked like the boat was speeding up—and it was. The throttle had become stuck in forward, full speed ahead and accelerating. Even with the one blade missing, the vessel went into warp speed. It was headed right for the front of the dock, bouncing on the choppy water. Everyone backed up. Several women screamed. A couple of teenagers dove into the lake to save themselves.

Had someone later hired an accident reconstructionist, he could not have explained how the bow of the boat had jumped the dock. The hull landed flat up and skidded forward, causing the back of the motor to catch on the end of the pier, in turn causing the entire motor—blades up—to again sail into the air, doing a flip. The already impaired prop landed again in the partly salvaged groceries.

Old Man Lamphear's minions were watching from a distance.

My mother was standing on the dock with her hands on her hips, yelling, "Gilly?!"

None of the three crew members said a word. We just started gathering the clobbered groceries so we could carry them up to the cabin, which we proceeded to do. Most of the contents were no longer contained in bags or boxes. Higgs carried two boxes of spaghetti, each of which had no seal at the end, so he was leaving strands of broken pasta in a trail behind him like Hansel and Gretel.

Higgs and I were so embarrassed that we didn't join the other teenagers for ping-pong and bullshitting afterwards. I think we went to a remote area and pitched horseshoes instead.

For the next day or two, any time my father got anywhere close to the boathouse, the employees and other guests would scatter. Plus he had to settle up with Old Man Lamphear.

THIRD SUMMER—FLYING LESSONS

The next year, my friend Jim "Bay" Basinger came with us. We stayed in the same cabin we had occupied the year before when Higgs was (or wasn't) there.

From the shore, and in the distance, we could see an amphibious plane land and take off from the lake. My father had always wanted to become a pilot (which he eventually did in his late 50s). Although he had spent more time than most people in the air (including much of a war), he said, "Sure would like to fly one of those beauties. That would be such great fun. Looks like he's taking up tourists. Would you guys like to go?"

We immediately signed up.

So the next day, Bay and I climbed into the seaplane. I was in the front seat and Bay in the back. The pilot looked to me and said, "Push that button there, would you, Sport?"

"Okay." I pushed.

"Now, see that thing over there? Slide that to the right."

I did, and it did something to a flap on one of the wings.

"Oh, and I'll need you to do this, and need you to do that." Bay's in the back seat with no buttons to push, but the pilot asks him to turn a crank on the roof. I finally said, "Wait a minute. We're sixteen years old. We can't even drive cars. We haven't taken Drivers Ed yet. Why are you asking us to do all this stuff?"

With that, the pilot showed us his right hand, which displayed only a pinky and a thumb. "I would have done all this myself, but a few weeks ago, I cut off three of my fingers in the propeller." I think this is when the idea of writing a book first came to me.

So with two newly minted assistant pilots sharing cockpit duties, the seaplane began to taxi, creating a huge wake that thoroughly torqued off several people in nearby canoes, who were shaking their fists. My father waved to us.

As the aircraft ascended, flying out of sight of the onlookers, the seven-fingered genius on the stick said something like, "You boys want to have some fun?"

Bay asked, "You're not going to make us steer also, are you?"

The pilot said, "No, but see that fire tower up there on the mountain? Hold on, boys!" (We *had* to hold on, because there were no seat belts.) With that, he aimed the plane directly at the fire tower and then suddenly banked upwards like a rocket ship. For the last fifty feet of the tower, our plane was moving parallel to it (i.e., straight up). Both of the guys in the tower, having endured this harassment before, gave the pilot the finger. He gave one back, using the only hand that could perform the task. Bay and I practically peed in our pants.

It is a proven scientific fact that when girls turn thirteen, they immediately discern that their parents are the dumbest people on earth. They attribute similar traits to older siblings. This combined with their inherent skill at whining makes them almost intolerable for several years. While Bay and I were airborne, my sister and her friend Sharon Kelley (both then in that phase) decided they wanted to go up in the seaplane too. My father said. "Absolutely not."

After we landed, Bay and I heard my sister and Sharon carrying on about wanting to take a ride in the plane. We wanted them to leave so we wouldn't have to listen to their whining. For that reason, we didn't call my father's attention to the pilot's missing fingers, which surely would have blocked the girls' prospective adventure. So my father, also apparently tired of the whining, relented, and the two girls climbed into the plane.

My father was scared out of his mind at this decision he had made, which went downhill when, at some distance, he saw the sea plane heading toward a bridge on a road near the lake. It wasn't a real low bridge, but it sure looked low from the marina. My father said, "What the hell is he doing?" With that, the seaplane flew under the bridge, banked, and came back to the lake.

Within twenty minutes, my father was making himself a Manhattan. Bay and I waited a few years to tell him about the pilot's digital handicap. We never told my mother.

Bay, Higgs, and Rob know these stories. But to Rob and me, the words "This is no fun," mean so much more than they might to the others. They remind us of a great trip, and many others we took together—learning to play golf with our fathers; soaking in their kindnesses and all the opportunities they gave us; watching them display their frustrations; finessing difficult golf terrain; and changing the contours of a car door.

Rob, Higgs, Bay, and I loved our fathers, and our other friends' fathers. We were all so lucky. So often, particularly when they were in positions of responsibility (such as umpiring, trying to oversee a Boy Scout troop, or attempting to control a Sunday School class), we did things *to* our fathers. But we also did things *with* our fathers, and we loved every opportunity. They were all good to us. My father, Rob's father, Higgs' father, Bay's father, Messrs. Thompson, MacIlroy, Estes, Freund, Hughes, McQueen, Jaeger, and others—they were truly excellent specimens. They wanted us to have fun, and *we* usually did, even though it didn't always work out all that well for *them*.

THE *CAPTAIN BILL*

In 1939, Joe DiMaggio was nicknamed the "Yankee Clipper" by Yankee Stadium announcer Art McDonald. Maybe that's why, for years, when the New York Yankees were training in Fort Lauderdale, Florida, they chose the Yankee Clipper Hotel as their home base.

Located on A1A at the south end of the traditional Fort Lauderdale beachfront, this structure was built to look like a ship, even though it was not named for a ship, or for Joe DiMaggio, but for an airplane. It's a few miles down the beach from the Elbo Room, where, in 1960, right under our noses, the movie *Where the Boys Are* was filmed (in which Yvette Mimieux, Paula Prentiss, and the perpetually tan George Hamilton starred, and Connie Francis made her movie debut). Big excitement.

Anyway, the beach adjacent to the Yankee Clipper is where, for years, I spent a lot of time with my family while visiting—and for a time living in—Fort Lauderdale. I didn't see much of the Yankee players, except when my father took me to a spring training game. I got to see Mickey Mantle, Yogi Berra, Moose Skowron, Whitey Ford, Gil McDougald, Ellie Howard, Country Slaughter, and others up close. This was pretty cool, but I was an avid Brooklyn Dodgers fan in the 50s, having amassed a sizeable collection of their Topps baseball cards, some of them having been preserved in almost mint condition. A future gold mine.

Almost directly across A1A from the Yankee Clipper was the Bahia Mar Marina, which, in the late 50s and early 60s, was the home to two excursion boats that attracted me. I wanted so bad to go out on both of them.

GILBERT E. "BUD" SCHILL, JR. AND JOHN W. "MAC" MACILROY
AND ROBERT D. "ROB" HAMILTON III.

In the late 50s, my grandfather, father, and uncle opened a branch of their New Jersey-based millwork business in Pompano and bought two tiny houses on the southwest outskirts of Fort Lauderdale. They would take turns commuting from New Jersey to man the southern business venue, and our families would be in Fort Lauderdale for weeks at a time. I spent half of eighth grade there.

Our house was on the far edge of the distant outskirts, beyond the cattle ranches, in the middle of nowhere. It took almost an hour to drive to the beach. Our development had thousands of houses, all of which were exactly the same except for the color of the cement, the names on the mailboxes, and the cars in the driveways. It was a wonder anyone could find their way home.

About a block down from our house was a sandy field. I wandered in there couple of times and ran into some other boys who lived nearby. It turned out they were Native Americans (whom we called "Indians" at the time). I made friends with these young lads and hung out with them whenever I could. They were just as goofy as I was.

Fort Lauderdale is known as the "Venice of America." It has an extensive canal system, branching off of the Intracoastal Waterway and the Indian River. Back then, some of the canals were lined with the beautiful homes of the beautiful people. My father would often drive us past the abodes of the likes of Mickey Rooney and Tallulah Bankhead. We didn't think there were any canals out where we lived—just sand, and grass, and look-alike houses, and cement trucks, and road pavers, and gas stations, and Royal Castle hamburger joints. It was really drab. To get away from the drab, we would drive up to the Yankee Clipper beach on weekends, keep an eye out for the ballplayers, and marvel at all the boats at Bahia Mar. Again, there were two that always caught my eye.

The first was the *Jungle Queen*. This was a triple-deck excursion craft made to look like a riverboat. Back then, you just sat on it and listened to a semiretired tour guide tell you about the primitive land that lay beyond: the land of jungles, and Indians, and alligators. These were brave Indians, who wore deerskin pants, and moccasins, and painted their faces and had feathers in their hair, and who, for reasons none of us understood, had perfected the skill of wrestling alligators. My sister and I always wanted to go for a ride on the *Jungle Queen*, to explore this primitive land and watch this dangerous activity we had heard so much about.

So one day, my father drove us the hour it took to get from our house to Bahia Mar, and we all climbed aboard the *Jungle Queen*. After about an hour out on the Indian River, the *Jungle Queen* moored at the much-anticipated Indian village. We thought we were in another world. Dangerous activity. A huge alligator pit. Enormous alligators. Fierce Indian men. One of the braves vaulted into the pit, charged a gator, grabbed him on the side and started rubbing his belly, thus paralyzing him (or her) into total inactivity.

This should have been exciting, but it wasn't. There was no biting. No thrashing. The post-wrestling inactivity of the gators wasn't much different than the pre-wrestling inactivity. None of it was very scary. In fact, it was a downright wimpy show.

I decided there was nothing to this wrestling alligators stuff. This was supposed to be the highlight of the *Jungle Queen* adventure, but it was a bust. I wanted to go out on a real boat, in real water. I wanted to go fishing for the day out on the high seas—on the *Captain Bill*.

In fact, just as we got back to the marina, and were exiting the *Jungle Queen*, we saw all the fishermen coming off the *Captain Bill*. They were red as lobsters and drunk as skunks, having been fishing all day on the famous craft. They had all caught fish and were loading them into coolers, beaming with pride and slapping each other on the back.

Bored with sleepy alligators, I nagged my father to take me out on the *Captain Bill*. He told me that someday we might just do that. Someday came a year or two later.

In the meantime, a few days after the "jungle" adventure, I was hanging out with the Indian boys, and one of them asked what my father did. I explained he was in the millwork business and that he was working up in Pompano. They volunteered that their fathers worked nearby. In fact, they could walk to work. "We'll show you." They did.

Off we went. Down one block, then a second, and then a third. Suddenly, I saw a canal. I didn't know there was one so close, especially one so wide. Then there was a clearing. It was the very same dumpy fake Indian village we had visited on the *Jungle Queen*. Three blocks from our house! So when our family had made a day of the *Jungle Queen* adventure, we had driven an hour in the car to the marina and then spent another hour in the stupid boat, only to return to a spot three blocks from our house. Pretty annoying.

As the boys and I approached this bogus "Indian village" by foot, I noticed the alligator pit with the two lethargic gators in there, each probably about ten feet in length. The only thing that kept them inside was their apparent laziness, their inability to hop, and the absence of ladders.

The boys had obviously been here before, watching their fathers "wrestle." One of the kids scaled the wall. The other climbed a tree on the edge of the pit and loosened a rope that was tucked behind a branch. He used the rope to swing out over the pit.

Although I had earlier concluded that these particular alligators were pansies, and that there was some trick to "wrestling" them, I wasn't, at first, thrilled with the idea of either swinging over the creatures or climbing into the pit. But I did both. And somehow, I manned up to the idea of rubbing the belly of one of the creatures. This was a piece of cake. Maybe they had just been fed plenty of chickens to keep them from being hungry, but they didn't snap at me. I felt I had accomplished something important.

When I got home, I didn't tell my parents where I had been, nor did I tell my sister, who would have turned me in right away.

This was one of two close encounters I had with alligators in the Fort Lauderdale canal system. The other was about three years later when I was water skiing in the canal near the intersection of Bay View and Sunrise, next to the park where Chris Evert was learning to play tennis. Right there, the canal was quite wide. My father was steering the powerboat. We had all sort of lost track of the fact that there were still some gators in the canals. So he's charging ahead and casually waving back at me, and I'm skiing, and out of nowhere, a big old alligator surfaces about ten feet in front of me. I had nowhere to go. My skis went right up his back and I sailed off his snout as if he were a ramp. Fortunately, I landed on my skis and kept going.

My father saw the whole thing. He panicked, lost track of where he was, looked out and saw land coming up on him at full speed. He yanked the steering wheel to the port side to avoid crashing the boat. Unfortunately, this propelled me with significant centrifugal force right at the beach. I had two choices. One was to fall back into the water, but there were some pretty stiff looking reeds sticking up, and I could have been skewered. So I chose instead to just hit the beach and slide into the sand. Except it wasn't sand. It was coral. My skis stopped short, and I slid about twenty feet up the coral surface. I took a piece of coral through my left hand, and my chest and legs looked like someone had sliced them open with razor blades mounted on a rake. Two guys had to hold me down in the emergency room, while another rubbed me mercilessly with a course washcloth soaked in alcohol. I looked like a mummy for days.

During the spring of 1960, my great friend from Short Hills, Rob Hamilton, went with me to Fort Lauderdale for about ten days. The two of us took our first airplane ride, during which the plane suddenly dropped a thousand feet in an air pocket, causing two stewardesses (as they were known back then) to temporarily experience weightlessness, touch their feet to the ceiling of the plane, and somersault into the laps of passengers, who, in turn, had soup bowls on their heads and noodles up their noses.

Upon arrival in Fort Lauderdale, Rob and I proceeded to get overly sunburned at the Yankee Clipper beach and had to spend two days taking turns soaking in lukewarm baths with Epsom salt, or some other soothing substance. The only exercise we could get during that interlude was to use my cork gun to shoot porcelain figurines off my sister's bureau. Speaking of which, at this point in my life, I was at the height of my marksmanship skill. I was deadly with a cork gun, having perfected the skill while spending a week at the Jersey Shore with Scotty Estes and his family, where he and I alternated using his cork gun to annihilate every fly in the house, before moving outside to get the rest of them. We got so good that, adjusting for breezes, we could nail those flies while they were still in the air.

Before heading home from the beach to recuperate from the toasting, I showed Rob the *Captain Bill*. We both marveled at it. We noticed that there was a small kiosk on the dock, where the vessel was moored. It had a sign advertising the *Captain Bill*, and wedged in all along the window of the kiosk were small *Captain Bill* business cards, which the proprietor obviously hoped would be grabbed by potential customers so they could show their friends and promote his business. We each grabbed one. In between Epsom salt baths and shooting the cork gun, we talked about how cool it would be to go out on the *Captain Bill*. We mentioned this on a daily basis to my father.

Rob and I had a friend from Short Hills named Woody Thompson. His family happened to be in Fort Lauderdale when we were there, and they came over to our house. The adults were a bit hungover from the night before, so we sat around our living room for a few hours while they decompressed. Rob and I had played up the *Captain Bill* so much that eventually my father and Mr. Thompson relented and agreed to take the three of us out the next morning on this glorious fishing boat. We were sure to have a fabulous adventure and catch lots of large fish. (Mr. Thompson's first name, by the way, was Grove, which made the nicknames of two of his sons, Woody and Chip, all the more appropriate.)

We stopped at a Howard Johnson's for breakfast on the way to the dock. I remember that because, looking out the window and across the street, I saw a Howard Johnston's, which was a replica of the Howard Johnson's, with the same design and colors, but an extra letter in the name. I wasn't too sure which one was built first, but this contrast gave me my first experience in the world of trademark infringement. Anyway, fueled with pancakes, Woody, Rob, Grove, my father, and I headed to Bahia Mar for a day of fishing.

We arrived at the slip at about 9 a.m. The Captain met us on the gangplank as we headed into the boat. Making small talk, Mr. Thompson asked him how the weather looked. "Couldn't be better. Perfect day for fishing. You'll love it." We were revved up.

Two deck hands helped us board and stow our stuff. One was quite pudgy, and the other was really wiry. Neither said much, and neither looked too smart, but their jobs were basically to bait hooks and clean up. It's the cleaning up part that proved to be a challenge.

The Captain was right about the weather—for the first fifteen minutes. Once we got out onto the open sea, things started to change. We were all gearing up for a lot of fishing. The two mates were walking up and down the deck, offering to put bait on the lines, but cautioning us fishermen not to drop our lines until we got far enough out—until we got to the "old salt's favorite fishing hole."

As we moved further offshore, the swells started. Pretty soon the *Bill* was rocking from side to side. It got worse and worse, until we all assumed we were doomed. The swells exceeded fifteen feet. There was no horizon. All we could see was water. If the boat was tilting port and you were holding that rail, you were basically doing a handstand. If, at the time, you were holding the starboard handrail, you were basically doing a pull-up.

No one on the boat caught a single fish. In fact, no one had a single bite. In fact, no one spent a single minute fishing or even wanting to fish. It was all we could do to dodge the fishing poles, lures, buckets of bait, and other paraphernalia that started shifting from port to starboard and back (some on the deck, and some in the air). Not everyone was agile enough to dodge these items as well as we did. And just about everyone got sick. The worst scene was one poor slob who somehow managed to get to a stationary bench toward the middle of the boat. He lay down on his stomach, grabbed the bench with both arms, hooking both ankles behind him like a human clamp. Thus he was able to stay in one place. This was both good and bad. Good because he didn't careen into us. Bad because, for the next forty-five minutes, it was like watching Linda Blair throw up in *The Exorcist*. We were afraid to laugh too loud for fear of throwing up ourselves, not from the motion, but from watching this guy retching on the bench.

During the tempest, the skinny mate, somehow able to stand, did nothing but mop up puke. As he did this, and as if to taunt the rest of us, he ate Cheese Nabs, which he squeezed into his mouth from the cellophane wrapper using one hand, while mopping with the other. His face bore no expression whatsoever. He almost seemed bored.

Miraculously, none of the five of us got sick, although Mr. Thompson was green and my father was mauve. Woody, Rob, and I, having been veterans of the Wild Mouse ride at Seaside Heights, New Jersey, were able to handle the ocean motion. We eventually made it back to the marina and entered the parking lot. Almost everyone was silent, including the crew. Walking on a slant, everyone just headed for their cars. I don't recall anyone tipping the deck hands.

I say *almost* everyone was silent. Woody, Rob, and I were talking up a storm. Not feeling the least bit sick, we made fun of everyone who was. Coming down the gangplank, we asked a couple of our fellow "fishermen" if they could go for a big juicy cheeseburger with mustard, onions, and fries. They bolted.

By the time we got back to our house, both Mr. Thompson and my father needed a drink. The Thompsons had to leave Fort Lauderdale the next day, so Rob and I would have to wait a couple of weeks to further compare notes with Woody.

Sometimes it's hard to remember when genius strikes, particularly as it happened to us so often in our early teens. I still remember the thrill of the caper Rob and I commenced on the day following the fishing trip. On that day, and for the rest of the week, we conned one of my parents into driving us up to the beach and leaving us there for the day. Every time we would walk past the *Captain Bill* kiosk, we would each take a couple of business cards, studying them as if interested, and put them in our pockets. As the days wore on, our thefts became more serious. We would take five each, then ten, then more.

For reasons neither Rob nor I could ever explain, we thought this was funny. We had the cards in our bathing suit pockets, in our shirt pockets and in our wallets. Every day, we purloined more cards. There would usually be about forty of them up on the board in the morning. By evening, there were about two, and we would have the other thirty-eight. By the time we had to return to New Jersey, there were no cards left at the kiosk, and our pockets and gym bags were stuffed with them.

Looking back on this through the prism of law school, our actions probably did not amount to petty larceny, since the cards were free and there was no sign that said "Take Only One." So I'm not willing to concede that a crime was committed.

We started to imagine Captain Bill at home at night, counting his future revenues from all the patrons who must be planning to go out on his boat, and explaining his anticipated business success to his wife:

"Baby, baby, baby, you know those earrings you were looking at last weekend down on Las Olas Boulevard?"

"Yeah?"

"Buy 'em!"

"What have you done now?"

"Wait a minute. I just had a spurt of generosity."

"What have you done now?"

"I just think we're going to be in the money. Business is looking way up."

"Way up, my ass. All I hear around town is that you took a group out a few days ago, caught no fish, two guys got hit in the side of the head by fishing rods, and everybody threw up. How do you convert that to cash?"

"Well, you know the great idea I had about putting the cards on the kiosk?"

"It was my idea, by the way."

"Right. Your great idea. Well, they're moving like hotcakes. Everyone in town is taking them, obviously looking forward to a day on the *Bill*. Probably telling all their friends. I anticipate we'll be full for most of the coming year. We may even have to buy another boat. Possibly a fleet."

"I seriously doubt it. The boat's a wreck, you're not getting any younger, you obviously can't gauge the weather, and both of your crew members are idiots. One looks like a manatee, and the other has the appearance and personality of a table leg."

And so on and so forth.

Again, we didn't know exactly how Mrs. Captain Bill took all this, but we figured the old salt was probably dreaming at night of gold chains, fancy cars, a country club membership, open Hawaiian shirts, young models on his arm, drinks on the house. Rob and I discussed this all the time, even after we returned to New Jersey. Even while we were in high school. Even while we were in college. Even now.

If you ever find yourself blessed with an overabundance of *Captain Bill* cards, there are many ways to put them to use. You can:

- Place them on the kiosks of other fishing boats.
- Include them with your tip at local restaurants.
- Use them to scrape cat poop and hairballs off a rug.
- Substitute them for worn out or misplaced Monopoly cards.
- Put a cluster of them under a table leg to keep the table steady.
- Insert them under the windshield wipers of random cars, particularly in the Northeast and Midwest.

According to an article a while back in the Fort Lauderdale *Sun-Sentinel*, the sixty-five-foot, blue and white *Captain Bill*, with a passenger capacity of forty, was mothballed in 1997, probably due to the long-term effects of our stealing all the business cards and the subsequent lavish investments the Captain made in preparation for the anticipated rapid expansion of his customer base. The headline reads, "Rising Expenses And Slow Business Combine To Sink Captain Bill, A Fort Lauderdale Fishing Institution For More Than Forty Years."

It turns out the original Captain Bill (the person) was Captain Bill Ennis, who started the business in 1940. By the time we made our voyage in 1960, Ennis had sold the business to his stepdaughter's husband, Frank Smith. I don't know whether it was Ennis or Smith who piloted the craft in the spring of 1960, although it was probably Smith, since, according to the article, when he took over in the 50s, Smith had fished only once in his life, and that was when he attended the University of Miami, where he played halfback (referred to by his coach as "drawback"), before going on to log three years with a

Milwaukee Braves farm team. This was obviously inadequate preparation for a life at sea.

When my father was in his eighties, my wife Ginger and I were visiting him in Fort Myers, Florida, where he then lived full-time. We were talking about the old days, including the two Bahia Mar adventures. He remembered that I had befriended the Indian boys. He did not remember, because I had never mentioned it to him, the part about me wrestling the alligators. When I told him, he coughed his gin and tonic up through his nose, swallowing an ice cube by mistake. Then I asked if he recalled the day we went out on the *Captain Bill*. And he said, "All I can remember was Grove turning green and that fool of a pencil-thin deck hand eating Nabs while mopping up puke."

I've said I was a Brooklyn Dodgers fan has a kid. A huge fan. I collected about a million Dodgers baseball cards, including, as I recall, every player on the 1956 team (the year they traded Jackie Robinson to the Giants and he retired). Of course, my mother, as so many other mothers did, threw my baseball cards out during my first or second year in college. Had she kept them, I would be able to afford the losses I anticipate from my investment in this book. So you can imagine my surprise, and consternation, when, in my late twenties, I opened an old box of stuff from my childhood room, thinking it might contain my baseball cards, and hoping to see Carl Erskine, Clem Labine, Don Newcombe, Pee Wee Reese, Roy Campanella, Carl Furillo, Gil Hodges, and my other "Bums"—and, hence, my fortune. I found instead, secured by a rubber band, about 200 *Captain Bill* cards, most of them in near mint condition.

SO *THAT'S* HOW
SHE GOT THE BIRD

Most of us were pretty good bullshitters, and a few of us gentlemen freeloaders of some note. Suds Estes and I thought we could run with the best of them, and by our seventeenth year—both of us newly licensed drivers—we were ready to take our show on the road.

In a happy circumstance of geography, our town was not far from a slice of the New Jersey Shore, and an easy drive—a few congested miles south on the Garden State Parkway to the Perth Amboy exit around Woodbridge, then southeast onto 9A, which promised a nifty traffic roundabout near Lakewood. There—with the top down in Suds' battered but surprisingly swift VW Bug—we would sometimes take a couple of goofy and carefree spins around the circle, then shoot off onto Route 33. About then we would begin to taste the salted air and feel the magical pull of the Shore. Like everyone else, we just called it "goin' down the Shore," and gave it a crowning capital salute.

The Shore ran, you must know, on a different set of rules from the rest of New Jersey, with a wonderfully expansive sense of hospitality and welcoming generosity. This is not to suggest the rest of the state was inhospitable, although the great *Time* writer Joel Stein has said, tongue somewhere in cheek, that Jersey hospitality seems to involve little more than "opening the front door." That's a start, of course, but down the Shore hospitality flew out these opened doors, and off the charts.

We could arrive unannounced at the homes of friends, and almost always be welcomed into their impossibly tiny houses, often invited to stay for a day or two. This was especially true if we arrived around cocktail hour, which down the Shore could begin as early as breakfast with a couple of early morning Bloody Mary "eye-openers." Early on, Suds and I figured out just when to arrive where. We favored, as you might guess, those happy homes where eyes were well-opened before noon, and everybody seemed to love everybody else.

These places were better than any hotel, which was never a likely option on our summer janitor jobs' salaries. The tiny seaside town of Lavallette seemed to attract an especially fun summer crowd, and we usually aimed for there. It was reassuringly un-swanky, and the word "charming" would be a stretch. Homes were mostly small, simple things, painted in pleasing sun-bleached shades of blue, and yellow, and white. Everybody seemed to want to meet everybody else, with the usual social barriers bleached away too.

This was particularly true of the teenagers, who were all over the place.

And on this Sunday, a fine mid-July day in 1963, the place was the beach, a surprisingly generous strip of soft white sand, although not the kind of powder-fine sand a first-timer might have expected. The surf breaking just off shore that day was unusually gentle, barely enough to kick up any salt-spray, and the few surfboards along the strip were reduced to beached props. And among the props, Suds and I spotted a couple of good-looking girls, which was an easy thing to do around Lavallette. Tall and athletic—one pushing six foot, the other maybe five-foot ten, although I think this is just one of those memories which has grown over the years—they had cute sunburned noses and a few freckles, and tans which suggested a carefree summer of fun and sun, unburdened with lousy indoor jobs, like janitors. They were clearly sisters. Maybe even twins, wearing matching two-piece tangerine-colored swimsuits, not quite bikinis.

We fumbled through introductions—always awkward moments—and like most girls we would meet down the Shore, they were remarkably forgiving. We quickly settled into a playful banter, everyone more interested in where we lived and went to school and why we were at the Shore than other things, like names.

I'm sure we got around to that, and knew their real names at least for the day, but Suds and I simply have not been able to remember them. What we do remember, however, is that they were both "rising seniors" at Montclair, even though the taller one seemed, curiously, a bit older than the other. Indeed, some time during the day, we found out that the "Older Taller One," as we have namelessly remembered her, had hit a bit of a rough patch early in her educational progress, and been forced to "stay back" a year. She was a little embarrassed about it all, we could see, so we never really pressed further to find out exactly which year had done her in. On the other hand, the other sister—we now remember her simply as the "Younger Smart One"—seemed to be delighted that they were now on their way to graduating Montclair together. Frankly, Suds and I had the feeling that they may have invented a cover story up in Montclair that they were actually twins. They could have pulled it off, but barely.

A fine little friendship was blooming that morning. Everyone seemed to like everyone else, and when Suds mentioned that we were hungry, the girls took the hint and invited us back to their cottage for a bite. But this was an amazing coup, particularly since we had known the girls for only about an hour. Renting for the summer, just a block off the beach, they said we would love their mother, "always quick with a smile and a snack."

We were in, off to another opened door.

Mother, in her very early forties, wearing an oversized "Colby College Tennis" shirt, greeted us warmly—the girls were right about that smile—and waved us in, sandy feet and all. Tall and also deeply tanned (this was all before dermatologists were invented), she was, we thought, a sure bet for that snack.

We didn't meet a dad, but the Colby shirt seemed to suggest, at least somewhere or sometime, a man in Mother's life. That seemed fair.

In any event, Mother Montclair sized us up quickly, figuring we must be nice varsity boys from some gentle town up the Parkway, and we were in. Neither of us believed, at least at first, that she had been trying out those popular "eye-openers," but who ever really knows down the Shore. What we do know is this. When she welcomed us into the tiny cottage, and asked us if we would like anything to eat, Suds went without warning for the homerun of meals, if that metaphor can stand.

"I'd love a turkey dinner."

The two girls and I thought he said, or certainly meant to say, a turkey *sandwich*. This would have been more in keeping with the nice spirit of hospitality developing around our happy new family-for-probably-just-a day. And a reasonable request in the middle of July on a Sunday noon in Lavallette, New Jersey, in a small cottage kitchen effectively filled with virtually total strangers. So I jumped in.

"Yep, a turkey sandwich would really hit the spot, or a BLT, or just a peanut butter and jelly. And this is really nice of you, ma'am. Please don't go to any trouble."

We were, as I have said, *gentlemen* freeloaders, and people used to say I should have gone into the diplomatic corps. And by then I was starting to really look at these girls, those cute freckles and all, and beginning to think longer term. Like with my head, not my stomach.

"No, don't be silly," replied Mother. "Your friend here said turkey dinner and *turkey dinner it shall be.*"

Yep, we thought, maybe she *has* been hittin' the sauce.

This was getting weird, but Suds showed no signs of backing off his absurd request. At least the girls didn't look like they thought this was dangerous Mother Montclair behavior.

"You mean with all the trimmings, and maybe pumpkin pie?" the Older Taller One chimed in, and I was beginning to understand her rough patch, education-wise.

Now I love a good turkey dinner as much as anybody. *But in its place*, which in my view was pretty much just Thanksgiving Day. Didn't anyone around here know this was July in Lavallette, flipping, New Jersey? Just who the hell's going to be selling big old whole Tom Turkeys around here today? I mean, maybe Mother could special order a nice sixteen-pounder over at the Safeway and have it in four or five days, and we could come back. And the pumpkin pie? Who grows pumpkins in July?

My buddy Suds was still thinking with his stomach, although I think he started the whole thing as a goof. Whatever, he was already too far in, and this was often the sad trajectory of most of our misadventures. Always south, and quickly. Things had already spiraled completely out of control, and we had been in the cottage for less than four minutes. This was close to a record for the two of us.

"Look, why don't you kids just grab a snack, go back to the beach, and I'll get this dinner ready. We'll eat about four." I had just been hoping for a snack.

No question, we thought, Mother had a drinking problem, or was running for Lavallette Summer Cottage Mother of the Year. Maybe even New Jersey Mother of the Year. (Or maybe, of course, she was just very gracious, playing by those special Shore rules. That was just the kind of logical explanation we would usually miss, about most everything that year.) At this rate, we figured she would be checking to see if we were both up to date on our vaccinations, and asking if we were getting enough Vitamin D and fiber in our diets, and even enough love in our homes. I began to think that I could be spending a lot of time in Lavallette, and probably Montclair, in my near future.

So off to the beach we went. Mother gave us the last of her sunscreen, as well as sodas and some snacks—healthy carrot sticks, as I recall—just "to tide us over." We fully expected her to check us for ticks.

She was so…well…*mothering*.

Suds was still thinking only about his Tom Turkey, the Older Taller One was all goofy about her pumpkin pie, and the Younger Smarter One happily going along for the ride. Even she started wondering aloud exactly what trimmings would await us back at the cottage.

I just thought everyone had lost their marbles, which seemed to be rolling around all over the place.

This was turning into a very interesting day, with the kind of story the ancient Greeks called a "unity of time" drama, where the plot confines itself to a single day, a "single revolution of the sun."

Some point to John Hughes' 1985 movie *The Breakfast Club* as a great contemporary example: a small group of high school kids spends a Saturday morning together in detention, sharing things about their lives and forming a tight bond, in just one day. Something like that was already happening to us. Unlike the Hughes' movie crowd, however, we were all in our bathing suits, and our sun had completed only about *half* its revolution that Sunday.

But when we returned to the cottage, after more pleasant beach time with the girls, what awaited us was what certainly looked to be the greatest *Lavallette Summer Cottage Hot July Sunday Sixteen-Pound Tom Turkey Dinner With All the Trimmings* ever seen anywhere, before or since, up or down the entire New Jersey Shore. Probably the entire East Coast.

The Older Taller One quickly spotted the pumpkin pie, and started squealing in delight, thanking her mom and giving her a big hug. Estes looked like he had just copped Shore Story Bragging Rights for the next century. The Younger Smart One seemed just as happy about the trimmings. I was happy that no one was hanging around Mother in white coats.

And this is the truly amazing thing. We both swear even today that we caught one of the girls whisper to Mother:
"Thanks for doing it again, Mom."
AGAIN?
This kind of huge, spontaneous holiday banquet in the middle of the summer was a regular occurrence around here? In this tiny cottage in the little seaside town of Lavallette? Just what the hell does this family do for *real* holidays, back at home base?

This was astounding, even a bit troublesome. Suds quickly saw the possibility that dozens of other lads were telling their own strange Lavallette Turkey Dinner Tales all over New Jersey, crushing his bragging rights in a bowl of cranberry sauce, which sat nicely next to the heaping bowl of mashed potatoes.

Perhaps she had just been a little sloppy in structuring her sentence, and simply meant to say "Thanks again." It was, I now remember, the Older Taller One, although all of us would often make these kind of gigantic meaning-changing word misplacements.

Or maybe we just had not heard her correctly, what with all the happy chatter.

Anyway, Mother had set a very nice Thanksgiving table as well, although on a faded yellow summer picnic table, which was the duty—and only—table in the cottage. Only a couple of things seemed to be missing. No little cardboard cutout Pilgrims, for one. And we quickly saw that she had set the table only for four. This was too much for me. Maybe Mother was trying to create a little relationship-building intimacy, and sacrificing herself again to the good summer times of the kids. Or maybe she just wanted to step back and enjoy her triumph. God only knows what trouble she had encountered in finding all the stuff for this feast, much less cooking it. It broke me.

"For the love of Pete, Mother, would you at least join us for dinner?" Suds still swears I had tears in my eyes.

She did join us, the only formal invitation heard that day, everyone bonding like the characters in Hughes' movie. It was a wonderful afternoon, absolutely fulfilling the promise of magic that our trips down the Shore were really all about. Maybe it was magic for Mother, too. We have always hoped so, and for all the other mothers in tiny but welcoming cottages all over the Shore that sunny Sunday, all creating their own magic for their sun-burned kids, and even gentlemen freeloaders.

We never, however, saw the girls, or Mother, again after thanking our new friends and heading home that Sunday evening. Sometimes you just can't improve on an experience, or a good story. Maybe the girls even went off to college that next year together, perfecting that fake twin thing. We have always hoped they did.

We never did figure out how Mother pulled it all off. Her performance did not, we were pretty sure, involve magic, like the kind of tricks "Orla the Great" would perform at our Boy Scout Troop and All-Sports Dinner in the spring, pulling all sorts of unexpected things out of his top hat.

But a turkey? No way.

Maybe lots of people keep a couple of frozen Butterballs in their freezers down around Lavallette for most of the summer, for the unexpected guest with a sly sense of humor. We just don't know.

As I said, the rules were different down the Shore.

We returned home a little later than usual that Sunday evening, missing what had been a more typical midsummer evening supper—a salad around my home, and light fare over at the Estes. That was usually no big deal, as we often would miss Sunday supper on those summer weekend trips down the Shore. My mother, who was pretty great too, just kind of shrugged, smiled, and asked if she could she fix me a sandwich.

"No thanks, Mom. I just finished a huge Thanksgiving dinner," I replied as I sped off to my room. "I'm really stuffed."

Yes, Suds and I were world-class bullshitters, but sometimes it really is best to go with the truth. Even as strange as the truth may sound, especially to the folks you love. They usually just let it slide, you know. And my mother did just that, and never brought up that strange reply in the gentle summer of 1963. But she must have often wondered just what we kids really did, down the Shore.

No story really ever does end of course, not even the Greek one-day ones. The first time my slightly younger wife heard this tale, she quickly came up with a reasonable answer to how Mother pulled it all off. Although it has never been the one I want, I think she's probably right.

"It had to be a BIG ROAST CHICKEN, you idiot," she said, rolling her eyes, "NOT A TURKEY."

"It just can't be done, thawing out a turkey, even if she could have found one, which was impossible, and no way could she cook a sixteen-pounder in three hours anyway. No one in Lavallette could have had a microwave then. Nope, just couldn't be done, not even with the help of Orla the Good, or whatever his name was, that magician you guys are always talking about."

I wished she had stopped there, but she didn't.

"So who's the 'Younger Smart One' in THIS family?"

Yes, maybe Suds wasn't the only one having a little goof that wonderful Sunday in Lavallette, New Jersey.

AND THAT'S HOW
WE EARNED OUR CHOPS

Joel Stein's squib on Jersey hospitality–that it doesn't go much beyond just opening the front door—still bugs me. He made this claim just before Super Bowl XLVIII (which was, as you may remember, advertised as the *New York* Super Bowl, even though it was actually played in New Jersey), urging the good people of Jersey to dial it up a bit, hospitality-wise, and calling for Jerseyans not to act like, well, Jerseyans. This was all done with a sly wink-and-nod, in the grand spirit of making fun of *anything* New Jersey, which is a national pastime. And now that you have learned of Mother Montclair, perhaps you harbor fewer reservations about any of your own Jersey visits. But another Halloween night caper—in October of 1961, when we were sophomores—should put to rest any doubts you may still have.

Knocking on doors well into dinner time—and certainly pushing the appropriate "trick or treating" age—Suds Estes and I had spent absolutely no creative energy on our costumes, which consisted entirely of matching "Groucho" glasses with attached moustache. You probably had a pair somewhere along the line, and they seemed to pass some minimal Halloween threshold. At least everyone seemed happy to greet us just as they had the parade of little bumble bee second-graders and eye-patched pirate fourth-graders and aluminum-foil robot sixth-graders an hour or two earlier. Out of candy—those little suburban bumble bees are especially voracious—many of these folks coughed up a couple of quarters, which may have been our strategy all along. But the greatest prize of all came atop a rather imposing uphill driveway, in a tidy brick and siding home on Coniston Road, when we were pushing eight o'clock.

We had almost called it a day—that driveway looked a little steep—but we decided this would be it, and trudged up to the door.

I'm glad we did.

When we knocked, and the door opened, we quickly recognized the gentleman of the house. He was as an elder in our Church, and his name I remember as something like a Mr. Herter, although I may be confusing him with President Eisenhower's Secretary of State around that time. Our Mr. Herter looked, indeed, quite the statesman, and just as we remembered him from most Sundays—tall, and impeccably dressed in a dark suit. He and his elegant house seemed to live in perfect harmony, each standing with an impressive, but not really off-putting, aloofness. Instead, it all came off as a reassuring statement of solid respectability, suggesting strong timber in our neighborhood, which usually tended toward the chaos of younger families and idiot kids.

He was just the kind of distinguished, God-fearing elder statesman who wouldn't much appreciate a couple of fake Grouchos interrupting his dinner well past the understood Halloween hour.

And actually we were interrupting his dinner *party*.

Through our fake Groucho glasses we could clearly see a pleasant gathering of four or five older couples, enjoying a rather formal Halloween evening around the dining room table, which was draped in a crisp white tablecloth and heavy with a full dinner spread and wine. The guests, too, looked like they had just come from church, dressed in their Sunday best. In fact, we quickly recognized this group as the very serious crowd who rested atop the leadership of Christ Church. Luckily, none of them recognized us, those Groucho glasses doing the job. And we were not, of course, decked out in our Crucifers' garb.

Suds and I weren't so sure how this would play out, but with just the slightest hesitation, we were welcomed into the home. His candy stash was long gone, but to the great delight of his guests—and to our astonishment—Mr. Herter reached over to a steaming plate of impossibly plump pork chops crowning the center of the table and picked out a couple of the very largest.

These chops were *magnificent*.

We could almost taste the stewed apple slices which were sliding off as he held the chops up for all to see. With a surprisingly theatrical flair for a man of his *gravitas*—perhaps a happy result of those fine wines—he grabbed a couple of napkins, wrapped those beauties up and handed them to us with a huge grin. Suds was eyeing a few other items on the table, but backed off when he saw that Mrs. Herter wasn't so happy with the disappearing dinner fare, or the new apple slice stains on her tablecloth.

Suds still swears that our generous host even said a kind word about our costumes, and wished us happy hunting as we were ushered out the door. Retreating down the driveway, we were laughing so hard we could barely chow down on those monster pork chops. They were not only too drippy for our candy bags, but the kind of Halloween loot which could raise troublesome questions at home. We polished them off before we turned off Coniston Road, and onto South Terrace for the short walk home.

They were the best pork chops we have ever eaten, even if we lost most of those delicious sliced apples in our hasty retreat.

Like I said, there was plenty of hospitality in our New Jersey, even if sometimes fueled by good wine.

A new kind of sensibility now apparently surrounds today's choice of Halloween costume, something to do with political correctness and not offending anyone. Or even not trying to pretend to be what one is not, which I thought was exactly what Halloween was all about. It seems a little confusing to me—like pretty much everything else these days. But I no longer go out on Halloween, so this is not a big deal, although this year I did catch the spirit. I sat outside on a folding beach chair in the driveway and handed out candy to the neighborhood pirates and bumble bees and dozens of other little kids. I got a little chilly, so I found a blanket and built a cozy fire in a small portable fire pit. I didn't plan it this way, but I looked pretty scary.

Homeless, frankly, with that blanket pulled over my head. At least I was enjoying a small batch bourbon—neat, in a plastic cup branded with the logo of that fancy club I had un-joined soon after Bud and Rob and I were asked to continue our evening elsewhere—and nothing out of a paper bag. One young pirate even played against character and offered *me* a Milky Way.

Sitting out there in the driveway, I had thought about wearing a pair of fake Groucho glasses which I found a few years ago. That would have been less scary than Homeless Man, and those fake Grouchos wouldn't have offended even Groucho himself. Just before my little Homeless Man fire burned out—and long after most of the kids had long since retired to their nests to count their candy loot—a couple of teenage boys wandered up the short driveway. They had gone all out—like with a baseball cap—and had that goofy innocence of all sophomores, and they looked to be up to the same kind of nonsense I remembered from that magical Halloween Night of the Pork Chops almost fifty-five years ago.

Had I been wearing those fake Groucho glasses, I would have happily given them to the boys—passing of the baton, you know—and even pointed them in the direction of a little dinner party I knew about just a few blocks away. But that's the thing about our stories: we just have to keep some of the best as ours alone. So I didn't clue them in on the dinner party, and saw no need to invite them in to share in my supper either.

Monster pork chops were probably not on the menu down the block anyway.

So I reached under my Homeless Man blanket, found a couple of dollar bills and (with none of Mr. Herter's theatrical flair) gave these two happy clowns the money. My guess is they never even thought monster pork chops could be a Halloween Night treat.

EPILOGUE

. . . the American men and women whose young lives had been defined first by the deprivations of the Great Depression and then by the sacrifices of the war came home to start families, build careers, build communities . . . Who would have blamed them if they had returned and said simply, 'I've done my share. Let someone else take care of the world?' They did not, of course. Instead, they gave us the lives we have today.

- Tom Brokaw, *The Greatest Generation*

THE MOST IMPORTANT PHOTOGRAPH I NEVER SAW

Floyd Patterson knocked out Ingemar Johansson in the sixth round of their third fight for the World Heavyweight title in 1961. This was the rubber match, after the ref had called the fight for the Swede following seven rounds in 1959, and Floyd had won by a knockout in the fifth in 1960. Floyd was one of my heroes, even though, or maybe in part because, he did some time in reform school before getting his act together and becoming a world-class athlete. Anyway, I watched all three fights on TV, the third one alone while "babysitting" three young boys down the street. That may have been both the first and last time I "babysat," not because I got fired, but because that line of work, in the 50s and 60s, was dominated by girls. By the way, none of the boys were "babies." The oldest was only two years younger than I was.

During the 1950s and first half of the 1960s, they lived four doors down and across the block from us on Canterbury Lane in Short Hills, New Jersey. We would play basketball out in front of their house. The oldest one was my sister's first ever "date." The middle one, wearing a cape, once tried to fly off the roof—he broke his leg. The younger one wandered into our garage one day and broke about 300 soda bottles (worth, then, two cents each) and a dozen eggs. Despite many interrogations by their parents, by my parents, and, later in life, by me, we never received a good explanation for either the jump or the garage rampage. Note that I have had multiple opportunities for interrogation, largely because the three boys (who all became very successful businessmen with wonderful families of their own) are not only among my very best friends, they are also now my stepbrothers.

The boys' father, Bill Woodman, was a fighter pilot. You fly a combat mission once, you're a hero in my book. You do it over and over, even more so. You do it in two different wars, you're really a big deal. Bill Woodman was a big deal. After serving in both WWII and Korea, and being decorated with the Distinguished Flying Cross, he stayed in the reserves for years, while pursuing a career in the aviation insurance business. Occasionally, while we were shooting baskets out in the street, he would buzz the neighborhood and tip the wings on one of the jets he still routinely flew out of Floyd Bennett Field in Brooklyn. But this story isn't about him.

My father, Gil, after being a lumberjack and attending architecture school at night, enlisted in the Army on December 8, 1941, the day after the attack on Pearl Harbor. Because of his terrible eyesight, he sneaked in and memorized the eye chart, which got him into Officer Candidate School. He rose to the rank of captain and commanded a company of engineers which (without him) was one of the first to land at Normandy on June 6, 1944 as part of the Neptune phase of Operation Overlord and the liberation of France. He didn't land at Normandy with his company because he had been plucked off a train headed for the boats and was flown to Scotland to build an airport. If this hadn't happened, he no doubt would have been killed in the invasion, as we understand was the fate of every man in his company. He would not have married my mother thirteen months later, and I would never have been born. He didn't tell me the Normandy story. Others did. Years later, in his eighties he confirmed it. And without even knowing about the Normandy story, his sister, my Aunt Ruth, after she turned ninety, told me that when my father returned from the war, he would dive for cover whenever he heard a siren or fireworks. So although his life was spared, it was not the same. Anyway, for volunteering to go to war and risking his life, I consider him to be a hero. But this story isn't really about him either.

Nor is it about his brother Hilly, who enlisted in the Navy on the day after the Pearl Harbor attack; nor about their cousin Bob, who is now buried in Arlington among other WWII heroes; nor about my Uncle Nook, who lost a leg in WWII; nor about my wife Ginger's father, Hubert Pierce, who was temporarily held back from active duty so he could build warships in Savannah and later joined his brother (who we were told endured the Bataan Death March) to fight the Japanese in the Philippines; nor about Ginger's maternal grandfather, who was too young for WWI and too old for WWII, but twice lied about his age and wormed his way into both wars. No, this story is about the mother of those three boys down the street.

The hero of this story, or rather the heroine, is Phyllis Ruth Rearden Woodman Schill, or "Betty" as she was called. She was born in Chicago in 1919 and lived for a while as a child in the Los Angeles area before moving to South Orange, New Jersey. She went to Columbia High School, where she met Bill Woodman, whom she married years later. She attended Oberlin College in Ohio as a piano major, then transferred and graduated from Syracuse as a music major with an emphasis in piano, which she played beautifully all her life (including once at the Hollywood Bowl). Her youngest son is also an accomplished pianist, as I might have been had I not, one Saturday morning with my parents not around, fired my piano teacher, Mr. Lundigan, to free up additional practice time with the fifth grade basketball team.

After the United States entered the war in Europe, Betty (then in her early twenties) could have stayed in New Jersey and remained safe and out of both harm's way and the heartbreak of the war zone. Instead, and over her father's objection, she joined the Red Cross and volunteered for overseas duty, serving in England, Ireland, and, eventually, in Germany during the occupation.

In 1989, after both Bill and my mother had passed away, Betty and my father (who had been good friends for many decades) were married in Colorado Springs. I was the best man at one of the happiest occasions of my life.

Seven years later, they decided to take a trip to Ireland. The trip was a bust in ways, because Betty got sick, and they had to come home early. Even that was a bust, because the airplane had mechanical trouble about a third of the way across the ocean, and it had to turn back to Ireland and start over. But when they got back to the States, I met up with them at their place in Sapphire Lake, North Carolina, in the mountains above Asheville. I was on my way by car from Richmond to Atlanta to join my son Randy at the 1996 Olympics. Betty and my father told me a story.

Betty had been assigned to an air base in either Ireland or Northern Ireland. We don't know the name of this base or exactly where it was. Betty said that every day, pilots would take off from this airport to participate in the war. She didn't say whether they flew from Ireland to Germany or had other duties over the skies of the British Isles. She did say that many of these brave pilots did not return, and dealing with the grief of their disappearances was part of her job. She and the other Red Cross volunteers were there to help with medical and psychological care. This could not have been fun, but it also could not have been any more important.

Anyway, during their truncated trip to Ireland, Betty and my father had gone looking for this airport. Somehow, and despite the change in landscape, they found it. It was small, and it was run-down. They didn't tell me the name of it, or where it was, but they sure enough found it. My father told me that as they approached it, Betty said, "This is it. I can't believe it's still here." They went inside the main building and looked around. They knew immediately that they were in the right place, because, as they came upon a beat-up old bulletin board, they stopped dead in their tracks. For on that bulletin board, secured with a thumbtack, was a picture of Betty. It had been there for half a century. In the photo, she was with a group of Red Cross volunteers and airmen—they were all dancing.

It didn't sink in immediately how strange and eerie and significant this was. Or how important that photo was, and would become in my memory—not so much because it was taken, but because it was still there.

Maybe I was tired, or just anxious to get to the Olympics, but for some reason, I didn't press for the details. I did tell Ginger about this story. And a couple of years later, we asked Betty and my father about it while visiting with them in Florida. But again, for some reason, we didn't press for the details. We should have. We should have

314

asked for the name of the airport, or at least what county it was in. And we should have called the airport and asked for the photo, or at least a copy. I can't explain why we didn't, and the fact that we didn't is very embarrassing to me. I guess we figured we had forever to tend to this search.

We didn't. My father died in 2001, a few days after the 9/11 attacks. He was clinging to life in a Florida hospital. Betty and I were essentially alone with him, since no one else in the family could travel, as all the nation's airports were shut down. We refused to let my father watch TV, for fear he would see what had happened and try to enlist again.

After my father passed away, we had a few more good years with Betty. But then we lost her too. And we never got any more details about the photo.

This is when Ginger and I started trying to figure out where the airport was. We were guessing. Ginger, who can find anything, tried to look it up, and at one point she believed she might have found an article about it, but the old airport she read about had been destroyed by fire in the last decade. So we gave up. We had nothing more to go on.

Funny, until 1996, on my way to the Olympics, I never knew Betty had even been in the Red Cross. Up to then, her only claim to fame, to my knowledge, was discovering, or at least disclosing to me, when I was about thirteen (the year Floyd Patterson lost to Ingemar Johanssen before regaining the title), the foolproof cure for the hiccups: "Hold your breath, and swallow thirteen times." Ever since that moment, I have never hiccupped twice in the same day. But I now know that Betty was a heroine to a bunch of airmen at a tiny spot in the British Isles during one of the toughest periods in world history. Like her first husband and my father, and my Uncles Hilly, Bob, and Nook, and Ginger's father and grandfather, she was an active and important member of America's Greatest Generation.

We'll never see the photo. But we'll always have the story. And we know it's true, because two of our heroes told us so.

AFTERWORD

We were pleased to see so many of the people you have met in these pages at our fiftieth high school reunion, held in October 2014. We went upscale, too, gathering at the Short Hills Hilton, although it now goes by the tonier "The Hilton at Short Hills." We think that's a bit much, but it was a wonderful time.

Jim "Bay" Basinger arrived on-scene early. An Anglican priest now, living in Virginia, he still can't skate. His delightful wife Donna recounted how, on an early date, he'd plowed into guests all over the rink, claiming he couldn't stop without a hockey stick. No one, of course, was about to hand him one. She married him anyway.

"Woody" Thompson, who actually found the Leech Patrol flag, has been married to his wife, Bonnie, forever, and remains what he always was—an unpretentious laugh-out-loud good friend to so many people. He, with a little help from his brother, Chip, added details of misadventures even we had forgotten.

Bob Haslam graduated from MIT and did, in fact, become a kind of rocket man…with the Air Force at Vandenburg Test Center. We remembered that they lost a couple of rockets there, too. Bob is now a patent attorney in California.

John "Nils" Ohlson held forth at the reunion in his inimitable way, wearing an impossibly loud Hawaiian shirt as the rest of us mustered out in classic blue blazers or business attire. He had a fistful of enjoyable stories about a life lived large "down under" in Australia. Throughout the reunion, tales about the years after Nils moved back home and started just showing up at people's houses in his RV for long stays, loud shirts in tow, were whispered. Wonderful.

George Freund is now a lawyer living in New Hampshire and Florida. When asked if he ever suited up with the Detroits, he responded that, since he was a worse skater than Bay, he was afraid to try out, for fear of being cut.

Scott "Suds" Estes, who married his delightful high school sweetheart, Janice, right after college, hit a kind of perfect domestic trifecta: one job, one wife, and one home. Suds played semi-professional hockey and, along with his son, won over thirty amateur national tennis and paddle-tennis championships, and today enjoys a second career as a tennis pro. He still goes down the Shore, but has never again tried to cop a midsummer turkey dinner. The whole Estes clan may be the nicest people you will ever meet. Just don't think you can ever beat any of them at tennis.

Bob deVeer, who also married his high school sweetheart, Sally, after college, enjoyed a successful career as a Wall Street investment banker, and lived for many years in Short Hills. Tragically, he lost both Sally and his second wife to cancer. Recently remarried to Mindy, he has never again tried to walk with a ripple tank, or, for that matter, tried to explain much of anything to do with physics.

Quite a few of the other players from our historically bad football team joined us, with guys like Ted Hellman, "Higgs" Higgins, Terry O'Brien, Greg Morgan, Don Hohnstine, Gary Happell, and Neal Welch, all looking about twenty years younger than everybody else, and ready to take the field once again. No one talked much about those awful defeats our senior year, although Higgs still claims we should have won "at least five games." We have always loved Higgs' spirit.

Billy Jaeger and Scott "Wiener" McQueen both ventured off to Dartmouth together, and years later reunited to run a successful network of radio stations across the country. After his successful business career, Billy retired to Hilton Head with his wife, Charlotte, and still remembers his father's blue coaching shoes, and gentle patience. Scott retired to Boca Raton, and missed the reunion, so we didn't find out if he has maintained his bowling chops.

We lost David "Spike" Hughes just before we went to press, but we think his family will enjoy learning of his bravado performance at the Livingston Lanes—and enjoy a quiet smile. He lived just across from our Glenwood School, and was one of our very first buddies.

We missed seeing "Big Al" Schultheis, who couldn't get to the reunion, but we caught up with him later to be sure he is aware of his celebrity status.

We have lost touch with Tony Intilli, and many of the great guys who left us along the way for private school. So we don't really know how their journeys have been, although a couple of our Pingry friends have popped up over the years in *The Wall Street Journal*, with stories of great success. They seem to have been magnets for money, not mischief, and we are very happy for them. They probably don't know how to dance either.

We saw many of our favorite girls, too. The lovely brown-eyed Judy O'Connell (her wall-papering days long gone), and another Judy who changed her *first* name to Jenny, Mary, the Twins, Diane, Dolly, Beth, Chris (but not her fun sidekick, Jayne), and Joanie, and Liz, and Macon from the West Road gang. Barbara, our favorite redhead from Glenwood, told us how pleased she was that that we had so fondly remembered her dad—the magical "Orla the Great." That was nice.

Two of our favorite Lauras, who often hosted unannounced teenage guests down the Shore, shared sad stories of the Hurricane Sandy tragedy, and none of us took that once magical drive to see just how much of what we remember was washed away. But another classmate, Francine LaVance Robertshaw, did send along her marvelous book about The Bluffs, a legendary cedar-shingled hotel which once sprawled along East Avenue in Bay Head. Too bad it is gone now, too. Lynne showed up, with her amazingly patient husband, having done the hard work of finding lost classmates, but she did not talk to us about bowling. She did, however, seem quite pleased that we had all taken showers.

We caught up with lots of other old friends, and made new ones, at the reunion, and we enjoyed hearing wonderful stories of their own misadventures in other neighborhoods. We just wished we had joined forces long ago.

We shared many stories about our parents. Most are gone now, several resting in a quiet courtyard memorial garden in the center of

Christ Church, along with some of the storied elders of the church. Named in honor of our Rev. Herb Cooper, it sits just outside the handsome leaded windows of the Crucifers' Room, and we like to think that they are all still keeping a watchful eye on a new generation of good-hearted but hapless young acolytes.

Some of us have talked about joining them there someday. It is a very peaceful place.

We also found our 1963 crucifers' "class picture" quietly hanging on the back wall of the Crucifers' Room, causing no trouble at all. But we were a little surprised no one had put it in deep storage. That would have left, of course, a very embarrassing space among the dozens of other crucifers' class pictures, although we would have understood. Completely.

There were, however, empty spaces around the tables where a number of our friends should have been, and that's *never* easy to understand, particularly the ones we lost long ago. Billy Fitzsimmons, "The Duke," Bobby Chandler, and too many others were missed, and remembered. We have lost over thirty classmates, out of some 320 in our high school class, including several in Vietnam, and we were pleased to see a memorial for them in our school.

We talked about finding out if any dancing school operations survive around town, trying to tame a new group of goofballs. But we thought it better just to leave that subject alone. We are convinced that our lifetime ban from the bowling alley remains in effect, but most of us don't bowl much anymore, anyway, so we didn't check that out either. Most of our camps are gone, and the *Captain Bill.* But you know that from the story. The Delaware River still flows south, but we don't know if it still brushes by a Fred Waring Golf Course. None of us ever drinks a Manhattan, and we no longer need to drive over a bridge for a beer. We pray that Fat Jack has done something a bit more appropriate with his musical talent, even though he would probably still be a hit around our gang.

The Village Center looks about the same, but with another new lineup of small shops. Boys don't seem to mess around with baseball cards so much anymore, and certainly not on the corner by Haggett's, since that closed long ago. Maybe no one flips cards against the walls of the Glenwood School anymore either, although the school still looks like a fine place to take a few first steps into the world.

Most of our teachers are likely gone now, and probably many of the other patient adults you have met in our stories. We only hope all of them—Mrs. Penalty, Mr. Weir, and the rest—had happy retirements, and maybe even looked back at our zaniness with a smile. We really do. Oak Pandick, our caring class advisor who went on to coach at Rutgers, died in October of 2014, just three days before our class reunion. He was ninety-three, and had hoped to join us. His passing was both sad and ironic. The legendary Jersey track coach Paul Beck died just a few years back. Long ago, Coach Beck had pulled extra duty as the adult-in-charge of the Glenwood sixth graders on lunch break, earning both our respect and love. Many of his former student-athletes made it to New Jersey for a memorial celebration, and a commemorative plaque has been placed along the backstretch of the high school cinder track. It doesn't seem to be enough for this great man.

Earl Battey lost his battle with cancer in 2003, at age sixty-eight. After his playing career, he worked with challenged youth in New York City, later became a high school coach in Florida, and was elected to the Minnesota Twins Hall of Fame in 2004, posthumously. We have also lost many of our other boyhood baseball heroes, although Don Newcombe is still going strong, having worked for years with the Dodgers organization. We still have a few well-worn baseball cards, wrapped in rubber bands and hidden away, and at least one autograph, saved for our grandchildren. Maybe even a *MAD* magazine, too, although they probably wouldn't get the goofy humor. Harry Chiti, it turns out, was from Charlottesville, Virginia, where all three of us did graduate work, and may have been there at the same time, and even a neighbor. Maybe we could have looked him up, just to ask him if it really was true that the Mets once traded for him in exchange for a player to be named later—that player being *Harry Chiti*, so he was apparently traded for himself. That's just the kind of goofy stuff we love. But he is gone now, too.

GILBERT E. "BUD" SCHILL, JR. AND JOHN W. "MAC" MACILROY
AND ROBERT D. "ROB" HAMILTON III.

And that's the thing about these stories, and our lives, and maybe the magic of it all: we never knew what was just around the corner.

ACKNOWLEDGMENTS

Doing all the goofy things you read about was easy. Remembering something close to what actually happened was a bit more challenging. And writing it all down, well, that was really something, with the three of us working not only as individual writers, but collectively, toward a shared vision of a manuscript and, finally, a book. Laughter, the glue of friendship, and the help of many, many people paved the way to publication.

We owe a singular debt of gratitude to Jerry Rudes, our agent. He tutored us on the fundamentals of publishing for a good six months *before* signing a contract, an act of exceptional good will.

Since then he has been a tireless and supportive advocate, and a gentleman of the first order who straddles the American and French fields of film and book agency with skill and good humor. This book would not have happened without him. We would not have fallen into his orbit without a kind introduction from the irrepressible Lloyd Kaufman. Thank you Lloyd.

Our publisher, Page Publishing, Inc., has been terrific. Stephen Matthews and Michael Yarnell have been particularly patient, transforming our manuscript into a *real book*, something we set out to do, but were never quite sure would happen.

Our editor, Randy Kaplan, *was* pretty sure it would, and his professionalism and early optimism were central to working through our manuscript. His critical eye was precise, thoughtful and always diplomatic, his editing timely, and his willingness to negotiate a phrase or two greatly appreciated.

We made some new friends along the way in Short Hills, including the Rev. Dr. Timothy Mulder and Ms. Juli Towell of

Christ Church in Short Hills, who helped us find, and granted us permission to use, the photograph of our Crucifers Class. And Lynne Ranieri, curator of the Millburn-Short Hills Historical Society, who opened her doors—and our eyes—to that treasure of local history. We thank each of them.

We also thank Bud's assistant, Teri Ann Tingen, who helped with copying, printing, and running drafts to Bud's house while he was laid up with an Achilles tear (another stupid story).

We also appreciate the exceptional writers at the St. Augustine Writers Conference, organized by the gifted Connie May Fowler, for sharing their inspirational personal journeys as writers, as well as the many other friends across our shared universe who have taken the time to read even a single page of our many stories, and often much more. All have been unfailingly gracious, and perceptive in their comments and suggestions, and the list is long. Rather than offending by an act of omission, we simply thank them all. We also give them blanket immunity for any errors of fact or judgment or any other stupid stuff in the book, as these are our fault, and ours alone.

Like many, we were saddened by the passing of Pat Conroy. His encouragement and support of new writers has been an inspiration. We have lost a legend, with a heart as large as his talent, and our thanks for his kind words about our book hardly seems adequate.

Finally, we thank our exceptional wives, who have been both inspiration and foundation for the project. What started as rolled eyes, emerged as their clever defensive ploy—a challenge to write our stories down. Ultimately, our response to their challenge blossomed into a book we think they may be proud of. We hope so.

ABOUT THE AUTHORS

All three lifelong friends somehow managed to survive their youthful misadventures, earn advanced degrees from the University of Virginia, and grow up into arguably functioning adults.

Gilbert E. Schill Jr: In his day, "Bud" could ride a bicycle indoors while balancing a slide rule on his nose and playing "Good Night Ladies" on the harmonica. A fan of water sports, he has water skied up the back of an alligator, had his foot skewered by a sting ray, and suffered an octopus up his nose. A trial lawyer and law professor, he lives in Virginia with his wife Ginger.

John W. MacIlroy: Fumbling footballs and first dates, and crowning his early years with a lifetime Little League batting average of .081, "Mac" went on to become an attorney, CEO and adjunct professor. Retired, he now lives on the coast of South Carolina with his wife Linda, a ceramic painted dodo bird named Dumont, and a small mortgage.

Dr. Robert D. Hamilton III: "Rob" flunked out of dancing school and prolonged his adolescence by picking up degrees from three universities, including a Ph.D., before becoming an award-winning university professor. Prior to academia, he lived briefly in the real world as a nonprofit executive. He now lives with his wife Jane outside of Philadelphia, PA. He still can't dance.

CPSIA information can be obtained
at www.ICGtesting.com
Printed in the USA
BVOW03*1351160617
486401BV00012B/5/P